The Legend of Benny

DOMINICK J. MORREALE, EdD

Legwork Team Publishing
New York

Legwork Team Publishing
80 Davids Drive, Suite One
Hauppauge, NY 11788
www.legworkteam.com
Phone: 631-944-6511

Legwork Team
Publishing

ISBN: 978-0-9841-5359-6 (sc)
ISBN: 978-0-9841-5358-9 (hc)

First edition 11/18/2009

Printed in the United States of America
This book is printed on acid-free paper

Cover illustration by Christopher Donovan

To my wife Gail who always inspires,
often resets my path and is forever there for me.

She is my soul mate.

CONTENTS

CONTENTS

PREFACE

The Legend of Benny shifts between modern day and Colonial times and as such, Old English and regional dialects are often intertwined with today's style of language. Contemporary characters in the book use regional language. The different styles of speaking are a part of history and are used to enhance the story. I hope you enjoy the variations.

ACKNOWLEDGMENTS

*T*he writing and completion of this book is yet another example of how my wife Gail encourages, helps and is always there for me.

Much thanks goes to my son, Randal, who sought out resources for the book's publication.

Encouragement came from the readers of my books, namely Carol Murphy, Sue Hansen, Anthony Castellino, and my son-in-law, Bob Wertz. Then there are the people who inspired me to create many of the characters depicted in the book: Pastor George and Gigi Gaffga, Rabbi Elliott and Sandy Spar, Dr. Greg and Robin Doroski, and Robert Harrington to name a few.

The Mattituck Library and the Riverhead Library are blessed with staff members who are always helpful. The Bureaus of Tourism for New York, Massachusetts, and the State of Connecticut have also provided much material.

Much gratitude and appreciation goes to Lois Dunne, the editor's editor. She defines the word friend.

Most of all, I must thank my publishers at Legwork Team Publishing, Yvonne Kamerling and Janet Yudewitz. They are knowledgeable and delightful individuals.

Chapter 1

Discovery

It was just after Thanksgiving when my story began.
This year I had decided I wasn't going to wait until the last minute to Christmas shop. Not that I have many people to shop for, at least not by myself. My wife and I usually shop together. This really means that I just shop for her gifts. I already knew exactly what I would be looking for when I left the house that morning. I wanted to add to her collection of antique glass electrical insulators, the type that are used at the top of electrical poles. I decided to look for one at one of the local antique shops. There are many along the main road of our quaint little town of Aquebogue, located on Long Island, New York, but I decided to start in Jamesport, which is only about a five-minute drive east.

Now that raises an issue, for which you need to have an understanding of the geography of Long Island. For starters, Long Island is shaped like a big fish. Its nose is pretty close to Manhattan, almost touching it in the New York Harbor. From there, it extends eastward into the Atlantic Ocean as it runs parallel to the state of Connecticut. Naming it Long Island was very appropriate—from tip to the tail, the island is about one hundred and thirty miles long. The tail actually splits off into two

fins, giving the island its fish-like look. Since the fins are parallel to each other, they've become known as the North and South Forks. Where the fins begin to spread apart, or fork, is known as Riverhead. The Peconic River enters the bay where the two forks begin to diverge. The town of Aquebogue is on the North Fork, just east of the split. Actually, there is no town; it's just a name and a zip code. Some folksy residents like to say that the town is a state of mind.

There are several antique shops in Jamesport, but I decided to start my search in the shop at the eastern edge of the town. I thought I'd start there and work my way back home. This antique shop is actually situated in an old white farmhouse. I hadn't been in it before, mostly because it is hardly ever open. Nevertheless, this time I was in luck.

The house is quite a rambling structure, with wings spreading to the back and sides. After parking the car I started to get out when I suddenly smelled the aroma of the season. It was that early winter smell of cold air and a wood burning fireplace, that wonderful memory-provoking smell.

I made my way to the front of the building where I found an elderly man hanging a Christmas wreath on the front door. I was delighted to see that the shop is still a house; the owner hadn't taken any walls down to make it more store-like. As I wandered inside, my sense of smell once again intensified. This time the smell of "old" struck me, bringing back memories of rummaging through my grandparents' attic. I stood in the main foyer for a moment and gazed into the rooms on both sides of the door. To the right was the parlor. It was heaped high with old objects that I'm sure most people would call valued antiques, but I have no intrinsic appreciation for those kinds of things. To me, the lamps, sconces, dishes and other items strewn about were just "old." They may be valuable but I just think they're clutter. Looking around I saw the fireplace hissing and crackling with warmth. It was located directly opposite the doorway and had two Lincoln chairs placed

Discovery

on either side. Those two chairs were the only pieces of furniture in the room that were void of clutter.

The elderly man finished his Christmas "decorating" and came inside. Walking to the fireplace he picked up a poker and moved the burning embers about, readying them for another log. "What are you burning? It has a great aroma. I smelled it the second I got out of my car."

"Fruitwood." He wasn't terribly long-winded and got right to business; "Know what you're looking for?"

I told him I was looking for an antique glass electrical insulator. I watched him as he thought about it. I studied his appearance while he decided whether or not he could help me. He appeared to be well into his senior years, but it was hard for me to pin down his exact age. His body showed signs of fatigue, but he held himself as erectly as possible. In his youth, he must have been quite tall and maybe even somewhat robust. Considering his scarcity of words, his looks, and the house, I guessed he was a native East Ender— that is, as opposed to those of us newly arrived, who only in recent years had discovered the beauty of the island's east end.

"Might," he finally said. That clinched it, he was definitely a native, and as we newcomers often say, he was more New England than those who live in New England.

Without another word, he left the parlor and carefully made his way down the hall. I guessed I was supposed to follow him, so I did. Trailing behind him, I glanced into the rooms on either side of the hall. The house had many more rooms than its outside appearance suggested. The old man paused outside a room on his right, then, apparently convinced that his recollection was correct, he turned into the room. It was the formal dining room, and much like the parlor, it was piled high with boxes and objects of yesteryear. The dining room table, which probably could seat twelve people, was much like a groaning board; however, instead of being overloaded with food, this one was stacked high with boxes. The old man went straight to one of the boxes and started

rummaging. At last, he found what we both had been looking for. He pulled out a green tinted insulator, but instead of handing it to me, he held it in his hand and carefully looked it over. He found what he was looking for. "Sort of recalled it had a chip. Not much value, unless you need to weigh down some papers."

I could see the chip was sizable, making the insulator undesirable for a collection. "Do you have any others?" I asked.

After a long reflective pause, he said, "Might, but I'd have to dig 'em out."

"If you would, I'd really appreciate it."

"Can't do it now. They're in the old part of the house, and it'll take some searchin' to find 'em."

Now, that news both excited and disappointed me, much as it would any antique hunter. All I could envision was a box of old insulators tucked away in some long forgotten room of the aged house. "I'll wait, or if you'd like, I'll help find them," I said attempting to calm down my excitement and at the same time, the potential disappointment of possibly being delayed.

I don't think he was terribly pleased with my suggestion. For a long time he didn't say anything. He studied my face and when he saw I was becoming uncomfortable with his stare, he turned away. He mumbled something I couldn't hear, then looked at me again and nodded his head, signaling that I should follow him.

Leaving the dining room we proceeded through the kitchen and into another hallway. The passageway became narrower as we descended several really old and creaky steps and entered an even older section of the house. "Mind your head," he cautioned me at one point. Looking up, I understood what he meant. A house this old often had some low main supporting ceiling beams, much lower than those in the rest of the building. I noticed something else. Up to this point, the best way I could describe his facial expression was "stoic." Well, at that moment, his face brightened, and I could swear that his eyes had a twinkle. I could only guess that perhaps this was his favorite part of the house.

Discovery

The temperature was much cooler, and the area was permeated with a heavy smell of must, even more than other rooms we'd been in, if that's possible. Coming upon a tiny room, the old man paused. Unlike the other rooms I had seen, this room wasn't cluttered. Except for a single sleigh type bed that didn't have a mattress, it was empty. In fact, the small bed almost took all of the space in the room. There was a small window, which was sorely in need of caulking and paint. I continued to look around the room, trying to figure out why we had stopped here. "Been told Washington bedded down here for a night or two," he said.

"Well, it certainly seems old enough. I once read, if you count all the signs that say Washington slept here, they would add up to more than twice his lifetime." The moment I said it I regretted sounding so abrasive.

"Can't disagree. And seeing I wasn't here, all I can say is, that's what I've been told."

"How come you don't have a sign outside saying that Washington slept here?" I did it again, another sentence I instantly regretted saying.

"No need to tell the world. Where a man beds down should be his business."

"Very true, but do you have any way of knowing the date he is supposed to have stayed here?"

"During the rebellion. Been told he stopped on his way to General Wayne's house."

"You mean the restaurant in Southold was once a real General's house?"

"So they say." He turned and exited the room. I stayed a second longer. I really wanted to ask or more accurately debate Washington's sleeping arrangements, but as I said, he wasn't much of a talker. I moved quickly to catch up to him.

Now the old man was standing in a room that must have been a combination kitchen, living, and sleeping room. To one side was a stone fireplace made with rocks found along the beaches of the

5

North Shore. The fireplace had one of those iron arms that swung out. It had a hook shaped end so a kettle could be hung from it. There was also a metal box built into the face of the rocks, the seventeenth century's version of an oven. There was no mantel but on both sides of the chimney the walls were recessed. The hearth was flat to the floor, with the stones extending out about three feet into the room. I imagined they, too, got warm and provided heat to the living area. The hearth's apron also helped to prevent sparks from hitting the wood floor. The floor had to be the original one. It was made out of pine that was held down by wooden pegs, although the pegs were so drastically worn they could hardly be seen.

The walls appeared to be the original rough-hewn pine planks that some time ago, had been freshened up with white paint but now had faded and were badly yellowing. As to the furnishings, the room pretty much appeared to resemble the other rooms in the house that I had seen. It contained an overload of cartons stacked beyond a safe limit, especially considering the low ceilings; a couple of straight-backed chairs, some made in the recent past but designed to look colonial, and an old maple table that was overloaded with cardboard boxes.

"How old is this area?" I asked as my eyes continued to absorb the room.

"Ten, maybe twelve years ago, a bunch of ladies came round. Said they were from the National Historical Society. Said the house was built around 1680, but didn't pay much mind to that."

"I guess you think they were wrong."

"Yep."

"Why?"

"Says so on that beam up there." As he spoke, he pointed to the beam above our heads.

I looked up, then to one of the straight-backed chairs. It didn't look terribly sturdy, but I figured it could hold my weight. "May I?"

"Can't see why not. Just don't go breakin' your neck."

Discovery

I moved the chair over and it proved to be stronger than I had first thought. I found the markings and although I was hampered by the lack of good lighting I could make out the words:

Built July 1661
Malcom Tallock

"Wow! That's something!" I excitedly said. "You didn't show them this?"

"Nope. They didn't ask. And seein' how they knew everything, I figured there was no need to confuse them. Some folks get along fine with what's in their heads. They don't need facts."

"This is just incredible. How long have you lived here?"

"Reckon about ninety years."

"Is that how old you are? I mean were you born here?"

"Yep."

"So your name is Tallock."

"Nope."

I could have had a longer conversation with a goldfish. I tried another approach. As I climbed down from the chair, I extended my hand to him.

"My apologies. I should have introduced myself." I did so and after the anticipated cautious delay, he finally responded. "Young. Ray Young."

"Are you a descendent of the person on the beam?"

"So I've been told."

Now, at this point, I figured he felt he had wasted enough time talking to me, because he cut me off.

"If we stand here talkin' you'll never find that thing you're looking for, and I can't be doin' my work. Besides, daylight is fading fast and you'll be needin' window light to look in the boxes."

He left the room and I realized he was leaving me on my own to look through the boxes. For some reason, I figured, he trusted me. Following his advice I immediately started my search.

I decided to begin by first looking into the boxes farthest away from the window on the table. While going through the very first box, I realized I was searching for the proverbial "needle in the hay stack."

The box was filled with all kinds of antiques. A hand-carved piece of soapstone caught my eye. It was a small carving of an ancient oriental vase; intricate and beautiful. Yet here it was, sitting in Mr. Young's collection of bric-a-brac, instead of being available for auction in the showroom at Sotheby's.

Looking through the boxes I knew I had to set up an orderly system so that I wouldn't find myself going through the same boxes over and over again.

When I started off on this shopping trip I knew it would take some time and effort, but at this moment, I felt the task was becoming fascinating as well as ridiculous. Hours were passing, I was getting cold, and Mr. Young was right, the light was already beginning to rapidly fade. For warmth, I thought about lighting the fireplace but quickly discarded that idea. One errant spark and the number of houses Washington purportedly slept in would quickly be reduced.

I moved a large box from the stack on the floor to the table. The box appeared to be somewhat heavier than the others, but I quickly browsed through it and didn't find any insulators. Nor did it contain anything that caught my interest, so I put it on the floor and because it was so heavy, I forcefully pushed it across the room. Actually, I misjudged the weight of the box and as a result gave it a harder shove than I should have. The box snagged on something, then upended, spewing its contents all over the place. I looked at the merchandise scattered about and all I could think of was, "oh hell, what antiques have I broken and now bought?" Then I noticed a portion of the wood floor had broken. A plank had dislodged. That's what probably snagged the box. And that meant I also damaged the floor—an antique pine and pegged floor.

Discovery

I began assessing the damage, looking over the antiques as I put them back in the box. None of the antiques were broken. What luck! I had gotten off easy. Then I looked at the piece of floorboard that I had accidentally broken. As I examined it, I thought, how strange? It hadn't shattered or splintered. It seemed to be in one solid piece. By the look of it, other than popping out of place, there was no real damage to either it or the floor. Hopefully all I had to do was put it back in place. But then I wondered how come there were no pegs or peg holes on it?

I looked into the open hole in the floor. Now, I'm no builder, nor am I an expert on how the early settlers built their houses, but I knew that houses like this one didn't have sub floors. With that thought in mind, I placed one end of the board into the hole and moved it about. I then hit what felt like several objects and another floor.

The floor lamp was within reach, so I moved it closer to the hole. I was right. This wasn't a sub floor; it was a wooden box that was suspended just below the flooring. It appeared to have the same shape as the plank I had dislodged and was somehow attached from underneath.

I couldn't extend the lamp cord any further and since the wattage was too low, I couldn't see into the box. At first, I didn't even consider the thought of putting my hand into the box. For starters, the box didn't belong to me and, even more importantly, it was probably loaded with spiders and mouse droppings. But then it dawned on me that this box had to be sealed. It had to have been covered with some kind of metal, or else anything placed in it would get wet from dampness and rot. The plank on top certainly sealed it tight enough. I convinced myself I wasn't going to take anything that I found, so, overwhelmed with curiosity I plunged my hand down into the hole. It was deeper than I had imagined and at first I thought it was empty, but then I felt along the bottom and quickly knew I had touched a familiar object. It was a book. No. There were two books: one lying on top of the other. They

were easily retrievable, so without thinking any further, I pulled them out. I placed the books on the floor under the lamp and plunged my hand back into the cache. Empty. I was perplexed. Someone took the time to build this elaborate safe and all they put in it was a couple of books? The books weren't even nicely bound, nor did they have gold leaf trim. They were just a couple of old, simple paged books, with a plain heavy-stock paper cover.

Before I even considered the possibility of the contents being private, I impulsively opened the first book. Randomly flipping through the pages, I had to look carefully because the print was so perfectly scripted; it almost looked as if it had been typed on a computer. Although faded to a tea colored brown, I marveled that every page was written in the same ultra neat, methodical script. The script was so neat that I would have bet that the writer had gone to a parochial school.

I turned to the front page and there in the same perfect script, except much larger than in the rest of the book, an acknowledgment had been written.

"As long as the tides rise and fall, I shall never forget the life and times of my beloved."

It was signed by a person named Rachael Tallock. I flipped the pages to the middle of the book and spotted dates at the tops of some of them. Suddenly, I realized it was a diary—a very old diary.

I decided to make my way back to the front of the building, leaving the safe uncovered so Mr. Young could see it for himself. As I went I peeked into each room to see if I could find the old gent. It wasn't until I got to the very front room, the parlor, that I finally found him. He was sitting in one of the high-backed chairs, right next to the glowing fireplace. His head was leaning back against the cushioned headrest, causing his neck and upper chest area to protrude to an abnormal degree. His Adam's apple—well it just didn't protrude, it was incredibly extended and to my horror it wasn't moving. I stared at the old man's Adam's apple for what

Discovery

seemed to me to be forever. That's when it dawned on me—maybe old Mr. Young wasn't just old anymore. He looked dead!

I thought, well, maybe it wasn't too late to save him. Maybe I could do artificial respiration on him. You know—the mouth-to-mouth kind. I carefully looked at his Adam's apple, his chin, his lips ... especially his lips. They were thin, not the bulbous kind, but they were cracked; could have been from age or even the weather. I thought to myself, "Mr. Young, head for that bright light because there is no way I'm going to put my mouth on those lips of yours." He must have read my mind. All at once he snorted. The sound was so loud and sudden that it scared the hell out of me. I reeled backward, but I could see his Adam's apple bobble. His snort was so loud that he woke himself up with a start.

"Are you okay?" I'm not sure if I asked him or myself.

"Didn't know you were standin' there. Scared the bejesus outta me! You really did!"

"Sorry about that." I wanted to add that maybe my coming into the room had actually stopped him from heading for that bright light, but I didn't. Instead, I handed him the books.

I told him how I came upon the books, and how I dislodged the floorboard. I also told him that a woman named Rachael Tallock appeared to be the author. "Looks like one of your ancestors has come back to haunt you," I quipped. As soon as the words came out of my mouth, I regretted saying them. Mr. Young placed the books on his lap and looked at them, concentrating. Then his face took on a look of pure anxiety. I had no idea as to what might be distressing him. Slowly, he took a pair of wire-rimmed glasses out of the pocket of his red flannel shirt. He placed the glasses on his face and since his nose had a sharpness to it, the glasses slid down his nose and landed on what seemed to be the customary place, just below the bridge.

There, on the title page in large print was the name Rachael Tallock. I could see Mr. Young's eyes fix on the name. I hadn't realized before that his eyes were so hazel. I thought they were

blue. Either way, their color changed as he piercingly fixed them on Rachael Tallock's name. They seemed as though they were going to burn a hole right through the paper.

I coughed. I mean I really coughed and not with the purpose of distracting his attention from the page at which he was staring. Nevertheless, my cough broke his concentration.

"Never was a fast reader," he said as he slowly looked up to face me. "There's a sayin' 'measure twice, cut once.' I always thought that had more to do with readin' than carpentry."

"Well, I didn't mean to interrupt you. I just thought I'd say goodbye and head for home." As he refocused on the book, turning the pages, I continued "You have a good day now," as I put my coat on and headed for the door. "And thanks for letting me go through the boxes." He didn't answer so I just shrugged my shoulders, buttoned my coat, and stepped into the foyer on my way to the front door.

"Hey! Young fella!"

"Don't stop," something told me. "Keep heading for the door and the great outdoors." But this elderly man was calling and I just couldn't ignore him, so I turned around and reentered the parlor.

"How am I supposed to read what's in these books. Even with these soda pop bottom glasses, I can't even see the words, much less read 'em."

I stepped closer and even though I had already scanned the books, I knew the flowing print was very small and every page was terribly faded. I looked over his shoulder at the page he was trying to focus on. "It's pretty fine printing. She must have been a very delicate and precise lady," I mumbled.

"So I've been told. And I would like to hear what she had to say. You know there was once one of them Egyptian kings, a pharaoh, who said, 'If somethin' was written, it must have been important.'"

Somehow I knew where this was leading, but I tried to get

Discovery

out of it anyway. "Well maybe you could get one of your friends or even a relative to read the books to you."

He gave that suggestion about a second's worth of consideration. "Out lived 'em all, except some nephews in Florida, and I can't very well ask 'em to come north just to have 'em read to me now, can I?"

I hesitated, considering what he was really asking me to do. I asked myself, "Was I really willing to invest all the time and energy it would take to read these books to this perfect stranger?"... I really can't explain why I agreed to do it, but I said I would take on the task. On my way out of the old house I couldn't help thinking—not only had I not discovered the proverbial pot of gold, I had also volunteered for a really big task. It must be something in my genes that compels me to volunteer. I agreed I would be back in the morning to start reading the books to Mr. Young. I also agreed to read to him for as many mornings as it would take to finish the books.

The next day, I arrived at Mr. Young's house well before our agreed upon time but he was already waiting for me. The fireplace was already simmering down and he had rearranged the comfortable Lincoln chairs so that we were now facing each other. He offered tea, which I declined, as I was anxious to get on with the task and complete it as soon as possible.

Once we were settled and Mr. Young had searched his pockets to find his glasses, I opened the book that had the earliest date markings and started to read aloud. The very first sentence alerted me to how challenging the task would be. As I recall, I think the book began with the words: "T'was the fourth night of the harvest moon of the year 1755, when he doth come to the house of the Father." I had to stop right there so Mr. Young and I

could sort out what that sentence really meant. We finally figured it out. The first part is simply a calendar calculation. The harvest moon falls in October and if we found a calendar dating back to 1755, we would just calculate the day of that month's full moon and add four days.

The second part of the sentence was actually the one that confused me more. I thought the words, "when doth he cometh to the house of the Father," meant when he arrived at the author's father's house. But, Mr. Young, having a great deal of knowledge about the colonial period, explained what it really meant. According to him, most of the people of the time lived by the Bible. Mr. Young quickly cited the chapter and verse in the Bible where it was interpreted to say only God was to be called the "Father." Therefore, according to Mr. Young, that part of the sentence meant that the person came to the house of God, in other words, the church. He also advised, as far as he knew, that his relatives were all members of the Mattituck Presbyterian Church and had been for generations.

"How can that be? How long has that church been there?"

"I reckon it was built around 1715, least that's what it says on the plaque hanging in the narthex."

I could have kept asking questions, but it dawned on me that we were on the first sentence and without any exaggeration; there were thousands of sentences left to go. So I killed the questions and pushed on with Rachael Tallock's diary.

Chapter 2

From Orphan to Family

1755. My father, Wayne Tallock, being a member of the church's Board of Sessions, was sent a messenger by Pastor Timothy, asking him to attend an emergency meeting. When Father arrived at church he discovered the topic of the emergency meeting. Pastor Timothy advised that a young boy had been orphaned and the church was being asked to assume responsibility for him.

Our mother was unable to bear any more children after Elizabeth, my youngest sister's birth. Father always thanked the Lord that he and Mother were blessed with three daughters, but my two sisters and I think that he longed for sons, or at least one son. Simply said, farmers need male offspring, not just to do heavy chores that are beyond the ability of females, but to be sure the land and name would carry on. I have often heard that continued family inheritance of the farm is, in many ways, even more important than the food it brings to the table. When Father went off to that Sessions Meeting, I had no idea how important family heritage was or would be in my lifetime. After all, at that time I was only four years old.

Now as I start to write about the course of events, let me

pause and say proverbs do what they are intended to do. They summarize and bring truth to what usually happens. That's why in school we learned to read by memorizing how each word in our Book of Proverbs was spelled. At the Sessions Meeting the proverb, "When a door shuts, a window opens," came true. My mother's lack of ability to bear more children, especially a son, was probably the main reason my father jumped at the opportunity he was presented with at the Sessions Meeting to raise an orphaned boy. However, as with most strokes of good fortune, there was a caveat.

The boy was brought to the church by an elderly couple who said they had only recently become acquainted with him and his mother. The couple had met them on a square rigger that sailed from Portsmouth, England. They were introduced by the ship's first mate who became aware that the man had medical knowledge. An introduction of this man to the child's mother became the mate's mission. He wanted to do something for this mother who was gravely ill. As a consequence, the man and his wife spent many hours during the sea crossing tending to the young mother. Their attempts were in vain. She died at sea.

Prior to her death, she told the couple about her life, who fathered her son, and her hopes for her son's future. Before boarding the ship, the young mother knew she was very ill with consumption and that her life would soon end. She had hoped to live long enough to bring her son to his father. Although her son was conceived out of wedlock, she was certain the father would recall the moments they shared together in France. She was positive he would accept his responsibility. He was a married man, which is why she had not previously informed him of the birth of their child. But her illness changed all that. Indeed, he might be taken aback to know that he had fathered a son, but she was certain he would make arrangements for the boy to be raised properly. Her fervent wish for her son's future, along with the name of his father, were confided to the couple.

From Orphan to Family

She died with this request on her lips, but the man told those at the Sessions Meeting that he and his wife could not possibly comply with the young mother's desires. Had the mother lived a few more days and told her story to others ashore in Greenport Harbor, then maybe her desire to inform the unknowing father might have been a possibility.

It was a sad moment as the couple disembarked at Greenport, but they tried to hide their ponderous concerns from the boy. As for the boy, he wept as his mother's body was unceremoniously buried at sea, but since then he'd been silent, totally silent. He became so silent that he appeared to be in a trance, not responding to either question or direction. He clung to the woman's hand and wouldn't let go. The lady surmised that he was in so much grief that shock had set in.

Once ashore the man made arrangements for a stagecoach to travel to Hempstead, their hometown and final destination. Since they were Christians of the Presbyterian Church, he also requested a stop in Mattituck. He and his wife had privately conversed and although they wished they could abide by the boy's mother's request, they realized they just could not. It would be impossible, or at least near insanity, for them to approach a married man and attempt to hand over a child to him saying, "This is your offspring." And to add to the complexity, was the recognized prominence of the supposed father throughout the colonies. It just could not be done.

The Sessions Meeting was held in the sanctuary and it was lengthy. The man recited over and over again the conditions set out by the dying mother. The boy and the wife sat in the parlor while the meeting plodded on. The parlor was quiet except for the ticking of the grandfather clock. The lady sat patiently on the couch, with the boy's head on her lap. Fear, sorrow, and grief had tipped him over the edge of exhaustion and he fell asleep as the good lady comforted him. While the lady was patient, the stagecoach driver was not. He insisted on arriving at the Perkins

Inn in Riverhead before dark. He spoke to the lady who empathized with his concerns. Since females were not permitted to enter the Sessions Meeting, she asked the driver to knock on the door and speak to her husband. He did so and that brought about the vote of the Sessions. They unanimously agreed to accept the child as a ward of the church.

As the man entered the parlor, the boy sat up. Instinctively, he knew that his sole source of security was leaving him. The lady hugged him and told him how much she would pray for him. Once the sounds of the departing stagecoach could no longer be heard, the boy became terrified. He was alone in the large parlor. At the tender age of five, he had already witnessed more than a lifetime's worth of grief and fright.

In the Sessions Room, the discussion continued. There were nine members present and they knew their only option was to ask a member of the congregation to care for the child. It was at this point that my father volunteered to accept the boy into his home and to care for him as his own. It didn't take long for another board member to recommend voting on the offer, and then there quickly ensued a unanimous vote of approval.

After that vote one of the board members made another recommendation; he urged that they vote to keep silent the information they were given concerning the boy's natural father.

Some debate followed about morals and ethics, then a vote on the motion was taken and passed. In essence, the boy's heritage and previous lifetime was to be expunged, erased, and forgotten. But, in this decision lies the caveat I had previously mentioned. The members of the board may have voted, but they drastically underestimated the intellectual workings of the five-year-old boy. He would not ever forget.

At the end of the Sessions Meeting the men said a prayer, and then filed into the parlor. One by one they walked past the boy as they made their way to the exit. For the most part it was a silent procession with simple nods in the boy's direction. Father and Pastor Timothy were at the end of the line. When they reached the boy, Pastor Timothy sat next to him and Father knelt down in

From Orphan to Family

front of him.

Pastor Timothy spoke first. "So, we've been told what you've been through. We want you to know that we're here to help. I'm Pastor Timothy and this is Mr. Tallock. He and his wife are good, kind Christian people. From now on they will be taking care of you. He will be your new father and Mrs. Tallock will be your mother." He paused, as if to allow the concept time to sink into the boy's head. The boy could not speak.

"What's your name?" Father asked.

The boy's tongue slid over his dry lips "Benjamin F. Young," he said in a barely audible voice.

Pastor and Father exchanged quick glances. Father then stood up.

"Well son, henceforth you shall be called Benjamin Tallock."

In essence, that is how Benjamin or Benny, as he prefers to be called, became a part of our family.

One might wonder how I acquired the knowledge of what went on at that Sessions Meeting. The answer is so simple that almost everyone who grew up back then could quickly and smilingly provide it—that is, if they cared to share a family secret. Simply said, back then our farmhouse was all of one room and a fairly small one at that. In most cases, parents would share their thoughts, dreams, and sometimes emotions, when they thought their children were asleep. It was in those moments that motionless yet awake children, like me, learned a great deal about the unspoken parts of real life.

I also learned a lot from Benny himself. It was many years afterwards and it took some prying but I managed to put his story together. Fact is, most of what I'm going to share happened before my very eyes, but some parts of Benny's story came from Benny himself; some from friends and some from foes.

19

Chapter 3

Finances & to Tell the Truth

Benny, the newest member of the family, who also happened to be my new older brother, never quite fit into our family. In fact, he stuck out more like the proverbial "sore thumb." Throughout our childhood mother often said, "chickens grow chickens." Back then I really didn't understand what she meant, but as I grew in age, I came to appreciate her proverbs. Growing up I was often told I looked just like my mother, but I know I think like my father. So chickens grow chickens that God fashioned after their parents, and people grow people, in much the same way. It wasn't long after Benny arrived that we began to understand how differently he thought, and reacted to certain situations.

We're farmers. As such, our family's goal was to operate a successful farm during our time, but that was not enough. The real objective was to be certain that the farm did so well, that it would always remain in the family. In order to achieve that goal, Father had to not only take care of the farm but also worked for the London Mercantile Company. In fact, it was the London Mercantile Company that paid for Father and Mother to come to the colonies. The company gave them the loan for the property and the setting up of the farm. It wasn't quite an indentured relationship, because

Father had previously held a responsible position in the company, but it wasn't far from it. The agreement was that Father had to repay all of the cost of travel and the purchase of the farm and he had to do this by continuing to work for the company—without salary—until the debt was paid. So, we lived off the farm, which really wouldn't have been so bad if Father had been there to work it. Unfortunately, Father had to travel for the company during most of the growing season and especially during harvest time. Father's company job wasn't very hard but it was dangerous. He was responsible for the company's *wampum* trade with the Indian tribes of the northern region and the Indians surely did trade a lot of furs for that *wampum*.

Now, we kids, along with Mother and Father, would spend many hours walking along the bay's shoreline looking for the right clamshells. I often thought how most people couldn't tell the difference between poor *wampum* and good *wampum*. Most of the Island's clam shells have a real rich and deep looking purple inside and the real good ones have a wide range of purple hues. The purple color inside clam shells is common to most clams found along shorelines everywhere, but the Indians explained to my father that only the Island's clams have the very rich hues that are highly desirable for jewelry.

We would hitch the horse to the wagon and head straight through our farm to the bay. Besides looking for the *wampum* shells, we would also wade out into the bay, using our toes to locate live clams. We'd reach down and pull up a clam and Mother would add to the excitement by telling us she would cook a clam pie or sometimes clam stew. We all loved collecting *wampum* and clamming and we never felt like it was a job.

Even as a boy, Benny never quite did things in a normal way,

Finances & to Tell the Truth

at least in comparison to the rest of us children. One day while we were collecting *wampum* and live clams, Benny took the horse and wagon and went back to the barn. When he returned to the shore, he unhitched the wagon and fastened a pull line with a series of farm rakes to the horse's halter. Then he walked the horse out into the bay with the rakes dragging behind. We all laughed at his antics. The muck he stirred up with those rakes created a huge mess. But, to our surprise, when Benny dragged the rakes up onto the shore, we saw that he had gathered a massive load of clams — many more than we could ever catch by using our feet, even after a whole day of toe clamming. But that was what Benny was all about. He spent most of his minutes, hours and days looking at situations and trying to figure out how to improve them. The simple things that we took for granted, he would turn into a study and ponder; often coming up with a better system or idea.

In school, Benny mastered his lessons but often got into trouble with our teacher, Miss Mary, for not paying attention. She would say his mind was wandering again and she certainly could not tolerate his drawings of gadgets and whatnots while she was teaching. She even kept him after school one day for what she said was an improper drawing he had made while she was teaching. She also said he was spoiled and undisciplined for wasting precious paper, and gave Benny a note to give to Father.

That night Father was furious when he read Miss Mary's note. He sent Benny to bed without supper. The rest of us sat at the table, said grace, and began eating when Father finally saw the drawing that Benny had made. He ordered Benny out of bed and back to the table to explain the drawing. Benny wasn't at all shy about telling Father how since he didn't like to go to the "out house" or privy when it was cold outside, he had redesigned a corner of the house to be fitted with a privacy curtain and an open-ended chute that was mounted to the floor. The open-ended chute then led to the outhouse pit. Father accepted the explanation and in fact seemed intrigued by the concept. Nonetheless, he ordered

Benny to return to his bed. Father kept that drawing with the deed to the house and other important papers and never parted with it.

You see, Benny was very bright and creative. He was also well-spoken and he always kept his wits about him. And, while he always denied it, I believe his bravery and willingness to stand up for his convictions were his strongest attributes. I must confess however, that I am writing these words with great trepidation, lest someone else should read them. This is my diary. For sure it's an odd kind of diary. I won't write every day and events may be left unsorted, but then again I am writing this diary for my sake alone. Writing about situations that affect me helps me to see them more clearly. Memories—that's it, my writings are more like recording my memories. I suppose you could say these are my memoirs.

I've often wondered how I could best describe Benny's personality. Writing about what actually occurred seems the best way and, I clearly recall one incident…. In our family Sunday is the Lord's Day. We generally would rise extra early on Sunday, then feed and water the animals. We'd collect eggs and milk our cow but the Lord's Day was not a workday, in the traditional sense. We would break the night's fast by eating biscuits that Mother had prepared earlier in the week and if the season allowed our hens to lay eggs, then we'd poke a hole on each end of an egg and suck it clean. And there never was a reason to miss church. Father's rule was simple: if the horse could pull the wagon over the roughened road then we had best be in that wagon. Sunday church was a must and once we got there, I can forthrightly say, I always enjoyed it. Pastor Timothy always seemed to present scripture in a way that made services feel very welcoming.

Sunday services were also a time of hearing news about neighbors, other colonies and the homeland. And Pastor Timothy would often add his own political view to a current issue affecting the colonies, though he did so as delicately as possible so as not to be offensive. After all, this geographic area from Ucquebaak (now

Aquebogue), an Indian term for head of the harbor, and Corchake (now Cutchoque), another Indian term meaning principal place, was established by the New Haven colony in Connecticut. Consequently, anything that happened in New Haven or England would have an impact on the locals.

The center of this territory is Mattituck or, as the Indians called it Mattatuck. It was bought by the Connecticut Colony which was the largest colony in New England. The leadership of the Connecticut colony bought Mattituck in 1640 for two large packages that contained some iron pots, knives, coats, hooks and needles. The Paummiss Sachem Indians thought they got a bargain. Actually, the Indians could not conceive of how anyone could truly own the land. They thought the land had always been here and it would still be here long after the settlers had passed on to the other side.

In turn, the New Haven colony granted parcels of land to fifty-one men, who along with their families settled the territory. Our father's company bought our farm from one of the original settlers, a distant cousin of my father. And, therein lies some of Pastor Timothy's problem. Whenever you gather fifty-one influential families together, you have divergent but equally strong points of view. Hence, if the Pastor wished to continue as Pastor, he had to make everyone in the congregation happy, or at least not make too many enemies.

Now, with this background, it should become clear how parts of Benny's character could cause him to run afoul of public view. On Pentecostal Sunday, Pastor Timothy drew his sermon from the Biblical Book of Acts. He described how Jesus told his apostles to stay together and how he told them that since they were baptized by water, they would soon receive the Holy Spirit. It was a rousing sermon that Pastor Timothy tried to have touch each of the congregants.

"After all, we have all been baptized by water and if we pray with deep enough conviction we should all receive the Holy Spirit."

Then the Pastor tried to reinforce the concept by asking what he apparently thought was a rhetorical question. "Has anyone here not been baptized?"

A moment of silence ensued and he was about to make his point when Benny stood up. "I haven't. I haven't been baptized. That is, not that I can recall," he said.

Our pew happened to be close to the front of the church, so almost everyone saw and heard Benny. I was seated next to him. Our sisters, Sarah and Elizabeth were next to me and then Mother and Father were seated next to them. Mother finally broke the silence with an audible gasp and an "Oh, dear me!" She then whispered to Father but we kids could hear her. "You and I talked about this. We thought his mother, being French, must have been a Catholic and would have had him baptized right after he was born."

Father attempted to whisper back but he has a deep voice and it carried, so others heard what he said. "There is no way to know for sure. And for sure Benny was too young to really know. Heck, maybe we should just have him baptized. Can't hurt, can it?"

Apparently Pastor Timothy heard Father because, being as quick witted as he is, he tried to defuse the situation. "Benny, right after this service I'll be sure to give you a good dousing. A good dousing, maybe in the horse trough," he mumbled, but in a way everyone could hear.

Pastor Timothy could always add a lighthearted touch to any serious situation. On the other hand, Father seldom found humor in life's serious dynamics, especially when he felt one of the members of his family was not acting appropriately. "Sit and be quiet," he muttered, with a stern look in Benny's direction.

True to Benny's character, though, he could not be silenced. His response to Father was low in voice but not without conviction. "I've never been sure if I was baptized or not. So, if I didn't answer Pastor Timothy's question, I would be a liar and I would have been disrespectful to him."

Finances & to Tell the Truth

From several pews behind us came a muffled statement: "Children should be seen and not heard."

Father didn't know who the muffled voice belonged to but he took exception to being chastised in public. He rose, and turned around. "I don't recognize the voice but let me say, that saying may fit when it comes to your children, but it's certainly not appropriate for Benny. What he said is true and he has the conviction to stand up for the truth. And for his virtue I can say I'm proud of my son."

As Father turned to face forward and sit down another muffled voice was heard. This time it came from a side pew. "Your son?"

Before Father could respond, Pastor Timothy commanded everyone to be silent. He demanded respect in the House of God. Continuing with his sermon he cited some of the attitude we had just heard in his depiction of witness accounts of the apostles' reception of the gift of tongues.

I thought Benny was going to get a tongue lashing on the way home, but Mother very calmly said she was sorry. She explained that it was her idea not to baptize him and her rationale was very simple. She suspected his natural mother, knowing her death was imminent, would have had him baptized. Furthermore, she believed that it was sacrilegious to be baptized more than once.

Benny was very satisfied with the answer. Nonetheless, he was baptized or "rebaptized," if there is such a word, several weeks later. But the point of all of this was that Benny had an obsession with the truth and he never backed down from his convictions.

I must admit, I really admired how he stood his ground when he knew that his belief was just and correct. Perhaps it was because of this personality trait that my admiration grew and grew into something that was much deeper. Then again, I shouldn't deceive myself. It wasn't just the stand he took concerning his beliefs that made him so appealing. It was also his appearance, tall and fair-haired, with a rather sharply etched nose and a very appealing smile. Those characteristics, along with the way he treated me

and, well, enough said or else I might be sharing desires and wants I should not be entertaining…. On second thought, just one final comment on the topic. As the years went by, I often wished that we weren't brother and sister. My deepest guarded secret was that one day Benny and I could court. What a blasphemous thought. Some secrets are best never to be revealed.

Chapter 4

Happenings
&
Emotions

It's been a long time since I've written in this book of memories. I think it's because there was a long period of stress and times of great worry. All of my private time was spent in prayer. For a while life was pretty much a matter of routine, but then that's the way it is when you live on a farm. We four children, that is, my younger sisters, Benny and I got up when the rooster called, did our pre-breakfast chores, and then went off to school. There were always chores. When we got home from school, we went right back to doing chores. The one nice thing about doing chores is that, in most cases, they're routine tasks, so your mind can wonder. Daydreaming took up a lot of space in my life and my childhood seemed to blend right into my teen years. As I recollect, my dreams turned from wanting a new doll to longing for a fancy dress. I really hoped to one day go to a grand ball the likes of which I'd heard the ladies talk about after Sunday services. Along with my daydreaming came the concerns of bodily changes. Hair grew where I least expected it to cultivate and there were protrusions — well, I've seen them on most ladies, but somehow I didn't expect to have them develop on me. And then there was the first of what I would later find out would be a regular monthly occurrence. That

first experience I was certain that I had swallowed a fish bone during the previous night's supper and it had slithered through my insides. I was sure I was bleeding to death, but somehow Mother's calm approach as she retrieved an old cloth, she kept in the chest Father had built, and her relaxed way of telling me how to use it, let me know things were normal.

"Say goodbye to childhood. You're a woman now," was her only comment.

Then one day after school Mother assigned the chores as usual and I, being the oldest girl, got the most difficult job. It was time to tighten the bed ropes so that we could sleep tight. The beds that Father had built were actually rectangular boxes with ropes strung out in a checkerboard fashion. These ropes supported the feather mattress. Loose or sagging ropes made for a lack of support and consequently a bad night of sleep. So, every so often we had to tighten the ropes, which was no easy task. I would rather have joined my sisters and mother who were down at the beach gathering *wampum*. They also planned to bring back some mussels for dinner. Mother thought Father might make it home from his trading trip to the North Country in the next day or so and he truly loved her mussel stew.

Benny was tending to the livestock, so I was alone to pull and twist the ropes as tightly as possible, then make a new knot and insert the knot into the notch in the wooden frame. Again, it wasn't an easy task, but there I was rope in hands, my bare feet spread out against the wooden frame for support and pulling with all of my strength. Well, wouldn't you know it, the rope snapped and I went tumbling backwards head over tail. I ended up against the wall with my posterior pointed in the wrong direction and my dress draped upside down over my head. My own anger would have been enough to deal with, but before I could right and collect myself I heard a distinct and unmistakable laugh — Benny's laugh. So, now I had to add embarrassment to my emotions. It was just too cruel.

Happenings & Emotions

Always the gallant one, no matter what the circumstances, Benny chose to come to my assistance rather than leave me to compose myself. He helped right me by pushing my posterior flat to the floor; and as I fussed with my dress he laughed all the more. I saw nothing funny in the circumstance but soon my disposition changed, and after considering how funny I must have looked, I too broke out in giggles. There we were, sitting on the floor laughing like fools, when his mood abruptly changed. He hesitated then kissed me — right on my lips. It was a quick kiss and I did not respond in either a proper or improper way. Besides being shocked speechless, I didn't respond because, well … mostly because I was a real novice at this kissing business. Benny moved back and all I can recollect is that I looked on his face, more precisely in his eyes. I tried to figure out some rhyme or reason for his inexplicable behavior. But then, I didn't really care why he kissed me. In fact, it was wonderful and I think, deep down in my heart, kissing him was something I really wanted. For what seemed like an eternity, we said nothing. Then impulse and desire took over and I moved forward and kissed him. This time it wasn't just a glancing touch of our lips. Suffice to say, I think we went from novice to top of the class during that kiss.

Something I hadn't noticed during childhood had just occurred to me. Almost all pleasurable experiences, be they bodily acts or thoughts of fantasy, come with a degree of guilt. This kissing business, especially out of wedlock and with my brother, instantly made me feel a horrendously powerful guilt. In fact, the guilt had already set in before we ended our kiss but I wasn't going to let it wreck a great experience.

"Benny! Whatever are we doing?" I said when we finally needed to breathe.

"I think … no, I'm sure, it's called kissing." There was not a hint of guilt in his voice.

"You know what I mean. You're my brother and we're not married." Talk about a bizarre sentence. I panicked and sprang to

my feet. I started fussing over my garments, making sure as much of my body as possible was covered up.

Benny just kept staring at me. "Rachael, ever since I was a kid, I've wanted to do that," he said solemnly.

Still stunned, maybe even more so by his calm, casual and yet very direct attitude, I mustered up my most incredulous voice. "Benny, let me repeat. We're brother and sister. What we just did is ..." I couldn't think of the word.... "Is ... is ..."

He didn't wait for me to remember the word I was trying to retrieve from my now totally confused brain. "Incest. I think that's the word you're looking for," he said in that same calm voice.

"Yes!" Guilt, guilt, guilt and more guilt!

"No, No. No! This doesn't qualify as incest. We're really not related ... I mean by blood. Mom and Dad are very kind and loving. They took me, an orphan, into the family, but that doesn't mean we're related."

"What a master of words! Is the devil making your tongue so quick to excuse us? Am I now to believe I just kissed and became completely flustered by a house guest?"

"You know what I've said is the truth, Rachael, and, it made me very happy. At last we've had this moment I have longed for. Aren't you happy?"

I couldn't answer. In a state of confusion, I lowered my head. The intermingling of so many emotions at one time was almost too much to bear. Then Benny wrapped his arms around me and my head collapsed on his chest. At that moment, I knew in his arms is where I wanted to be, now and forever.

For several weeks, Benny and I settled into somewhat of a routine, that is, a farm life routine. This was not out of choice. We were constantly in the company of other family members. If others weren't continuously present, then I guarantee oxen teams pulling us in opposite directions could not have kept us apart. We survived by exchanging private glances with each other. Yes, I do confess, those moments of knowing and longing spurred on my emotions so much that my love for him could never dwindle.

It was also a time of much activity in the house. Several years earlier Father had added on another room which served as a bedroom for him and Mother. This hampered any opportunity for us children to know all of the gossip and secrets of the family and neighbors. Now he also added a room for us girls. Benny still bunked in the living area but the new girls' room served to separate the sexes. No more moments of pretending to sleep while looking across the living area and hoping to catch Benny's eyes in the flickering light of the fireplace. Just knowing he was there, right across the room, with no walls to separate us, was incredibly exciting and romantic. I had no idea that our secret romance was about to come to an abrupt end.

One night, as Father concluded the evening's meal prayer, he announced that we would have a special topic to discuss over dinner. He paused dramatically as we all looked at each other in puzzlement. "We'll be discussing Rachael's wedding," he said.

For a moment no one spoke.

"Rachael. Rachael who?" I asked in a voice that surprised me.

Mother was quick to respond. "Why, that's you of course, dear."

The reaction around the table ranged from my sisters' jubilation to blank starring from Benny. Mother was so delighted that she reached across the table and grasped Father's hand showing a sign of affection that had never before been witnessed by us children. I, of course, had plenty of time to observe all of this behavior because I was in a complete state of denial. There was no way they could be talking about me.

"Dear, don't you want to know who Father has arranged for you to marry?" Mother asked me, breaking through my haze.

"Oh, yes of course." At that I snapped out of my trance and came back to the unpredictable world of reality.

Mother turned to Father and nodded. This was his segue into a well-rehearsed presentation. First he cleared his throat;

then he began. "I spent a great deal of forethought before even attempting this arrangement. Above all, I needed to consider your future. Mother and I want you to be well cared for and we want you to be in a God respecting family that has a history of good bloodlines. Good stock, so to speak."

Now that truly got my attention. "You mean, like what we do when we send out our cows for studding?"

"No, I mean like the Royal families do."

I wanted to say, what's the difference, but held my tongue.

"Anyway, those were our thoughts when I approached Zack Jones. He and I are distant cousins and when we met, we figured we were four generations removed. That should make having children pretty safe. So I suggested a marriage between you and his son, Charles."

I didn't know what to do or say. Time stood still. Finally Mother spoke. "Dear, aren't you happy? We thought you would be ecstatic and overwhelmed with joy."

What could I say? How could I answer? "I, I,..." But no words came out. With great shame—really guilt—and a very heavy heart, I lowered my head and I didn't realize I was crying until I felt the wetness of tears through my dress top. Still, I knew I had to say something, so I started trying to speak again. "I, I ..."

"She can't marry Charles. She's already spoken for." Benny said, in that calm and very confident tone of his.

Time stopped and a long shocked silence ensued. It was quite a while before we heard, "Spoken for? By whom?" Father sputtered and his voice was anything but calm.

"Me. And I apologize for not speaking up sooner. I should have asked you for Rachael's hand a while ago. That would have saved you the effort of seeking a match for her." Before anyone could speak, he continued. "So, Father, er, Sir, may I have Rachael's hand in marriage?"

Then it struck me. Benny and I had never talked about marriage. In fact, we never talked about any of this. All I could

Happenings & Emotions

recall was us kissing. My voice was higher pitched than I intended. "Benny, you never said a word ..."

"We didn't need to talk. When we kissed ..."

"Kissed! Kissed!" Father was getting really worked up—like a horse on fermented oats.

"Kissed!!" He ranted, his voice even more thunderous.

At this juncture the conversation became quite hard to follow. Voices overlapped and the increase in the pitch also added to the oftentimes, unintelligible conversation. Comments were being thrown about "willy-nilly." However, it is important to record it as closely as possible, even for remembrance sake. It went something like this:

FATHER: Kissed! (He said it over and over again and the more he said it, the more agitated he became.)

MOTHER: God have mercy! (Praying is something she does frequently, but this time she made the sign of the cross. I know Catholics, and I think Lutherans, make the sign of the cross when they pray, but we Presbyterians don't usually do ritualistic things. Maybe that's why we're called "the frozen chosen." Anyway, mother's crossing herself was truly astonishing.)

FATHER: Benny! What are you saying? She's your sister!

BENNY: Well, she's really not my sister, Sir. I mean we're not related by blood.

FATHER: Ridiculous! We took you into this house and this family and that makes her your sister. What else have you done to her? (he shouted.)

MOTHER: God Almighty! Help us! (Another sign of the cross—no, make that two, but I don't think she made it all the way to the left side of the cross, on the second signing.)

BENNY: We kissed. That was all. But, I will say ... (He looked at me and gave me a quick smile before continuing,) ... we kissed as lovers and not as siblings.

MOTHER: Oh sacrilege!! Blasphemy!! (She added another couple of crosses.)

35

FATHER: You have disgraced yourself, our daughter, and the entire family, (he roared at Benny, pointing his finger accusingly.) Why didn't you tell us what he did to you? (he demanded, facing me.)

ME: Because it wasn't he, it was we. (I suddenly stopped crying; found my voice, and jumped right in to support Benny. Now, is that a sign of true love or what? In fact I said,) I love him Father and I love kissing him. (My admission shocked everyone, even myself.)

FATHER: You could not have been compliant in such lurid behavior. He had to have forced you. And if not, then you had to be under some kind of evil spell.

MOTHER: Dear Lord! How could our Rachael have gone so far astray? (She made several more crosses.)

ME: Mother!! You make me sound like a harlot!

FATHER: Such words! Not in my house! And in front of my children! Children, go to bed! (We all jumped up, including Benny, but Father quickly clarified.) Not you two! You two! (He waved at my sisters.)

ELIZABETH: But this is exciting. Can't we stay?

FATHER: No! This conversation is not fit for the ears of decent young children. (So they reluctantly left the table. But I am certain, they soon had their ears snug against the bedroom door.)

BENNY: Sir. (His calm manner of speaking persisted. He hesitated and looked at me.) There are two things I must say. First, I humbly apologize for not being forthright sooner and secondly, I'm asking for Rachael's hand in marriage.

MOTHER: I'm going to faint! A sister and brother marrying. Oh dear God! What have we done to deserve this?! (Hey—no crosses; I wondered if she gave up.)

ME: (At first I was enthralled by Benny's request for my hand, but then I just didn't like the way he went about it.) Hey! What about asking me first? Asking dad without asking me first is no better than a match marriage. (I guess that got his attention because Benny then got up, walked around the table and stood next to me. Suddenly, he dropped to one knee. I was mortified. Yes, I wanted a proposal, but not in front of our parents, for goodness sakes! But there was no stopping him.)

BENNY: Rachael, I have loved you in the past. I love you even more now and I pray I will love you even greater as we grow old together. Will you marry me?

ME: (Sugar plums were dancing in my head.) Yes! Oh, yes! (I said, as butterflies bounced in my stomach and tears gushed from my eyes. I heard my sisters cheer from behind the bedroom door. Their roars of delight encouraged my tears of joy to flood my cheeks.)

MOTHER: Oh my word!! (she said crossing herself yet again. Right then and there I made myself a promise: If my heart didn't stop and I survived this whole ordeal, I was going to ask her about this crossing thing. But Father's next words indicated he too was more than curious about this sudden penchant.)

FATHER: Dear wife, what in blazing sunsets are you doing? Making the sign of the cross is … is … blazes! I don't know what it is. Just stop doing it! (he ranted.)

Was he angry! He got up, left the table and walked about the room, talking to himself. Every so often he would look over at me, then at Benny, pause, and then resume moving about the living area. This went on for quite a while and we knew better than to interrupt him. At last he stopped and came back to the table. It seemed that a great deal of time had passed, but it was probably only five minutes, and all the while no one said a word. But by then Father's anger had oddly seemed to dissipate, only to be replaced by another emotion. Now it appeared that he was genuinely distraught. "Well … What I thought was going to be a surprising evening for you, Rachael, turned out to be a shocking one for me," he slowly said. "Mind you, I'm not at all concerned about the Jones family. They'll survive and I'm sure their son will find someone else. I guess what I'm saying is that, no one should

come between people who are in love."

Mother smiled at him and it was apparent that they shared an entire conversation without speaking a word. He looked at Benny, who was now standing at my side, and then focused on me.

"You have our permission and our blessings. But I ask one thing of you. Let some time pass before you marry and keep your intentions to wed within this house. Deep down in my heart I'm not at all that shocked. Truth be known, I am responsible for what has happened," his voice faded off.

When I began this chapter I foretold of periods of happiness and stress. That night proved to be full of both — in the extreme....

Chapter 5

Heading North

The one belief I share freely is that nothing happens by accident. The Lord preplans everything. Pastor Timothy calls it "predetermination" or "predestination." But, in the case of my pending marriage to Benny, I think the Lord served as a co-conspirator. You see, even at a time when Father was greatly stressed, such as that night when all of this was discussed, he still conjured up a plan. Father didn't share his plan with us that night but he certainly knew all of the steps we would take.

Needless to say, sleep was almost impossible after that night of revelation, confusion and ultimate happiness. What a convergence of emotions! I doubt if anyone caught a wink of sleep that night. The next morning we all got up late and rather than sitting down to breakfast, we quickly took biscuits and tea and started out to do our chores. Livestock, especially cows, seem to be less productive when we humans disrupt their schedule.

On my way out of the house I heard Father say something to Benny that caught my attention. "I'm going to need some help on my next working trip to the North Country. I'd like you to come along and give me a hand."

Stepping through the doorway, I stopped and wondered what he

really meant. Father had never before claimed that he needed help on his trips to the North Country. I therefore thought of all kinds of notions that he could be considering.

Benny must have had the same questions in mind. "That would be an adventure and I'd love to learn how you go about selling the *wampum*. I mean, trading with the Indians and all. But if I went with you who would do the work here on the farm?"

Father had obviously already considered the issue. "We're past the planting season and the ladies can handle the routine chores. What they can't do will just have to wait until we get back. We'll only be gone for a few weeks. Indians don't take a lot of pelts in springtime. That's the time for the young animals to be born. The adult animals are needed to feed and protect them. Another thing I've learned is that Indians are afraid to take too many pelts. They believe they will offend the animal spirits if they take too many at this time of year. They fear the spirits will stop the animals from having young ones and that would mean an end to pelts. More importantly, it could end their food supply."

It was then that I realized Father was planning to prepare Benny for the future and although he may have done it reluctantly, he had accepted Benny's plan to marry me.

It took several days to prepare for the trip. Father always took the Company's two horses, one for riding and the other to carry supplies and *wampum*. Hopefully, on the return trip the packhorse would carry a goodly amount of the pelts. This time Benny would need to take one of our farm horses. We had two horses, which left one for Mother to use with our wagon. We had planted some cool weather crops like cabbage and kale. We'd need the wagon to take some produce to market. We'd also need the horse to take us to church and in case we had to get to Doc Gregg. In other words, Father and Benny would have to do with three horses.

The same situation was true for the two long guns we had. Father and Benny would take one and the other would be kept at the house. Of course you might think that decision was simple, as a long gun would be needed for protection at the house but that's not the main reason. The gun's primary use was to keep the deer from devouring all of our crops. In fact, that had become one of Benny's major tasks, not that he found it to be so terribly arduous. He really was quite a marksman and his early morning and evening vigils not only served to protect the crops but also provided us with our main source of meat. Before leaving Benny made sure the gun was clean, the flints dry and the pouch filled with powder.

Usually, the days before Father was to leave were filled with apprehension, especially for Mother. To say her nervousness was justified is an understatement. Each time Father ventured north, there was the very distinct possibility that we would never see him again. On those trips, danger surrounded him every day. At any time he could encounter a situation that could end his life, either by natural circumstances or at the hands of evildoers. And the North Country is so vast and such a wilderness, that he or his remains, could easily disappear, never to be seen again. Now that Benny was going along with him, Mother was a little relieved but paradoxically, she was doubly apprehensive.

It was odd but once they left she seemed less nervous. I think she spent even more time in prayer, which seemed to have a calming effect on her.

The night before they left, Mother cooked us an elaborate dinner of venison roast and root vegetables. She had simmered the roast for most of the day and the aromas helped to distract us from the fact that the men of the house wouldn't be around for a long time. The meal was everything the forecasting aromas had predicted — delicious beyond description.

Just as supper ended, Father asked Benny to check on the horses, which seemed odd, because it was a request we'd never heard him make before. Then he suggested that I accompany Benny, in case he needed help. It was at that moment that I, and I suspect everyone else in the house, realized Father was truly a

romantic at heart. Benny and I started for the barn and we hadn't taken but two steps when he reached for my hand. We walked there hand in hand. Once inside the barn, Benny lit a candle. As we checked the horses we talked and before we knew it, we were once again in each other's arms. It was a wonderful moment but knowing that our family was thinking about us, made us both feel awkward.

We started back towards the house, again holding hands, when Benny stopped and turned me toward him. "I know men have said this to women ever since language was developed, and I said it when I proposed to you, but that was in front of our family. I really want this to be just between us. I have always loved you but never more than now, and I pray I will love you even more in the years to come," he said.

His words were so touching that I paraphrased them to him. "I love you today, more than yesterday but less than tomorrow."

Expressing our love was only a part of what happened to me at that moment. At that moment I also fully understood that I was a woman, a woman in love.

Chapter 6

Seeds of Discomfort

Once the men left for the North Country, things seemed to get very quiet around the farm. Oh, our chores increased and Mother and I said repeatedly that we never realized how much Benny really did around the farm. Still, it was quiet.

That is until Sunday came and we went to church. We had gotten up extra early so we could do our morning chores, hitch up the wagon, get washed and dressed, and make it to the church in time for services. However, the time issue became questionable. We were certain the road had become bumpier than normal for this time of year. Usually the spring rains caused ruts to form and holes that we have laughingly called "craters." This year the craters were so large that our horse stopped in front of several. Apparently, he was fearful he might not make it out to the other side. Nonetheless we made it to church with time to spare before Pastor Timothy had begun the service.

We climbed the steps and as we entered the narthex our quiet spell was broken. Not that those who were gathered in the narthex were noisy—far from it. If anything, they were overtly quiet, sullen and even mournful in their whispery voices. This was a far cry from the usually warm comfortable feelings that

permeated our church. We approached the closely banded group to extend greetings but Mother respected the atmosphere and merely nodded hello. I followed her lead. The tone was broken by Bertram Hard; a well respected church elder and community leader.

"This is 1775 and our King is treating us like medieval serfs," he proclaimed.

His wife, Adel, was quick to put her hand on his arm. The gesture she made was meant to warn him to be careful of what he was saying.

But another congregant, Wendel Rivers, had already made up his mind that Bertram was out of order. "You're a subject of the King and your words sound like treason," he said in a commanding voice.

"Let him speak. Besides, we're in church and all of us here have sanctuary," countered another man.

That statement brought a large murmur from the crowd. In fact, the silence that permeated the atmosphere when we first entered the church was now replaced with random bantering and ranting. To be more specific, the ranting was about King George's most recent tax. People were challenging or supporting all sides of the issue. What was causing consternation was the fact that, not only did this tax seem unfair, but to add insult to injury, it was only being levied on the Colonists. The other citizens of the empire were not subject to this tax.

The inflamed rants continued until Pastor Timothy entered the narthex and briskly walked to the bell cord. He began pulling on the heavy cord. "If we pray to God for guidance, I'm sure he'll answer. So let's go into the sanctuary and pray," he calmly said.

As the crowd followed Pastor Timothy into the sanctuary, my sisters and I tagged along behind Mother. When we got to our pew I asked her what our neighbors and fellow parishioners were arguing about. Before answering she took a moment to consider the facts, "It seems to me that arguments of this type always come

Seeds of Discomfort

down to money. In this case, King George wants more of our money and now many of our fellow Colonists are saying, 'enough is enough.'"

"Are we saying that, too?" She looked surprised by my question.

"Well ... actually, yes. Your father works very hard and we certainly don't want to pay any more taxes than we have to, but we certainly don't want to defy the King."

I wanted to ask more questions but couldn't because Pastor Timothy called the service to order.

Now, I need to share a little truth, or more likely a little confession. Maybe it's because of my age or even that I have an overly active imagination but I sometimes don't pay attention to the sermons at church. Instead, I often drift off into daydreams with my eyes wide open. And the church atmosphere is certainly most conducive to letting one's mind drift. On sunny days the stained glass windows render a soft glow to the sanctuary that has an almost hypnotic effect. On cloudy or inclement days the soft light coming through the stained glass, combined with the candles glowing from two chandeliers and the wall sconces, makes for all the comfort of a pan-warmed bed on a winter's night.

But on this day things were different. After opening prayers Pastor Timothy thumbed his Bible and I could tell he was planning to deviate from his customary reading and sermon. He fiddled with the pages until he found the verse he wanted to share. "In Luke 16 we read a parable about a wealthy man, a king in his own right. The parable also speaks of a beggar whose body was riddled with sores. The two men die. The beggar goes to heaven and the wealthy man is doomed to hell for eternity. Through the fires of hell the wealthy man sees the beggar with the patriarch Abraham in heaven. He asks if Abraham would let the beggar dip his fingers in water and press them to his scorched lips but Abraham says, 'your wealth on earth sealed your faith and the beggar's poverty has earned him heaven.'"

It wasn't hard to figure out Pastor Timothy's intent by citing the parable. He was drawing an analogy between the Colonists, who for the most part were not beggars but certainly not well off financially, and our own King George, who had riches beyond compare. In fact King George didn't need any more riches, especially those gained by imposing more taxes on the Colonists. However, as Father always says, while most people have enough pennies, they have a pound appetite that never seems to be satisfied. Anyway, the point to Pastor Timothy's sermon was that, in the end God will deal with all people in accordance with their lifestyles here on earth. I was sure his sermon would bring an end to the kind of debate we encountered when we entered the narthex that morning.

Instead, the debaters didn't even wait for the service to end. Bertram was the first to erupt. He impulsively stood up. "And the Bible also says God helps those who help themselves. If we do as you suggest … that is do nothing, we relegate ourselves to being slave colonies. And I, for one, would rather die than be a slave!" he said in a forceful, bordering on belligerent voice.

I instantly knew Wendel was going to counter Bert's position and he did so in a commanding tone. "Bert! You keep speaking words of treason and you may get your wish. King George has the power to make you a slave and if you don't like it, he may grant your wish and see to it that you die."

With that, the debate got louder and louder, with Pastor Timothy trying in vain to regain control of the church. Finger pointing gave way to fist waving as the mayhem escalated. That's when our normally calm Pastor had enough. He raised the heavy church Bible up in the air and slammed it on top of the altar. The sudden noise rattled around the walls of the church, startling the congregants.

The entire congregation fell silent. It was apparent that Pastor Timothy was going to speak but for the longest moment he just stood there, with his brown-grayish hair disheveled, probably

Seeds of Discomfort

from slamming down the Bible. "Have you forgotten, you're in the house of the Lord? Remember what Jesus did to the vendors in the temple? They were quiet compared to you people!"

He paused and a smile crept across his eyes demonstrating that he had found levity, even in a moment like this. His smile broadened ... "Besides, most of you usually sleep during my sermons. What happened this time?"

That drew some laughter but he was quick to raise his hand requesting silence. He obviously didn't want another outburst. "These are not easy times and I'm concerned we are edging closer to a point when each of us will be forced to make a very difficult decision. It's not hard to forecast that we will be making the kinds of decisions that will pit neighbor against neighbor and even kin against kin."

Another long pause, then he said "I'm going to end the service now. Put away your hymnals. We won't be singing any more hymns. Instead I'd like each of you to leave in silent prayer. Yes, pray that the Lord leads you to the proper decision, but pray more that whatever is decided does not lead to conflict between us Colonists. So, go and pray."

In silence, we left the church. Presumably everyone was leaving in prayer, except that I had a major problem with Pastor Timothy's directive. Oh, I understood the part about praying for divine intervention so that we would not witness neighbor assaulting neighbor, but what about the larger possibility or predicament? Shouldn't he have directed us to pray for peace between our mother country and those of us in the colonies?

I simply prayed for peace.

Chapter 7

When Views Clash

On the morning Father and Benny left home and headed

towards the North Country, the weather was typical of Long
Island in springtime. Although the sun was breaking in the eastern
horizon, it was still very chilly, windy and a good measure of
dampness crept into everything. Father knew the boats available
for ferry service across the Sound to Connecticut usually departed
in the early morning. The boat ride would take the better part of
the day and most ship captains planned to make it to the New
Haven port before nightfall. Of course, all such plans were subject
to the will of the winds and the mood of the waters. Father knew
this day's windy conditions would be a factor.

When the London Mercantile Company selected Long Island
for its base of field operations, they gave most consideration to the
region's supply of high quality *wampum*. They also drew a straight
line on a map to the habitat of the northern Indian tribes. They
paid little regard to the dangerous journey Father would face each
time he traveled across the Sound. The Sound has a well-deserved
reputation for being a treacherous body of water. Somehow, the
London Mercantile Company didn't even consider that Long
Island sticks out more than one hundred and thirty miles into the

ocean. To suggest that Father head up island and cross the Sound near Manhattan, where its width is less expansive, rather than head directly north was equally ridiculous. It would mean many days of extra travel to cover Father's assigned territory.

His territory covered most of southern Connecticut and the northern area of the New York colony. Traveling directly north across the sound to Connecticut was the shortest and most efficient route. Had the company's administrators thought to station him in Connecticut, they would have saved him a great deal of travel time. But then again, there's the issue of the *wampum*. How would he get it? Suffice to say, there really was no easy answer. So Father's route would take him across the Sound to New Haven, where he traded with the Pequot Indians. He also traveled further east along the Connecticut shoreline to swap goods with the Narragansett tribe. Then he made the long trek north and west across the Hudson River towards Albany. There he would turn directly north and make his way into the Adirondack Mountains and on to Lake Champlain. Father had said, although he never saw one, he had heard that the British Military Engineers had made maps of this entire area. In fact, the French had maps dating back to the sixteen hundreds.

In the Adirondack region he would travel for days and cover more than a hundred miles in order to trade with the Mohegan, the Onondaga and the Oneida tribes. Of course, he would travel even more days and many more miles heading further north where he would then trade with the Mohawk Indians. They were England's best ally and yet they were feared the most by the Colonists, because they were fearless fighters. Actually, their tribal name was Kanienkeh, but the Colonists who faced them in battle gave them the nickname Mohawk, which comes from another tribe and means "man eater." Thank goodness Father didn't have to do business with them. Mostly, they live north of his territory and the London Mercantile Company bosses hired some pretty tough characters to deal with them. The company's philosophy was to

When Views Clash

face force with force.

After trading off all of the *wampum* for pelts, Father would head south to the Isle of Manhattan. There he would bring his goods to the offices and warehouses of the London Mercantile Company, located on the corner of Wall and Stone Streets. I've never been there but from what Father has said it sounds like an area that just bristles with people moving in all directions. Father has been to Boston but he said it couldn't compare to the bustling activity of New York, not that he liked going to New York. He always said he couldn't wait to drop off the pelts, resolve his finances and head for the East River Ferry to get off that island. According to Father the pace in Manhattan and especially where his office is located, is so hectic, he would still be doing paperwork while the pelts he brought in would already be graded, crated, and sent off in ships bound for coat manufacturing in London. By the time he got home those pelts were already half way across the high seas.

That was the journey that lay ahead of Father and Benny as they made their way to the Mattituck docks. From our farm to the docks along the Mattituck inlet it was about an hour's horseback ride. Later Benny would say it was the easiest part of the trip. Once Father chose the ship and paid the fare the real task of getting the horses on board began. Horses have two main weaknesses. The first is that they aren't the smartest of the four legged creatures; and the second is that they are just about the spookiest of all critters.

The men made several unsuccessful attempts at walking the horses up the plank and onto the ship. On most tries the horses merely stopped at the beginning of the plank and bolted backward, but on one attempt a horse lunged forward and to the side. It ended up with its hind legs on the dock and its front legs suspended between the dock and the boat. Luckily the horse wasn't injured but it did take a lot of effort to get all four of its hoofs back onto the dock.

Finally, the captain realized they had to take another approach. He got a large cloth and a piece of sail canvas that had been cut into a six inch wide by six-foot long strip. Then the captain placed the cloth over the horse's head while Father and Benny stretched the canvas strip around the horse's rear. The strip went from side to side and Father held one end while Benny grasped the other end. The captain yelled, "now!" and he tugged on the reins while Father and Benny yanked the bay mare up the plank. It wasn't easy and the biggest concern was the possibility of the horse stepping off the plank, simply because it couldn't see where it was going. But it worked. In fact, it worked for all three horses.

As expected, the horses were very jittery during the crossing. They had been confined with boards that were assembled into a stall, but still, the motion of the boat had to be very upsetting to them. Father and Benny took turns staying with the horses, trying to keep them calm. At one point, Benny came back to relieve the men and serve his time.

"I need to get something off my chest. I have a motive for taking you on this trip," Father said.

"I know, or at least I think I've figured it out. You want me to learn what you do so I can earn a living and support Rachael," Benny responded.

Father hesitated, then nodded. "That too, but there's something else and I'm just going to tell you straight out. I don't want any misunderstanding. If you and Rachael go through with this crazy idea of marrying, then you can't live on the farm. Or for that matter, you can't live anywhere near the rest of the family."

Benny was shocked. "Why?"

"Benny, you're my son. By birth or not, I've raised and cared for you as a son. Rachael is my daughter. How do you expect me to feel? Don't you see? When the rest of the community hears about this they'll laugh, and believe it or not I can handle that, but then they'll talk about what a weird, evil family we are. They'll

When Views Clash

even accuse us of being unchristian and I've heard of families being shunned by the church for actions that are far less sinful than what you are intending.

It's not only going to affect you and Rachael, it's going to cause Mother and me to become outcasts. And, what about your sisters? How are they going to be treated by the community? Do you think it will be easy for them to marry? Who will want to become a member of this family?"

Benny couldn't respond. He couldn't even hold his head up.

"What I'm planning is to take you to the North Country. There's plenty of good farmland north of Albany. Some land there, you can still stake a claim on. If you and Rachael still want to go ahead with your plan, then I'd want you to move north. Folks in our community only need to know that you've moved to a new territory. They don't need to know you'll be doing it as a husband and wife." Father paused, took a long breath and exhaled. "I had hoped and prayed that one day you, my son, would take over the farm, but Mother and I will figure out something else. It will make a good dowry for one of your other sisters."

Benny continued to remain silent. Father had made it clear where he stood, and that's when the conversation ended.

The landing in Connecticut was chaotic but that was to be expected. After settling the horses' and their own stomachs, the men left the seaport and headed east along the road that parallels the shoreline. Father had hoped to travel a good distance towards the Pequot encampment before sundown but the ferry crossing took longer than anticipated. He mumbled something about "favorable winds being a rare, if ever occurrence, as far as he was concerned." As a consequence, they stayed overnight at the Red Lion Inn. Benny was really happy to get there for two reasons. First and foremost, since Father had made his comments concerning his vision of Benny and my relocating to the North Country, there had been little if any conversation between them. Father was angered by the whole situation and withdrew into

silence. Benny perceived that we were in effect being sent into exile, a thought that also provoked his own silence and he thought the inn might be a good diversion for both of them.

Benny's second reason for being happy to arrive at the inn was simply the excitement of it being the first time he was staying at an inn. The inn also allowed for Benny to have conversations with others, which boosted his spirits, however it was filled to near capacity and he had to share a bed with two other men. That was a disheartening circumstance. Disheartening may not be the appropriate word. Surprised ... no, shocked might be more like it. When Benny entered the bedroom, he was greeted with a body odor that was so intense it burned his nostrils and flooded his eyes with tears. "Chin up," he told himself as he made ready to join his bedmates. He convinced himself to "make do," things couldn't get worse, but to his horror, things got much worse. In the predawn hours his bedmate on the other side got up and made a bowel movement in the chamber pot. That was more than Benny could handle. He bolted from the bed, grabbed his clothes and boots and got out of the room as fast as was humanly possible.

Father, having had other experiences of inn stays, faired much better. He, too, was assigned a double bed that was also slated to accommodate three men. Father paid for the room but on previous occasions, he had found these kinds of situations to be so uncomfortable that he had resorted to sleeping in a chair in the parlor. Granted, the upright position wasn't terribly comfortable but it was a far better option than bunking with two other men who were strangers.

With boots and clothes in hand, Benny entered the room and spotted Father.

"What took you so long? I figured you'd be here sooner," Father said, with a wry smile.

"You should have warned me. That was really disgusting."

"It's just one of those things you just can't warn another person about. Think about it. There are two other men in your room and

When Views Clash

two in mine that don't seem to be bothered by the situation. I just can't figure out what one man's limit is as compared to another's."

"I just can't wait to leave."

"We'll leave after breakfast. There's about two hours till dawn, so grab a seat and get some sleep. And always remember it's worth the price of the inn if it's raining, snowing or there's lots of ice out there. It's even worth it if you're just too tired to make camp. I'm a good customer; they know me, so I'm almost always assured of a roof over my head and shelter for the horses. That's why I don't complain and I make do."

Benny thought for a moment. "I get your point and I guess there isn't another inn around here?"

"Not until we get to the Connecticut River and then take the toll road north. But I'll warn you now, don't expect the sleeping arrangements to be much better. And another thing to remember, here you get a hot dinner and a good breakfast. That's a lot better than trying to eat the hard dried jerk meat we brought from home."

Benny accepted this advice but more importantly he realized Father was exposing him to a true learning experience—one he would never forget and one that would help guide him through life. He fell asleep on the floor next to the fireplace and didn't wake until the smell of freshly baked biscuits and smoked ham peaked his senses.

Father and Benny's trek east to the river and then north past the Toll House Inn, on the toll road was very time consuming but the scenery was so beautiful that Benny ignored the passing of the hours. A day after they left the Red Lion Inn they approached the Pequot Indian's main encampment. They had seen Indians along the way but members of this particular tribe are a shy lot. When Indians would see Colonists coming towards them, they usually stepped off the roadway and into the woods, not to be seen again.

This encampment was different. It was void of shyness and although its location changed with the seasons, it always

maintained a certain degree of lively activity. Benny expressed his surprise to Father about how closely the encampment resembled our own village of Mattituck with a few small differences. Instead of shops where products were sold by merchants, the Pequots had communal huts where food was kept for distribution to tribal families. There even seemed to be an area of food cooking stations where meals were being prepared for the whole tribe.

It took a while for Father and Benny to maneuver through the encampment towards the center where the Chief's hut was located. As they moved forward the Indian children followed causing quite a ruckus. Apparently, visitors were a good reason to celebrate and express joy. "Good to see happy children, but whatever happened to the old adage that children should be seen and not heard?" Benny said to Father with a grin.

Father smiled as he answered. "Indian life is simple, especially for the children. They help their elders gather food and wood for the fires but for the most part they're free to be kids. Oh, there are certainly rituals of adulthood ahead but Indian boys and girls learn to be free spirits. Growing up as children you heard about budgets, mortgages, seeds to buy and crops to look after. They have no such concepts."

"Sounds good," Benny said reflectively "but, I don't see any harm to the way we farm kids were raised. And as far as being a free spirit ..." He was about to say more but the gathering in front of them began to spread apart. He guessed they were nearing the Chief's hut, but he really couldn't distinguish it from the other huts.

They slowed down their pace as they approached a hut with colorful geometric patterns painted on its deerskin coverings. From the inside, the hut's flap, which served as a door, opened and an elderly Indian man stepped out. To Benny he looked to be about the oldest of the Indians who were present and he was quite different looking from the Indians Benny had seen in the Mattituck area. His skin was more weather-beaten, almost leathery looking.

When Views Clash

In truth, he looked more like a Colonist who worked and lived along the shoreline or at sea. His hair was parted in the middle and flowed back into a long braided ponytail, that was predominately gray, streaked with black. He had few teeth but Benny had already noticed that was common among the Indians. Still, the nicest thing about him was his smile.

"My good friend. Too many moons have passed since you last came to see us," he said, greeting Father with open arms.

While the Chief was speaking Father dismounted and he too opened his arms to exchange greetings with his friend. As they embraced Benny realized Father and the Chief not only did business together, they also had a bond.

Now ... since this is my memoir, I can say this. I can't write down the Chief's name because I can't pronounce it and if I could say it, I wouldn't be able to spell it.

Father then introduced Benny to the Chief and within moments they were all seated on the ground right in front of the Chief's hut. Other Indian men carrying pelts joined them, forming a circle. The trading began immediately. It was almost as though the Chief wanted to get the business out of the way so that he could enjoy the company. To Benny, the trading itself was fascinating. It was done by the Pequots spreading out their pelts on the ground in the center of the circle. Father and Benny did likewise by displaying their *wampum* on a canvas and placing it near the pelts. When Father picked a pelt, the Chief selected a shell. Each of them looked for certain qualities in their selection. The shells with darker and more brilliantly purple hues were favored by the Chief, and Father looked for the pelts that were large and had few blemishes. Pelts that had fur missing or bald spots from disease or fights with other animals were less desirable. Sometimes the Chief would signal that he wanted more than one shell for a given pelt and that's when he and Father would negotiate. On many occasions that situation was reversed with Father wanting more pelts for a specific shell. The trading was rapid and within a short

time it was finished. That's when the Chief motioned to a few female Indians, who were standing around the periphery. The sign was their signal to bring food and drink.

As the men dined on venison that had been roasted over cedar wood, served on mats woven out of the local tall grasses, they conversed about many things. Among the tribe only the Chief spoke English, a skill he had picked up at the Toll House Inn. There he frequently traded game for blankets, utensils, fishhooks, and other items that had become tribal necessities. The Chief directed his attention to Father. The other Indians spoke in their native language and Benny tried to get a feeling for what they were talking about. Fortunately, they used a number of hand motions along with their dialogue and it was apparent to Benny that most of the men were talking about a sport. The conversation was extremely enthusiastic in nature, with some of the men becoming very excited.

In the midst of all the hand motions and chatter, the Chief spoke calmly but loudly to Father. "Your chief, the man you call King, he very bad father."

"What?" Father was baffled by the comment and thought he had misunderstood. "What makes you say that?"

"The man you call King, who lives on the other side of the great water, he does not like his children."

Baffled even more, Father questioned, "why would you say such a thing?"

The Chief reflected, not only on the question but also on Father's face before answering.

"I say this only because you are a friend. A man I trust. If my brothers, the Mohawks, hear of my words they would be angry. What I say is for your ears and heart. Not to be spread like seeds in the wind." Once again he considered what he was about to say before speaking.

"A good chief is the same as a good father. He tries to make life better for his people, his children. He does not take away. He gives all of himself and all of his goods, until he has no more. Then he finds ways to give some more. This King of yours, he takes away from you Colonists and he keeps taking. He does not make your life better. He makes the life of Colonists very hard."

Father clearly understood. "So you've heard of our tax problems. Yes, it is a very heavy burden on us, but the King must need our money to pay for all the costs of running the kingdom. Where are you hearing all of this?" Father abruptly asked.

"The Toll House Inn has many travelers. They speak plainly and with large voices. I do not speak, I listen. Then I speak to my friends, like you."

"Well, it's true. Compared to others in the kingdom, we are being taxed too much, but that's because the King has no one from the colonies to tell him our true feelings. That's what we want. We would like the King to have people around him who are from the colonies. Much like you, Chief, you have your people around you and they advise you. And I know you listen to them and consider their ideas. We want the same thing. We want our King to have representatives from here in his council."

Father smiled. "I'm sure our King is ..." Father's smile faded and he weakly added, "... I just hope our King is considering this."

The Chief was not convinced.

"A father who takes from his children 'til they cry out to be heard, is not a good father. He will not listen. He will become more angry. He will lash out. Bad fathers think the whip will make their children obey. This King is not right. He also does not see that the great water between himself and his children has made them less fearful of him. He does not see that his children have grown and his whip can be caught and taken away."

That night Father and Benny slept in a hut provided by the Chief. When he sleeps, Father snores but Benny said he could tell the Chief's words had bothered Father. That night there was no snoring, just a great deal of tossing and turning from Father's side. At daybreak they packed up the horses, ate some dried

turkey, said their goodbyes and headed south on the toll road. There wasn't much conversation and Father set a quick pace. It was as though Father were trying to escape a bad feeling. His pace was hastened by the dryness of the road and the previous heavy volume of traffic that had pounded the wheel tracks smooth. On approaching the Toll House Inn, Benny asked where they would be stopping for the night. "I'd like to make it to the Idle Hour Inn. It's in New Haven," Father said to Benny's surprise.

"But isn't that well past where we ferried across the Sound?"

"Yes, but I think we can do it."

"Is that where you usually stop?"

"No." Father often gives two types of answers: a simple, straightforward, non-explanatory one, or a long-winded, elaborate one—this was the short version that implied he didn't feel the need to explain or justify his reasoning. To Benny it had to be irritating.

As was his custom, Benny couldn't just accept an unexplained answer and so he pursued it. "Why?"

And Father, knowing Benny would probe, presented an answer that didn't satisfy but was hard to question. "The faster we travel the quicker we will be home and our task accomplished."

Father's manner of speaking was sharp, to the point and subliminally loaded with anger. Benny surmised Father was still seething over the notion that Benny and I were planning on marriage. And I really couldn't find fault in Father's judgment. Imagine a father being informed that his son and daughter were planning to marry. It is a ridiculous concept—so ridiculous, that it's almost comical. As they rode Benny had to deal with mixed emotions of compassion and humor. He didn't know if he should act sullen or laugh. He decided to display neither emotion but he did admit, at times, it was hard for him to keep from laughing.

They rode for hours, stopping only to rest the horses and relieve themselves, eating dried biscuits and jerk meat as they

When Views Clash

traveled. Darkness was setting in as they finally saw the flickers of lantern lights in the distance. They were exhausted and the horses were depleted of energy when at last they arrived at the Idle Hour Inn.

At first all Benny wanted to do was settle the horses, rent a room and get some sleep. They were fortunate. Even that late hour, the inn had a room available and better yet, they would not need to share it with anyone else. Right after registering, they went upstairs and down the hall to the room. It was more than adequate, with a large bed and a window. Father always loved fresh air in a room so he opened the window. At the same time Benny discovered the water pitcher on the dry sink was filled with hot water. He poured some of it into the bowl and since there wasn't enough light for a shave, he just washed up and told Father it was a fine reward after a long day's ride.

Father placed the bundle of pelts under the window to try to minimize their odor. The drying skins still had remnants of flesh that was rotting away and the odor was terrible. Although he and Benny were getting somewhat used to the stink, they had to consider others at the inn.

After taking care of the horses, Father insisted on going to the inn's pub. He was a firm believer that no one should go to bed on an empty stomach. Father and Benny washed up and now eager for a hearty meal, made their way down the stairs, through the lobby and into the adjoining pub. Once inside they were quite surprised by the noise level. The pub's low wooden ceiling, hard wood floors and the density of patrons, all talking at the same time, didn't make for good acoustics. Benny and Father stood in the inside doorway wondering if it was at all possible to find a table, when a rather short, balding, man made his way through the crowd and greeted them. He looked to be a spry man in his late sixties.

"Gentlemen, velcome, velcome, velcome. Vil it be a table or the bar?" His accent was distinctively Jewish.

"Dinner, if you can find us a table," Father answered.

"Von moment," said the man as he turned to make his way back through the crowd.

Benny spotted the little black skull cap on the man's head. "Is he a Jew?" he asked Father.

"Yes, yes. But don't speak so loudly of such things." Father's hand motions also told Benny to lower his voice.

"But I don't think I've ever seen a Jew before."

"Benny, wake up! You haven't seen much of anything that you've seen in the last two days before."

"That's true. But some things are just so much more surprising that I ..."

He was interrupted by the reappearance of their Jewish greeter.

"Vat a nice table I got for you," he said, motioning them to follow him.

Once they were seated he asked if they would like wine, grog or ale to drink?

Now, Father, at one time or another may have imbibed in all three of the offerings but as for Benny, that's another story. At home, he usually drank milk from our cows or water from our well, or sometimes he even drank cistern water. On occasion, and a rare occasion at that, he would have beach plum wine that we made, and I suspect beach plum wine was probably the strongest alcohol product Benny had ever tasted. So when he asked the little Jewish man, who they discovered was the innkeeper, for an ale, Father was surprised. Nonetheless, Benny got his ale and although he wasn't quite sure he liked its bitter taste he kept his appraisal to himself. However, Father looked at Benny's face and knew the bitter brew was not going down that easily and he smiled to himself.

"The problem with witches brew is that it tastes better when you consume a lot of it. But then other problems replace the taste," Father said with a chuckle.

When Views Clash

As he always does before a meal, Father started to thank God for the food they were about to eat. At that moment the innkeeper returned and since prayers are not a normal occurrence in the pub, he was surprised but made light of it. "I see you know my wife does the cooking here, so you're praying even before you eat it."

"No, no," Father protested. "I've eaten here before, but that's not why we're praying. We're thanking God we've made it here safely and we're grateful for the food we're about to receive."

"Oh. Then I'll tell my wife you're a repeat customer despite her cooking." With that the innkeeper once again disappeared into the crowd.

Benny was confused. "We didn't even tell him what we would like to eat."

"No need. His wife only prepares one item for the day, so everyone eats the same thing."

When the innkeeper delivered the dishes heaped high with mutton and boiled potatoes, Father and Benny ate with delight. The only problem was the intensifying noise level. Once again, Benny found that there was a silence between himself and Father, but this time it wasn't desired on either of their parts, it was due entirely to the extraneous noise.

There were several British army regulars standing at the bar. It seemed soldiers were everywhere these days, so Benny didn't give them a second thought. While he was studying the crowd he noticed a large group that had congregated in the front of the pub near the outside door. It was a mixture of men, most were probably in their late teens or early twenties. Benny recalled he was in New Haven, the home of several colleges and universities, the most famous being Yale College. He also realized this group was probably comprised of a couple of professors and their students. The surrounding noise prevented him from hearing what they were saying but considering how animated some of them were, he figured the topic had to be really interesting. Benny considered moving closer to the group but dismissed that idea as he thought

it would be insulting to Father. He kept his attention focused on the group and hardly noticed the soldier who had left the bar and made his way toward them. The soldier said something to one of the young men who had just made a statement. Within seconds, everyone in the pub knew something was amiss and a hush came over the room.

"Those are treasonous words!" shouted the soldier.

"I've said nothing that is treasonous!" retorted the young man, "and I'll even say it again. I am merely quoting a well known supporter of the Crown, who also believes, 'No island nation can govern a whole continent.' And the man who said it is none other than Thomas Paine."

"And I'll tell you again. I don't give a damn where you learned it. What you're sayin' is treasonous."

The young man decided not to argue with the soldier. Turning around he waved him off and started to sit down again but the military man wasn't finished. "Don't you turn your back to me, as you've done to your King and your country! If you're not a traitor, stand up and pledge your allegiance to the Crown and England," he yelled in a commanding voice.

The young man was taken aback. Seeing this, one of the professors stood up in his defense. "See here, I'm a barrister and professor of legal letters and I tell you, you don't have the authority to make such a demand."

"Shut up and sit down old man or you'll find yourself trying to get out from under my boot. Then you'll know how much authority the King's loyal men have."

"We have courts to deal with the likes of you," the professor shouted back, standing his ground.

"And we have gallows for traitors like you," the soldier exclaimed as he reached to unsheathe his sword, a maneuver that instantly signaled for his three comrades, standing at the bar, to come join him. As they did, they left their long rifles leaning against the bar's edge and drew their swords, flanking the lead

When Views Clash

soldier's sides, and forming a wedge.

The other patrons scattered from the brewing altercation; only the innkeeper, the little Jewish man with the bald head and yarmulke intervened. He pushed his way past the crowd of patrons and inserted himself between the lead soldier and the professor.

"Put avay your veapons! These are teachers of law and their students. They are not common criminals that you should threaten them like this."

But the soldier would not back down. "Little man, if you stand here, in front of us, I'll consider you one of them. And as for them being students and teachers ... well, they need to be taught a good lesson about the real law. But, we'll be fair. Let us take that one student, the one who thinks he can quote others who preach treason and get away with it. We'll teach him a good lesson for the others to learn. If he survives the cat o' nine tails, he'll tell others to obey. If he doesn't survive, he'll still tell others to obey." He then quickly passed his sword over the innkeeper's bald head. "Now, out of my way or you'll go down, too." He didn't wait for the innkeeper to move on his own. With his free hand he shoved the little man out of his path.

Now, Benny had never really been in a physical confrontation before and no one will ever know what possessed him, but he got up and quietly slipped behind the crowd to the bar. There he retrieved one of the soldier's long guns that had been left leaning against the bar. He pushed his way through the crowd and approached the soldiers from behind. Then he raised the barrel, simultaneously cocked the flint and jammed the gun's point between the shoulder blades of the lead soldier.

When Father saw Benny pick up the rifle from the bar, he gasped. When he saw Benny shove the gun's barrel into the lead soldier's back he was horrified. "Oh Benny, what have you done?!" he moaned to himself. But Father too, felt he had no choice. He moved to the bar and grabbed another rifle. Then he stationed himself behind the crowd. He really didn't know what Benny was

going to do, but just in case one or more of the patrons behind him decided to show just how loyal they were to the King's men, he would protect the rear.

"I've got your back!" Father shouted to Benny with a great deal of conviction.

The lead soldier took a sideward glance, so he could see who was threatening him. "The Crown doesn't take lightly to those who point weapons and threaten the men of the Royal Brigade. There will be no mercy. You'll hang for this," he said with intense fury in every word he enunciated.

"Pardon, but as I recall, the Crown also frowns on its men telling one of its subjects he was about to be whipped, and probably put to death." As Benny spoke he was surprised at his own calmness.

"Well, now there will be two of you that I'll break in half with the whip. Then you'll be hanged." The soldier was almost growling.

"Maybe so, but first let me ask these learned men of letters the question that started all of this. Or better yet, why don't you first drop your swords to the floor." The soldiers did as they were told.

"Now, if we can make room, I'd like our soldiers to sit at the long table in front of them and face me." There was some shuffling as the students and teachers moved out and the soldiers sat down. "Okay, now back to my question," Benny continued. "Would one of you distinguished professors please tell us, is what the student said punishable by death?"

The three law professors, looked at each other. It was apparent by their voiceless conversation that two of them were yielding to the oldest member. The senior member of the group moved to the center of the area near Benny. He looked first at the accused student, then at the accuser, the lead soldier, and finally at Benny. He was silent for a few moments, while he gathered his thoughts. With a deep rumble he cleared his throat and then launched into a legal diatribe. The inn had become not merely his courtroom but his legal stage until his conclusion. "Under statutes of common law of the Colony of Connecticut, which has been sanctioned by the House of Commons in Great Britain, Patrick, the accused, could be labeled irresponsible, disrespectful and even insulting. But these charges are not punishable with regard to imprisonment and especially not, as the accuser maintains, remediable by corporal punishment."

"Oy vey, vat he say?" blurted out the innkeeper.

"I think he said he's innocent," another patron shouted out.

"In a pig's eye!" ranted the lead soldier but to his further dismay his shout drew laughter from the other patrons.

"All right … all right." Benny took one hand off the gun and waved it over the crowd to regain their attention. "Do you agree with your colleague?" He asked the other two professors.

The first professor nodded his head affirming the opinion. The second professor had a response that was more like that of a lawyer. He took his moment to answer and stretched it into many moments.

"Let me be clear. A verdict of not guilty is mandatory. As a witness to what happened, it is easy to see that no laws were broken. Therefore from a technical view of the law, he is innocent. Another view is that of the spirit of the law and from that perspective, he may have spoken in poor taste and acted offensively to some people who were present. However, with reference to the legal aspects of the spirit of the law, he is equally innocent."

Benny felt pretty good. He had managed to stand up to a military force that was about to perpetrate a wrong. His efforts seemed to be successful but would not truly be so until the lead soldier acknowledged and accepted the verdict of the law professors. "Do you accept and will you comply with the opinion of these legal experts?" he asked the lead soldier, looking straight at him.

"Yeah." the soldier said sounding like he was about to regurgitate. Benny then looked at the other soldiers and one at a time they agreed. With a feeling of joy and a sigh of relief Benny eased off the hammer of the long gun and laid it down in front of the soldiers on the table. "Thanks for listening and understanding," he said and then turned and started to make his way to congratulate Patrick, the young student.

In a jackrabbit move, the lead soldier rose, grabbed the gun and cocked it.

"Don't take another step or I'll shoot you for disobedience!" he yelled at Benny's back.

Benny froze. He slowly raised his hands and turned to face a crazed looking soldier, who had just experienced a defeat and wasn't about to give up. "I thought you just agreed with the professors," Benny said.

"Yeah, I did, but you've got to be punished for pointing a weapon at a member of the King's army."

The elderly professor stepped forward. "But that, too, is justified and dismissible in court. You see, that man was trying to prevent you from committing a very serious crime."

"I've heard enough of your fancy words that twist things until the bad guys sound like the good guys." The soldier was now shouting. "This brazen creature will do as he is told. You will march out of here, in front of me, or I'll blow your head off right where you are standing."

"And the second shot, you will not hear, cause the ball is aimed to go in one of your ears and out the other. Now put the gun down." Father's voice commanded.

One of the other soldiers, who knew the situation could only get worse, put his hand on the enraged soldier's rifle and made him lower it. "Let's just get out of here," he said.

Benny wasn't sure it was over. Before the soldiers could round up their swords and rifles he motioned for Patrick to quickly join him. "I'll get him back to the college grounds and then I'll be on my way," he loudly said to the professors. They promptly left through the front door and out into the dark night.

When Views Clash

"Stick close and be real quiet," Benny told Patrick.

They made their way to the side of the inn; then hid near the wood line. They waited in stillness and silence for a little while. Then, just as Benny had suspected, they could hear the soldiers exiting the inn. The rattle of their sabers was a dead giveaway. Within moments the soldiers walked close to where Benny and Patrick were hiding. The lead soldier was admonishing the others to "... move quicker and stop all the noise. We've got to catch the traitors before they make it to the college. If they make it to a house, we may never find them."

Benny waited until he was certain they were out of hearing range when he motioned for Patrick to follow him. They made their way to the back of the inn. There he leaped up onto the rim of a barrel that collected rainwater that fell from the roof, and hoisted himself up onto the flat roof itself. It took a good deal of athletic agility and when Benny turned around he realized that Patrick was having difficulty accomplishing the feat, Benny leaned over the edge and helped Patrick up onto the roof.

Together they raised the window to the room Father and Benny had rented earlier. Benny led the way in by diving head first onto the pelts Father had earlier arranged under the window. Patrick followed but the second he landed he let out a gush of air. "Whew.... What a stink!" he exclaimed. He sat up and continued to rant. "Smells like the college latrine, except this time we're not standing next to it, or squatting over it. We're in it!"

"If you're around them for a while you don't even know they have an odor," Benny laughed. "Anyway, better to deal with the smell than get our own hides whipped by that army nut."

"You're right and ..." Patrick stopped speaking as he choked up. He swallowed hard. "And you saved my life. Given a chance that nut would have whipped me to death and dumped my body in the woods. That would have been the end of me." He paused, as if to consider what he had just said. "You know, I can never thank you enough. I hope you're never in a fix like that but I promise, if

I can ever help, I'll be there for you."

Benny was about to assure Patrick that he had simply done the right thing, when a noise came from the doorknob. Both of them scrambled to their feet and since the darkness prevented them from finding weapons, they made fists and prepared to attack. As the door inched open Benny heard Father's voice. "Benny, are you all right?"

Once again Benny found himself sharing a bed with two other men, but this time he didn't mind. The three of them spent most of the night talking until finally the need for sleep overcame them. Prior to finally giving in to sleep, Benny and Father set up a plan to accompany Patrick back to his living quarters. There he would pack his things and then head for home. Once things seemed to be under control, he could return to college. Hopefully, in the interim, the nutty soldier would be moved to another post.

At dawn they set up the horses, and went to the pub for breakfast. The innkeeper came to their table while they were enjoying a wonderful breakfast. They talked about the excitement of the previous night and Benny was emphatic that the storytelling of heroics and deeds was much more dramatic and exaggerated than what had really happened. The innkeeper also told them of another heroic deed that had also occurred that night. Apparently an unidentified patron had taken it upon himself to go to the military post commander and share what had happened in the pub. As the innkeeper was closing his door for the night the commandant entered and said he had sent out a platoon to capture the wayward men. He also wanted to verify the facts, which the innkeeper gladly provided, thereby substantiating the patron's story. With that information in mind, having Patrick take a leave from college was no longer necessary.

The innkeeper pleasingly reinforced that all had ended well but Benny wasn't so confident. Intuitively he felt they had not seen the end to the previous night's episode.

Chapter 8

Causes for Alarm

I would like to say that while Benny and Father were off

having an adventurous time, we at home were experiencing a tranquil and restful period, but, unfortunately that was not the case. In fact, the events that took place, while our men folk were away from home, caused us women a great deal of consternation and anxiety.

It began as a continuation of the controversial event at Sunday service—the debate concerning the treatment and attitude of our King towards us Colonists. Only a few days after the Sunday incident we heard of actual fistfights between neighbors. Apparently the differences between those who support the view of the King, otherwise known as Loyalists, and those who were called Patriots because they were requesting more influence in the King's decision making, had escalated beyond words. These are emotional issues and some people simply cannot detach their feelings for a cause from their feelings to wanting to punch the dickens out of the opposition. So now our little tranquil town was becoming a house divided. People were either supporters of the Crown, and calling themselves Loyalists or were against the King's seemingly unfair impositions and referring to themselves as

Patriots. To be sure, the occasional sparring between our town's folk fortified the positions of each side.

As for Mother and us girls, all of this friction didn't really matter. My sisters went to school and Mother and I continued to run our farm. In the privacy of our home we shared our view of the situation and we could honestly find good aspects on both sides of the issue. Not that it mattered to anyone else but we resolved to keep ourselves as neutral as possible. In essence, that meant we would not align our house with either side.

Well, neutrality isn't always easy to maintain, nor is it always safe to be neutral. Maybe if you live on some mountaintop or on an isolated island in the middle of the ocean, you can stake a claim to neutrality, but if you live in a community, surrounded by forces and influences, then you'll likely have to choose a side. And, how you go about supporting that side may be very dangerous. You see, we tried to be neutral and stay away from debates, arguments or any other confrontational situations. "Mind our own business," became our motto. Then one day, our feelings changed.

That day, Mother and I were tending to our cornfield. Each year we plant several acres of late harvesting corn along the roadway in front of the house. This was the first year neither Father nor Benny were present to do the tilling. Before leaving they had planted the early spring crops but this particular corn is planted well after the others have already begun to sprout. Mother and I didn't want to miss a planting and we wanted to also prove that we could do the job. To that end, we hitched up the horse to the plow and, to be honest, we weren't doing all that badly. Of course our furrows weren't all that straight and both Father and Benny would have admonished us for not waiting for them to return, but again it really wasn't all that bad. In fact, it seemed to us, that the horse quickly got the idea of what was to be done and he sort of straightened out the furrows as we went.

We were occupied with the rows when the dog started to bark. At first we looked around and saw nothing unusual. Then,

Causes for Alarm

we heard the sounds of horses in the distance and in short order we saw them coming—the King's army; Red Coats, many of them, coming down the road. A lead mounted rider bolted from the ranks, spurred his steed and within moments was in front of us. He pulled back on the reins, making the horse half spin around and rear on its hind legs. "Secure your dog!" he shouted. "Our mounted men, as well as foot soldiers, have orders to put down any animal that could be harmful to them or impede the mission." Then, as quickly as he approached, he retreated to his place in the ranks. And we, just as quickly, did as instructed.

The column of troops was impressive, both in number and regal appearance. When they reached our house, the Captain—at least that's what rank I thought he held—commanded his troops.

"Brigade! Eyes right!" He then tipped his head to us and as the troops passed us their heads swiveled in our direction.

Mother was even more impressed and pleased than I. She made all kinds of complimentary remarks about the soldiers. "How polite, how regal, such a gallant group of men; truly nice to the gentler gender, makes you proud to be part of the kingdom ..." I had to laugh because she was so awed by the flattery directed at her, while the reins to the horse and plow were draped over her shoulder.

We couldn't stop talking about how exciting it was to have our very own military parade right in front of us. We talked through our chores, while making dinner, and half way through the night. Yes, there was no doubt about it, we decided; we were a part of the greatest power on earth and our King was a righteous man who was doing what was best for the entire kingdom. Even the Bible tells all people, right down to the lowest slaves: "Serve wholeheartedly, as if you were serving the Lord." I think that was Ephesians 6:7. In other words, we are subjects of the King and we should be loyal to him. Anyway, that was our conviction, as we went to bed that night.

The next day our convictions had a complete turnabout.

Early in the morning Mother and I had gone to town to purchase provisions. We needed some basic staples, such as, flour, molasses, salt for preserving, etc. That meant we would go to Malcom Smith's General Store. It's located across from the Parsonage lawn on Main Street.

The Parsonage lawn is also considered to be the town meeting place or the town square. Twice a year, for the Harvest Festival and at the end of the spring planting, for the Growing Festival, the entire community comes together on the square to give thanks to God and enjoy a day of food and merriment.

Upon arriving in town we were surprised to see that the Parsonage lawn had been converted into a military camp. Compared to the normally tranquil field, where children romped and played, it was an odd scene. There were men moving about engaged in all kinds of activities. Some were just setting up their tents; others were manning huge kettles of food; and still others were unloading large wagons, some containing firewood, others food and supplies. In short, they were establishing a village within a village.

The men had most of the roadway that fronted the shops blocked with the wagons. There were just so many of them. Mother had to maneuver our wagon around to the rear of the General Store and we entered via the back door. There we were greeted by Mr. Smith, the proprietor. He is always a gentle person, contrary to what you'd expect because of his huge size.

"Ladies, what a pleasure it is to see you. I do hope we can provide you with what you need. Unfortunately our store has almost been cleared out by the military."

"Oh, I'm sure we can make do. But we are delighted for you. Such an unexpected surge in business must be wonderful." Mother was smiling with delight for the Smiths as she spoke. She always liked Mr. Smith and his wife.

At first Mr. Smith didn't respond. Then he slowly looked about to make sure no one else could hear before he softly spoke in a very low voice.

"It would be a great day for sales if we were to be paid. All we got for a great deal of stock was a promissory note. When I said we would like cash, the officer said we'll either accept the note or they'll confiscate the goods as requirements necessary for the King's army and we'll get nothing at all."

Mother's facial expression turned from a smile to a frown in an instant. "They can't do that. It can't be legal."

"I'm afraid they do have that kind of power. And we shopkeepers have been told not to complain. Voicing resentment would be considered to be disrespectful towards the Crown and that's now punishable. It could mean going to jail."

"How reliable is the promissory note? Do you know how long you'll have to wait before you get real money?"

"They said I'll get paid when the quartermaster arrives," he said with a shrug of his large shoulders. "And they don't know when that will be."

We were all silent for a moment, reflecting on Mr. Smith's predicament, when a ruckus broke out in the front of the store. Mr. Smith excused himself and moved quickly to check on the situation. We were right behind him when we heard Obedia Hawkins shouting in anger. His words were not directed to anyone in the store, however; he was venting his anger, but not at the people who caused it.

"Obie, calm down. Shouting isn't doing any good." Mr. Smith advised.

"But they stole all of my firewood and gave me this worthless piece of paper." He was still shouting.

Mr. Smith tried again. "You'll get paid. You'll see ... it will work out."

"Malcom, how can you think like that? You've heard all the same talk the rest of us have heard. They haven't paid anybody in Boston or New Haven for all the stuff they've taken. They say we should consider it a donation to the cause."

Mr. Smith wasn't so convinced. "Not true. The New York shopkeepers have been paid. And on a regular basis, too."

"Right, but they're all Tories. They're in bed with the Red Coats. We're considered to be either on the fence or out and out rebels."

The door opened and in walked our local blacksmith. Like most men in his trade, he was simply known as Smitty. He wasn't as agitated as Obie, at least not on the surface.

"Mind your manners fellas. The Red Coats just finished building a rack at the other end of the commons. Anyone caught acting a little too disgruntled is going to spend some time with his neck and wrists clasped between some mighty big timbers."

"Same thing they did in New Haven," Obie moaned.

Mr. Smith continued to try to calm everyone down. "You know, that's just for show. I'm sure we can discuss things with them and they'll understand our frustration."

"Malcom, you always see the cup half full, and that's your problem." Obie was no less agitated as he continued to speak. "To them discussing means complaining, so don't go chatting with them too soon or you'll be one of those they'll make an example of."

Doc Gregg, a highly educated man who served as our village medical person entered the store. Everyone became silent, waiting for him to speak. He glanced at all of us who were standing in a circle.

"Judging by your faces, I'm not the only one having a bad day," he said.

"What did they take from you?" asked Obie.

"Oh, just my time and my work. I've been pressed into service. It seems, a lot of troops out there are in need of having teeth pulled and there are some who have sores that just won't go away."

Doc Gregg sighed, extended his hands, palms up, "So, I've been ordered to serve. I've also been told I'm to take care of the troops first, then, when I'm sort of off duty, I can take care of

Causes for Alarm

the medical needs of the town folks." For a moment he stopped speaking and looked around the store. "My fear is, when they leave, they'll force me to go with them," he said softly.

Mother really didn't like what she had just heard. "They can't do that. We need you here, besides, you're not an indentured servant, you're ..."

Doc, as he was known to us, stopped Mother mid sentence. "Truth be known, they can do anything they like to me. I, like the rest of you, have no say."

Obie let out a warning as he glanced out the window. "Officers heading this way. Should we head out the back door?" he asked looking at Mr. Smith.

"Hold your ground," Smitty calmly said. "Besides, they know we're here. They've probably been watching us and they've got the back door covered." He smiled at us. "Shoppers, let's get on with our shopping and storekeeper, it's time to get back behind the counter and tend to business."

We scattered and started to play our roles when a young officer graciously opened the door and stepped aside to let a Major enter. Within seconds the door was closed and the Major stepped forward with two junior officers flanking him.

"It is a good morning and I'm so glad you are gathered here," said the Major. He obviously surmised that we had just dispersed. "Do please regroup here in the front of the store so it won't require me to stress my voice." Truth is, he didn't look like he stressed any part of his body. For an officer he certainly didn't look trim or fit. And, I don't want to be too callous, but he must have had his uniforms made by Omar the tent maker.

Before speaking, he made a grotesque rumbling sound that started deep in his gut and moved up through his nostrils. He was trying to loosen his vocal system, but it sounded like some of his innards were about to be propelled through one of his head's orifices and sent flying across the store. As his bodily sounds decreased and we gathered around, he resumed speaking.

"I'm Major General Stanley Placeham. I am finding your little hamlet to be quite charming. It reminds me of some of the villages along the coast back home. And speaking of home, I've come to tell you that we will need to have some of our officers supplied with living arrangements in your homes. It is customary that they receive good sleeping arrangements and the home keepers will be kind and accommodate the officers' schedule for meals. And I shouldn't need to remind you but when you share this information with the others who inhabit this village; you will tell them that their duties include keeping the officer's clothing in repair and washed. Of course, it goes without saying; that the house owner will care for any other needs that may arise. I myself am staying in the parsonage. The good Pastor Timothy and his wife, whose name slips my mind ..."

"Grace." I filled in the blank

"Yes, very good, very good. Well, again the Pastor immediately saw the need for me to have good resting conditions. He gladly offered to move out to one of the parishioner's houses, while I use his house. We will also make the parsonage headquarters. I would also say that your Pastor should be recognized by all of you town folks, as a model servant to the Crown and the King's men. I have nothing else to say at this time." Having concluded his business, he was about to leave.

Mother interrupted his plan. "Sir, what about a household such as ours, where our men folk are away at work?"

"Well madam, need I remind you that chivalry is a virtue among our troops. In fact, I think of them as impeccable soldiers. But fear not. You will not be required to have an officer stay at your house. On the other hand, I'm sure an occasional uniform to wash or a meal to prepare should make you feel good about doing your duty for the realm."

With that, they were gone and we were stunned. It was several seconds before anyone spoke.

"I can't believe Pastor Timothy simply turned the parsonage

over to them," said Mr. Smith.

"Well, it is customary to share your house with the officers. I mean that's done all over the kingdom," said Smitty.

"Does anybody know how long they'll be here?" I asked.

Obie was quick to answer.

"Good question Rachael, but none of the Red Coats will give us that answer. Seems its top secret. But I got a little insight when they took my firewood. There were two officers there and one said to the other, the four cords they took should do and when they leave in a couple of weeks he didn't want to have his men haul any up to Boston."

"Well that could help answer a number of questions." Mr. Smith's broad face seemed to narrow as he pondered the information. "It sounds like they'll be here for two weeks but knowing how the army works, that means three weeks. That's not such a long time. We can deal with that. Now we also know where they're heading. I didn't think the island's North Fork would be a great place to make camp, especially for the number of them out there. But Boston does make sense. Colonists up there always seem ready to stand up for what they believe in. They're different from the other colonies."

Obie lowered his voice and gave Mr. Smith a long hard stare. "Sounds like I just gave you a piece of the puzzle. Also sounds like you got more than a passing interest in this information. Who are you planning to share this info with?"

"No, no Obie. I was just fascinated by what you had just said. Nothing more to it."

Obie's facial expression suggested he suspected something else. "Would you like to know how many troops are out there?" he casually asked.

"Sure!" Mr. Smith quickly responded.

"Bet you would," Obie said. "Gotcha."

Mr. Smith dismissed Obie with a wave of his hand. "Just curious, just curious. Okay, I've got to get back to work."

With those words our circle dispersed, with everyone going off to get on with business. Mother and I placed our order with Mr. Smith and he promised to do his best to fill it.

"Now I feel bad that we, too, must sign the I owe you book," Mother said as he finished going over the list. "It's another promissory note."

"Yes, but I know, as soon as your husband is back home, you'll come back and pay what you owe."

We said our goodbyes and left Mr. Smith to load the wagon and then visited some other shops along the main road. The print shop was one of Mother's favorites. There she bought a copy of the day's news. It cost a penny and for as many times as I've been with her when she purchased the newspaper, it always amazes me that she leaves the shop saying the same phrase: "I know it's an extravagant waste of money but I just love to read about what's happening around the town and the colonies. I even love to read about the latest things that are happening in England." After saying this, she paused, took a moment to enjoy her private thoughts, then her face blossomed into a radiant smile which quickly transformed into a calm and serene look.

"You know your father and I do so enjoy the same things. We love to read the news together after dinner. I miss him so."

The wagon ride home was especially pleasant. Mother's feelings towards my pending marriage to Benny seemed to soften. We talked about things she felt I would need to have, such as kettles and good oil lamps. She even broached the subject of a trousseau, but in no way could she even think about discussing the bodily encounters that begin when people wed. I suspect she believed those areas were best left to the process of discovery.

We were nearing home when our happy mood came to an abrupt end. From a distance we could see yet another gathering of Red Coats. This time they were stopped in front of our farm and the closer we got the more we saw that some of them were scurrying about the property. Since no one was at the house, they

Causes for Alarm

apparently assumed making themselves "at home," was allowable. We could see a couple of them trying to catch one of our chickens. Others were tying up a pig they had managed to wrestle and secure.

Mother snapped the reins on the back of the horse to make it move faster. "I guarantee, when I get finished with them, they'll not walk off with a single feather or pig's ear," she said angrily. She was even angrier as we got closer to the troops. "Last time I read the newspaper, some Colonist wrote, 'both fish and company stink after three days.' These impeccable soldiers, as the Major called them, have just arrived and they stink already," she said.

Chapter 9

Over Rivers,
Across Mountains
Then Near Death

After leaving the inn, Benny and Father traveled west
along the road that borders the Connecticut shoreline. They rode for
several hours before turning north and this time the conversation
seemed to never stop. It was certainly contrary to the previous
day's ride. The talking started when Father complimented Benny
on his heroic act of the previous night. Of course, he also told him
how dumb he was to challenge what seemed like the entire British
army. Benny sort of accepted the compliment, sort of because he
really believes it is everyman's responsibility to prevent unjustness
toward others. The being dumb part, he accepted entirely. He
couldn't argue with the truth; what he did was dumb. If for no
other reason, it was simply dumb because he placed others in
danger.

But Benny didn't want to dwell on the merits or stupidity
of his own behavior. He wanted to talk about the philosophy the
young law student was espousing. And who was this Thomas Paine
fellow? And, of course, the underlying grand question, where was
all this debate heading?

The questions seemed simple enough but as both Benny and
Father discovered, the solutions were complex and in most cases,

if implemented, would readily collapse our entire world. One thing was for certain. their conversations made the trip go very fast.

They turned onto the River Road. This road runs along the east bank of the Hudson River and has some of the most beautiful vistas any man has ever seen. Bucolic rolling hills that gradually sloped down to the pine tree lush riverside and a mountain range in the distant background made for a view that totally pleased the eye and mind. When Benny first saw the river he was awestruck. Father assured him that God's artistry would become even more pronounced as they went further north into the mountain ranges. At first Benny could not believe the scenery could become any more beautiful. As their distance north grew, he became more of a believer.

"You always said you loved the scenery on your trips. Now I understand why."

"I only wish your mother could see this. I've heard a lot of trappers who've worked in the far northwest say there's a waterfall that looks like the whole ocean is spilling over it and it drops so deep you can't see the bottom."

"Well, I'm more than satisfied with what I'm seeing right now. And, you know, if King George could see this, I'm sure he'd have a better feeling for this part of his kingdom."

"Oh, I would think he is well informed. His royal surveyors have mapped out this entire region and what they saw has been reported to him in great detail."

"I don't know how you can describe this kind of beauty."

"I suspect that's because you and the King are probably not looking at the same beauty."

That confused Benny. "What do you mean?"

"It's simple. You're looking at the aesthetics of God's creation. King George, like most monarchs, hears about this beauty and converts the beauty into huge parcels of forests, fur-coated animals; mountains potentially covering up loads of gold and diamonds. You see the richness of the land; most monarchs see how rich the land will make them."

Benny took time to reflect on his father's words.

"Well, since he's the King, I guess it's his for the taking anyway."

"Not so fast. It doesn't always work that way. Sometimes the monarchs don't get to reap the rewards. Remember, New York once belonged to the Dutch and I'm sure their royalty had some great plans for all the riches they once owned."

"I guess you're right. In fact, at one time didn't the French own all of this North Country?"

"Most of it."

Benny considered another issue. "None of that matters anyway. The French, the Dutch, they don't count. England has the biggest and most powerful navy on earth. And the army outnumbers all of the other armies. That makes England the strongest power of all. No other country is going to take away anything from King George."

Father wasn't quite so convinced. "I have to say, not so fast again. There was something to what that young law fellow was reading. The man he was quoting ..."

"You mean Thomas Paine?"

"Right." Father thought the point he was about to make was so important that he actually stopped his horse. "The idea that an island nation could govern and really control an entire continent, and we really don't know how big this one is, is simply preposterous. And I think King George knows and understands this problem. I don't think he fears other countries like France or Spain. His biggest concern has to be us."

"You mean us, the Colonists?" Benny said as they started moving again. Although he asked, Benny already knew that was exactly what Father was insinuating.

"Sorry to say Benny but more Colonists are like you — they've never been to England; and were raised on the frontier; which is a hard life that instills a lot of independence. You don't have that

emotional bind that ties you to the mother country."

"So you think England could have a problem from within its own colony, I mean us?" It was more of a confirmation than a question.

"Yes, and I think we're beginning to see that the King has had the same notions and is beginning to take action to control it. His men are taking tough stances and giving no quarter. He has passed rules about fees and tariffs that are really intended to financially weaken the colonies. And he's inserted some very rigid magistrates and governors to enforce his policies."

"Where did you learn all of this?"

"Mostly from reading between the lines of the newspapers. You know how much your mother and I love to sit by the fire and read the paper at night."

The next stop was a little Indian village just south of Kingstown, on the east side of the river. Trading went quickly, which delighted Father. He wanted to cross the river before nightfall, but of course they couldn't leave too soon. This was a Mohegan village. The Mohegans are a gentle and peaceful tribe. They live in drastic contrast to their "cousins," the Mohawks, who reside further north. Mohegans love to talk and would talk themselves silly, before picking up a weapon against other tribes. For certain, they wouldn't even give consideration to making war on Continental men. Father often said civilized men could learn a great deal about civility from this tribe.

Over the years, Father had become a friend to some of the men of the tribe and it would have been an insult if he and Benny had abruptly departed right after trading. So they stayed a while and enjoyed a meal of fire-roasted game, including a huge turkey that the Indian women had coated with a mixture of crushed leaves and animal fat. Father was also pleased to see Benny make friends among the young men of the tribe. One day, a member of this group would replace the Chief and become the leader with whom Benny would engage in business. Farewells were said over

Over Rivers, Across Mountains ...

and over again. After leaving the Indian village they went to the Kingstown Ferry Station and booked passage to cross the Hudson. There is always a brisk breeze flowing down the river canyon, so the ferry made a wide arc bowing north and quickly approached its port on the west bank of the river.

Darkness was approaching as they entered the hamlet of Rhinebeck, which was a very pleasant looking village. In many ways it reminded Benny of Mattituck. They went past the church to the town's inn. Known as the Beakman Arms, the Inn is famous for the bed linen in the rooms being changed on a weekly basis. Most other inns change the sheets once a month, weather permitting. In cold or rainy weather, when hanging laundry is not practical, the periods between changes may be longer. And unlike most other inns, the food at the Beakman Arms is usually very good.

After settling in they went to the pub and while eating Benny couldn't help but hear the other diners talking. The tidbits of information he picked up led him to the conclusion that pub talk was limited to the weather and politics. He also began to realize that Father's concept of the King's relationship to his colonial subjects may be very accurate. He was more assured of Father's perceptions when he heard some other patrons openly criticizing the King's economic policies that were being imposed on the colonies.

"You and that Mr. Paine are right." Benny wisely whispered across the table. "The distance from here to England has encouraged some people to become very brave."

"We'll see. Just remember, the future comes too quickly. Anyway, right now we have a more pressing concern. Tomorrow we'll continue north and from now on we must take extra precautions."

Benny's face suggested he couldn't figure out what Father was saying. Father then realized he had never told Benny of the dangers that lay ahead of them in the North Country. He leaned

over his plate which he had just wiped clean with a piece of bread. "Let's start with what I said on the ferry ride crossing the Sound. I said that if you insist on marrying Rachael ..." He deliberately refrained from saying, *your sister*, for fear someone might overhear ... "Then, I recommend you and she move here to the Rhinebeck area. Do you remember?"

"Give or take, that's about what you said," Benny spoke as he cleaned his plate with his knife.

"Yes ... Well, I said this area for a reason, several reasons in fact. Now you've seen the town. It's very much like back home and the people are pretty much the same. And most important, it's safe here. You see, any further north and I wouldn't consider it safe. North of here is Mohawk territory."

"But the Mohawks aren't on the war path. It's just the opposite. They're our allies. They love us Brits. Besides, the King and the Mohawk Chiefs have signed a treaty." Benny's voice was a little too loud.

Father made hand motions intended to quiet Benny down. "Yes, yes, but here's the thing. This idea of peace between the Mohawks and England is, as you say, based on a signed treaty. Now Benny, you're very bright, so think about it ... a signed treaty?" Father paused to emphasize the concept. "Look, King George has his barristers draw up a document. Bear in mind, most of those court officials have never set foot in the colonies and can only think of Indians as men splashed with red dye. So this legal document has a great deal of words and terms like *whereas* and *henceforth* and *therefore* in it. The King likes it and signs it. You know, he does that famous twirl signature with his fancy plume. Then he sends it to the Chiefs to sign. Benny! Surprise! The Chiefs can't read. So, somebody tells them the document says that you and the great Chief in England will be friends. And the Chiefs put their x's on the page. But what does it all mean?" He waited a second then inserted his own answer. "It means nothing! The King thinks he just outfoxed a bunch of red men and the Indians don't really know what it means. So whenever Indians see an opportunity to make personal gains at the sake of a white man, they do it, or if they want to redecorate their tepee and think a new scalp would look good hanging from one of the support poles, well why not?"

"That can't be!" Benny was shocked that his father would say such things.

"And why can't it be?" Father asked with his palms up.

"Our officials wouldn't stand for it. They'd send the troops in."

"Good point, but it overlooks one thing. The Indians may not be able to read but they certainly aren't stupid. Let's face it; they just wouldn't leave scalped bodies lying around." He stopped speaking, looked Benny in the eye and continued. "I've been doing business for a lot of years and every time I get to the North Country I hear about some settlers that have disappeared or a trapper who hasn't returned from the woods. Believe me, settlers don't just wander off their farms and get lost and trappers don't go into the woods, and on out the other side and keep going. See, I'm thinking, peace treaties are broken all the time. Only thing is, up in the North Country, the Indians don't know they've broken them or even care a hoot and a holler if they break a thousand treaties."

"So, what do we do?"

"We take extra precautions. We travel only in daylight. If possible, we stay with a group and stay alert. From now on you'll see a lot of natural beauty but only look and enjoy after you've carefully scanned the area for potential trouble. And remember, Indians can be as close as five foot into the woods and you may not see them. They know how to blend into their surroundings."

"What about going into their camp grounds to trade? Isn't that like walking into a fire?" Benny was confused.

"Not really. See, when we approach a compound the Chief will have already been alerted. The hotheaded young warriors wouldn't dare hurt us. The Chiefs like our *wampum* and want us to bring more. But, and this you have to understand, between

camps, that's another story. A couple of renegades, especially if they've gotten hold of some alcohol, would make us disappear in a heartbeat. They'd also take off with our shells and whatever skins we have."

That was enough to convince Benny and so, the next morning, when they left the inn and started north, he was on full alert. The terrain they were traveling on changed and not for the better. The roadway narrowed and the forest grew much thicker. It seemed that the woods had encroached so much on the road, that it was becoming more of a path leaving them a very limited passageway. Benny realized that wagons would have difficulty traversing this section of the road. The further north they went the harder it was to walk or even ride. The incline got much steeper, and the road surface became rockier. Given the travel conditions, Benny and Father had no choice but to dismount and walk along with the horses.

They had left behind a smaller set of mountains with lower elevation and had begun to climb the Adirondack Mountains. Associated with the increased elevation was a decrease in temperature. At several points they could see valleys and more mountains in the distance that were still covered with snow, despite the fact that it was springtime.

"If there's this much snow now, what happens in winter?" Benny asked.

"You get a lot of snow. Some years, I've come up here at this time and there are still several feet of snow left on the ground. But the road isn't so bad. Travelers pound it down as they come through with their horses," Father told him.

Father and Benny chatted for hours. Only hunger and the need for sleep stopped their steady trek northward and their endless talk. To cure their hunger and need for sleep they stopped at an inn that was owned and operated by a French family. The bedding was mediocre but the food was superb.

For several hours they continued on their northerly track.

Over Rivers, Across Mountains ...

Then they came to a fork in the road. "Here's where we turn northeast," Father advised. "If we were to take that other route we'd head northwest ... straight up and over those mountains."

Within a short period of time Benny saw that they were descending in altitude. At one point he could see the valley below.

"Is that going to be our next stop?" He motioned to what appeared to be a village far ahead, in the center of the valley.

"Yep and this one has something I reckon you've never seen before. It'll be a surprise for you."

"What do you mean?"

"You'll see, but first we'll do our business."

When they reached the valley floor Benny was surprised to see a town and not a small village. The town appeared to be somewhat larger than their hometown and much busier. Father was also surprised.

"Only a year ago, when I was here last, there weren't all these shops, I don't even recognize the village. Right there ..." He pointed to his left; then made a wide arc with his outstretched hand. "All of this was a Mohawk settlement. Now look, it's a commons, with a corral, livestock and even a blacksmith over there. But where did the Indians go? I mean, where will we get our pelts?"

They pushed on to what they supposed was the center of the town. But there were so many roads and paths in every direction that it was hard to tell. Finally, they pulled up next to a man loading a wagon.

"Do you know where the tribe has moved to?" Father asked.

"Yes Sir, just the other side of town. Straight down this road. It'll be on your left but you'd better get there quick. They're about to be moved again."

"Why?"

"Well it's simple. We need the land so the Injuns gotta go." The man looked somewhat astonished that he had to explain such

a simple thing.

"But the Indians own the land. How could it just be taken from them?"

"Fella, that's about as wrong as you can get. See them Injuns owned the land and lost it 'cause they sided up with the French. And them Frenchies ... Well, we old Union Jackers kicked the you-know-what outta them." As he finished speaking his face broke out into a wide smile, displaying a near toothless grin; that progressively grew wider, and even more hideous. But the scarcity of teeth didn't stop him from speaking. "Yeah, we beat 'em but we didn't throw 'em out. The French stayed, though most moved out into the woods. As fer them Injuns, we just corralled them over to the other end of town but, as I say, they ain't gonna be there long."

Father abruptly ended the conversation by nodding his head and nudged his horse forward. With Benny and the pack horse behind him Father rode forward, on to the relocated Indian compound which would soon be moved again. There was no mistaking that this was an Indian camp and yet, there were glaring features of the camp that were compellingly strange. Father had never before seen such conditions in an Indian camp. Usually, tribe members were active and engaged in their duties, but here there was a downtrodden atmosphere. The braves and squaws appeared to be operating in a daze.

Father led them on, deeper into the camp. They didn't see a greeting party or escorts. "Never seen anything like this," said Father turning to Benny. "Can't believe they'd let us just wander in here and up to the tribal common. Always had to be escorted and sometimes they took my weapons. Can't figure this out." They arrived at the tribal commons and stopped in front of the Chief's quarters. Tribal members were still drifting about but there wasn't any sign of life coming from the Chief's tent. Finally, a flap was spread open from the inside and someone peered out. Moments later the Chief appeared. His greeting was a mere nod of his head

Over Rivers, Across Mountains ...

He displayed no enthusiasm at seeing Father, despite the fact that he and Father had shared business dealings for many years.

Father was truly puzzled. He and the Chief had previously enjoyed each other's company. They had been engaged in business but they had also established a bond of real friendship. Father dismounted and stepped directly in front of the Chief.

"There was a time when my friend was eager to see me. Have I done something to offend you?" The Chief glanced away from Father and his eyes focused on the ground. His face was saddened. He did not answer. Father took the initiative. "Whatever lies on your heart can be lightened by sharing it with a friend." The Chief's face lifted. He studied Father's face for a while; then motioned for him and Benny to follow as he slowly walked to the tribal long hut.

Inside the tent, seated cross-legged on the deerskin covered earth the Chief spoke. "Just like our prey, we have walked into the iron jaws of a trap and now we are captured with little struggle left in us."

"Who would set such a trap and where are these iron jaws you speak of?" Father was confused.

"That is the terrible part. The trap cannot be seen and yet it was set by those who would befriend us." Father didn't respond. He realized the Chief would explain in his own time and his own way. "When the French came they went into our woods and took our game," the Chief continued. "They trapped many beaver, fox and raccoon. They built some houses by chopping down our trees for their walls and roofs. They took and we shared. Then your brothers, the English came. They killed many French and yes they also killed many of our tribesmen as well, for we had sided with the French. But that was war and many Indians, French and English were brave and gave their lives in the war."

The Chief paused for a long time and it was easy to see that he was reflecting on his personal losses because of the war. He gasped for air; the filling of his lungs would help him get through his sorrow-laden tale.

"Then peace came and many of our tribes, mostly the Iroquois and the Mohawks, became friends with your Red Coats. Your high Chief, the King, wanted peace, so along with his men, we shared the pipe and let our tepees fill with smoke. Soon our braves were putting down their weapons because your people gave them the taste of firewater. And soon after, our men who were once mighty hunters and warriors became servants. They even gave up their spirits for the want of firewater. In exchange for the white man's poison my people helped your people clear the forest for farmland. They even helped build a place of many houses; what you call a town. Our women and children ... they are even sadder. They die, in great numbers they die before our eyes and yet we see no reason. They cough, cannot eat or drink, and their bodies become very hot with fire in their blood. They die when the days are long and full of sunshine; but more died during the last time of short and cold days. The women who survive are no longer able to bear children. No children mean our tribe will die. We have become weak. Our men are no longer the braves they once were. Our women have become fruitless and our children are dying."

Father wanted to express his sorrow but the Chief had more to say.

"Your people know we are weak so they take from us what they want and feel free to treat us like captured slaves. They take our land at will. They move us by mounting their horses and push against us and our tepees until we move to where they will permit us to stay. As for me, I am no longer a Chief of braves but a man who looks on as his men drink and lay in their own vomit. I see our children die. I sit and watch as our women die. I look on with pain as those who won't die walk without life."

Father could say nothing. He and the Chief rose to their feet and Father embraced his friend. Father and Benny left the camp and headed back into town, deeply troubled by what they had just witnessed.

"That was really terrible. Isn't there anything that we can do

Over Rivers, Across Mountains ...

for them?" He asked Father.

"I feel as bad as you do but you must understand. They are a people who have been smothered and trampled by a changing world. At one time they flourished in this land, then — and it was only a couple of years ago — the Dutch, then the French and then we the English came marching in. We are a modern people, with modern ways. I am sad to say they are either going to have to adapt or they will disappear."

The ponderous experience and the thought of what the future could hold for the Indians lead the men to trudge on in silent sympathy.

"I didn't see the name of this town. Do you know what it's called? And what about that surprise you mentioned on the way into town?" Benny asked as they arrived at the inn.

"It's called Saratoga Springs. That's an Indian name meaning 'hillside of the great river.' Some translate it to mean 'place of great happiness near the swift water.' As for that surprise, let's check into the inn first."

Not long after registering, getting the horses settled for the night and storing their goods, Father and Benny left the inn and walked down the road, stopping in front of a large building that looked like a small fort. It had stockade walls for sides and the main entry was arched with large double doors. They entered and Benny immediately saw that the foyer opened to an outdoor area that encircled a large pond. It was actually more than a mere pond. It looked more like the Roman pools that Benny had read about in school, beautifully landscaped, with rocks around it and people sitting everywhere. Most people were in the pool. Benny was baffled.

"It's cold out. What are they doing in the water? They'll catch their death."

"No Benny, they'll be all right. This is a mineral spring and the water is very warm. It's like what the Greeks and Romans had." Father smiled and started to disrobe. "Come on, undress

down to your skivvies. This place is for men only and once you're in the water you'll be warm."

Benny didn't take long to get the message. Within seconds he had disrobed and was in the water.

"Hey, this is different. It feels like someone put whale oil in the water. It's great."

They soaked for hours and all their aches and pains from arduous walking and endless time riding seemed to melt away. Cleaned up and mellow from the long mineral bath, they were able to enjoy a restful night of sleep. Even Benny's last words before dozing off didn't appear to distract Father from falling asleep. "Oh how I wish Rachael could have been with me tonight. She would have loved the bath," was what Benny said, to my later delight.

The next morning, well rested but not really eager to leave Saratoga, they packed up their horses and were about to leave the inn when another man approached them. "If you're heading north, mind if my partners and I join you?" he asked. "You know what they say, the bigger the number the better and safer the trip."

Father quickly agreed. In fact he was quite delighted. The gentleman's statement was correct. The larger the traveling group, the safer the situation. Also, the man and his partners seemed to be businessmen and therefore didn't appear to pose any danger. Together with the three businessmen, who said they were New York bank representatives seeking to establish branch offices, Father and Benny started north again, but, within an hour of leaving Saratoga they came upon a fork in the road. One of the fellow travelers said they would take the northwest route. The men intended to travel to a series of lakes that were set in such a pattern that they resembled the fingers on a hand. According to Indian folk lore, the Great Spirit laid his hand on one of the finest areas of land on earth and left the imprint of his fingers.

Father and Benny planned to take the northeast route, so they said their farewells to their short time fellow travelers and went their separate ways. As they traveled, Father described to

Over Rivers, Across Mountains ...

Benny where they were going. He told him of a long lake that runs north and south and is somewhat narrow. The lake had several Indian and then French names and now is known as Lake George. At its northern point, Lake George is very close to Lake Champlain, another large lake that reaches to the far north and is similar in shape. Father told Benny there were several Indian camps along each lake and there were also two main forts, which meant the area was pretty safe. They rode on in silence, basking in the glory of being citizens of the mightiest empire on earth.

Father heard something unusual yet quite recognizable and pulled up the reins on his horse. The noise he heard was the sound of galloping horses coming up on them from behind. Benny and Father readied their weapons as they moved to the side of the road.

They recognized the riders as the horses came into view. There were six mounted riders, all members of His Majesty's Royal Forces. The men quickly approached Father and Benny, and the lead rider, an officer, extended a greeting on behalf of the Crown. "In what direction are you traveling?" he asked without any preliminary discussion.

Father motioned north. "We're heading for Lake George."

"I see. Have any Indians on horseback gone past you?"

"No Sir. Is there a problem?"

"Afraid so. Appears as though a band of red men attacked three white men on the westward fork. Killed the men and took their horses."

Benny, who would normally respect Father's position and let him lead the discussion, could not restrain himself. "They weren't three business men,... bankers, were they?"

The officer gave Benny a quick glance, "That appears to be the case. They had bank papers on their persons, but tell me, how would you know that?" he said, his voice ripe with suspicion.

Benny was really saddened by the news and rather than answering the question he whispered an expletive. "Damn."

Father picked up for Benny and explained how the three men

97

had been their traveling companions up to the fork in the road. Satisfied with Father's statement, the officer lost his suspicious tone. He was especially congenial when Father asked if his group was moving on to the fort and whether he and Benny could join them along the way. The officer told him that would be fine but since there was a long way to go, they would be making camp prior to darkness.

This turned out to be the first night Father and Benny used their outdoor sleeping rolls. Benny loved it. He said over and over again how much he loved sleeping under the stars. The clarity of the night sky dazzled his mind. He felt as though he could touch each star and he was mesmerized by the sheer number of them. Back home on the island, the skies never looked so clear and bright.

"Wouldn't you love to be here in a few hundred years or maybe even a thousand, when we'll probably have figured out how to get up there?" he whispered to Father, who was snuggled up in his sleeping roll."

"Benny, now you mind me. You keep thoughts like that to yourself. Talking like that makes you sound pretty queer to some folks." With that critical and stern comment he turned over and faced away from Benny. "It's almost as crazy as saying, you're going to marry your sister," he added, with his back to Benny.

Late the next day they arrived at Lake George, and there at the most southern part of the lake was Fort William Henry. Although darkness was setting in, Benny could see how large the fort was and how strategically it was located. Its cannons, of which he suspected there had to be at least a hundred, were placed so they could protect the waterway and the surrounding land as well. Benny was so fascinated that the next morning he rose particularly early and satisfied his curiosity by wandering about the fort. He explored every area, room and alcove that he was allowed to enter. His fascination was intensified rather than reduced by what he saw.

Over Rivers, Across Mountains ...

When he finally got back to where he had left Father he found him ready to depart. "Now is when our work really begins. From now on, every day we'll visit as many Indian camps as we can." Father's words were really the establishment of goals. And so, they worked their way north, up the eastern shoreline, stopping frequently to do business. They went as far north as the tip of the lake where it connects, or comes close to Lake Champlain. There they approached Fort Ticonderoga and spent the next two days trading with the Indian camps around the fort. It was only after Benny asked a few times that Father finally agreed to enter the fort and camp on the grounds for an evening. In fact, their pack horse was so loaded with pelts that Father felt that the safety of the fort would allow them a more restful night of sleep. He wasn't terribly concerned about the trip back to the company's home base in New York. Their means of travel south would be fairly safe but for now traveling with such a large quantity of goods, without a military escort, on isolated roads and making camp on the roadside, could be very dangerous. And the danger could come from white as well as red men. He was particularly concerned about a few legendary French trappers who had earned a reputation for, as Father put it, accumulating a whole year's worth of trapping in a matter of minutes. That's why Father thought an evening at the fort would be a welcome reprieve from constantly being on guard.

Benny eagerly explored the fort. It troubled him that he couldn't spend as much time exploring as he truly wanted, but the knowledge that they would be on their way home soon well compensated for any disappointments. The fort, built around 1755, was fairly new. The French who erected it favored stone in its construction. Benny was impressed by the size of the living quarters. As he wandered about he spotted steps leading to the second level platform. No one was there to stop him so Benny decided to climb them and explore the upper battery area. He was awestruck by the views at the top. Pivoting around, Benny realized he could see for miles in every direction. That's when he

realized the fort was actually on a peninsula between Lake George and Lake Champlain, an incredibly strategic location. He also visualized how the cannons were mounted not only to defend the fort itself, but also the waterway between the two lakes.

But then Benny noticed that many of the cannons were laden with rust. He wondered how the military men could let this happen. These cannons were far too valuable and critically important for the troops to allow them to fall into such deplorable condition. Even the harshness of winter this far north was no excuse. Benny wondered if any of the cannons still worked. He grumbled to himself that the officers in command could never have been farmers; every farmer he ever knew kept his equipment in the best shape possible. Maintenance was the key to successful farm operations. He moved to one cannon to inspect it more closely when he heard Father calling. He knew it was time to leave and head south.

When they left Fort Ticonderoga Benny realized Father was in a very good mood. "So, how come you're in such a good mood?" Benny asked.

"We're heading south and that means we're on our way home." Father's jubilance was growing by the moment.

Benny smiled in agreement but in his heart he felt a little pang of depression. After all, home was a place from where he and Rachael, his wife to be, were soon to be exiled.

From Fort Ticonderoga they set a quick pace south along the lakeshore. They actually retraced their route, in the opposite direction, when they headed north. Since they weren't making trading stops, it took only two days for them to travel from Fort Ticonderoga to Fort Henry, albeit they took breaks in consideration of the horses, especially the burdened pack horse. They stayed overnight in the security of Fort Henry and the next day they traveled a short distance east to Glenn's Falls. Father was most relieved when they reached the riverbank of Glenn's Falls. It was crowded with people boarding or debarking vessels.

Over Rivers, Across Mountains ...

Nevertheless, Father dismounted and dropped one knee to the ground. He paused making his heart ready.

"Lord, we praise You, and most of all we thank You. You have guided and protected us and for this and all the other gifts You graced upon us we thank You."

Benny stood next to Father and reined in the horses. "Amen," he said, joining Father in his prayer.

Glenn's Falls is not as busy as most of the harbors near our home. The little harbor area doesn't have enough river traffic to warrant several stores but there is one general store. Father went to the lone ship to book passage. Then he walked to the General Store and stocked up on dry provisions for the voyage home. Benny was waiting for him. "What are we doing?" he anxiously asked Father.

"We're going to take that boat." Father pointed to a boat that looked more like a barge with sails on it, "and head for New York."

"You mean we're going to take this stream all the way south to New York?" Benny couldn't believe what he had just heard. He looked at the waterway in front of them and shook his head.

"Do you remember, on our way up here we crossed a very wide river, the Hudson?"

"Yes, but this isn't the Hudson."

"Oh yes it is. It's just that right now we're almost at the beginning of the river. It's not quite the very start but it's just about the first spot where a sizeable boat can maneuver."

Benny needed no further explanation. The very thought that they were headed home and stopping off in New York was exhilarating. Like most children growing up on Lange Islandt, as the Dutch called our island, Benny had always heard about New York, and had dreamed about visiting it. They made their way to the vessel. It was a large, odd-looking boat that was almost flat bottomed, yet it had sails, not a lot of sails, just a main and a jib. And the strangest part was the center keel that rose up into the ship. The main sail just missed the keel's top, as it

swung about.

Loading the horses went smoothly, and as soon as the horses were secured in their stalls, the ship's captain ordered the first mate to let loose and shove off. The captain seemed very capable of giving orders to his subservient first mate, the only other working person on the ship. From behind the stern wheel, the captain watched as the mate waded into the water and pushed the vessel into the center of the stream. Then the mate hopped back into the boat and hoisted the main sail. He scurried about securing lines and setting the jib. Benny realized that he and Father were the only passengers on board. He turned to ask Father about this, only to find Father setting out their bed rolls at mid ship on the deck.

"What are you doing?" he asked Father.

"Once we pick up a southerly wind and hit the down river current, we'll be in Albany in no time."

"What happens then?"

"This boat will fill up with passengers." He said it as though Benny should have already known. "And, by the time we get to Poughkeepsie," he continued, "we'll be overcrowded and mobbed." Father finished staking out their territory and decided to take a well-deserved nap. Benny, on the other hand, was too excited to nap and didn't want to miss a thing. He wandered the boat from stem to stern and when he walked by the captain at the wheel, he paused to watch the man carefully negotiate the waterway. "Not as hard as it looks," the captain announced.

"Looks pretty difficult to me."

"Yeah, but ya do it a couppla hundred times and ya get so ya don't sink it too often."

Benny laughed and said, "I'm glad you said that Sir. I sure do feel a lot safer now."

"First trip down the Hudson?"

"Yes Sir. Came north for a bit on it, but this time we're going all the way south to New York."

Over Rivers, Across Mountains ...

"Been to the city before?"

"No Sir."

"Then you'll be in for a real treat. Ya know it's not as old as London but it's sure got some good history. Did ya know, there was this Dutchman named Minuit. Peta Minuit, that's it. He was a gov or somethin'. Anyhow, he thought he was pretty darn smart. He met with a pack a Injuns and bought the whole darn island from 'em. Ya know, Manhattan Island? By the way, Manhattan is Injun talk for land of many hills. Anyway, he dealt with them Injuns and made a hell of a bargain. Some trade, it was. Gave them Injuns a bunch a beads for the whole island." He paused to laugh at the punch line that was still going around in his head. "Only problem was," he said still laughing, "th' Injuns he dealt with didn't own the island in the first place. He made his big shot trade with the Canarsee Injuns. They were just visitin' the island. They lived way over on the other side o' Brookline, ya know, cross the river, near the ocean. The real owners, them poor Lenape Injuns, never even got a single bead; not that it mattered none. Them Lenapes been dyin' off anyhow. Ain't but a couppla handfuls left of 'em. Ain't nobody figured out what's making 'em die off, neither."

Benny nodded his head as the captain continued to talk.

"Yep, that there Minuit was a Dutchman; and them Dutch owned it. Then we up and took it from 'em. Give it a new name too, we did. Yep, a bit more than a hundred years ago now, t'was in 1664. Our own Charles the Second named it after his blood cousin, York. Fella was a duke, ya know. And ..." He raised his voice to emphasize his forthcoming piece of knowledge. "Did ya know, that there is one growin' city, growin' quicker than green on da bottom a this here boat. They tell me, twenty some years ago t'was about three thousand buildings, now they say there be about four thousand houses and big buildings. And talk about people, well they say that little island's got about twenty two thousand folks livin' on her."

"That's really something," Benny commented, while he

103

slowly began to move away. He wanted to do more exploring and he knew there was no easy way to break off this conversation with the garrulous old captain.

"Hey, ya know what's raising Cain with the city," the captain said raising his voice as Benny started to drift away. "I mean, after all them battles over her, ya'd never believe it woulda become infested with 'em Jews. Yep, plenty o' 'em too. Comin' all the way from Brazil. Ya know, that land below us. Ya know about 'em Jews? Killed Christ, they did."

Benny didn't hesitate to respond. "Did you know, Christ was a Jew?" he said, a serious look on his face. "And He came to earth as the Savior of the Jews. And His earthly lineage was from a long line of royalty, all Jewish. And, as He was dying on the cross, He called out to God the Father to forgive them, for they know not what they do. And, if He forgave them, who are we?" Benny's serious expression gave way to a smile. "Have a blessed day," Benny told the captain still smiling as he turned and walked away.

As Father predicted, the river got wider, much wider, and the boat became crowded. At each succeeding port many more people got on than got off. The crowded conditions didn't seem to bother the captain and he only had to shout words of warning once as they entered an area just north of Manhattan Island, where the river is bordered to the west by another colony, New Jersey. As near as Benny could tell, the southern flow of river water clashed with the northern push of the Atlantic Ocean in this area. And to make matters worse, they entered the area at high tide, when the ocean's onslaught was at its strongest.

"She's gonna get rough, so everybody hang onto somethin.' There ain't no stoppin' if ya falls overboard," yelled the captain.

Fortunately they made it through the rough currents and from there on, it was smooth sailing right into New York Harbor. Even maneuvering into the dock side seemed to be simple enough. Any questions Benny had as to what made Manhattan such a valuable property of the Crown were erased during that last leg of the trip. The harbor's deep waterway and convenient dockage were ideal for navigation and the too numerous to count ships in port were a testament to the island's value as the trade capital of the New World.

The company's offices and receiving station are on Wall Street, almost at the foot of the docks. Once on shore, Father hurried to the company's office to finalize this trip's business. On the way, he gave Benny a guided tour of the city, with a thorough narration so that Benny could truly appreciate the many wonderful sights he was seeing. Father pulled the pack horse next to the company's loading dock and with the help of the receiving clerk's staff, the pelts were sorted, counted, weighed and arranged in order for the company's merchandise appraiser. The process was time consuming but did not take nearly as long as the paperwork, which was the next step. Benny stayed close to Father so he could learn about each process. When they were finally finished with the appraisal tallies, Father and the receiving supervisor each signed the exchange document. Benny was delighted to see the process come to an end but to his surprise, there was still more paperwork ahead. They went through the building to the administrative offices, where they entered the loan department. After another wait, Father turned in the exchange document. In turn, he received a note confirming that the mortgage on the farm had been paid for another year. The loan officer also counted out some money and handed it to Father.

Finally they returned to the horses. Father waited until they had walked up Wall Street. "We did good. Very good," he said. "After paying our mortgage, the loan for Mother and me to travel here from England, and after taking out our trip expenses, we still have enough to live on until the next trip. Yes, we did good. Thank God. He has blessed us. Let's get to an inn, then you can go and explore the city."

They stopped at the Fraunces Tavern for a meal and then

went next door to the Grace Inn and registered for the night. The inn was opposite a village square that has become quite famous for a specific activity. The businessmen who work in the area, on their off time, often play a game that has caused this fame and has ultimately led to changing the name of the square. They play a game called bowling, right there, on the green; hence the area is now known as Bowling Green Square. I would venture to say that many a meal break from the surrounding offices has been spent playing and wagering on that sport.

Anyway, the Grace is a rather small inn. It doesn't serve meals, so most guests go next door for good dinners. The Grace does have a spacious parlor and most guests gather there for leisure and relaxation. After Benny had boarded the horses in a nearby stable and brought their personal belongings up to the room Father had rented he was raring to go off and see the city. "Where do we start?" he asked Father.

"We? Not me; I'm exhausted. I just want to read the newspaper and relax in the parlor. Besides, I've seen the city many times. Don't go north of the ditch; not much to see up there and besides, that's an unsavory part of town. Lots of what they call shows and theaters, so there's those kinds of folks up there."

"You mean there's actually a ditch that separates the city? I mean between good and bad?"

"I don't know that I'd call them bad folks, just different. Mind you, I haven't seen them but I hear tell they're kind of different. I mean the ladies wear all that stuff on their faces and the men prance about like they're always on a stage. And yes, there is a ditch but the city has been filling it in over the years. Now they call it Canal Street. Never really was a canal but Ditch Street doesn't sound too appealing, so leave it to the politicians. They'd make a fur coat out of a possum."

Benny said he would be back before dark and off he went. He walked across Bowling Green and was surprised to see how congested it was. There were many military men, mostly officers,

Over Rivers, Across Mountains ...

mixed in with the civilians. There were hardly any children there, mostly men, and many were simply traversing the green to get from one building to another. Without trying to be obvious, Benny looked at the men very carefully. They were clerks, accountant-type people and some, the better dressed ones, he thought had to be bankers or the heads of big companies. Benny realized he stuck out like a sore thumb. Compared to the men around him, he was quite poorly dressed. His dark brown britches were worn and tattered, although they were in good repair. His long twin tailed jacket had all of its buttons but was bare threaded at the elbows. His shirt lacked the front frill and was made out of hemp and not the fine cotton he was seeing on most men around him. The shoes others wore were highly shined and most had buckles. In comparison, his were scuffed from walking untold miles, in conditions clearly not meant for pedestrians. In fact, holes had even developed in the soles of both of his shoes. Fortunately, Benny had learned a trick that an Indian had suggested to Father. Apparently, during a trading session Father was sitting cross-legged when a Chief noticed a hole in his shoe. The Chief gave Father a piece of deer leather; then carved it so it perfectly fit the inside of his shoe.

Benny also thought about his tri-cornered hat and almost laughed out loud. In recent weeks it had seen its share of bad weather and almost continuous use. He decided not to pay attention to such petty things, though. Besides, he didn't know any of these people, so it didn't really matter.

He moved onward, walking south on Wall Street towards the harbor. In minutes he reached the area where the street meets the water. He then realized why it was called Wall Street. The docks had been rebuilt and fortified but he could still see the remnants of the original wooden retaining wall. It was built by the Dutch to keep the English out. "How foolish." Benny thought. However, it does serve to keep the harbor water out of the street.

After taking in the sites Benny spun around and headed in the opposite direction. He made a couple of turns and came back to

Wall Street. There in front of him was the most beautiful church he had ever seen. Trinity Church is built of stone and spirals high up into the sky. The beauty of the impressive structure overwhelmed him and, in fact, even after wandering the rest of the southern portion of the city, Benny felt Trinity Church was the prettiest building he had ever seen.

The sun was beginning to set, so Benny decided to head back to the Grace Inn. Grateful for God's small favors, his walk was indeed a brief one because he had such a fine sense of direction.

Benny could hardly believe how happy he was. He had just walked around the greatest city in the colonies. He was on his way home. He had it in his mind that we were soon to marry and to his delight the trading trip was a rousing success. Everything was perfect. As Benny turned the door knob to the front door of the Grace Inn, he felt happier than he could ever remember feeling. He opened the door and walked into the parlor. He was about to share his feelings with Father, but then his good mood evaporated the minute he saw Father lying on his back on the floor. Several people were standing around Father and some others were kneeling beside him. Benny saw the blood coming out of Father's mouth and seep down the side of his face and neck. His eyes were closed and he was motionless. His pants were wet from the release of his own urine.

"No! Father no! Oh God, no!" Benny screamed.

The people tending to Father as well as the spectators quickly turned to face the frantic young man. At first Benny was blind to anyone but Father. He ran, and fell to his knees right next to Father.... Then he cradled Father's head on his knees saying, "Why? Why? How did it happen?" Benny looked up at the faces staring at him. "How did he die? Why?"

No one answered his plea, but a man standing near Father's feet began reciting a verse that Benny had heard many times before. "May perpetual light shine upon him and may his soul rest in peace." The man ended his prayer for Father's soul by making the sign of the cross. As he learned after his birth mother had passed on, Benny knew that the death of a loved one ends a chapter of one's own life, changing it forever.

"So where's the man with the *vibes?*" someone shouted from the foyer in a commanding tone. Everyone turned to see who would dare to disturb such a solemn moment. But as quickly as they turned to face the loud voice, they spun back, as Father's supposedly dead body jolted up from the floor and began to shake and vibrate. Benny had been on his knees but he fell over, startled by the shock of Father's sudden and violent thrusting— return to life.

Father's limbs snapped about without control. As his eyes opened wider than Benny thought possible more blood spurted from his mouth.

"Clear away! Clear away!" shouted the man with the bellowing voice.

"He's alive. He's alive," Benny uttered it like a prayer of thanks,

"Hallelujah," shouted the man who had said the blessing over Father's body.

"Of course he's alive," said the man with the commanding voice. "As are most people who've had a bout with the vibes. Now clear away! I've got work to do. And somebody get me some rags. I don't like kneeling in blood and piss. Makes me stink for the rest of the day."

Benny was so horrified and elated at the same time that he couldn't speak, his thoughts scattered hither and yon. Had Father come back from the dead? Or maybe he didn't die after all.

"Young man, do you know him?" asked the boisterous man.

"He's my father," Benny responded still in absolute shock as he looked up at the rather burly man with the commanding voice.

"Good! Then what say you snap to and give me a hand, or he really may die." The man gave Benny a moment to refocus then he

continued to speak. "Let's get him on his side, that way he won't choke to death on his own blood."

"Where's he bleeding from?" Benny asked. He looked for a wound but couldn't see one.

"Probably his tongue. Most people who get the vibes gnaw their teeth and sometimes they bite their own tongue and that's why we're going to do this ..." The man pulled out a piece of leather from a pouch that was strung over his shoulder, "I'll spread his jaws and you put this between his teeth. Be careful, he'll bite down pretty hard. Put your finger too close and you might lose it."

Benny took a second to assess the leather. It was actually a piece from a bridle. Then he nodded to the man and both worked to insert the leather strip into Father's mouth. The man then put his knee behind the small of Father's back, thus preventing him from rolling into a flat position and possibly choking on the fluids accumulating in his mouth.

"What do we do now?" asked Benny.

"Not much. Just keep him on his side and wait. If we get lucky, the vibes will last only a minute or two more. But, I've seen them last for hours, not that the person who's going through it will remember. They usually come out of it and ask, 'what's going on.'"

"What caused this?" Benny asked perplexedly.

"Some people say bad blood or too much of it. There's some people in my profession who think blood-letting helps. Many even carry leaches and put them all over a person who's in the midst of a vibe bout. But I can't swear by it."

"Profession? Are you a doctor, Sir?"

"Yeah. That is when I'm not trimming beards or fixing a wig." The man kept one hand on Father's shoulder to steady him on his side.

Benny was fascinated by this burly man and if he weren't so preoccupied with Father's condition he would have studied him closer. He did notice the man was larger than most men and based on appearances he most probably was also very strong. The man's arms and shirtsleeves were covered with a strange outer garment. It had sleeves that went over his shirt sleeves, with tie strings at the top. This was presumably worn to keep him clean. His black, curly hair straggled over his thick eyebrows. In Benny's opinion he didn't seem to fit his chosen profession. Nevertheless, Benny was just relieved to have his help.

"How did you know Father needed help?" Benny asked the man.

"Miss Grace sent for me."

Benny scooted around so that he was close to Father's head. He leaned down and speaking softly told Father he was going to be all right. He told Father that he was going to pull through this and that he was very much loved by his whole family. Father's spasmodic jolts continued as Benny whispered in his ear. After a while the spasms slowed down and then stopped. A few moments later Father's breathing became more relaxed and he appeared to be asleep.

"Sure sign he's out of the woods." the burly man said.

"Thank God!" Benny whispered into Father's ear.

Ever the praying man, Father nodded his head.

"Amen. Praise the Lord," he said.

The next morning, when Father woke up, he looked around the room and didn't recognize it. Benny was sitting in a straight-backed chair, but was leaning backwards so the top of the chair was pressed against the wall. Although he was in a deep sleep, he sensed Father had awakened and so he pulled himself back to consciousness, Father and Benny looked at each other for a long moment.

"I don't remember going to bed. How did I get here?" asked Father.

"It's a long story but first, how do you feel, Papa?" Benny had never before referred to Father as Papa and he had never before addressed him with such a warm and humble tone.

"Don't know. My head hurts, tongue's chopped up. Bit it or

something during the night. Why are you …? What's going on?"

Benny took some time to explain the events of the day before. "Death?" Father asked. "He died for me." He paused a long moment but Benny didn't interrupt. He knew Father had more to say and he did. "Remember therefore from where you have fallen; repent."

Benny knew Father was quoting the Bible but he couldn't identify which scripture he was referencing. Moreover, he wondered if Father was talking to him or to himself. However, other than Father's seemingly disoriented chatter, he didn't appear to have sustained any major physical problems. He appeared to be tired and very weak but other than that, his limbs and body were intact. For the remainder of that day Father rested and only once did Benny leave his side and that was only because the burly man came to check on his patient. Before leaving, Benny asked Father for his money sack, so he could make travel arrangements for them. Father, with Benny's help, managed to get out of bed, retrieve the sack from his travel bag, and hand it to Benny. "He has said, 'I have set before you an open door and no one can shut it,'" Father told Benny.

Benny noticed that the burly man seemed bewildered by Father's words. Then Benny grasped Father's shoulders and moved him back into the bed. "It's time to rest," Benny told Father, embracing him gently.

The burly man offered to stay with Father while Benny made travel arrangements. He said he had intended to sit in the lobby and read his newspaper, an activity he could easily do in the room so Benny accepted the offer. Before leaving Benny and this gentleman exchanged mailing addresses and spent some time talking. Benny promised to keep him informed of Father's progress.

There are basically two ways to travel home to Long Island from Manhattan Island. The most common way—at least for those who could afford it— is by voyaging on an eastward-bound sailing

Over Rivers, Across Mountains ...

ship that travels along the coast. Benny seriously considered this means of getting home but then decided against it. He simply wasn't sure how he would manage Father on a ship, especially if he had another episode of the vibes. Instead, he decided on the alternative way of traveling, over land by wagon.

So, after leaving Father in the hands of the burly man, Benny retrieved the horses from the stable and made his way to a wide road known as Broadway. He knew where he was going, straight up Broadway to Canal Street or as Father called it Ditch Street. The area he was going to was more rural, and he hoped to find a used wagon to buy. Very quickly he found an older wagon that was longer than most, with wheels intact. Luckily, all of its spokes were in place and solid and even the tailgate hinge was in working order. The owner, a blacksmith, came strolling out of his shop when he saw Benny looking over the wagon. He promptly told Benny that the wagon was in fine shape and quoted him the selling price.

Benny had learned to negotiate from accompanying Father on this business trip. Using his new skills, Benny and the blacksmith finally settled on half of the originally quoted price. The wagon cost far less than passage by boat would have cost. Although this was a two-horse wagon, Benny had only taken one horse out of the stable. Nevertheless, with the bill of sale in hand, and one horse hitched up to the wagon, he climbed on and rode off. Benny tested the wagon by going farther along Canal Street, all the while checking out the sights, looking for an area where food products and produce were sold. Benny knew that with so many people in the city, there just had to be a major area where such goods came in from the countryside to be shipped to restaurants, inns and smaller vendors. Realizing it was getting late, Benny made his way back to the inn; leaving the horse and the new wagon at the stable. He paid the bill, asked that the innkeepers grease the wheels, and told them they would be leaving very early the next day.

Dawn had yet to breach the horizon when Benny departed

the Grace Inn with two horses pulling the wagon and one tied to the back. Father was stretched out in the wagon's flat bed. Benny had used the bedrolls as a mattress and also to cushion the ride for Father. It had been a moonless, dark night. Benny would not have even been able to direct the horses and wagon had it not been for the oil-lit street lamps. They weren't but a few minutes away from the inn when Father mumbled something about seven lamps and seven churches and then he fell asleep again. Benny wondered what seven lamps he was talking about, but then he figured that Father must have been counting street lamps.

They had been heading east toward the river. Daylight was just breaking as they reached the road that runs north and south along the bank of the East River. Benny took the road north and even though there was barely enough daylight to see, he was still able to discern a considerable amount of activity in the distance. As they got closer he saw that it was a market of some kind and then he realized this was where the goods from England as well as the other colonies came into port. And, considering the number of wagons that were loaded with goods and heading to the port, he realized that this is also where domestic area goods were being brought for wholesale and shipment. Getting closer, Benny could see the many ship masts in the breaking daylight. Never before had he seen so many ships gathered in any one harbor.

There was heavy congestion on the roadway. Wagons of all sizes and shapes seemed to be moving in every direction. Benny laughed to himself because the area looked like one big ant colony. He maneuvered the wagon through the crowded roadway only to find another hub of activity a few minutes further along. Benny realized that the congestion increased every time he entered an area where a ship was being loaded or unloaded. This went on for quite a long while. Then Benny came to an area that was different. Although there were many boats docked, they were mostly small boats and they were all unloading, not loading. Benny's nose told him exactly what was going on before he could actually see what

Over Rivers, Across Mountains ...

they were doing. The boats were unloading fish and other seafood. He had driven right into New York's fish market. From here the fish would be sent to restaurants, inns and food stores all over the southern tip of Manhattan.

Benny was glad to get past that area. He kept smelling his clothes to see if the fishy odor had clung to him. In between sniffing he spotted the sign he was looking for, the sign that announced boat service to Queensland and Brookline. The East River would be the last body of water to cross before they would be on Lange Islandt. The sign was old and still used the Dutch spelling.

But Benny was worried at the notion of loading the wagon onto a boat to cross the river. As it turned out, the ferrymen were so accustomed to moving wagons on board, fully loaded with horses attached, that it took them no time and little effort at all to load the wagon onto the boat. Once the flat-bottomed boat was loaded, it was towed across the river by ropes that were harnessed to mules and guided by workmen on shore.

And so, with Father asleep more than he was awake, Benny made his way back to the island. The road that hugged the northern portion of the island was well traveled. It went through many small towns and villages. At dark Benny pulled up to an inn just outside of a town called Westbury. There Father and Benny ate dinner and then slept in the wagon. Because Benny was concerned about a reoccurrence of father's vibes and the accompanying, dangerous gyrations, he felt the sides of the wagon offered the safest sleeping situation. Benny also felt, if they could rise early enough and travel late into the day, they could probably make it home by the next evening.

Chapter 10

Farming
&
Recruitment

Mother has a very strange ability. For many years I didn't know what to call it; then one day in school I learned the word "phenomena." Since then I've called her ability "Mother's phenomena." I've also learned her ability has another name. It's called "premonitions." Some people have "hunches," but that's not what I'm referring to. When Mother has a premonition, it almost always concerns something substantial and never anything that anyone would wager upon.

The morning Benny and Father left Westbury, Mother had a premonition. She didn't share it with us, but I knew from the way she was behaving that something had happened. She rose early, rushed through her chores, shot a Canadian goose, cleaned it and set it in the fireplace for roasting. That may not sound like much and to tell the truth it doesn't take too much luck to kill a goose. Hundreds of them sit in our field and they don't move out of the way of people. If you aim at one and miss, the odds are you'll get the one behind it. The hard part is cleaning and preparing the bird.

"Why are we having such a fussy meal?" I asked Mother.

"Oh, I just thought it would be nice," Mother answered

trying to end this topic of conversation.

"Mother?" I said suspiciously, shooting her an inquisitive look.

"Well, just in case they come home today. I'm sure they'd love a home cooked meal."

I helped her get the goose on the spit and in place over the fire. It would be a long day of continuously turning the spit but between my sisters and me it would get done. We also went down into the root cellar for potatoes, onions and carrots, the last of last year's produce. Towards evening, the dog started barking. Mother was ahead of me as she made her way to the road and looked east. From our side of the road, the south side, that means we looked right. Nothing. We waited a while and still we didn't see or hear anything.

Father always takes the boat from Manhattan to Mattituck, then he takes the road right through town to our home. We got tired of waiting and we also became concerned about the food cooking in the fireplace so we started back to the house. That's when we heard the squeaking and clanking sounds coming from the west. We tried to see the origin of such a clatter, but we were blinded by the intensity of the setting sun. The sounds grew louder and we finally recognized the noise to be a horse-drawn wagon. Curious, we wanted to see who was coming our way, and imagined that they'd probably be going to Mattituck. Using our hands to shield our eyes from the sun. the silhouette soon came into view but the brilliant sun continued to make it impossible to see who was coming. At last the outline of two passengers on the running seat could be made out, and it didn't take but a second to realize who they were.

"Benny!" I screamed.

"And Father!" Mother said a second later.

We both couldn't wait for the wagon to get to us and began to run toward it … Benny saw us running and pulled up the horses. He jumped from the wagon and sprinted toward me. We met, or more precisely collided. He lifted me off my feet and we hugged and kissed and kissed and hugged.

"So much for brotherly love!" Mother said as she sped by us over to the wagon and Father.

"I love you," Benny said over and over, between kisses.

And for the first time ever I told him how much I loved him and that the two of us would always be one. He opened his mouth to say something, but then he abruptly placed me back on my feet, and joined Mother and Father.

Intuitively, I knew something was wrong. Although the sun was still blinding, I could see that Father was still perched on the wagon seat. I rushed to catch up to Benny and then I heard Father say something to Mother, who was standing next to the wagon. "Things saith He that holdeth the seven stars in His right hand, who walks in the midst of the seven golden candlesticks."

During my entire lifetime I had never seen Father look the way he did at that moment. His long brown hair with graying temples was a mess. His brown eyes were opened wide and his normally chiseled facial skin sagged. His speech was clear but he surely wasn't making any sense. He stopped talking and stared straight ahead, not looking at anyone. Benny stood behind Mother and waited for Father to finish his comments. Then he placed his hands on her shoulders and turned her around. Mother's face was streaked with tears.

"What happened?" she asked in an unsteady voice.

"He had an attack of the vibes. It happened three days ago. There was no warning. It just set upon him." Benny didn't like speaking about Father as if he weren't present. "Let me pull the wagon up to the house. We'll get Father cleaned up and we'll talk."

With the help of Sarah and Elizabeth, we got the wagon stored, the horses into stalls and fed. Benny helped Mother clean up Father; then he soaked in a tub of warmed up water until Mother had me knock on the bedroom door to tell him dinner was ready. The feast Mother prepared was scrumptious, although the festivities were greatly subdued because of Father's condition.

After dinner, my sisters volunteered to clean up the dishes. Mother tucked Father into their bed; then joined Benny and me on the porch. Benny told us everything that happened. After he finished the story, the three of us sat in silence. Time seemed to drag on until finally Mother broke the quietness.

"Whatever God wills, will be done," she said. "I will give him so much loving care and will pray for him, of course ... I'm sure he'll be back to normal within no time at all. For now, I also have other concerns. What's going to happen to the farm? Where will we go? What will the two of you do? I'm sure Father shared his plan of moving you to the North Country ... Can things get anymore uncertain? Even our community is falling apart."

The last comment she made surprised both of us. I could see it on Benny's face. Mother was talking about our immediate family crisis and all of a sudden she spoke about a community problem? Maybe she needed a diversion from the pain of our family's situation. Benny and I just let her ramble on.

"What with the Tories and the other Colonists arguing and openly threatening each other ... and yesterday when Rachael and I went to town, we heard about the brewing hostilities in Boston. I just don't know what we're all going to do."

Benny let Mother's questions and emotional thoughts settle into us for a moment, then said "I've thought about most of these issues you've raised." Benny paused before continuing, "For the last couple of days, that's all I've thought about. Riding on a buckboard for hours at a time hurts the backside so much, that it gave me motivation to think about more important matters. First of all, Father will need a great deal of care and we'll all help and ... yes we'll all pray for his recovery. When I think back to that day I thought he had died, I am so grateful that God has allowed him to remain with us. Let's all just keep praying to the good Lord that Father will improve every day."

"Now, the next couple of points cannot be separated. They're all linked together and it all starts with Rachael and me ..." We were seated on the two person bench Father had built. Mother sat across from us. Benny took my hands in his. "We want to marry, and sooner, not later," he said.

I couldn't resist. I melted and fell into his arms. Raising my head, I softly kissed his lips. Benny sat up straighter but didn't let go of my hands as he continued speaking. "The farm ... we all know the company holds the mortgage and to pay the mortgage Father had to trade fur pelts with the Indians. But in truth, trading with the Indians is about to become a thing of the past. If nothing else, on that trip I learned the Indians are dying off and if they don't die from disease, their tribal culture, including trapping is crumbling. Things are changing and we too must change. We've got to get out of the fur trading business and find something that has a future."

"But how can we pay the mortgage without the income? We'll lose the farm for sure." Mother was fighting back tears as she spoke.

"I have some ideas that we should consider. On the way home from Manhattan, I saw some things that have changed my way of thinking about the farm. Up until now we've raised enough produce and stock to feed just ourselves for the year. Manhattan has thousands of people that need to be fed. They get their produce and meats and seafood from farmers and fishermen who live near the city. What if we increased our farm capacity and also increased our livestock ..." Benny paused to gather his thoughts, then continued. "... And, instead of searching for *wampum*, we should consider catching more fish. The fish we catch will never stay fresh on the long journey to Manhattan, but we can salt or smoke it until we collect enough to make the trip profitable."

"But who will do all of this work?"

"Think about it. For all the time and effort it takes for us to gather the *wampum* and the many days of traveling to trade for fur, we can easily spend that time doing farming and fishing. And yes, it will take a lot of effort from all of us but that never stopped

us before."

"Oh, but, you can't stay here," Mother wailed. Then in a more calm voice she added, "What will people say if you two get married? I mean, how can we face our relatives, friends and neighbors?" Mother's tears flowed heavy as she spoke. "My daughter, marrying my son ... Oh dear me."

Benny cut her off. "Your bastard son! Who loves you very much. But, mind you, in a very different way from how I love your daughter. And, quite honestly, I don't care what others think or say. Rachael and I are not going to head for the North Country and abandon you, Father or our sisters. Once Father recovers and our plans for the farm work out, then we can reconsider where we'll settle for good. For now, let's face life as God has placed it before us." He stopped and took a deep breath.

"Mother, what do you really think? Do you have any other ideas?" he asked her.

Mother sat still for a long time, "So be it. But I've never thought of you as a bastard son. To me, it is as if you came from my womb. No child could be loved more than I love you. And I know Father feels the same way." With that said she got up to check on Father but not before gently kissing both of us.

Before leaving, another thought occurred to her. "Tell me, Benny, how do you think we will be affected by what's happening in Boston?"

Benny looked puzzled.

"In town yesterday, there was a lot of talk about the problems between Colonists and the English troops escalating," I responded. "And King George pronounced before parliament that we Colonists must be obedient, even if we have to be taught obedience."

"It's well known that King George is a reserved man who has fathered ten children with his queen," said Benny "He loves to dress up like a farmer and work in the gardens and farms around the castle. I can't believe he would escalate a conflict, especially one that is so far away from the mother country."

Mother was not so optimistic, nor was she ready to disregard a potential problem. "If it does become a war, which side will we join? Have you children thought of that?"

Benny wanted no part of the pending crisis that was beyond the realm of his immediate environment. "We all have enough to do just to care for Father and save the farm. I don't even want to think about the world outside of our land and house. If war comes, we will remain neutral."

Normally, when Father returned from his springtime business trip he would start the process of planting our crop for the year. This time Benny would be taking over the task and his first step was to pace off the parcel to be planted. Even though it was springtime it was still bone chillingly cold outside. But then, that's typical for the island, especially for the far east end that sticks way out into the ocean. So I bundled Father up and took him out with me. We went to see if Benny needed any help. To my surprise Benny had already paced off the area to be cultivated and it was at least twenty times larger than our normal planting parcel.

"What are you doing? We can't work all of that, especially the wooded patch," I yelled across the field.

"Yes we can and we will," he casually responded, as he moved closer to us.

"We couldn't harvest all of this area, let alone plow, cultivate and seed it."

"Sure we can and don't forget we're not planting the whole field at one time. We need to bring in a constant harvest to sell off during most of the year, not just one harvest when everything is cheap."

"But that's not how we or any other farmer does it. We plant, wait 'til fall and harvest."

"Just because that's the way it's been done before doesn't mean that's how we have to do it forever more."

"Where have you seen farming done the way you're describing?"

"I haven't," Benny calmly said as his facial expression slowly changed and his face broke out into the smug grin I had seen so many times before. It seemed that Benny had a plan worked out in his head and was about to put it into action. "Okay. We now know how much we're going to plant."

From his pocket he pulled out a piece of paper showing the dimensions of the area, as well as the lines and names of different vegetables. Obviously, his plan was to start harvesting in a few weeks and continue doing so until the next winter.

"Let's hope Mr. Smith at the General Store has all the different kinds of seeds we need," said Benny pointing to sections of his diagram. "Will you go and ask Mother if she needs anything from the store or if she'd like to come along," he added without skipping a beat. "I'm going to recount the rows to make sure of my math, then I'll hitch up the wagon and we'll head for town. Oh, don't forget to get the money pouch. We're going to avoid using credit as much as we can."

"To him that overcometh I will give to eat of the tree of life which is in the midst of the paradise of God." Benny and I just looked at each other. Was Father trying to tell us something?

Mother decided to come along and we had a good time on the way to Mattituck. Benny expanded on his plan, or should I say dream, and Mother and I kept poking fun at his ideas. But when Benny mentioned that he needed a keg of vinegar, the mood changed from teasing to serious. "I would hope we could serve a better wine than vinegar at your wedding," said Mother to our surprise and delight.

I had been sitting on the wagon floor with Father when I realized this was Mother's way of saying she was giving her permission and blessing for Benny and I to marry. I managed to leap to my feet and throw my arms around Mother with such force she almost fell off the buckboard. We hugged and cried. And hugged some more.

"Look what a mess I am. I look a fright and we're going to town," Mother said through her tears, trying to smooth her skirt.

Benny stopped the wagon, put his arms around both Mother and me. "You look wonderful," he told Mother.

"I know thy works, love, service, faith and patience," said Father from the back of the wagon.

Receiving Mother's blessings for us to marry was one of the happiest moments of my life. Mother was aware that relatives, friends, the entire community, especially the church, would mock our decision to marry. But getting Mother's blessing meant to me that she would face anything for the sake of our happiness. At that moment I was happy, so happy and so much in love that my stomach felt like it had butterflies in it. Benny's speechlessness and radiant face told me that he, too, was thrilled to have Mother's support.

As we entered town and approached the parsonage lawn we saw a man in the stockade, with his head being stretched away from his shoulders by the wooden clasp around his neck. To our surprise it was our woodcutter friend, Obedia Hawkins, known as Obie. The stock's strangling hold on his wrists made his big workman's hands turn blue. His face was distorted with pain. It appeared as though his legs had given out some time ago and now his chin and the back of his head were held taut against the stock. There was little life left in him.

Benny jumped from the wagon and moved through the crowd of spectators, who were mostly friends and well-wishers who pleaded with Obie not to give up. Some stood in silent prayer. We know that the British use the stockade to set an example. This form of torture is not intended to deliberately kill but to so severely punish a person that he would never challenge authority again, nor would anyone who witnessed the punishment. Benny

pushed his way through to the front. "What did he do?" Benny asked Malcom Smith who was standing near the so called rack.

Malcom took a deep breath. "He told the soldiers, who took his firewood, that he needed real money to live on. He told them that the script paper they had given him was worthless and no one would accept it as cash. So now they're making an example of him. The Sergeant just told all of us shopkeepers, we had better accept the script or we'd get worse punishment." He looked at Obie and shook his head. "He'll never make it 'til dawn."

Pastor Timothy and Doc pushed through the crowd to the stockade. "What did the Commandant say?" Malcom asked as soon as they were within hearing distance.

"We tried, even begged, but he would not reconsider," replied Pastor Timothy in a sorrowful voice with his head down. "The punishment stands. Obie is not going to be released until tomorrow at dawn."

"I'll get my chisel and bust the lock," said Smitty, the blacksmith.

"Careful!" said Malcom as he took hold of Smitty's arm. "Talk like that could get twenty of us in racks. You know what the Crown's officers are trained to do. Even if we talk about challenging their authority, without even making a threat, they'll pick off a bunch of us at random and punish us even worse."

"Can you open the lock without breaking it up?" Benny whispered walking closer to Smitty.

"Picked a lock or two in my time," he responded from the side of his mouth.

"Good. Meet me behind the General Store in five minutes. Just get there by taking a roundabout route."

Benny whispered the same meeting arrangements to Malcom, Pastor Timothy and Doc.

"What in the world is young Benny up to?" Malcom said to Doc and Pastor Timothy before leaving. "He'd better not get us nailed Pastor."

Farming & Recruitment

"He's too smart for that. He's one of the most clever young men I've ever met," replied Pastor Timothy, with a frown on his face.

"Guess he gets it from his father," said Malcom as he walked away.

"Yes. Both of them," said Pastor Timothy to himself.

Once they were gathered in the little secluded area behind the General Store, Benny wasted no time laying out a plan. He was brisk, precise and in total command, so much so that the only response from the others, was the nodding of their heads. They unanimously agreed to his plan without any discussion.

"We're going to create a diversion," Benny told them. "One that will require Major General Placeham to move all of his troops, including the ones guarding Obie, to combat the problem. Malcom, you and Pastor Timothy and you too, Doc, are going to start a fire as soon as it gets dark, a big fire. Right in the woods to the north side of the parsonage. Smitty, get your lock picking tools. You and I will get Obie out of the rack as soon as the guards are ordered to go and fight the fire. If the fire is big enough and close enough to the parsonage, it'll take 'til dawn to put it out. Just before the guards come back to release Obie, we'll put him back into the rack. With an eight hour or so break from the torture of the rack, he may live. We just have to pray he lives until dark. Everybody ready?"

"Not so fast there Benny," cautioned Malcom. "If we light a big enough fire, we could burn down our Pastor's house."

"He knows that," Pastor Timothy said, as he looked at Benny's face. "But he also knows the Major General wouldn't raise a finger to help us even if the whole town were on fire. However, the good news is that the parsonage is now his house and headquarters and he's storing all of his papers in it, not to mention hordes of wine, food and other delicacies. He'll do anything to save his parsonage."

"Okay, but that makes us against the Crown and I'm not so

convinced I want to do that." Malcom was still worried.

Benny decided to handle this issue. "We're not taking sides. We're trying to save the life of a friend. And if you get caught, just act like you saw a fire and tried to help put it out. Smitty and I will handle breaking Obie out of the rack."

"If we get caught, we're dead men," said Benny looking straight at Smitty. "Do you want out of it? Just say so and we'll all understand."

"I'll get my lock pickin' tools," said Smitty without hesitation. "See you at dark, on the road near the rack."

While Benny and the others were plotting the rescue mission, that Mother and I knew nothing about, Mother and I decided to move forward with the shopping plan. We drove the wagon to the front of the General Store, went inside and started to shop. Benny came into the store from the rear. We did a lot of shopping; we bought more seeds, vinegar, salt and spices than we had ever bought before. After the wagon was loaded, we headed towards home, but once we reached the outskirts of town Benny halted the wagon, kissed me goodnight and told me not to worry. He would be home in the morning and so he started walking back toward town.

Mother and I knew he wouldn't tell us what he was up to, and he hadn't given us enough time to express our concern to him. As the day drew to a close, the sunset was beautiful. I sat on the porch and tried not to worry, but I fussed and fidgeted trying to figure out what plan Benny had hatched in his head. He always seemed to come up with ideas that other people couldn't understand, let alone conceive of themselves. The last twinkle of light disappeared over the horizon, and Mother had already lit the candles when I got off the bench to get ready for bed. Then something caught my eye. It looked like another sunset, but this light was coming from the east. I realized that it actually was coming from the town. In moments the little glow grew and grew.

Mother stepped out onto the porch. "The whole town must be on fire."

Farming & Recruitment

"You don't think Benny had anything to do with this, do you?" As I spoke my concern grew deeper. I didn't like the feeling of dread that was slipping over me.

"I hope he did," she responded with surprising conviction.

"What?"

"Don't misunderstand me dear. I only meant, if Benny started it, then it's under control."

The fire burned all night. The smoke was very dense and the evening dampness forced the smoke to billow about on the ground. Even as far away as our farm is located from town, the smoke severely limited visibility. Still the early glow and intensity of the fire was an incredible sight. Mother and I knew if Benny had anything to do with that fire he would have made sure that it wouldn't intentionally hurt anyone or destroy valuable property, not unless the fire got out of control and the town was truly burning down.

Mother and I wrapped ourselves in blankets and spent the night looking at the sky above Mattituck. My sisters stayed up for a while and watched with us, but soon they became tired and went off to bed. Father was safely tucked into bed, so the night's vigil was left to Mother and me. As dawn broke we could see the smoke but no flames. There was still no sign of Benny. Our vigil continued.

At the rack, Benny stood watch; and just before dawn Smitty helped Obie reinsert his neck and wrists between the timbers. Smitty then put the hasp back in place and the lock through it. Joining Benny, the two walked to the other side of the road to wait. "Last night, we got him out just before his legs gave way," Smitty said as they walked. "You know, he would be dead if he were left draped in that torturous rack overnight."

Their wait was brief. Pastor Timothy and Doc soon

approached with two guards and a sergeant. The guards were grumbling that they had to fight the fire all night and why the hell couldn't they release this useless woodsman later? In fact, why didn't the officers think to press him into service and have him fight that awful fire? The Sergeant unlocked the hasp and released Obie, who fell toward the ground but was quickly caught by Doc and Pastor Timothy.

Doc brought over his small wagon and after our Pastor helped load Obie on board, Doc took him to his office. Smitty and Benny walked to the General Store where Malcom was sitting on a stool resting after the long tiring night of starting fires and extinguishing them. Malcom smiled as his fellow conspirators entered the store.

"Well, fellow Patriots. Was it worth it? Is he alive?"

"Barely, but Doc will get him back to health."

"Where did you get the term 'Patriot' from?"

"Oh, some of the officers said that's what the troublemakers in Boston call themselves."

"Troublemakers? You mean people who want freedom from England are calling themselves Patriots?" Benny was surprised they gave themselves a name.

"That's right. And since we carried out a mission against the Crown, we're now Patriots."

"We set the fire to save the life of a friend. We didn't join sides. We're not an organized group. I for one, see myself as a neutral person in all this nonsense."

Pastor Timothy pulled his wagon behind the store and entered as Benny was finishing his claim to neutrality. They chatted for a while longer then Pastor Timothy offered to give Benny a ride home. After the long night Benny was delighted with the offer and accepted; they soon left town and headed west.

"Well young man, you are to be congratulated," the Pastor said to Benny during the ride to the farm. "You not only saved Obie's life, you did it without a single shot being fired. You're very clever." He then chuckled, mostly to himself. "However, in the process I was almost burned out of my house!" he said with mock indignation.

"Sorry about that Reverend but it was the best idea I could think of at that moment. How did the parsonage fair?"

"The north side got a bit charred but the damage isn't too serious, just superficial. Structure's solid as ever. Besides, it was worth it, not only to save Obie's life, but to watch Major General Placeham scurrying about. Lord forgive me but in the middle of battling the fire I laughed uncontrollably when I saw that grotesquely overweight man running around and shouting orders. He looked so ridiculous but he did as you suspected he would. He ordered every military person on the grounds, including those guarding Obie, to fight the fire."

They talked about Father, and Benny said he thought Father was making progress. Pastor Timothy mentioned Doc was researching the ailment.

"I understand Doc's written to Harvard Medical School for information and advice. Benny, you know we are your brothers and sisters in Christ and we will do everything we can to help," said the Pastor. "You know Doc, if Harvard answers his inquiries and say they have a way that could help, he'll have your dad in his buggy and on the way to Boston in two shakes of a lamb's tail."

Benny couldn't find any words to say. He simply nodded.

Pastor decided to lighten up the conversation. "Well, that is, Doc would head for Boston if there is a Boston left. You know, there's this band of Patriots who are spearheading a breakaway from England. They call themselves the Sons of Liberty."

"They should call themselves the Sons of Civil War or Revolutionary War. Pastor, it's very easy to get caught up in this so called fight for independence, but I firmly believe reasonable people are needed as leaders, people who first and foremost understand that a war of this size would mean thousands and thousands of deaths."

"I certainly agree but both sides would have to have reasonable leaders and right now King George is anything but reasonable," the Pastor responded. "He keeps saying we Colonists don't need representation ... we need to learn obedience. That's why men like Paul Revere and John Adams have called themselves the Sons of Liberty. They say if we can't represent ourselves, give us freedom."

"I'd still like to remain neutral," Benny argued.

"I'm a praying man, Benny, but there's not a prayer of staying neutral."

"Then the Sons of Liberty are going to have to win or lose without me."

"Do you care if they win or lose?"

"Sure I care. I'd rather we Colonists be independent but I'd also rather we find a peaceful way of achieving our independence."

Pastor Timothy thought about what Benny had just said. In fact, he gave the comment a lot of thought.

"I'm happy to hear which side you're on and truth be known, you're not alone," the Pastor said. "There are a lot of good statesmen saying the same thing. Even Washington and Franklin have been saying there has to be a peaceful resolution to this crisis, but it just keeps escalating. I'll say it again. It takes two sides to reach a compromise and the King has surrounded himself with war hawks whose sole aim is to beat the Patriots down."

The Pastor was just finishing his statement to Benny when his wagon came into our view. Mother and I quickly went to the road to get a better look. Even Father made his way to the road. I squinted and strained my eyes every way possible but couldn't make out who was coming up the road. In desperation and fervently praying that it was Benny who was coming home; I started to walk toward what I finally recognized as a wagon. At last I saw the silhouettes of two people on top of the buck seat and knew the passenger was Benny. I picked up my pace, first walking quickly, then a slow run, and finally a race to the wagon. When Benny heard me screaming his name he jumped off and came running to meet me, arms wide open. In mid road we reached each other and I flew into his arms. We hugged and kissed and hugged some more. I admonished him not to ever do anything like that again, even though I didn't know what he did. I told him he had worried me to no end.

And then one of those moments happened that become embedded in one's mind forever. Benny was standing with his back to Pastor Timothy's wagon. I glanced past Benny and my eyes met Pastor Timothy's deep blue eyes. With his slightly graying beard and long hair, he looked like a version of Moses. The meeting of our eyes was so intense that it stopped me in my tracks. I don't know if I was feeling guilt because of my open display of affection towards Benny, or if I was relieved that at least now our Pastor knew of our love for each other. It didn't matter. The meeting of our eyes was and still is a source of inner relief for me. Without saying a word, his eyes told me that this twist of life that has bonded Benny and me was all right. His eyes brightened and he smiled.

With his arm around my shoulder, Benny turned to face our Pastor.

"Aside from Mother and Father, you know more about us, or me, than anyone else. Would it be wrong of me to ask for your blessing?"

Pastor Timothy stopped smiling, got off the wagon and slowly walked to us placing one hand on Benny's shoulder and the other on mine. By this time Mother, holding Father's hand, came up to stand comfortingly next to me.

"Heavenly Father, I know of no other people who are more deserving of Your blessings and grace than these two young people. They have always been devoted to You and have always followed Your commandments, especially when it comes to respecting one's mother and father. I ask You to shed Your blessings upon them in the name of Your Son Jesus Christ. Amen."

He then asked God to oversee Father's recovery, provide

strength and bless him.

"And have made us kings and priest to our God; and we shall reign on earth," Father said looking heavenward.

"Amen," added the Pastor.

Mother offered refreshments, so we walked to the house with Benny leading the horse and wagon behind the rest of us.

"I see you've taken to quoting from the Book of Revelation," Pastor Timothy said to Father.

"That's it! That's it!" Benny exclaimed. "All of those quotes he's been saying. They come from the Book of Revelation."

"Why? I mean, why is he quoting Revelation?" I asked.

"He doesn't usually respond to our questions or comments, except to quote scripture," Mother added.

"Do not be afraid. I am the First and the Last. I am He who lives and was dead and behold I am alive forevermore," said Father to my surprise.

"He answered that time," Pastor said. "He's telling you, me and all believers that he's been spared or we've all been spared but we'd best make our lives as holy as possible. He's saying we should live life as though the end were here and we won't have any regrets."

"Good advice, for people of all times," Benny chimed in.

For the next few weeks, as a family we worked at a feverish pace, not only on the farming part of Benny's plan, but also on his fishing, clamming and hunting ideas. We planted the fields we had farmed for years, then cleared and cultivated new areas. We seeded with a wide range of vegetables and started Benny's "rotation crops." We went from fishing for single catches to fishing for mass harvesting. At night we set up lanterns on a raft in the brackish waters of the pond on our bayside property. Fish, especially crabs and eels, were drawn to the light and we either scooped the crabs up with nets or speared the eels. The crabs were smothered in seaweed and kept in a cool spot in the barn. We smoked the eels in the little shed Benny and Father had built. At last some of the green leafy vegetables were ready for harvest. We all helped load the wagon to the brim with vegetables, fish, crabs, and clams. It was truly a wagonload. As soon as we finished, Benny gathered sleeping gear and he and Father left to go to the Manhattan markets.

Unfortunately our family's frantic work to get our products to market paralleled world events that were just as frantic. As Benny and Father traveled west to Manhattan, Mother and I went east to Mattituck. Upon entering the town we saw the military rushing to break camp. The army's cannon haulers, supply wagons, medical, ammunition, cookware, and every other kind of wagon you could imagine were scattered all over the road. Mother moved our wagon to the bumpy side of the road to get around them. When we got to the General Store, Mr. Smith said he heard the Major General had gotten orders to head for Boston. The situation had gotten very bad up there and it didn't look as though war could be avoided. King George had sent his three leading Generals to get the Colonists under control. Generals Henry Clinton and John Burgoyne had arrived, and to everyone's surprise, even General William Howe showed up in Boston. He had said that he would never come to the colonies. Mr. Smith guessed that the King had given him orders to the contrary.

We left town with our supplies and our bad news. Were Benny and Father safe, we worried. What would happen now? Would Benny be forced into joining one of the sides? Could we still farm peacefully?

Benny had no trouble selling all of the products. In fact, some of the wholesalers wanted to formalize a supply arrangement, but Benny went to several taverns and discovered the proprietors would pay more for some of the products than the wholesalers.

They especially liked the smoked eel, which they placed on the bar to entice customers to stay a little while longer and pay for more drinks. Benny made enough money to go to Wall Street and make a payment on Father's debt. Even after that, there was quite a tidy sum left for us to live on and support the farm. Benny's plan was successful which made him feel jubilant during the return trip home.

He followed the same route as he did on his initial trip to Lange Islandt. This time, as he moved north along the East River and took in the view of New York Harbor, Benny noticed more ships at anchor than he had noticed on the last trip. The ships were mostly English war ships. He couldn't help but make a mental note of how many ships there were and how big they were. He then began to get a little bit angry. He couldn't understand a king that would spend a fortune on ships, men and gear, but wouldn't ease off on unfair taxes. Surely this armada had to cost much more than all the taxes the King pressed on the colonies. Where was the logic?

Benny arranged to be ferried across the river, and just after landing on the Queens County side, he and Father encountered a road block. It was set up in a location that prevented anyone from attempting to go around it to avoid detection. Benny stopped the wagon at the end of a growing inspection line. He stopped a good distance from where all riders were being questioned and all the wagons were being searched. The blockade was manned by regally uniformed British troops. The troops looked more impressive than they usually did because of their new red coats, clean britches and shiny boots. Benny knew that this group of regulars was fresh off one of the ships in the harbor. The procession moved at a slow pace. The soldiers were not only searching all the wagons, they were also extensively interrogating each person. Benny resolved to wait patiently but as he moved up in line, a clearing of woods appeared on his right side. A camp had been set up in a clearing and Benny was surprised by the men milling about the camp.

Farming & Recruitment

They were dressed in blue uniforms and as Benny drew closer to the camp he could tell they weren't from England. They were speaking a foreign language. He couldn't identify the nationality.

A red coated, English officer, much younger than Benny, approached the wagon. "Where are you coming from and where are you going?" he asked Benny.

"We were at the market in Manhattan and we're heading home to Mattituck."

"Where is Mattituck?"

"Along the North Fork of the island, on the east road."

As Benny answered the officer's questions about why he and Father were in Manhattan, for how long and with whom they had conversations, another British regular walked to the back of the wagon. From the camp came a blue coat and together these two men began to search the wagon. Other than bedrolls, empty crates, a barrel, and Benny's long gun, the wagon was empty. The Blue Coat lifted up the long gun and said something in his language that Benny couldn't understand. "Mine," Benny said, pointing to himself.

The Blue Coat grunted something, took the gun and started to walk away.

"Hey, that belongs to me!" Benny shouted and started to get off the wagon. He was abruptly stopped by the barrel of the British officer's long gun.

"He can't just take my gun!" Benny said dropping back to his seat. "I'm a citizen of the Crown. You're supposed to protect us!" Benny's anger was increasing rapidly. "Get my gun back from him! He's leaving!"

"First off, you being a citizen of the Crown remains to be seen. And right now, the Crown is pretty angry at you Colonists. That's why we're at war." said the first officer.

"War?" Benny yelled out. "We're not at war!"

"Oh yes we are. Shootings at both Concord and Lexington. Happened two days ago, April 19th."

"Oh no," Benny said softly as he slouched back onto the wagon's bench.

"Sorry fella, but our Hessian allies over there don't want Colonists running around with guns. They say better we take them now than have someone use them on us later."

Benny sat up straight. He was about to protest and demand that his gun be returned when Father put his hand on Benny's knee and pressed down. It was the first time Father seemed to respond appropriately to what was happening. Benny looked at Father and smiled, heeding his caution. The officer motioned for Benny to move on. Benny snapped the reins and turned to look at Father. "It's wonderful having you with me again," he said.

Having his long gun confiscated upset Benny, but it was rather short-lived. He soon purchased a new, albeit used long gun at the General Store. Actually, I think Father's progress towards recovery had the greatest impact in restoring Benny's positive outlook. We all rejoiced and gave thanks as we saw Father's health steadily improve. He even began helping out around the farm and doing things of his own accord, without direction. Best of all was the radiant glow that emanated from Mother as Father progressed. Since that day he arrived home, in such a bewildered condition, she had never given up hope. She nurtured Father and poured a tremendous amount of love into him. She never treated him like an invalid or a helpless soul, but always showed respect and quietly helped him without making a fuss. The care, help and love she provided was never about her; it was always about her husband—a man she loved without reservation and with a great deal of dignity.

The cloud that overshadowed all of the good things happening in our lives was the war. Every trip to Mattituck was highlighted by news reports. Sometimes the reports turned out to be true, but as often as not, they were just rumors or falsehoods. We heard of the scores of Patriots who were killed at Concord. We also got word that the Sons of Liberty had already surrendered, but praise the Lord, those reports turned out to be false. We all knew our colonies had joined together and formed a governing body, the Continental Congress, but then we heard some of the southern colonies had disagreed with the notion of declaring war on the mother country. What made it even more confusing was the fact that the war had already begun and fighting was intense in several northern colonies. So the issue was two-fold: what was true versus what was false; and what was the chronological order of events?

There were some things, however, we could be sure were true. We knew that a Virginian who fought in the Indian Wars by the name of George Washington, was made General of the Continental Army and I might add, it would be hard to find anyone in the colonies who didn't know what he looked like. The newspapers frequently had drawings of his face and often critically depicted his large and pointed nose.

Boston was under siege and boat-loads of British troops had already arrived. In fact, it was Benny who provided us with the most accurate news. On every trip to New York he would purchase a newspaper and, as we all knew, anything printed in the newspaper must be truthful and accurate. Benny received the news with genuine interest but he would not allow the events to interfere with his goal of planting, gathering produce, harvesting seafood and hunting game. Everything we did had one purpose: gather products and get them to market. And, as the harvest season progressed, Benny increased his trips to the market.

We worked very hard, but we also had many moments of pleasure and fun. Some nights, after we set up the smokers, we would sit on the porch and just talk for hours. When everyone else went to bed, Benny and I would sit on the swing and enjoy each other and our newfound love. Butterflies in our stomachs were a common occurrence. Physically, we respected the established boundaries but our embraces surely tested the limits. Life was good and with a promising future that naturally included marriage, life would become even better. So days blended into weeks and soon

the cold season was upon us.

But just when everything was going so well, another of life's twists occurred. It had been a long labor-intense day. We had eaten our supper and were about to sit around the fireplace when our dog became restless and started to growl.

"Probably deer heading for the corn field," Mother said.

"I thought about it, not likely." Benny moved the smokers so they should be blanketing the field with dense smoke. "If there's anything deer won't go near, it's the smell of meat being roasted, smoked or cooked any other way."

"What about a wind from the north?" asked one of our sisters.

While we were talking Benny was making sure the two long guns were ready, but he answered the question. "Only in the dead of winter does the island get northerly winds and that's not too often."

The dog's growling became deeper and louder. Benny cocked a gun and moved to the door. All of us were startled and jumped when someone knocked on the door. "Who's there?" Benny asked, in a deep voice.

"Hello Ben. It's me, Pastor Timothy."

Benny lowered his gun and unlatched the door. As Pastor Timothy crossed the threshold he looked around at each of us. "I'm so sorry to have startled you," he said ruefully.

"'T'was nothing," Mother said. "Just that we don't get too many night visitors out here ..." She abruptly stopped speaking as two other men followed Pastor Timothy into the house.

Our Pastor cleared his throat, then introduced us to the two gentlemen. One of them he referred to as Colonel Henry Knox, and the other was none other than George Washington, the Commander of the newly organized Continental Army. Here he was, in our house. After nodding hello and extending salutations Washington promptly moved next to the fireplace. What a towering man I thought. And as tall as he was, he was equally gracious.

Farming & Recruitment

There were no pretenses. Being out in the cold night air chilled him, as it would anyone of us. Mother quickly filled the kettle with water from the bucket and I scurried to the cupboard to fetch some tea for brewing. Benny was right alongside of me gathering some cups, glasses and a decanter of our homemade beach plum brandy. The General and the Colonel gladly accepted a glass although Pastor Timothy declined. The General asked if we could send some tea to his attachment outside. He said they were four soldiers in all and could they put themselves and their horses up in the barn? "How presumptive of me," he quickly added. "When your Pastor said this would be a welcoming and safe house to stay, I automatically assumed you would know of our needs for bedding for the night."

"It is our pleasure," Mother said. "House guests are rare but always welcome and we're delighted that you, of all people, would honor us by coming here."

Benny, on the other hand, was disturbed about something and he wasn't discrete in concealing it.

"I just don't understand how you could be here ... I mean, on the island."

"Pardon?" General Washington was taken aback. Both the question and Benny's tone of voice surprised him.

Benny forged ahead. "I mean, I don't understand how you could leave the army in the middle of a siege. The army is still in the hills surrounding Boston and holding the King's army under siege, isn't it?" He plowed right on without leaving time for the General to respond. "And wasn't it General Howe who said when he's ready he'll march his troops up the hills and whip the pieces out of the Continentals? So how could you, the leader of the whole thing be here?"

"Benny!" Pastor Timothy said and was about to chastise him for addressing the Commander in such a manner. But the General himself interrupted by raising his voice. "Stop!"

When a figure as imposing as the General says stop, every

person stops. The General then resumed his normal speaking voice. "If we've engaged in war for the right to be heard then everyone has the same right. Therefore, without disclosing anything that is vital to the war effort let me answer." He paused, and I'm not sure if it was to gather his thoughts or for effect. "I must start with a preface. General Howe is a very formidable opponent. He is so formidable and knowledgeable about the arts and techniques of warfare that only God's intervention, by way of miracles, or a lapse in Howe's functioning, could save our cause. For God to send us miracles is worthy of prayer but beyond our control. And, while a lapse in Howe's functioning is equally out of our control, a study of his past functioning does reveal some aspects that could give us an opportunity, if we are wise enough to understand and capitalize on them."

At this point I decided that General Washington may be brilliant, but who could understand him? Interestingly enough, he took many pauses between sentences. Maybe he was giving us time to try and figure out what he was saying, or perhaps he was carefully editing his own words so he wouldn't reveal anything.

"One of General Howe's characteristics is that he doesn't like to engage in long battles or campaigns during cold or inclement weather. His previous engagements show he doesn't even advance his army in winter. Given the cold and wet season the Boston area is currently experiencing, leads me to calculate that my absence" — his eyes looked straight into Benny's eyes before he continued to speak — "to do other pressing military duties, is quite safe."

"Thank you Sir. I appreciate your response but I must also apologize. It was inappropriate of me to ask a question like that, especially the way I asked it. I'm sorry to have been so rude to such a distinguished guest in our home," Benny said respectfully.

"Apology accepted. Nevertheless, I reiterate, the question was legitimate and warranted a response." The General glanced at Pastor Timothy. I could tell they had a silent communication between them. Once satisfied he and the Reverend were considering the same option, the General refocused on Benny. "That raises another issue. I would like to speak frankly and openly. If you wish we can speak in private."

"What you need to say to me, can be said to all of us." Benny decided to lighten up the mood. "Besides, they'd torture me with nagging 'til I'd tell them anyway."

"As you wish. But we came here tonight not solely to rest, although rest is very much needed. Our objective is to enlist your assistance in a special war project."

Benny's resistance sprang to the fore. "I'm a farmer. I'm not a soldier and I don't want to be a soldier."

"The good Reverend here has already shared your sentiments about fighting and soldiering with us. So, please clearly understand that we are not asking that of you. However, based on what we've been told about you, I am asking you to perform a service. You and everyone else here must understand the need for complete secrecy about our presence here and what we are about to talk about." He looked at each of us and didn't move on to the next person until he received an affirmative nod from each of us. Satisfied that no one in the room would break the confidence he was about to share, he looked at his attaché. "Colonel," he said.

As if he were being called for a stage performance encore, Colonel Henry Knox stepped forward. As he did, the General along with Pastor Timothy retreated to be closer to the fire and to carry on their conversation. The rest of us were now, so to speak, in the hands of the Colonel.

Though Henry Knox is much smaller in size than his commander, he has an impressive physical appearance. He is young, possibly in his early thirties but then again, the Continental Army is primarily comprised of young idealists. His eyes are dark brown and, in spite of his youth, his hair has thinned so that he looks almost bald. It's quite a surprise that he hasn't taken to wearing a wig. While most men of the times wear their wigs because fashion dictates it, it was obvious that the Colonel could

use one to cover up a substantial hair deficit. Actually, fashion is one reason men wear wigs but the bigger reason they wear wigs is simply due to head lice—pesky little critters that multiply like fire in a kindling pile. Rather than trying to wash or scratch them out, especially in the cold season, it's easier to shave the head and cover it up with a wig.

All talk of hair aside, Henry Knox's face is nicely chiseled but there is one characteristic that is not physical that overrides his looks, and in fact impacts every aspect of his appearance. There is no other way of describing this aspect except to say he is a veritable worrywart who deeply distrusts anyone who is not a military man. The Colonel began to address Benny but also made sure that each of us could hear his message.

"I'll begin by saying, if you reject or even have concerns about what I'm about to propose, just say so and we'll be gone."

An abrupt interruption came from the General. "He means, we'll depart after we've rested."

The Colonel nodded and gave a quirky little smile. "To be sure, to be sure, but my point must be clear. You are under no obligation to agree to this assignment, so, if you wish us to cease with this notion, just say so."

Benny didn't like the prologue. "It might help to make a decision if you would just say what you want me to do." His tone wasn't terribly cordial. In fact it sounded almost as if he were becoming irritated.

The Colonel wasn't accustomed to being spoken to in such a manner. "In the army, when a soldier is given an opportunity to speak he simply says, 'Yes or no, Sir.'"

"Well I'm not in the army, so, what say you get on with the proposal?" Benny had now gone from mere irritation to downright annoyance.

Rather than follow Benny's suggestion, the Colonel addressed his own concerns. "Therein lies the heart of the problem. I had suggested we seek out one of our troops or an officer who could accomplish the task and still maintain the standards of soldiering, such as obedience, following orders and respect for authority. You know, army regulars are always better than non-regulars. But Reverend Timothy ..." he nodded his head towards our Pastor, "being a person who has a great deal of influence among members of our newly formed Congress, has persuaded the General to consider involving you."

"I'm flattered that our Pastor would recommend me to assist the army. I'm equally surprised to hear of his influence among Continental leaders, but, unless you share the plan with me, all of this talk may be for naught."

Knox finally relented. "Very well, we've got Boston filled up with Howe and his troops. We've got them under siege. See, we're up on the hills surrounding the city, but when Howe decides to come up one of those hills he'll roll over us like a barrel going downhill. So, we've come up with a plan to knock him on his ear. You see, if we had some cannons to fortify the hills, as he and his men make their way up, we could blow them dead, right back down the hills. Or, if we had cannons we could attack the city and not wait for Howe to attack us." Knox paused. What he was saying was either common knowledge or could be figured out by simple deduction. But now it was time to disclose the aspects of the mission, all of which was apparently top secret.

"We don't have cannons. We need them and we know where there are many available. They're at Fort Ticonderoga. Your role will be to get us to the fort, pack up the cannons, and get them to the hills of Boston. Will you do it?"

Benny disguised his surprise at this sudden request. "Just a couple of questions. The last time Father and I were up in the North Country the Red Coats occupied both Fort Ticonderoga and Fort Henry. Has that changed?"

"Yes. Our troops, a group of Vermont Freedom Fighters crossed over the northern pass and took both forts by surprise. Our troops now have them secured."

"But the English regulars and their allies, the Mohawks, are still in the territory. Aren't they?"

"Yes and that's one reason why you're being asked to participate. Your job will be to get us around the regulars. The Indians probably won't be much of a problem."

"Oh, and why not?"

"We just don't think the Indians know that much about warfare."

Benny wanted to correct the Colonel and say most army commanders could learn a great deal from how the Indians wage war, but he didn't want to side track the conversation. "What else?"

"We expect you to help us get the guns and bring them across to Boston. Then you can return to your family and your farm."

"Excuse me, Colonel, but that's not a very clear answer. So, let me break all of this into easy questions that can be precisely addressed. First, how many troops are you taking to the North Country?" Benny continued to speak in a very sharp tone.

"Not many. We can't spare them from the siege ranks."

When I heard what the Colonel said, I got suspicious and Benny must have read my mind. "So, exactly ..." He emphasized the word *exactly* before continuing; "... how many soldiers will be making this trip to get the cannons and move them to Boston?"

"Well ..." Knox paused for a long time, not a good sign of what was to come. "Er, I'll be going, then there's my brother, William. He'll be joining us."

"And?" This time Benny's voice betrayed his shock.

"And? There are no other regulars but I anticipate recruiting men as we go," Knox said defiantly. "And should we be successful and obtain, say fifty cannons, I would venture to say we will need about one hundred men to transport them."

"What happened to your notion that regulars are always better than irregulars? Now you're going to try and recruit as you go, assumably from the irregular Patriots?"

Knox's defiant posture didn't change. "These are the fortunes and predicaments of war. Now, are you going to join us?"

"Wait a second. It's not that I don't trust your experience in fortunes and predicaments of war, but just how much of a regular are you?"

Knox's defiant attitude deflated. "My heart is totally committed to our cause. Freedom is an absolute necessity."

"That's nice, but again that's not what I'm asking. Let me ask as clearly as I can. How many military battles have you fought in?"

"None," Knox said lowering his head, his defiance completely gone.

"How long have you been in the army?"

"A little over two months." Knox took a deep breath before continuing. "I was made a Colonel because I was one of the first to sign up from the Boston area."

"Now I understand your comment about how the Indians know so little about warfare. You've never seen them in battle, have you? You weren't even in the French and Indian Wars, were you?"

"No, but I've read about them; and I've read many books on the art of warfare. Books, that's what I've done for a living."

"Huh?" Benny said, by now utterly amazed.

"Oh, I own a bookstore in Boston. My wife's running it while I'm away and it is hard on her, with the young one and all." Knox snapped himself back to the moment. "But, all of this stuff about my military past doesn't change the need for those cannons to be moved to Boston. Now, we've got to get on with our plans. Are you with us or not?"

Benny didn't respond. He just kept staring at the Colonel.

"Well?" Knox was getting nervous. Benny's stare was getting to him.

Benny then turned to me. "Can we talk for a moment?" Without hesitating he turned and walked onto the porch.

I followed. Once outside my eyes adjusted to the dark but the rest of my body didn't adjust to the cold. I tolerated it. On the path I could see the sentries near the road. Benny was sitting on

our swing and I sat down next to him.

"It would take God's intervention for the Colonel's plan to work, another battle of Jericho." Benny was rambling so I just sat and listened.

"He really has no plan. No army. No equipment. And really no idea of what he's talking about. I'll bet he never even looked at a map. If you go east from Fort Ticonderoga, you run smack into the highest mountains in the colonies. You cannot carry cannons over those mountains. I've seen those cannons; there's nothing light about them. They've got to be a couple of thousand pounds each, and I mean each one. And he's asking for help! How ridiculous! No wonder the General never said anything."

In an instant I knew he had made a decision to help. "So, how do you plan on helping him?"

Benny looked at me and shook his head. "I really haven't made up my mind yet, but the chances of his success are so slim and the need is so great that I'm really considering it, but I wouldn't make a decision without talking with you first. Somehow you always know what I'm going to say or do before I even know myself."

"Strange how love works. Isn't it?"

"Yeah." He confirmed my statement in a romantic tone.

For several moments we sat very quiet and very much in love. We could have sat there together forever but the moment disappeared as fast as the front door opened and Pastor Timothy walked out onto the porch. He made several throat clearing coughs, that I'm sure were intended for us to be aware that he was standing there.

"I'm heading home," he said. "Before I go, I'd like to ask a quick question."

"Oh, good," Benny said in a tone that was far sharper than I've ever heard him use toward the Reverend. "I've got a couple of questions for you too," Benny responded.

"Well, then why don't you begin. I only have the one question and it doesn't require an immediate answer."

Farming & Recruitment

"I don't think any of us in town were aware of your contacts with the new Continental government. Would you care to share with us who they might be?"

The Reverend paused, looked away from us, then turned and looked at Benny. "The spring has sprung and the mouse has been caught." Then he slowly nodded his head. "I'm sure you know with whom I've had communications. In fact, I'm rather glad it's finally out in the open. I would rather have told you over a fine supper and some wine, but I've been sworn to secrecy. And, I would point out, I wasn't the one to spring the trap. Obviously our commanding General didn't get the word. Anyway, let me give you the short ... or it may turn out to be the long, of it."

"When you were delivered on the church's front steps, so to speak, our Board of Elders made several decisions. We were overjoyed that your mother and father here volunteered to take you in. However, the Elders also arrived at a decision after your new father left the church and took you home. The rest of the Elders decided to notify the person who, allegedly, is your natural father. After all, your natural mother was on a mission to bring you to him. I was instructed to attempt to make contact. Truth is, it wasn't a difficult task. I wrote to him and explained the situation. To my surprise he wrote back and invited me to meet with him, in Philadelphia, for lunch."

"After several more letters we set up a time and met at a tavern. He was an incredible host and the meal was exquisite. And how he loves to talk; he constantly quotes Poor Richard's Almanac. Then again, he claims to have been its ghost writer. I don't know, maybe so. He surely is witty enough. But our culinary indulgences and side chatter are not what your ears want to hear. So I will be as frank as possible and I would preface what I'm about to tell you with my deepest belief that he is an honest and forthright gentleman. I must say, however, he readily admits to being a philanderer; without my asking, he confessed to many dalliances; so many that he cannot count all of them. But—and I emphasize

the term 'but' — he vividly recalls your mother and he does so with great warmth and sensitivity. She was not a casual entanglement like so many of the others. He was so fond of her that he planned for and paid for her to cross the sea. Prior to hearing him reveal that fact, I had always wondered who had paid for the voyage you and your mother took. I suspect he had planned to establish a residence for her on this side of the ocean."

"However, he openly admits of his surprise to hear about you. With much sensitivity he says he and your mother were very much in love and you being conceived is not inconceivable. And he adamantly says, if needed, he would provide for your needs, the same as he has for his wife and the eleven other children he has raised and provided for in an admirable way. In fact, his eldest William, is now governor of New Jersey. Things got complicated when he heard that you were being cared for by a loving and faithful couple, and so, he elected to stay out of your life, but he often advised that, should you need assistance he would render it in an instant. Anonymously of course." The Reverend lifted his hand and jabbed the air signifying he had more to say. He was just trying to find the right words. Then his reflective moment ended.

"I tell you, he's quite a man, dignified, with overwhelming intelligence with a commanding presence that fills a room when he enters. And, you'd never guess, but I'd also add that he's quite religious, in his own way."

Benny had heard enough. "Religious? Sorry Reverend but I would use other adjectives to describe him. Although I'm not a cursing man, I'd say he's a cad, a cheat and everything else embodied in Satan."

"Not so Ben. His beliefs are very strange and yet he is deeply committed to God. You know, I've given him a lot of thought and he so closely resembles a major figure in the Bible that it's astonishing." The Reverend stopped talking and his finger went up again and jabbed the air again. "I might as well tell you. Your father resembles King David. King David was a great King with glorious attributes and yet he reduced himself to accepting temptation and cavorting with Bathsheba. He even committed murder. He had her husband moved to a front line which then advanced on an oncoming wave of enemy troops. They called it the suicide line with no hope for survival. And despite those evil deeds, God still loved David and said he was a man after His own heart."

Benny remained silent, but looking into his eyes I knew he was calculating whether or not to engage in a debate. Wisely, he simply said, "After all these years ... at least now I know who my birth father is. I suspect every other person in the colonies would be proud to have a father of such stature ... but not me. And thanks for not as yet mentioning his name, although, with the clues you've given, it's easy to figure out. Right now the sound of his name to my ears would be revolting and my stomach would turn so, that I'd get sick."

Pastor Timothy was not about to let Benny disparage or disrespect his father, "Now hold on. He never meant any harm to your mother or you. He's an upright man and he doesn't deserve ..."

Benny interrupted saying, "Right now, I can't help feeling the way I do. In time, I'll probably do as I've been raised to do, forgive others their trespasses and honor thy father and mother. Not right now."

"I'd like to discuss this further but now is not the time. I don't want to detain the Colonel much longer. But please, one more question. Why did you recommend me for this strange mission? And please don't say it was because I'm familiar with the North Country; I've only been there once."

"Well that's a much simpler question to answer than your first one but in truth, I'm glad I've shared all I know about your birth father with you," the Reverend said. "Knowing that much about your natural father, and your heritage, and not being able to share it with you was quite a yoke to bear. But you see, what I

just shared has a great bearing on your second question. I told the General you'd be the one for the mission for two main reasons. First, and you are correct, it is because you've been there and because you're not like other people. Benny, over the years I've watched you. You see things others miss. You learn quicker than the others and you develop ideas that are very effective. Starting that fire so we could rescue Obie is just one example of your quick thinking. Then there's your fortitude. That comes from being nurtured by good parents. It's a quality that your father has instilled in you. And most importantly, you have heart, a quality bestowed upon you by your birth father and given all accounts, also by your birth mother."

I've never seen Benny so embarrassed. Having no adequate response, he rose to say goodbye to our Reverend and to go back inside.

"Before I take my leave, will both of you answer my question? May I have the honor of marrying you two?" Pastor Timothy had a warm twinkle in his eyes.

"I can't wait!" The words spilled out of me without any conscious thought or consideration. Talk about an impulsive, but truthful response.

"I can't wait either … but we will wait." Benny's answer defused my overly zealous response. "I loved you when we were younger," he said looking at me. "I love you more now, and I know my love for you will keep growing and be its deepest as we age together." Benny paused and used his thumbs to wipe the tears that were flowing from my eyes. "We'll marry after this mission. I'll not hide or be quiet about it. You and Mother can organize the wedding and a celebration to follow. Whatever perception people have about us will change that day. For those who can't resist thinking and speaking about how our relationship is strange … well that's not our problem. It's a problem they'll have to live with. Not us." He then turned to Pastor Timothy.

"I must admit, to the people who don't know our circumstance,

Farming & Recruitment

a marriage between what appears to be siblings is a bit bizarre. To clear up the matter, I would like as many of our community to attend as possible. And that's where we'll need your help. During your sermon, Reverend, would you please explain the real circumstances?"

"It would be my pleasure. There's nothing like the truth to dispel rumors and wagging tongues. And if you two and your mother will permit, I'm sure Grace would love to help with the preparations for the celebration."

Benny and I grasped each other's hand and said thank you to our Pastor.

"I can't believe how much was said in so short a time," Benny told the Reverend. "Much to think about during the quiet hours ... but for now there's a Colonel sitting by the fireplace who has some good ideas. He just doesn't seem to be organized or know how to get things done. I may not be much help but I'm going to try to help him accomplish this mission."

"Amen and may God show you the way." said Pastor Timothy.

Chapter 11

North Again

The General rose from the chair nearest the fireplace
and thanked Mother, who had just informed him that the bedroom was ready. He would be using Mother and Father's room and they in turn would share my sisters' room. Benny had already advised the General and the Colonel that he would help. He and the Colonel were discussing the next stage of the mission while the General remained quiet, listening intensely.

"Before heading north I need to go into New York and make some purchases for the Boston front. Our quartermaster gave me a list." As the Colonel spoke he pulled a sheet of notes from his coat pocket.

"Do you have that list memorized?" Asked Benny.

"Memorized? I hardly know what some of this stuff is. I can't be expected to memorize it and why on earth would I want to do such a foolish thing?"

"Excuse me, but what do you expect to tell the British regulars when they search you and find it?"

"Search me? Are they really searching people?"

"Sir? This is war!" Benny couldn't believe he had to say such a thing to the Colonel. As for the General, he simply turned to

155

the fire and warmed the front of his body. "And don't think you can get around the checkpoints. If they catch you, they'll send you straight to a stockade," Benny continued. "And if the regulars catch you with that kind of note on your person, you may spend the rest of the war in a brig. But if the Hessians are on guard duty and they catch you, you're guaranteed dead, right on the spot."

The General spun around. His eyes widened. He came to life. "You said Hessians, didn't you?"

"Yes Sir. I've seen them. They're on guard patrol with the regulars."

"Son, this is important. Where and how many?"

"I've seen them on the last couple of selling trips to New York. They're at the road checkpoints. I don't know how many there are, but I have counted the number of ships in the harbor, the troop transport ships that is; and while I couldn't tell how many regulars there are versus how many Hessians there are, I do know the total number of ships has grown."

"You do? How many are there?" The General perked up even more. Benny described to him exactly what he had seen. The discussion, or should I say interrogation, went on for quite a while. The General allowed Benny to present vague answers at first, but then probed and prodded him until Benny was able to recollect more exact information. Finally, the General was satisfied with the data he had garnered from Benny.

"You have just saved me a reconnaissance expedition. I had received such sketchy information about the British fortifications, numbers, fleet size and so on that I was personally heading to New York to see for myself. No need now. So, on the morrow, I will return to Boston." The General smiled at Benny. "Therefore young man, I will resume my position on the front lines. I'm sure that will please you." He chuckled out loud. "Well then, I'm off to dash out some correspondence and then to retire for the night."

We all nodded good evening as the General moved from the fireplace towards the bedroom door.

North Again

"I know your desire to remain out of the conflict, but I must tell you, you've already performed a great service for our fledgling attempt at independence. I am grateful." Then, as if this night had not been strange enough, the General's eyes became very piercing as he stared at Benny.

"You have an uncanny ability. It should not go to waste. The future of these colonies is dependent on men such as you. I'm certain, some time in the days ahead, we will have an opportunity to consider your future service to the colonies."

Benny is a very proud man but he's also very humble. To this day I've never heard him mention that the General of the commanding forces thanked him.

After the General left, Benny and Knox set out to organize a plan. Knox wanted both of them to go to New York, where he could conduct business and meet his brother William. His brother would then accompany them to the North Country. But Benny had another plan.

"Henry, you head north after doing your business. I'll meet you," he told Knox.

"Where? When? And why go separately?" Knox's voice increased in pitch as he spoke.

"The why is simple. Getting to and then through Manhattan may not be so hard for one person. Once there are two or three of us, we may look somewhat suspicious. We'll be stopped for sure and we may not make it out of the city. Traveling from different directions would be safer. Also, if something happens to you or me, the other can move the mission forward. Get a map and find the village of Rhinebeck. We'll meet there in four days. If one of us doesn't show up on that day, the other moves on ... oh ... and be sure to get rid of the map."

"Mister Ben ..." Knox drew out and prolonged the name. "Caution is one thing but you are taking it to a ridiculous level. And, trust me. If I ever get caught, I'll never give up any secrets."

"Henry, I pray you never get caught but if it were to happen,

157

you'd spill all the beans as quick as a hen lays her morning egg. You might want to act like a clam but if a Hessian shoves a wood splint under your left index finger, you'd be a screeching donkey before they got to your right hand. Get rid of the map and don't write any notes."

"I guess you're not going to tell me how you're going north to Rhinebeck or any of your other plans." Knox said with some chagrin.

"I'll see you in four days, at the Beckman Arms in Rhinebeck." Benny said, effectively ending the conversation.

The next morning the house was filled with hustle and bustle. I helped Mother make tea, hot cakes, and smoked sausage. When the General tried the sausage, he proclaimed it to be the best he had ever tasted. This statement generated a smile and a twinkle in Father's eyes. Father was very proud of his recipe and how he used apple wood to smoke the links. I was even more delighted to see how much Father had recovered. His recuperative progress had not been rapid but it was definitely even and steady. He had not suffered any major setbacks, physically that is. Emotionally, he appeared to be having difficulties accepting the fact that his body could not respond as his mind wished. The culmination of his dilemma happened when he realized he couldn't accompany Benny on the forthcoming mission. Benny also sensed Father's disappointment, so very quietly, he asked Father to join him on the porch.

"I need your help," he told Father. "The Colonel has no idea how hard a task lies ahead. Moving cannons, especially if there are a number of them, over such rough terrain is near impossible. He thinks we can go to the North Country and raise an army of men to do this. It's not going to happen. We'll have to help him. I'd like you to go to Reverend Timothy and together with him, make some arrangements for help."

Father, whose language had substantially deteriorated as a result of the vibes, so much so that he could not yet speak

North Again

properly, was surprised by his son's request. He stretched his hands out, palms up. By doing this Father was showing that he was confused by Benny's request. Not only confused but more to the point, probably unable to accomplish the task. Benny didn't let Father's concerns stop him. "You are the only man I can rely on. When you speak to the Reverend, explain how we need other men to help. See if Obie, Doc, Smitty and even Malcom Smith can join us. I simply can't wait for them; I have more recruiting to do. Anyway, it's best we don't all travel together, especially between here and the North Country where there's a high concentration of British regulars. If the men are willing to help, tell them to meet me at the Lion's Head Inn in Connecticut. We'll meet three days from today." Benny paused and looked into Father's eyes before continuing. He knew he was giving Father a heavy burden but he also knew Father needed to feel useful. "I need you to do this. Without the help of men I can trust, I don't think this mission will succeed. Can you do it?"

A long moment passed. Father had been sitting in one of the porch armchairs, somewhat slumped forward. He straightened up his back and slowly nodded his head. He then tried to utter the words, "I'll do it." The words that came out were really unclear but to Benny, they formed the best sentence he had ever heard.

I can emphatically say the last moments Benny and I spent together, before he left, were beyond any emotional time I had ever experienced. I cried, tried to smile and wept again. We were in the barn, getting his horse ready, and we fell into each other's arms as though we had been grasping for one another for years. Oh, my imagination extends reality, of course we had our limits. We weren't raised under a Puritan religion but Reverend Timothy's Calvinistic sermons helped to give us the notion that impure thoughts were as sinful as the deeds themselves. If Pastor Timothy and Calvin were right, then I'm guilty as charged. But, I'm not sorry nor do I regret my thoughts. Simply said, we weren't in the midst of satisfying our total desires. Yes, it was lust, but

Benny, having more willpower than I, stopped.

"After marriage we can do anything we like and never feel guilt or a need for repentance," he said. I agreed, but to tell the truth, I would have disregarded all virtue and morality. I think, at that moment, I would have given in to lust.

I don't know where Father went off to as Benny made his way down our path to the road. He probably knew he couldn't bear to watch his son march off to war. Mother and I, along with my sisters, watched, cried profusely, and hugged each other as Benny disappeared down the road to Mattituck and the docks. Several hours after dawn the ferry completed the crossing of the Sound and docked at the wharf in New Haven. As Benny had anticipated, the wharf was well patrolled by British regulars and as soon as he and the other passengers disembarked, they were detained for questioning. They weren't allowed to leave the dock to move on with their business until cleared and released by the troops. Cleared meant going through a vigorous interrogation. Benny had anticipated the interception and he was well prepared to deal with it. I am so proud of Benny's ability to plan ahead and anticipate the moves of others. He is truly wise beyond his years.

"It's like playing chess," he would say. "Only consider the current move after pondering the future moves of your opponents." When the regulars questioned him, he pulled out both a sack of *wampum* and a mortgage statement from the company. Wisely, he told them that the company is a major supporter of the Crown. How true. In fact, we often jokingly called it the Tory company. After being cleared and released, he moved west along the King's Road, tracing a route he had traveled before.

It didn't take long for Benny to get to the Yale College area and the Lions Head Inn. To his surprise, while registering and securing a room, the rather short, rotund and balding innkeeper, whom he had taken a liking to previously, recognized him and greeted Benny with an embrace and a warm welcome. Storing his gear in his room and freshening up, Benny went down to the

North Again

meeting room of the inn for something to eat. The innkeeper seated him at a corner table and recommended his wife's chicken soup with matzo balls and dark Russian bread. Benny agreed to the recommendations and upon his return with the food, the innkeeper joined Benny at the table. Benny enjoyed the man's company but he was somewhat surprised that an innkeeper would intrude on a customer's dinner.

"So vat brings you here ... again?" the innkeeper said.

"I'm on another trading trip with the Indians. You know, pelts for *wampum*."

The innkeeper raised his eyebrows. The movement, when combined with his chunky face and bald head, caused rows of wrinkles to appear on his scalp. The innkeeper spoke with a deep Yiddish accent, and as he spoke his eyes rolled back and forth. The total image was quite humorous.

"So? Vere are the pelts? Last time you ver here you stunk up one of my rooms vit 'em. Yet this time you bring none. So?"

"I'm taking a different route. I'll start trading further north."

"Mister Benny, it's not so long ago, I was living where the Hapsburgs roamed. You know Austria? I was a Rabbi there." He paused to reflect on what he had just said. "No! I'm still a Rabbi, just very few Jewish people here, so my congregation is ... as ve say, vat congregation? But this is only a stop. Someday I'll go to New York and start really being a Rabbi again. But, that's not my point. Are you listening?" He knew Benny was listening, so that was just a figure of speech he used to maintain attention. "My point is, I'm a clergyman and you shouldn't lie to a clergyman. So ... vats the real story? And call me Saul."

Benny didn't know why but he had complete confidence in his newfound friend. Even so, he didn't reveal the whole plan, but he did share that he was looking for the college student named Patrick — the one who had started the whole ruckus the last time he was there.

"So you think you can just valk onto a college campus and recruit people? You're a putz," said Rabbi Saul. Although Benny had no idea what the word meant, he knew it had to be derogatory. "Everybody knows the college is filled with radicals," the Rabbi continued. "And the professors are the vorst of the bunch. If the British army had its way, they'd march in and shoot them all. But that would cause a revolution." Rabbi Saul smacked his bald forehead. "Putz! This is a revolution. Well, you know vat I'm trying to say. Even the Tories vouldn't tolerate that kind of behavior. So the regulars vatch the campus all day and night. If you go there, I guarantee you'll be arrested."

"So what do I do?"

"Me. Everybody knows me. And I go there all the time. Many of the professors are my friends and I even lecture there sometimes. I'll go and find this Patrick for you. How do you like the matzo balls?"

"Your missis can sure cook!" Benny exclaimed, taking another huge bite of the fluffy cracker meal ball that had been soaking in rich chicken broth.

The next day proved to be quite delightful for Benny. At last he met Ruth, the Rabbi's wife, the creator of all the wonderful meals Benny had enjoyed. In the morning, as Benny sat in the same corner of the inn's restaurant there were only a few other patrons present and Ruth had once again treated him to a delicacy of smoked white fish, hummus, blintzes and eggs. He told me the blintzes were similar to rolled hotcakes that were stuffed with crumpled cheese and covered with blueberries.

As Benny enjoyed the culinary delights, Patrick strolled in to the restaurant. The Rabbi had been successful. Benny rose from his chair as Patrick walked right up to him. They greeted each other in the European style, their happiness at seeing each other again apparent to anyone looking at them.

"Rabbi Saul gave me a briefing on what you plan to do. I'm with you," Patrick told Benny. "Of course, my father may want to shorten my life or at least my college career when he finds out I've abandoned my classes for the cause of freedom. But either way I'll have no regrets. As soon as the war started I began considering how to do my part. Your coming here is an omen. Count me in."

Benny and Patrick spoke at length, sharing their views on the war, the strategies being used and the form of government or leadership that was evolving. They talked over breakfast and through lunch when the door opened and in walked Obie.

"How could I not come? I'm only alive because of you," Obie said as Benny's heart bounced with joy.

Just before bedtime Doc and Smitty knocked on Benny's door.

"Need some roommates?" Doc said when Benny opened the door.

Father and Reverend Timothy had succeeded in their mission.

It was early, just after dawn, when Patrick returned on a horse he had borrowed from a professor. After breakfast and hugs from Ruth and the Rabbi, they said their farewells. But Rabbi Saul would not let them depart until he said a prayer and placed his hand on each person's head. He blessed them and asked that once the mission was over they would write and stay in touch.

They rode in pairs, heading north and west without incident and without sighting any British regulars. They crossed the Hudson and made their way to the outskirts of Rhinebeck. Benny was reluctant to enter the town as a foursome. Instead they made camp a good distance from the road and Benny rode on ahead. He left his long gun with the others, because a man with a long gun tends to attract more attention than an unarmed person. Benny intended to do a reconnaissance of the Beakman Arms Inn. Although this was only the third day since he'd left Colonel Knox, he thought it was possible that Knox could arrive early. If not, then Benny planned to spend the next day waiting on the road outside of town.

He paced his horse slowly and as he entered the town he noted that a British guard post had been set up. As he approached the town's entrance, two members of the security guard force waved to him to halt his horse and dismount. He did as they ordered and before they could ask he produced the same papers he had showed at the wharf. His documentation and lack of a weapon satisfied the guards and he was allowed to pass. Benny decided to walk alongside his horse and stopped a few feet into the town so he could put away his papers. Doing this, he observed a horse-drawn wagon pull up to a little cottage. The cottage housed the guard post soldiers. A man, not in uniform, stepped out of the cottage to help the wagon driver with a delivery. Benny was close enough to hear some of the conversation between the driver and the man. From what he could tell the man was thanking the driver, who was the owner of a local general store, for supplying them with so much food. Benny thought about the conversation which served to magnify just how divided the Colonists were over the war. He recalled walking about Manhattan and how many large companies were overtly loyal to the Crown. On the other hand, he thought, most ordinary people were disenchanted with England and wanted home rule. Benny pondered this quandary as he remounted and once again slowly paced his horse through the town, hoping to be unnoticed.

A steady, strong, but slow pace made him look more like a person with an objective to reach and less like a wanderer, thus casting off suspicions. As Benny reached the front of the inn it seemed more beautiful to him than the last time he was there. He casually looked around; then decided to go inside. He thought he would take a look in the pub to see if Knox was there. If he wasn't there, then Benny thought he might find him in the dining area. Stepping inside, he stood still for a moment to allow his eyes to adjust to the dark.

"May I help you?" he heard a woman's voice ask before he had a chance to look around.

North Again

"Oh, no thanks. I'm just waiting to be joined by some friends." After Benny spoke, he realized he could have made a mistake. To his relief, he could see the woman's head bow; then she disappeared into the darkness. He soon recalled the room with beautiful wooden walls and a back door all carved of dark oak. Yet he couldn't help wonder why such a prestigious inn would be saving on candles. Benny knew that candles weren't all that costly and a few lit here and there would not only make for better visibility, they would also make conditions much safer. Now that his eyes had adjusted, he looked into the pub area and saw that Knox was not there. Benny figured that Knox probably hadn't arrived as yet. The room was deserted; not a patron to be found. Benny even noticed that the waiter's apron had been tossed over the bar's counter. Business was so slow, he mused, even the wait staff had taken time off.

It was probable that the Colonel was still en route, so Benny decided to return to where the others were camped. He could keep watch for Knox from there. But before leaving the dining room he walked over to the window. This window was another feature that made the inn so popular. It's larger than any other pub window in the region and it was famous for its view of the main street, so much so that local patrons often made reservations well in advance so they could have a table with a view. Benny lingered a moment, enjoying the luxury of looking at the town through the famed pane of glass. He was ready to leave when he spotted two riders heading toward the inn. Long guns in hand and riding with distinct authority, they were easily identified, at least the lead one was. It was Knox and the one next to him had to be his brother. Benny wondered, was it possible to look more obvious? They certainly didn't look like traveling sales people or merchants. And the last thing they resembled was farmers. How in the world did they get past the guards? Benny was bewildered, but thought "No matter, they were here."

Benny was about to go to the door to greet them when

he spotted something odd. A man, on foot was moving rapidly along the storefronts and keeping pace with the Knox brothers. He stayed just far enough behind them so as not to be seen. Yes, Benny thought, the man was definitely following them. And, as they got nearer to the inn, Benny realized it was the same man he had seen at the cottage. Now he got it. This man was out of uniform because he was a "trailer" a member of the guard force who trailed unsuspecting people to find out what they were up to. If the people they trailed were involved in anything not approved or appreciated by the Crown the trailer would signal for the troops to arrest them. In addition, this trailer would be able to identify any others with whom the unsuspecting travelers might rendezvous. This way he would find more treasonous Colonists to question and arrest.

Benny sprang into action. He quickly grabbed the apron off the pub counter, donned it and opened the front door. Before Knox could say anything, Benny quickly moved down the steps and next to their horses.

"Say nothing!" he commanded. "Get off and quickly go inside. It's dark in there so your eyes will take time to adjust. Don't wait. Walk straight ahead and out the back door. I'll meet you there."

"But ..." the Colonel tried to say something.

"No! Not now. Do as I've said. We're in real danger right now." Benny took the bridles of their horses, as well as his, in hand.

As the Knox brothers scooted up the steps and into the inn, the "trailer" approached Benny.

"Where are you taking those horses?" he demanded.

"To the stable Sir, for the evening."

"Good. Now, where did those two men go?"

"Not sure Sir, but they said they wanted to go up and be refreshed before supper."

"Good again. Now, go and stable the horses. Then go down to the guard post and tell them I ..." He paused to emphasize who he was, "the Sergeant, wants four troops here immediately. That will save me a walk and I can also keep an eye on things here. Is that clear?"

"Yes, Sir!"

The Knox brothers were waiting as Benny had instructed. "Mount quickly and follow," Benny told them as he threw aside the apron.

"But ..." Knox again tried to voice a protest.

Benny ignored Knox's plea to be heard and instead rapidly led the way from the rear of the inn. Instead of going south on the road, the way in which he had entered the town, he headed east. This way he avoided both the Sergeant seeing them from the window and the guard station. At last the Colonel stopped trying to interrupt with "buts." He finally got the idea that he had walked into a trap. Being trapped was bad enough, but if Benny had not been alert he, too, would have been caught. Knox's lack of perception and judgment could have caused the failure of the entire mission, and maybe even caused their deaths.

The entire next day, the group of seven took evasive actions to avoid towns and settlements. Knox wanted to go directly into the city of Albany, an area where he was certain he could recruit others to help on the mission. Benny explained the dangers of approaching total strangers with such notions, but by this time he knew the Colonel was not a man who readily heeded advice. Doc, being a person of substantial perception, recognized Benny's dilemma and intervened. He presented the Colonel and Benny with a viable alternative.

"Why don't we split up? Our town folk will go with Benny and you and William go on to Albany."

Knox didn't like the idea. "I'm in charge and, as the commanding officer, I don't like the concept of splitting our ranks."

Doc wanted to tell him that he, Obie, Smitty, Patrick and even Benny weren't in the army. He wanted to tell him that they just

were helping in this particular mission, but he knew that wouldn't go over well with the Colonel. And it didn't make sense to cause anymore unease, so Doc simply presented the logical concept that having all seven of them get caught would doom the mission. At last Knox recanted, and asked Benny for suggestions.

"We should bypass Albany," Benny said. "Maybe I'm wrong, but bigger cities seem to lean more in favor of being Tories and I don't think we can just stop citizens on the road and ask them to join our cause. Do you know of any militia groups operating in this area?" he asked the Colonel.

"No. From what I understand all organized militia were asked by the General to join the front lines. Mostly they went to Boston. Some are deployed in the Philadelphia area. We do have a friend here, a judge, but I don't think he's involved with armed forces."

They were all puzzled and very quiet. Finally Benny stopped his horse, turned it around to face the others.

"I think we should do two things. We should ask as many as possible of the militia who captured the forts to join us. I understand that will leave us very short-handed, so I also have another suggestion. I'd like to go on to Saratoga and ask an Indian Chief I met there if he would volunteer some of his braves to help us."

"But the Indians have sided with the Crown," said Obie. "As I understand it, the Cherokee along the southern Appalachians have signed on with the Crown. Up here the Mohawks sided with England and the regulars have been supplying them with long guns. Shows how much the Crown understands how the Indians think."

"But they're just Indians. They can't be of any consequences," said the Colonel.

"Colonel, I've heard you say something like that before," Benny interrupted. "And with all due respect, I'd say you're underestimating the Indians. I've seen what they are capable of. Last time up here they attacked a group just like us and took their scalps."

North Again

"I'd always thought those stories were just that, stories. But, if you say you've seen their deeds, then we'll have to believe it."

Obie spoke up again. "But that brings me back to my point. Why would this particular Chief want to help us?"

"Obie your question is very good and I don't have an exact answer, but I do know many of the tribes feel just like the Colonists. Yes, the regulars may be giving them guns, but that doesn't make up for the bad way they have been treated. I'm sure some of the Indians are feeling disgruntled, especially the chiefs who have seen their once proud people become humiliated. I'd like to speak to a chief I know who I think wants to see pride again in his people."

Knox nodded in agreement. "Okay, but what do we give him in return?"

"Henry, you will give him your word, your word that if and when we succeed, you will see to it that his tribe, above all others, will be well cared for."

Chapter 12

Conflict in Mattituck

By this time Benny and our other townsmen had only been gone a few days. At first all we could do was to pray for their safe return, but then we were faced with a predicament. It all started in church during the Sunday service. After the opening prayer, Pastor Timothy followed his normal routine and asked the congregation to pray for people who are sick, or dying, or those who are faced with unusual circumstances. He then added, "And we pray for our men folk, both those who have joined the Continental forces and those in the British regular forces. A soul is a soul no matter what earthly side the soul chooses. Amen."

Despite his efforts to portray the church leadership as neutral, a challenge arose from a number of the congregants. The rumbling of voices could be heard and Mister Rivers, one of the disgruntled parishioners, bellowed out "Why should we pray for traitors?"

The Reverend was quick to respond. "Not traitors, Patriots or Regulars. Souls! And we shouldn't care about anyone's political persuasion. It's their soul we should pray to save. And with the grace of God, may they pray for your soul ... and mine as well."

But Mr. Rivers wasn't concerned for the souls of traitors. "I don't care about the souls of men who betray the Crown. Hell is where they belong!" That was harsh but his words didn't worry me. God is too smart to listen to the recommendations of men such as Rivers.

"We know who they are," he continued. "There's no coincidence that a bunch of them sailed off to Connecticut. You are our community leader; you must turn their names in to our British commander for prosecution," he said, pointing a finger at Pastor Timothy. "Until then, their lands and homes should be confiscated. Their families should be displaced and sent to live elsewhere. We don't want them here."

He had certainly gotten my attention and I could see Father was well aware of what Rivers had just said. But Pastor Timothy answered the charge.

"Contrary to your view, I am not your political leader; I am your spiritual leader. On your behalf, I will not take up a public cause, pro or con. If this position is unsuitable to you or others of the congregation, then I suggest you take it up with the elders. If the elders concur with you then they can ask me to leave. You see, you can and do have a voice in this church."

I don't know how many people in attendance got the inference. He was actually demonstrating a major reason why the Colonists have taken up arms. We want a voice in our own government. That point aside, I was again alarmed. What would we do without Reverend Timothy as our spiritual leader? But that issue was quickly resolved when Clem Hawkins stood and commanded the floor. Hawkins has been an Elder in our church for more years than most of us can remember. He's also highly respected in the township for the years he served as a captain of one of the largest ships in the whaling fleet. And, as an aside, his house on Manor Lane has one of the largest widow's walks in the colonies.

"Pastor Tim ..." Hawkins was one of the only men in the community to address the Reverend using an abbreviated first name, "I for one, appreciate your spiritual leadership and

Conflict in Mattituck

whatever your political position is, it's none of my concern, that is, so long as it doesn't interfere with how you religiously lead us. No, I don't want to wait for rumors to fly about. I'm calling for a vote of confidence in you as our Pastor. Now ..." He looked about the congregation and for a moment his eyes settled on Rivers. "If somebody has facts that would stop the vote then that person should speak up now. If no one comes forth with facts then let's get on with the vote."

The church was silent and most eyes were fixed on Rivers but he had nothing to say. Then to my surprise, and I think the surprise of everyone else present, Father rose to his feet. Mother grasped at his long coat but he was not to be stopped. With tremendous effort he raised his hand.

"I call the question." Granted, his words were weakly said but at least for those who were sitting around him, the message was clear. He was seconding Hawkins' call for confidence and, more importantly, he was showing his support for our Pastor. The loud applause that followed his statement gave testimony to how the congregation felt about Father.

"All in support of our Pastor please say aye," said Hawkins. The shout of ayes had to be heard out of the church and down main street.

"Opposed?"

Not a murmur was heard. Even Rivers didn't utter a sound, but to everyone's surprise he got up and made his way out of his pew and into the aisle.

"Some of us have to do what's right. Long live the King!" Mr. Rivers then marched back down the aisle and out of the church.

Unfortunately, I tuned out the rest of the service. I was deeply concerned about what Rivers and his cohorts were going to do. One thing was for sure, although they may not pose any more threats to Reverend Timothy's leadership, they weren't going to let the issue of our men going off to help the Continentals rest. I wanted to visit the General Store and consult with Mister Smith,

but this being Sunday, the store would be closed. Dropping by for a visit might raise all kinds of suspicions. Being Benny's sister, fiancée or whatever would definitely arouse suspicion about why I might be visiting. Yet, we had to figure out how to stop Rivers and his buddies from raising havoc with the lives of our men on the mission and, at this point, the lives of their families too. Later that night, I figured that I would saddle up and ride to the store. Of course I'd leave the horse a distance away and then walk to the building. The Smiths live above the store and have a stairway attached to the back of the building.

I didn't share my plan with anyone but as soon as it became dark I went to the barn. I lit the candle in the reflector lamp and went to get the saddle. For a moment I thought it had been misplaced, but soon I realized it was gone and so was our riding horse. The plow horse was still in its stall. Just before I left the house, I saw Mother mashing dried herbs at the table, so I realized that it had to be Father who had taken the horse. That realization triggered an urgent alarm in my head. There were no other saddles but we had an extra bridle, so I placed it on the plow horse, doused the light, jumped on her bare back, and headed for town. I knew where Father was heading but what he was going to do once he got there was a mystery. Even further alarmed, I rode to the Rivers' farm which was a prize piece of real estate that was located very close to town. The moon was full and made for good visibility, yet I couldn't see Father or our other horse. Then I realized, before the vibes, Father had generally been very stable; he wouldn't just ride up to the farmhouse and do something crazy, like shoot Rivers. But now, I just didn't know what he would do. Finally I had to start thinking about what to do myself and not fret about Father.

Trying to convince myself not to worry sounded good but the only thing that relieved me was spotting Father. He seemed to be casually riding down the path from the River's farmhouse.

"What are you doing here?" I asked him.

Conflict in Mattituck

His response to that question and to the rest of my questions was very garbled, so I had to piece together much of what he said. Father started by telling me about a friend he had met a long time ago, back when Father first started working for the company. Father met this man on one of his trips to the North Country. Like Father, the man, of Italian heritage, was a fur trader, working for another company. In fact, he was the only Italian fur trader on the circuit. Father said he had learned a great deal of people skills from this man which he used in his own dealings, especially with company officials.

Father told me that this Italian fellow shared with him how he had handled a particularly tense situation—a case where he needed a man to do something that the man had complete control over, but the man wouldn't cooperate. The Italian fellow's solution was to act recklessly toward the other man, to the point where he almost seemed insane. Following this concept Father had gone to the Rivers' farm, and had killed a chicken by hitting it with the butt of his long gun. After doing this, he had waited for Rivers to come to the barn, when like all farmers, Rivers made his evening call on the barn to give the animals water and close the doors for the night. When Rivers arrived Father snuck up from behind and put his gun to the back of his head. Then he made him take off his shirt. After which he tied Rivers to a post and gagged him. Father is pretty good with knots so even with his dexterity problems he was able to securely bind Rivers.

Then he cut the chicken's throat and let the blood spill all over Rivers' shirt. With the bloodied shirt in hand he went to the farmhouse and knocked on the door. I'm sure in telling me the story he downplayed how upset Rivers' wife was when he told her, using the bloodied shirt as proof, that he and others had assaulted and hurt her husband. He even confessed that he and other members of the militia had attacked Rivers because of his statements at church. He told Rivers' wife that the "Townsmen Militia," as Father referred to himself and the others in his mob, believed Rivers to be a traitor to the cause of freedom. In fact, Father assured her that if it weren't for his own pleas on behalf of Rivers, the Townsmen Militia surely would have killed the man. Father told Rivers' wife that the militia would not have any remorse about her husband's death, and that it would be a source of warning to other traitors.

"But if you do what I'm about to tell you to do, then I'm sure the militia will let him go. Then you can nurse him back to health." He waited for her to think about what he was saying. Then he sternly added, "There is only one condition. You are going to write and sign a letter telling what your husband has been doing."

She was hysterical, her thinking was obviously distorted, and so she agreed. In her frantic state, Father admitted, she would agree to anything. Father dictated and she wrote. What was written is so unbelievable that I will always consider it to be totally immoral and evil. It is the most outlandish and corrupt thing I have ever seen. And I can't believe Father engineered it. For memory's sake and how the letter impacted our family and community I'll write it verbatim:

November 1, 1775

Dear Colonel Knox:

It was our pleasure to provide you with supper and overnight accommodations while on your journey to the Isle of Manhattan.

We hope you did not think of us as being too forward for advising you to take the northern route to the Isle. The southern route continues to be plagued by British checkpoints. This situation is not possible to avoid.

I am penning this letter on my husband's behalf. While falsely appearing to be a strong supporter of the Crown, he was assaulted by several militia and is now too injured to write to you himself. His vocal stance and public position

Conflict in Mattituck

allows him to infiltrate the British positions without question.

We pledged to secure information for you. We traveled through the checkpoints without incident. A Tory going to the Lloyds Bank of London, to secure a loan is readily allowed past the guard stations. Once past, we observed the war ships in the harbor. Fifty-six war ships were present.

Approximately half appear to be troop carriers and the rest war vessels. We do hope this information will help you and General Washington.

Mary Rivers

She not only signed it, she was told by Father to write another copy that she would give to her husband. Without any doubt the poor lady was tremendously bewildered but she had the wherewithal to ask what was to become of the letter and her husband?

Father told her that the letter was to be hand delivered to the British Post in Huntington. He told her that as soon as he walked out of the door, one of the other men would hand carry it, overnight, to the post and explain to the officers that Rivers' husband was intercepted and upon searching him, the letter would be found. Father also told her that her husband would be brought back to the farm by sunrise. She should look around for him, as the other members of the militia didn't want her to recognize them and they would not come to the house. Mary Rivers wondered why Father didn't care if he was recognized.

"That's easy to answer. Your husband's threats were made directly against my son. A man who loves his son would attack with all the fury God gave him to protect his child. Consequences mean nothing to me as long as my son is safe. But I tell you and swear upon the Bible, if anything should happen to my son or any other member of my family, I will kill each and every relative of

the entire Rivers' clan."

Father and I rode on to the General Store. We handed the letter to Malcom Smith, he said he would promptly get it into the right hands. He also cautioned us to be careful but Father said he wasn't worried. Confused by Father's lack of concern, Smith asked how Father could feel so confident that Rivers would not retaliate. In his broken language pattern, Father told us it was because of the second part of what his Italian friend had taught him.

"First, you go at your opponent with complete fury. Then you conceive of the most extreme punishment possible. Warn your opponent that the slightest attempt to disrupt your plan or retaliate against you will mean that punishment will be inflicted. Let your opponent know that there will be no compromises. So, when I was tying up Rivers and when I left his wife, I told them, any contrary moves at all, would result in the entire Rivers family being 'routed.' In other words, any unacceptable behavior shown by Rivers would mean his entire family, all living relations, would be killed."

From childhood to adulthood, this was the only time I had ever seen my father display such a cold-hearted, murderous and unchristian attitude. And what really frightened me was the feeling that he would not hesitate to carry out such a dastardly deed. There were no limits to how vicious he could be, when it came to protecting his family.

Chapter 13

More Recruits
&
Fort Ticonderoga

Meanwhile, Benny and the six other men were making

steady progress towards Saratoga Springs. Although the distance they traveled each day was somewhat curtailed by the short autumn days, they made up time by taking few breaks. They only stopped to give the horses a rest, and when a stream or pond was present, to give them water. They ate dried beef and at one point Benny unraveled a smoked eel he had wrapped in tarp and stored in his saddle bag. Even though they enjoyed the smoked fish, Knox suggested it was time they stopped for a good meal, as well as to pick up provisions and supplies. A plan evolved that allowed Benny and Henry to move out ahead of the others and go straight to the Indian compound. The others would divide up and Henry's brother, William, would take some of Henry's money and go to one of the general stores in Saratoga Springs. Later they would register separately at an inn. Hopefully, by conducting their activities separately, they could avoid suspicion. Doc was delighted with the plan.

"Good timing too. It's getting pretty cold and I wouldn't be surprised if we got some frost or even an early snow tonight. A warm bed sounds better than my bedroll and the hard,

cold ground."

After they set up the plan Obie moved out ahead of the others to serve as point man. Since the beginning of the trip north, one of the men had always moved about a half mile ahead of the others as the point man or advanced guard. If the point man spotted something unusual he would fire his gun. If he encountered a British patrol he would say he was shooting at a rabbit or deer. When he felt that his lead was sufficient he would slow down his horse's pace from a gallop to a trot to enjoy the pristine countryside. Although the scenery was peaceful, he always made sure to stay alert and kept his long gun cocked.

The noise that caught Obie's attention came from a distance up the road. It was foreign to the wooded environment but it was a sound he quickly recognized. "There was no doubt about it. It was a wagon and a heavy one at that," Obie thought to himself. Obie raised his long gun and aimed at an imaginary rabbit, well off the road but he made sure he could still see the road ahead, out of the corner of his eye. The deep sounding clanks of the wagon wheels churning the rocks on the road meant that the wagon was either overloaded or was a specialty wagon. It wasn't long before a single mounted rider came into view and immediately afterward, a very large, cumbersome, solid-walled, prisoner coach came into Obie's side view. Obie maintained his pose until the advanced guard yelled out, "Halt!"

That's when Obie pulled the trigger firing at the imaginary rabbit and immediately whirled around. "Dang! What's wrong with you! You just chased away supper. You want to explain that to the wife and kids?" he yelled at the guard in pretended anger.

"Oh!" The guard, a British army Private, was surprised by Obie's verbal outburst.

"What in bloody hell is going on?!" Both Obie and the Private heard the bellowing loud voice of the Sergeant who was in charge of the patrol. He had been riding solo to the rear of the wagon but now, as he bellowed out obscenities and rants, he whipped his steed and sped quickly to approach Obie and his underling.

"Private! Your orders were to keep the road clear. No stopping. Now, what is it about your orders that you didn't understand?"

"My fault." Obie started to move off the road as the Sergeant got even closer.

But the Sergeant wasn't about to accept any excuses and one coming from a citizen and in all likelihood, a Patriot, was absolutely not acceptable. "Not so fast and stand your ground!" he continued to bellow as he pulled his horse right in front of Obie. "What are you doing out here? And don't tell me hunting. Two steps out of any town or village up here would get you all the game you need. So, what are you really doing?"

"The game's bigger out this way," Obie snapped back, with a touch of arrogance.

That comment and tone didn't sit right with the Sergeant, who was unaccustomed to anyone showing him the least amount of disrespect or arrogance.

"Okay, wise ass. I can deal with that kind of answer." He then turned to the Private. "Put him in shackles and toss him into the prisoner wagon with the other wise asses. All traitors, they are." he ordered. He motioned with his long gun for Obie to raise his hands and move to the rear of the wagon.

"I'm a loyal citizen of the Crown and I haven't done anything wrong. You can't just arrest me for no reason," Obie protested.

"I certainly can and don't talk to me about being loyal to the Crown. I don't believe you. Same as I don't believe the rest of you Continentals. I can't believe we declared war and we don't know who the hell we're fighting. Half of you so-called Patriot soldiers don't wear uniforms and the rest shoot at us from behind trees. You don't even know you are supposed to stand up in lines and hold rank. We should treat everyone of you as the enemy. Shoot at all of you is what I say we should do." He paused long enough to get himself even angrier. "Now, Private, get him into the wagon and let's get moving before I throw you in there with him!"

One of the two men riding on top of the wagon climbed down to unlock the back door of the wagon and Obie was ordered to climb in. Before doing so, he gave one last go at the Sergeant about how good citizens of the empire were supposed to be protected by its soldiers and not abused by them. Obie was really just stalling for time so Benny and the others could get away or find good hiding places. He ducked his head to avoid the roof beams and gave a final shout before the door was slammed shut and locked.

"I'll write to the governor about this. You've treated me like a criminal."

The wagon they had put him in was large and could hold eight passengers, or more precisely, prisoners. Currently, it held six men. Adding Obie made it seven. When Obie entered the wagon he couldn't see anything because it was pitch black inside. The walls were made of heavy oak planks and the only air circulation came from a porthole in the rear door, making the wagon a moving fortress.

"Welcome to hell," said one of the prisoners.

"Stop complaining. When you see the dump they're taking us to, you'll think this is a carriage built for a king," said another.

"Well, welcome anyway. Although, I should say I'm sorry you had to join this sorry lot," said the first prisoner.

Obie was uncertain of what was going to happen.

"Yeah, could be with you for a while. Then again, who knows what could happen," he mumbled.

Benny and Patrick had left their horses with the others and moved up the road to see what Obie's warning shot was all about. They clung to the wood line and did their best to stay out of sight. At last, Obie and the prisoner transport unit came into sight and they could see Obie being escorted and forced into the wagon. His horse was tied to the rear of the wagon and it was obvious that the Sergeant was reprimanding one of his soldiers. Benny and Patrick quickly made their way back to the others and went about laying out a plan of action.

Within moments, the prisoner convoy appeared in the distance. As planned, Benny left his horse and long gun in the woods, walked to the road and raised his hands. He did it in such a manner that suggested the advancing patrol should stop. It took a few minutes longer for the patrol's Private to see this man in the road, with his arms and hands waving over his head. However, the message didn't sit very well with the private who usually did what was required of him. After all, he'd just been scolded for letting the last obstacle stop the progress of the patrol and he certainly recalled the warning he had just received from the Sergeant. "Stand clear! We will not stop!" he yelled, raising his musket. Benny stood his ground and said nothing. "Stand clear, or I'll shoot!" he yelled, even more forcefully. But Benny kept his pose.

The Private drew closer and slowed his horse. Consequently, the entire patrol slowed to a near stop. The Sergeant whipped his horse, sped around the wagon and came up next to the Private.

"For God sakes, man! Can't you do anything right? You there! Fool! I command you to move out of the way!" he bellowed at Benny, showing the Private how the situation should properly be handled. Still, Benny didn't respond and his pose didn't change. The Sergeant and his underling both rode up to within a few feet of Benny and stopped their horses. When they saw that there was only an unarmed and quite possibly very foolish man in front of them, he lifted his gun and let the barrel point toward the sky.

"What in bloody hell do you think you're doing?" the Sergeant yelled as he leaned forward and peered down at Benny.

"Just releasing your prisoners and taking you and your men as prisoners," Benny finally responded.

"Shoot him!" the Sergeant ranted at the Private,

"Keep the gun up or you'll be shot." Benny spoke calmly and pointed with his forefingers to both sides of the road. As though rehearsed many times, Knox and his brother William appeared on one side of the road, while on the other, Smitty stood quietly as all

three took steady aim at the Sergeant and his man.

The wagon driver, trying to be as unobtrusive as possible, reached for his musket. "Your life is too worthwhile to be wasted," said Patrick from behind him. The driver and his side rider quickly raised their hands.

"Thank you. Liberty is a reach and worth death, but we should strive for the least number of deaths as possible," Patrick told them.

Surrender was inevitable but that didn't stop the Sergeant from grumbling. As he was being chained and ushered into the now vacant prisoner wagon he cursed the Private and blamed him for this predicament. "If you had followed orders and just shot the bloody bastard ..."

To add fuel to the fire, when Benny saw the condition of the prisoners' footwear, he ordered the Sergeant and his men to remove their boots and toss them out of the wagon. He also asked Smitty to secure the wagon door and make it almost impossible to open.

"I didn't mean to get you into such a mess," Benny said to Obie, giving him a sorrowful look.

"I knew you'd get me out of there. I have faith. Remember, you saved me before. I'll never forget that."

"You'd do the same for me. We can count on each other." They started to shake hands but then quickly embraced each other. When Obie told me of the episode he recalled Benny saying, "that lumberjack could certainly bear hug."

Henry approached them. He was very pleased with how well the capture of the patrol had gone, but he was also concerned. "What are we to do with the real prisoners you just released? We can't just turn them loose. They're probably all murderers or rapists or even both. Can't we fit them back in the wagon, with the regulars?"

Benny raised his hand as though he was stopping another wagon patrol. "Well, let's consider them for a moment. First off, we're pretty far west. That mountain range ..." He pointed west to some pretty steep mountains," ... over there is basically our border. The King has said, none of us, his subjects, are to settle beyond those mountains. And that's true for the entire Appalachian range." He paused to think his way through his idea. "Now that means something. You see, out here murderers and rapists aren't usually treated like other criminals. If you kill someone and get caught, well, there might be something like a trial but more than likely, you'd be hanging by a noose from a tree before the next morning. And, as far as a man who commits rape, he'd be hung up on the tree nearest to where he got caught and you could wager that not all of his body parts would still be attached before they hung him."

"Ouch," Obie said, grabbing for his crotch. The others laughed. "I sure got the point," Obie said.

Benny wasn't finished. He walked over to the prisoners and all of the others gathered around.

"I want each of you to tell us why you were in jail." He paused for a moment. "Or would it be better if I asked the Sergeant in the wagon?"

"No need," said one of the men, as he moved to the front of the six prisoners. "We're all in the wagon for the same crime. Truth is, we were all brought before the magistrate together. We're debtors who haven't paid the banks back; not that we didn't want to, but each of us was unable pay back all that we owed. Most of us are farmers and we couldn't grow enough to feed our families, buy supplies for next year's crop, and pay back the banks. In my case, the price of seed went so high that ... well, I just went broke."

Benny's compassion for his fellow farmers was overwhelming, but he forced himself to be objective. "Where did you buy your seed?"

"The England Seed and Farm Products Company."

"Do you know who owns the company?"

"Sure, we all do. It's the same people who own the bank."

Benny nodded his head and turned to Knox. "A word please,

William, Doc." He also nodded to the others and they knew he wanted them to join him, as well.

"It's an all too common practice of the banks," he said as soon as they were away from the prisoners. "They lend the money knowing it'll be rough for the farmers to pay them back but then, since they also own the supply company, they raise the prices. The farmers fail; their wives and children are forced to live with relatives and the bank repossesses the farm. But now the bank has a cleared farm, and usually a house and barn. The farmer goes to jail and the bank resells the much improved farm at a higher price. The bank makes much more money. Unfortunately, the farmer and his family become destitute and ruined."

Doc nodded his head. "It happens all the time, but you can't stop it. Every young man wants a farm. They marry and some get a dowry or borrow for the down payment. They work hard but the system only allows for the smartest or, mostly the luckiest, to succeed."

"With your permission, I'd like to do something," Benny said to Knox. He then shared his idea. After which he and his comrades walked over to the prisoners, who surmised their fate was about to be discussed, and they were anxiously awaiting the outcome. Benny quickly stated his plan. "The Colonel has decided upon an offer he would like to extend to each of you. There are options. First, you can return to the prison wagon and serve out your time. Secondly, we can set you free right now, but that would mean you'd be an escaped prisoner and if you are caught, there'll most likely be no mercy. You'll probably be hanged. The banks would make sure of that. Thirdly, you can join the Colonel, and enlist in the Continental Army. At the end of your tour, the Colonel will hand you documents stating that you were seized and pressed into service. He will also reward you, that is, if you provide good service. He will give you a letter absolving you of your promissory note and set you free from the charges against you." Benny took a long pause. "How do you want to proceed?"

More Recruits & Fort Ticonderoga

Without hesitation, each man stepped forward, signaling that they were joining the service. Benny then gave multiple orders. "Get the horses unhitched from the wagon. Get the boots of the regulars and put them on. Get organized for travel and leave the wagon in the middle of the road. Hopefully the regulars will be rescued."

"I am recommending you for a commission as an officer. And I am awarding you a field promotion as of right now. The rank of sergeant is now yours and I'm sure the General will make it a permanent promotion," Colonel Knox announced to Benny while all of the men were present. "Your abilities and performance are exemplary."

Benny was grateful and humbly thanked the Colonel. But what he held back from saying was that he really didn't consider himself to be a member of the army. He had promised to help on this particular mission, a task he felt he owed Pastor Timothy and his friends. He was not a committed person to the army and would not be a soldier after this mission. But for now Benny decided to remain silent about his future plans.

They left the wagon in the middle of the road and confiscated weapons, horses and anything else that could possibly serve them on the mission. They were still shy by two horses, so some of the men had to double up and even ride bareback as they were also short of several saddles.

Although their numbers had nearly doubled both Benny and Knox knew this was far short of the number of men needed to carry out the arduous task ahead of them. At the next major fork in the road, Benny left Patrick in charge as he teamed up with Knox to go to the Indian encampment in Saratoga Springs. William and Doc were headed in the same direction but were traveling a good distance behind. Their task was to secure supplies and provisions. As they approached and moved through the town, Benny pointed out how rapidly the community was growing. Even since he was here last, he saw that there were now even more new buildings being erected. At the far side of town they neared the Indian encampment. Knox's reaction was the same as Benny's when he first visited the area. "This is deplorable."

Chief Stillwater didn't hesitate to grant a meeting with them. Upon entering the tent Benny recalled how Father said this leader was once very proud and walked upright. It was obvious that the burden of his tribe's social ills and the white man's encroachment were heavy on the Chief's shoulders. And yet, one of the Chief's primary concerns was for Benny's father. Benny extended Father's regards and then explained the current circumstances. He introduced the Colonel and told of his special mission. At this juncture Benny knew he had to be very careful.

"This is why we've come, to ask for your help. We need men. Your braves could help us carry out this most important task. We need you to lend your braves to us." Throughout, Benny deliberately never mentioned compensation. He knew that the Chief would need to consider the concept first; then they could negotiate for the services of the braves. Most important was to get the Chief to accept the idea of his men helping the Colonists.

But the Chief was listening for the words that were not said. "Has young Benny mixed up things? Does he not know the Mohawks have agreed to fight on the side of the Red Coats?" The Chief didn't give Benny time to answer. Instead he kept asking questions. "As tribal Chief I sit at the council with the Mohawk Chiefs. Am I to say we have decided to help the Colonists instead of the Red Coats? And then what will happen? Do you suppose the Mohawk tribes will approve or do you think they might decide that I've betrayed our nation? Do you think I should consider your request or do you think you should reconsider making such a request?"

Benny didn't respond right away, wanting to make sure the Chief had raised all of the stumbling blocks. Then he finally responded.

"In our book of faith there is a true story about a giant. This

188

giant was leading his huge army against a much smaller army. The giant and his army were so sure they would win the battle that he challenged any man of the smaller army to a one-to-one duel. The giant walked towards the small army, with fierce weapons, and he wore metal over his body for protection. In the midst of the small army was a warrior and all this barefooted man wore was a lion's cloth. His weapon was a slingshot. The giant and this young man moved toward each other on the battlefield. The giant raised his spear in one hand and held up a shield in the other. Then he threw the spear and it landed between the legs of the young warrior. In turn, the young man loaded his sling with a rock. Then he took aim and let it fly. The rock soared across the battle field and it went just above the shield and it struck the giant in the forehead. With a thunderous sound, the huge giant fell backward onto the ground. He was dead and his army was shocked and horrified. In fear of this young warrior, holding only his sling, the giant's army ran in retreat."

"So, is it your belief that the Colonists, like the young warrior, will win?" asked the Chief.

"Yes, Chief. The Red Coats may outnumber the Colonists' army but the leaders and men of this young country are determined to have free will. Because of this determination I think they will win and this will be an independent country."

"So, instead of following the direction of the Mohawk Chiefs, I should listen to you and take up sides with the Colonists? But I see yet another possibility. If I do nothing, our tribe might then be in a better position, no matter which side wins."

Benny knew that the conversation would reach this point. He also knew that it was time for negotiation. "I watched you and my father negotiate over *wampum* and pelts, so I knew we would reach this point. We will make it tempting for you to help us. I introduced Colonel Knox to you, but I didn't tell you who he is and why he's here." Benny looked at Knox and realized he had never seen the man smile so happily. "This man is an aide to the

Chief of all the Continental Army. He is a very powerful man and he pledges, if and when the Colonists win this war, he will see to it that your people will be cared for."

"How?"

"Food, clothes and the most important thing, the lands you hunt will be yours forever."

"You would give me back what belongs to me in the first place?"

"Chief, you are not treated by the white man as though the land belongs to you. They take it away from you. Just look at this town. Your camp was once in the nice woods at the other end. Now you camp in a swamp, the unwanted land."

Benny may have gone too far with that last sentence. The Chief lowered his eyes. The truth was painful, "Are you making a promise before your God?"

"Before my God, I promise to do my best to fulfill this pledge."

The afternoon had become colder. The Chief gave some commands, loud enough so his people outside of the tent could hear. Two squaws entered the tent with their arms filled with logs and kindling. They immediately began to start a fire. Another squaw brought in a long stemmed pipe. The Chief lit the pipe, took a deep draw and passed it to Benny. After Benny took a pull he handed it to Knox. Both Benny and Knox knew the smoking of the pipe meant that the Chief had agreed to the offer. They would receive help from the Chief. Both men were delighted; actually quite jubilant.

Unfortunately, their jubilance was only momentary. It diminished when the tent flap opened again and in walked two very young braves. This was to be the help the Chief was offering. Now, I must say that Benny never has an unkind word to say about anybody. But, he said the only honest way to describe these two braves was to call them scary. They looked very much alike. They had the typical thick black hair of an Indian and they wore a

More Recruits & Fort Ticonderoga

bandana around their forehead with feather quills stuck under the bandanas. They were lean, but skin and bones would be a more appropriate description of them. Their deerskin clothes, however looked supple as well as warm The Chief rose and spoke to them in their native tongue. "I thought you negotiated a great deal but if this is all we get, we are in trouble," Knox said to Benny.

"It may be the best the tribe can offer," Benny said. "We should be careful not to underestimate this offering." The Chief ended his conversation with his two braves, then he hugged each of them. Benny watched carefully and saw something in the Chief's eyes that only for a fleeting moment revealed a deep emotional affection between the Chief and his braves.

"They will follow your orders," The Chief said to Knox. "They speak your language and understand they represent our tribe," he added softly, but with conviction. "They also understand they hold the future of our tribe in their hands."

The meeting ended and the Chief walked them to their horses. As they mounted the Chief had a need to say more. "One more moment." He looked very solemn as he spoke. "The first time I heard the Bible story of David, I was a boy. A French missionary told it and explained how that young man with the sling, David, killed the giant and then became King of all the people. In your telling of the story, the young man represents your young country. After your young Colonists defeat the giant from across the great water, will it become a leader of countries?"

Benny was impressed and intrigued by the Chief's logic, but how to answer was not easy. "Only time will tell, but one thing is for sure. A nation is only as good and strong as its leaders. I've met the leader of this nation's forces and I know of the willpower and determination of many of the other leaders, men like Colonel Knox here or Adams in Boston or even Patrick from Yale. If men like this shape this union of colonies, then yes, it will one day be a leader of nations."

They had stayed longer than Benny had anticipated but when

the Chief offered accommodations for the night, both he and Knox gracefully declined. The four horsemen, Benny, Knox and the two braves, left the encampment with many children following them to the edge of the encampment. When Benny had first arrived he felt that the Chief had the look of a worrisome man. Now, looking back at him he realized the Chief's worries had grown by leaps and bounds. Benny promised himself that these two young braves would get back home to their tribe in safe and healthy condition.

As they moved through the town of Saratoga Springs, yet another surprise awaited them. William and Doc were seated on the buckboard of a wagon.

"What in the world are you two doing with a wagon?" Knox's question was laden with humor.

"Now, Henry," In the presence of the other men, William didn't usually address his brother so informally. "Just think about it. We're shy a couple of horses and saddles. We also needed extra horses to carry food and supplies. This rig answers all our needs, and we got the wagon and horses at a good price, if I do say so myself."

"Besides,..." Doc interrupted, "we'd have a devil of a time getting all of this stuff onto a couple of pack horses." As he spoke, he lifted a tarp off the back of the wagon. It was filled to the rim of the sideboards with provisions and gear.

"Why didn't you just buy the store?" Knox asked, looking at the supplies.

"We keep getting recruits," Doc then glanced at the braves. "I see, you've got two more, and they look like they could use a square meal or two. We may just have to buy up a whole lot more; besides, we still have lots of money left."

"Well don't forget, we've got a long mission ahead and I hope you got receipts. We have to account for every cent of that money."

"You two did real good. The wagon will probably come in very handy and one thing is for sure. Napoleon said, an army moves on its stomach. We have a lot of stomachs to fill. Now, if your horses are tightly secured to the back, let's try to catch up to the others before it gets too dark."

It was dark, very dark before they caught up to the others. They made camp and the next morning William and a couple of the new recruits made coffee, a couple of dozen scrambled eggs and some *jack cake*. Even Henry complimented his brother for making the right purchases and organizing the meal. After a good sleep—though with so many of them they could not stay at an inn as Doc would have preferred—and a hearty meal, they were able to resume their trek north. They put in three more long days. and passed what remained of Fort Henry. It had been burned down and there was still much confusion as to which side had set the fire. Nonetheless, it was a landmark that meant Fort Ticonderoga was only about twenty miles further north. The next day, they reached Lake George. The trip up to the North Country had gone very smoothly. The road now hugged the eastern shore of the lake and as Benny recalled it would be an easy ride to the fort. The hills and gullies had now given way to the lowlands around the lake. Benny and Knox rode next to each other and what started as idle chatter soon evolved into strategic planning.

"It should get a bit colder tonight than last," Knox said.

"The colder, the better."

"Right you are. I wouldn't mind a deep frost, and then some light snow on top."

Benny knew what Henry was aiming at. "Don't mean to intrude on your plans but would cold and snow have anything to do with moving the cannons?"

"Right you are. The weather has all to do with how we get the cannons moved."

"Makes a lot of sense to me. I've seen those cannons. Including the mountings, each one has to weigh about two thousand pounds, enough to sink a wheel wagon pretty deep, even with a small amount of rain."

Knox nodded his head.

"Pray for cold weather. A warm rain could wreck this whole mission." He kept nodding his head. "Yep, weather could make or break this entire mission."

Luckily, the temperature had begun to drop. It was late autumn but up in the North Country, very often fall turns to winter very quickly.

One of the braves Benny had asked to serve as point man approached and advised that there was a spot ahead where it would be wise to make camp. It was a clearing and easily defendable if they were attacked, especially by the Mohawks. They camped with the knowledge that the next day they would reach their destination.

Fort Ticonderoga came into view and while the men knew they didn't complete the hardest portion of the mission, there was still great excitement. The braves came back to the group as they felt that the Colonel should lead the men into the fort. Knox kept his eyes on the fort and the closer they got the more intensely he studied it. It had been a while since he had left Boston and he felt that quite honestly, anything could have happened since he last heard of the cannons and the fort. Like Fort Henry, it could have been burned down or worse yet, the British could have recaptured it and made off with the cannons. As they got closer Knox could see the walls were still upright and then the portholes for the cannons could be seen. At last, some of the cannons themselves came into view. Knox was at once relieved and jubilant.

"Look sharp men! Double file. Sit up in your saddle and eyes front." Benny fell in behind the mission's leader and he too felt a surge of patriotism along with a stab of excitement.

The gates were opened and they were warmly greeted by the fort's occupying force. Only a few months ago the fort had been captured by Ethan Allen, Benedict Arnold, and a group of some eighty-three of Vermont's finest Green Mountain Boys, surprising the Red Coats who had been occupying the fort. The regulars had

More Recruits & Fort Ticonderoga

believed if an attack were launched against the fort it would have to come from the south. The regulars had not yet heard that war had begun, so they were doubly surprised when they were invaded and the forces came from the north. Allen and Arnold led their troops across the northern tier, then crossed Lake Champlain. The surprise was so successful that very few shots were fired.

Allen and Arnold had already moved on to other fronts of the war, so Knox met with the new commanding officer. However, Knox was so anxious to move the cannons that he bypassed the formal greetings and made his way to inspect the guns. He was joined by William and Benny. The number of cannons still in place delighted them, but the condition of the weapons was a bit alarming. Many of the cannons were rusted and their wooden carriages were rotted away. The rust was so bad that the cannons' future usefulness was, at the very least, questionable. They stopped next to one of the cannons. "Do you think we'll ever be able to use it?" Knox glumly asked Benny.

Benny put his hand into the nozzle and slowly maneuvered his fingers about the cannon's interior. "I'd be more afraid it would just blow up instead of spit out a ball."

"How did they get like this?" William sounded dismayed.

"I'd only be guessing but they're French made and I think the French use more raw iron in their cannons than we do in the Colonies or in England. I'd also question how they were cared for. If you look around, you don't see any of them covered with canvas and ..." Benny did a three hundred and sixty degree scan before continuing. "... I don't see one grease bucket. Up this way, near the lake, which means lots of moisture in the air, iron rusts pretty quickly. These guns should have been smeared with grease at all times."

"Benny, we need these cannons. Can you get the men and salvage as many as possible?"

"It would go quicker if you can talk the fort commander into letting us use his men. He'll do it or he won't be a commander

much longer."

That night the weather turned colder and a light snow fell. In the morning Benny, William and Knox met again. A night's sleep, indoors, in a barrack bed, with a fire roaring in the fireplace, was enjoyed by all the men, but now Henry was anxious to start restoring and salvaging the cannons.

"It won't take the three of us to organize the restoration of the guns. Henry, you might want to start working on your plan to get them transported and they won't be much good without powder and shot."

"Thanks Benny. I didn't want to leave you with the hard task, while I ran off to take care of other jobs, but, you know what you're doing with the cannons and I'd just be in the way. On the other hand, I can organize the trip ahead. William can handle transportation."

Benny nodded in agreement. "In the long run, it'll save time. In the meantime, we'll get as many guns as possible ready for action."

Given the cold weather, Knox asked William to get sleds. Buy them, make them ... in other words, anyway he could, he was to bring in as many sleds as needed to transport the cannons. They wished each other luck, exchanged some planning ideas, then the three men launched into their assigned tasks.

From a personality point of view, William is very much like his brother Henry. More academically proficient than vocationally skilled, he seemed awkward in situations that required manual ability. Yet, when tasks required reading, writing or arithmetic, he easily excelled. Based on this assessment of William, Benny suggested he take Smitty with him in his attempt to have sleds made to order. Benny felt Smitty's knowledge of how to make things from iron and wood could augment William's bookish approach. Together, they should do well.

So, William and Smitty started their search for sleds right within the walls of the fort. In fact, some of the Green Mountain

More Recruits & Fort Ticonderoga

Boys, who had successfully captured the fort only several weeks earlier, were gathered near the main gate. William and Smitty approached the group and were delighted by the eagerness of these Vermonters to help. A couple of them had, at one time or another, worked as coopers and they had some useful ideas about cutting the barrels in half. Then they could put some rails on the bottom but Smitty found too many design problems with the concept. He thought the shape of the barrel would make it too close to the ground and any alteration would make it too top heavy and prone to tipping over.

Smitty sketched out a simple and somewhat traditional one person sled. It had one major alteration: instead of a flat platform, it had a gully running up and down the length of the sled bed so that the cannons would remain in the middle. He planned to remove the cannons from their wooden carriages, which would then be transported separately.

After giving the plan one last review William and Smitty authorized the men to begin working on a sample that could be used in a trial run. Feeling optimistic about their decision and the fact that they had initiated and envisioned the completion of a major task, William and Smitty started to say their goodbyes.

Their euphoria was short lived.

"You ever been over them mountains?" asked one of the older Green Mountain Boys, shaking William's hand.

William was quick to answer. "I'm from the other side of them. Boston actually, which is to the east and somewhat south of the mountains." William kept shaking hands and had moved to the next man when an uneasy feeling came over him. He whirled his head back toward the man he had just spoken to. "And?" he asked. The man only shrugged his shoulders in response. William, being from the same geographic area often demonstrated the same behavior but at a moment like this, he didn't appreciate the "tight-lipped" experience.

"Tell me what you are referring to!" he snapped at the man.

But barking, shouting, or screaming at people from the north eastern colonies wasn't likely to make them more responsive or talkative, either.

The man took his time to answer. "You do know you're going to be going over mountains. And mountains don't just go up and down. They tend to have sides that also slope. And, they're rocky too."

"So, what you're saying is, you don't think the sleds we just designed will make it?"

"Yep."

"You think they'll flip over?"

"Yep."

"They're too high?"

"Yep."

"Not wide enough?"

"Yep."

William was frustrated. He looked at Smitty, "Do you think we need to reconsider our design?"

"Well, I guess so. I mean, he obviously knows the terrain better than we do."

"I knew it was too easy." William said and waved goodbye to the Vermonters. Smitty caught up to him and they walked out of the open fort gate.

Smitty was still puzzled and asked, "Why didn't we get that guy to help with the design? He seemed to know more that we do."

"I'll never deal with people I have to drag information out of. He should have been forthright and offered his knowledge without my having to pry it out of him."

Due to the safety offered by the fort there are usually merchants, traders and vendors near the front gate. Outside the gate this day there was a typically large crowd of people. And as with most forts, the gathering resembled an outdoor market place. William and Smitty made their way through the crowd. They hadn't been here before so they weren't sure where they were going. However, they couldn't go too far. As they soon discovered, they were nearly surrounded by water. It finally occurred to William that the fort was actually built on a peninsula. They saw the docks ahead of them and noticed boats still in the water.

"I guess the owners don't believe the lake's going to freeze," Smitty commented as he waved his hand at the boats.

"Either that or they plan to pull them out as soon as the freeze starts setting in. I've seen that in the Boston seaport area. They wait until the ground freezes which help the boats glide easier, but it is a timing trick. Wait too long and ice can form around the boat sides. Then it's a race to save the boat from being crushed."

One boat in particular, was very different from the others. "What a weird looking boat. Isn't it?" Smitty was never really fond of boats.

"That one there ..." William was pointing to a very large boat. "It's called a gondola. It's originally an Italian design, from Venice actually. But I don't think the bow is usually as tall as that one. And they certainly aren't normally as large as that vessel. You know, in Venice they have to negotiate all those small canals to get about."

"No, I don't know anything about Venice and for that matter, I know very little about Italy. But ..." Smitty kept looking at the gondola and his mind churned. "... but ..."

At first William didn't think much about what caused Smitty to stop talking in mid sentence; then his mind must have caught onto what Smitty was considering. He exclaimed, "No! No! There are no buts about it! By gosh!"

They both stopped looking at the gondola and turned to face each other. "It'll work. All we have to do is get the cannons down here before the lake freezes," William said.

"Could get cold tonight, but I don't think it'll be enough to freeze the lake over."

"With all those merchants by the gate, I'm sure we can hire some teams of wagons and oxen or even horses, to haul the

cannons down here." Then William turned and started a quick pace back to the fort, "Come on, let's get back to tell my brother and Benny."

"But let's stop by the gate and get more information so we have our facts in order, then we can lay out a plan for the Colonel and Benny."

William and Smitty were in luck. Benny had just finished inspecting and numbering the cannons. Henry had also just arrived having completed his dealings. He had been meeting with Major General Philip Schuyler, the temporary Commander of the fort. The other men of the group had a fire roaring and were roasting some venison that the two braves had brought back from a hunting trip. Some of the other men had ventured out of the fort and shopped for bunches of root vegetables. All together, the aromas promised a fine meal to come. Henry led his group to the fire where they were joined by the others.

He was the first to announce his day's successes. "The Commander here at the fort is a fine gentleman. He has ordered the release of any and all the cannons we want to take. And he will release, to my command, any number of the Green Mountain Boys, as we need."

Benny pulled a piece of paper from his coat pocket and carefully looked it over. He was thankful he had the help of one of the Green Mountain Boys who many years ago, had been a gunnery sergeant in the British army. He taught Benny the names and types of cannons that were at the fort. He also noted each cannon's weight, the amount of shot needed, and so on. Benny took his time before speaking. He wanted to be certain of his facts and calculations.

"As near as I can tell, we can salvage fifty-nine cannons. Most of them, forty-three to be precise, are heavy brass and iron. Our guess is that they probably weigh about a ton each. There are also six cohorus, eight mortars and two howitzers. And ... and ..." He paused to think of a good adjective for one other cannon in the collection, "and there is one cannon, we don't know what to call it, except that it's gigantic. It easily weighs three thousand pounds. Mostly made of brass, some iron. Probably could launch a mortar clear across the lake."

"I also inventoried the munitions room. It's well-stocked with mortar and fine powder. In all, if my calculations are correct, we have to haul about sixty tons from here to Boston."

"There is one major problem, however; almost all of the cannons are on wood carriages that were made during the French and Indian War. They don't look like they've seen even the slightest amount of care. In brief, most of the carriages are rotting away. Some are so badly rotted that they crumble at the touch. Therefore, I would suggest we transport the cannons without the carriages. We can have new carriages made up once we get to Boston."

"If you can salvage one carriage for each type of cannon, we can put them in an advanced dispatch and once we get to the other side of the Hudson, we'll send them ahead," Henry interrupted, "That way our men in Boston can get a head start on their construction."

"A great idea and we can certainly do it." Benny couldn't conceal his enthusiasm.

Then William spoke up. "Smitty and I have mapped out a plan and now that we know there are about fifty-nine cannons, we'll be able to refine it. Actually we came up with some ideas but a couple of local folks we talked to at the gate really helped. In fact, if you ..." he directed his point to his brother, "approve of the plan, we can get the equipment and men needed to carry it out ... within minutes. So, here's what we propose: we take the cannons out of their porthole positions and move them by oxen cart down to the dock. Down at the dock a large gondola is still in the water. We have arranged to rent it. On it we take the cannons off this peninsula and down the Chute River. The Chute flows to an area known as the Bridge Landing. There, we offload the cannons and

place them on other oxen carts. We take them a short distance to the northern most point of Lake George. There we load them on boats and float them down the entire length of the lake. But, and mind you, this is a big but ..." He took another deep breath, "here's the key to the entire operation: time and weather." He emphasized the words and paused to let them sink in. "We've got to move fast. People at the gate say this is very rare weather. Normally the lakes and rivers are frozen by now and there's plenty of snow."

"So, why not wait for snow?" Henry asked.

"Because, moving down the lake is much quicker than getting across snow."

"Can't argue with that," Henry conceded, "but our plan calls for changes along the way. That means a lot of advanced preparation." He hesitated to gather his thoughts. "I mean, let's say the lakes don't freeze and we boat the cannons south. We'll still need sleds when we get to the southern landing of Lake George. Right?"

"It's a good plan but it needs an advance or point person to carry it out. And, if it's well coordinated, a great deal of time can be saved. Think about it. While work is being done here to load the cannons, someone can go ahead to the bridge landing and organize the oxen carts. Once that's done, then an advanced group can move ahead and organize the boats needed to go south on the lake."

Henry caught on and finished Benny's concept. "Then that advanced group could race south and organize the rest of the trip. All of this means, no waiting around for sleds to be built or bought. All of that can be done while the cannons are already being moved and making progress. It's a wonderful strategy."

Benny liked the plan but he wanted to be totally satisfied. "Everyone think. Before we move ahead with this plan, let's be sure there aren't any real obstacles we've overlooked."

Everyone fell silent and each person quietly, in his own mind scrutinized the plan. Finally, Henry spoke. "It will save time and we can do it. Are we all agreed?" He looked about and each man nodded, affirming the plan.

Henry took another moment to think. "But I'm not sure I should do the advance work. Maybe ..."

Benny didn't let him finish. "Pardon, but you are the only one who can do it. You have the General's authority. None of the rest of us has the rank or power to command things on behalf of the Continental Army."

Henry nodded. "Of course you're right. I just didn't want to lose sight of the cannons."

"Sir, you set up the exchanges and we'll get the cannons there," Benny said in a determined voice.

"But I'll go with the first trip on the gondola, just to be certain it's going to work." Then Henry walked closer to the fire to warm his hands. "This mission could determine the outcome of the siege of Boston, the entire war, and our becoming a free and independent country." He stood in silence, as did all of his troops. Without a call to worship, each man prayed in his own word and to himself. After a few minutes of silent prayer Henry solemnly proclaimed, "Amen!"

Then he completely changed his mood. "Is that venison done yet? It's probably going to be our last hot meal for a while, so let's enjoy. Then we'll race the weather to accomplish our mission."

One of the braves carved the venison and the men helped themselves. The venison was really delicious and as they ate, the men relaxed and chatted. The noise level was quite high, and Benny used this circumstance to his advantage as he approached Obie and initiated a private conversation out of hearing range of the others. "I'd like you to take on a special assignment Obie. I'd like you to go with the Colonel, sort of keep an eye on him. Keep him out of harm's way." Benny paused. He was having a debate with himself. He hesitated sharing more of his concerns but then he realized his sharing would help Obie understand his assignment. "Obie, Colonel Knox is a special person. He has only

one goal. The freedom of our colonies and to achieve that freedom he would give anything ... including his life. He's a good man who doesn't consider his own safety. I'd like you to stay with him. If you would, be his bodyguard and protect him, especially from himself."

Chapter 14

Creative Ideas
&
Heroes

Fort Ticonderoga is an impressive structure. In fact,
as Benny described it, not only is the structure itself an expansive
work but its location could not be more ideal. The idea of building
it on that little peninsula, that juts out between Lake Champlain
and Lake George must be credited to French Governor General
Vaudviel of Canada. His idea was to construct the fort in 1755 so
that he could stop the British from moving north and taking over
the waterway and consequently the very valuable fur trade. The
fort's design is very complicated. It looks somewhat like a star,
and it is incredibly strong. Benny had learned that the French had
built side by side walls by framing them out of wood; then filled the
space between the wood walls with dried mud and straw. Finally
they had stones brought in from a nearby valley and faced the
entire structure. Inside the fort there are three story high barracks,
enough barracks for four hundred men. The fort walls average
twenty feet in height. The portholes for the cannons were evenly
spaced and the larger cannons pointed directly ahead, out onto the
lake, where ships navigating north and south had to pass.

As I mentioned, strategically, the fort is ideally situated. It
sticks so far out into the lake that ships coming from the north and

heading for Lake George were forced to come within range of the fort's cannons. Between the two lakes is a short passageway called the Chute River. Although this waterway is short in distance, it's really not entirely navigable. It has too many dangerous rapids and minor falls. It is for this same reason that the mission's men had to offload at the Bridge Landing, which actually has a roadway crossing over to Lake George.

Once the French finished the fort's construction they named it Carillon. Putting it into service was a proud but short-lived moment for the French. Barely two years later, in 1757; The English captured it. They renamed the fort Ticonderoga, which, according to the local Indians, means land between two bodies of water. Benny heard the fascinating story of how the Green Mountain Boys took the fort away from the British. Ethan Allen, who led the Boys in the raid, was really surprised by the lack of sentries and vigilance on the part of the British. Even more surprised was the British Commander who opened the door in the middle of the night to find Allen standing there with a long gun and saying, "Surrender or else!" It's hard to believe but the Boys captured the fort without any resistance at all.

Anyway, back to the moving of the cannons. The meal and respite was over. The men were given various assignments and they quickly scattered to tackle them. It was early evening which meant torches and lanterns lit the way. Knox had gone down to the gate just before the vendors and merchants packed their wares and prepared to go home. He negotiated with several of them and patriotism aside, many offered their services especially for the fee Knox offered.

William and Smitty had been given the task of securing hoists to lift and maneuver the cannons. They had seen some in the fort itself but the ones they saw didn't have wheels and would have been too cumbersome to move about. So the two men left the fort and secured the service of several carpenters. In turn, they discussed and decided upon several options, including modifying the stationary hoists and building new mobile units.

And, talk about cumbersome: Benny had his hands full trying to move the cannons from their positions on the upper wall. It wasn't until the ex-gunnery Sergeant stopped by and made suggestions that a solution was resolved.

"If you're trying to make love to that thing, it needs a longer fuse to get it hot," the Sergeant said seeing men with their arms around a smaller cannon and attempting, to no avail, to move it. I'm sure in the telling of the story Benny cleaned up the Sergeant's words, but the point was well taken. Benny and his men simply had no idea as to how to move this or any of the cannons.

"You can't move it without a hoist, at least not from its porthole."

"But we released it from its carriage," said one of the men who had just been struggling to move it.

"Well, now that's a good start, but the cannon itself weighs about two thousand pounds. So, if you don't care much for your lower equipment, go ahead and try to lift it. But if you don't want your nuts moving to where they don't belong, then I suggest you go and get a hoist."

"I'm not following you, Sarge. If we bring a hoist up here, how do we get a cart up here to load it on to. I mean, we are two stories high."

The Sergeant looked astonished. He shook his head in disbelief.

"Too late. I guess your nuts already got shot up to your brain and stopped you from thinking." He motioned everyone away from the cannon.

"After you place the hoist here, above the porthole, and tie up the cannon, you lower it to the ground on the outside of the wall. So bring a block and tackle with the hoist."

Benny had remained silent during the verbal exchange but as soon as a hoist was in place and the Sergeant showed the men where to place the block and ropes, he got the concept. Benny

wasn't happy with the idea of dangling a two thousand pound object over the side of the fort wall, but the Sergeant showed them how just a couple of guide ropes, pulled by men on the ground, could safely place the cannon in the bed of a wagon.

The first cannon was the most difficult. After that, even the heavy brass cannon was easily moved and placed in the bed of a waiting wagon. With the first rays of dawn the gondola left the landing with its initial load of cannons. The ever-concerned Henry Knox was also on that first trip from the peninsula to the Bridge Landing. Henry is a very large man and poked fun at himself by comparing himself to a cannon as the gondola left the shore.

"That hunk of iron and I are about the same weight. But it has one advantage over me. If it goes overboard, it'll sink straight to the bottom of the lake. If I go over, I'll bounce around like a fat goose shot in the rear and then I'll sink."

The trip south in the Chute River is very short but that's not to say it was easy. The river's current was directly against them. Unlike most rivers in the northeast which flow from north to south, the water flows from Lake George to Lake Champlain via the river. And, especially at this time of year, with all of the rain that has fallen in the region, Lake George is very full. The water current is very strong, causing conditions that have to be handled with great skill and knowledge of that specific waterway.

Henry watched the rowers put their back into the oars and the helmsman struggle to maintain the tiller. He eventually called for help from one of the men stabilizing the cannon. The helmsman had to have a good feel for the water. Brute strength against the tiller could easily tip it and end a good plan. As a consequence the helmsman repeatedly cautioned his helper, "Easy, easy ..."

At last the first of many round trips was made by the men aboard the gondola. Henry got off as soon as the nose of the boat grounded at the landing and watched the men use the hoists to load the cannons onto the wagons. It was a short trip to the north landing of Lake George. There, as he had arranged the night before, was a flotilla of small, mostly flat-bottomed boats that would carry the cannons and men some thirty two miles to the southern most landing of the lake.

Henry reveled in delight as to how smoothly the operation had gone thus far. As he watched the cannons being unloaded from the wagons to the boats of the flotilla, William, Smitty, and Obie arrived on the wagon they bought in Saratoga Springs, with horses in tow. The two braves, who were mounted on their horses, pulled up next to him. The braves both greeted and said goodbye at the same time and rode off.

"Where are they going?" Henry asked.

"Benny gave them two assignments. They're going to scout ahead for any wandering British patrols or columns and they're going to continuously hunt, so we can have food for the men," answered his brother.

"I thought we got rid of this wagon. Why are you still using it?" Henry was puzzled.

"Benny wants Smitty and me to try and stay ahead of the boats. We'll have food and whatever equipment that might be needed ready."

"Road could be pretty muddy but I guess we do have to feed the men. I know Benny quoted somebody when he said an army moves on its stomach and who knows what equipment we may need. Best be prepared." Henry paused for a moment then added, "I'm glad Benny thought of these things. I just forget about stuff like that or, to be honest, they just don't ever even occur to me."

William was puzzled. "Why are you smiling?"

"Oh, just thinking. I knew he'd be a good officer." Then he realized the wagon had two horses hitched up to it.

William answered before Henry asked the question. "Smitty picked the two best he could find for your trip south."

"Why two?"

Obie answered that question. "Sir, one for you and one for me."

"Where are you going?"

"With you Sir."

"With me? Why? I don't need help negotiating for sleds and oxen. Or for that matter finding my way around."

"Right Sir, but I'm to stay with you. Benny asked me to."

"A chaperone? Now he's assigning a chaperone to me?"

"No Sir. I'm just keeping you company."

Henry's round, pudgy face turned red. All in all, he looked somewhat comical. Being very tall, and stout to the point of over weight, and having a round red face made him look ... well, comical is the moat appropriate description.

"Benny has overstepped his authority! I'll just not have it. I am hereby countermanding his order. Obie, you can go and tell him."

"Sorry Sir, I can't do that."

"But I just gave you an order!"

"Yes Sir, I heard. But see, here's the situation." Obie took a second to run his hand over his stubby brown beard, which either needed to be shaved off or properly groomed. "It's like this. You're talking army and I'm good at abiding with proper orders. But when Benny asks me to do something, now that's different. It will be done." He then looked very sternly and said the next words in an even sterner voice. "Now, Benny asked me to keep an eye on you and so help me God, I'm going to do what he asked."

Judging by the redness of Henry's face, William was certain he was going to explode and his perception wasn't too far off.

Henry looked at Obie, who kept that stern appearance on his face. Henry's look turned into a stare and just when everybody thought a rant of unprecedented degree was about to unfold, he calmly spoke.

"Fine. Just be sure to keep up with me and don't become excess baggage." He then turned and walked back to the boat loading.

The cannons were being laid onto the boats' decks. Henry was satisfied the task was being handled correctly by the community people as well as the troops from the fort and so he walked back to the wagon.

"We'd better get moving. It looks like we're going to get some snow and I'd rather travel in the mud," he said to Obie.

William spoke up. "Henry, be careful. This mud is about to turn to ice and I think it'll happen before the snow starts to fall."

"You're probably right. But more importantly let's pray the lake doesn't freeze before the boat makes it down to the other end."

"Benny said he'll be in charge of the cannons. And you know him, one way or another he'll get them to the other side," William said, much to Henry's surprise. Henry wanted to argue, "But you just met the man and hardly know him," but he swiftly discarded the thought.

Henry and Obie mounted their horses.

"Oh, while you're praying, please add a couple of words for our good fortune, so that we may secure the sleds we need," Henry told his brother.

It wasn't until much later that afternoon that Benny arrived at the bridge landing with the second load of cannons. As soon as the first cannon was hoisted onto a wagon he jumped on board. He was anxious to see the boats Henry had readied but before he left he ordered the men manning the gondola to make another round trip. He, too, was worried about the apparent changing weather. Once Benny arrived at the landing he was surprised to see so many different kinds of boats. Among them was a scow that Benny thought was the best of the lot. The scow was actually a flat-bottomed boat that was also flat on top. It had a squared off front and the rear was equally square. Benny said its main function was to transport large amounts of cargo such as stone or sand.

"What in the world is that one called?" Benny asked one of the ex-prisoners who was getting another boat ready to be loaded.

"You being from Boston, I guess you don't get to see many

lake or river types of boats. They're not the kind you work around a bay on. Most of these don't have much of a keel and they're all flat bottomed. That one over there has a French name. It's called a Bateau. If you ever hunted for fur, you'd be familiar with it. The stern and bow being raked up like that, lets you get it close into the shoreline without going aground. The sides being flared out like that, means you could toss the animals you've trapped on board and, again, you don't need to run aground."

"Not the best craft to transport cannons I guess." Benny felt a surge of concern come over him.

"True. But it'll work a lot better than that Piroque over there." The man pointed to a canoe type of vessel that from the top didn't look like it had much of a bottom, although, the skimp and narrow bottom was also flat. "At least, on the scow we can load a couple of cannons and a load of mortar. We'll be lucky to balance one cannon in the Piroque."

The teams of men, some the owners of the crafts, worked at a quick pace using the hoists to move the cannons onto the vessels. Benny and the man watched for several minutes; then they turned to go back up to the road, when one of the Indian braves appeared on horseback. Benny looked at the Indian who simply nodded his head in a way that told Benny they needed to talk. Benny excused himself and walked up to the Indian.

"Do we have a problem?" he asked the native who was dressed from head to toe in fur.

With a simple nod of the head the Indian let Benny know that there was a serious problem. The brave dismounted, knelt down, and picked up a rock. Using a combination of broken English and while drawing in the wet, muddy bank of the lake, he described the pending danger. Benny listened and studied the drawing. It was easy to decipher one part. There was a war party of Indians—those who had sided with the British—in the vicinity. What Benny could not figure out was just how unfriendly they were to the Colonists.

Creative Ideas & Heroes

"Do they mean to fight us?" Benny asked the brave. Supplementing his words with the use of many hand and full body signs, Benny got the question across.

The brave answered with that universally understood sign: he shrugged his shoulders. The brave wasn't sure they had a hostile situation on their hands, yet he didn't want to risk not alerting Benny and the men. A surprise attack on the lake or even along the shore could devastate the mission. The mud drawing needed some verbalization, or at least hand signals to help Benny understand it. Benny dropped to one knee and studied the lines, circles and dots while the Indian made hand motions and facial expressions that brought meaning to the mud script. As Benny stood up, William and Smitty approached.

"I'd say you look like you're having a good time playing in the mud, but your face tells me it's not fun you're having," said William.

"You're right. I wouldn't call this fun." Before continuing Benny raised his hand and put it on the brave's shoulder. The Indian may not have understood all of the words Benny was about to say but the intent was to tell him, he did a good job and it was appreciated. "Thanks to our friend here, we may not be happier but we can sure make things a lot safer. Here, take a look." He knelt back down and using the drawing in the mud he explained to William and Smitty what was happening. "The Mohawks are gathering. But not in one place. They've set up two camps. One directly east of us, the other to our south. Apparently, they're a little confused by what we're doing. They must have thought that we would be traveling over land and they could hit us from both of these directions."

"With our backs to the water," added William.

"Right. But here's the interesting part. According to our brave here, they're just sitting."

"Probably waiting for more of them to arrive or maybe even some Red Coats to get here," Smitty said.

213

Benny had a puzzled look on his face. "Or, they're not sure of what to do. By this point their scouting parties must have reported back to the Chiefs that we're moving cannons. I'll bet the Chiefs are a bit confused."

"How so?" William voiced.

"It's just a guess on my part, but ..." He paused; wondering to himself how crazy was his idea. Then he decided to share it. "But the Indians are just like any other group of people who find themselves in the middle of two groups having a fight. They want to be on the side of the winners. And here's the confusion. The British recruited them but we, the Colonists, took the fort away from the Red Coats, and they didn't even put up a fight. And here we are moving what were the British cannons and the Indians are figuring, we're about to use them on the British."

"So you think they're confused," mumbled Smitty.

"I'd say so and I think we should keep them confused." Benny moved his foot through the mud script. "I'm convinced of it. But let's not take a gamble. William, would you ride back to the fort. Talk to the Major General. Tell him we could use more of his troops to protect our cargo. Explain the Indian situation to him.

Smitty, you organize a protection ring around this area. It may slow the loading and unloading process but take some men off that duty and use them to set up a defense.

And you my good friend ..." he pointed to the Indian and then to himself, "... and I are going to try and meet with the Mohawk Chiefs."

"How you gonna do it? Just stroll into their camp?" William said in a voice of disbelief.

Benny's answer wasn't very long. "Yep."

The Indian brave had a prearranged meeting place with his brother brave. Once they had rendezvoused with him, all three men made their way to where the Chiefs were camped. They made no attempt to conceal their movements and in short order; they were spotted by the advanced Indian guards and surrounded.

Creative Ideas & Heroes

One of the braves exchanged some words with the guards and that brought about some quick maneuvers, leading to their forced dismounting from their horses and the stripping of their weapons. The three of them were then forced to sit on the ground. Benny said his rear end had never felt so cold. He figured they must have sat for a couple of hours. In fact, it was after sitting for a long period of time, that he finally realized that he and his Indian companions were actually prisoners.

At last a brave rode up the path. He exchanged some words with the Indian guard and together they approached Benny and his companions. He spoke in English. Well, sort of. "I talk how you talk," he said.

"You speak English," Benny said with delight.

"Yes. I talk, you come."

So Benny and his two Indian companions mounted their horses and followed the *sort of* English-speaking Indian. They made their way to a trail that was easy to follow. It appeared to be a route that had seen a good deal of traffic. To Benny's surprise, through the trees he caught a glimpse of the camp. He surmised that the Mohawks had become very brazen. Then he realized, why not? Having the British as allies meant having the protection of the most powerful army in the world. The Mohawks must think the Colonists were crazy for going to war against the mightiest military they had ever seen. And, during the French and Indian War, they had seen column after column of Red Coats plow through their territory.

As they got closer to the camp Benny recognized the signs of a camp community. He could smell the campfires in the winter air, the meats roasting on open pits and soon he could see the smoke filtering through the woods. A little further down the path the woods opened to a large field. Benny was instantly struck by the size of the camp. It spread across the entire field, which was at least twice the size of our town. There were so many tents that he couldn't even count them. To the far side of the field was a body of

water, much bigger than a pond but not as large as Lake George or Lake Champlain. Many Indians were gathered at the shoreline. It was a hub of activity. There was water gathering, washing of pelts and even fishing on the other side. The cold weather didn't seem to hinder them.

They wound their way through the camp and came to a center area where a large number of men were seated on pelts, spread on the ground. Several fires for warmth were lit and attended to by squaws. Benny's companions were ushered off.

"Down," said the Indian who had come to get him.

Benny dismounted and with his hand he brushed off his coat. Then he noticed his pant legs had mud on them. He brushed them, too. For a moment he wished that he were able to make a better appearance. Even his tri-cornered hat had seen better days. And a shave ... how he wished he had shaved off his stubbly whiskers. Benny reflected a moment longer. He considered how an officer of the British Empire would look in this type of situation. No question about it, an officer would look regal. They always look regal. It's part of the mystique. A look that, in itself, has their foe feeling that they are in the presence of a formidable force. Funny, Benny thought, how regal people can be so intimidating.

Then Benny regained his mental composure. He straightened up, reminding himself he was not a British officer. He reminded himself that he really didn't think of himself as an officer of any army. He was just a Colonist. He was a farmer standing alongside of his fellow Colonists in a fight for justice, especially for farmers.

The escorting Indian took Benny by the arm and moved him toward a horseshoe-like gathering. "The Chiefs say you speak. I tell what you say."

"I thank you for your willingness to tell the Chief what I'm going to say," Benny graciously said. He was being purposely extra nice to the escort/interpreter. He knew, how this man's interpretation of his words or even his tone and posture, would add clear or distorted meaning to the Chiefs. He then turned to directly face the Chiefs. Before saying anything his eyes glanced around the assembled men. He started looking at the left side of the horseshoe, carefully searching each man's face. One, looked familiar somehow. Couldn't be, he thought. Then, as his eyes continued across the faces of each Chief, he recognized another Chief. He fought the urge to say, "Hello" or "I'm sure my father would love to see you," and he forced himself to keep a neutral, placid face. But as his eyes moved from left to right he recognized even more men and some even nodded to him, acknowledging their past acquaintance.

When Benny was sitting on the cold ground, waiting and hoping the Chiefs would let him speak, he mentally rehearsed what he would say. He began speaking in a strong voice but he spoke slowly. He wanted the interpreter to have as much time as necessary and hopefully he would pick words that would be the most positive.

"I am pleased and grateful that you the Chiefs of a great nation have allowed me to come before you. I am also pleased to see so many friends seated on the council. For years my father has done business with you and he considers each of you to be his friend. As you know, I have followed in my father's footsteps. And I, too, have had the honor of meeting many of you." This opening statement caused much turning of heads. Some of the Chiefs were surprised to hear that others knew this Colonist who stood before them. "Let me not take up your time. I would like to tell you why I have come." Then, without fancy talk, he cut right to the heart of the matter. "The Red Coats have asked you to partner with them. They have probably told you of the rewards you will receive should they win this conflict against their own people. And that is true. If they win, you will win." He stopped speaking and began to walk back and forth across the opening of the horseshoe. Once again, in the center of the opening, he turned to face the arch and walked straight into it. That brought him closer to the Chiefs. Then he continued in a deep and convincing tone. "But they will not win.

They cannot win! They may have many ships and many men but they are a long way from home. This great distance means it is not easy to keep control. The great pond between here and their far away home will prevent them from having the easy victory they claim will be theirs. Their men will long for their women, their children and their homes. They will march at us but they will not have their hearts in their duty. The Colonists will not march against them; instead, we will use the techniques you have taught us. From behind trees and rocks we will take our aim, then shoot, then disappear into the woods and brush."

Dead center, at the top of the semi circle, a Chief raised his hand. Benny saw him and stopped speaking. He waited as the Chief said something. Then the interpreter did his job. "Chief of all Mohawks says, you speak the truth when you say they have many men, many more than the Colonists. And many of the Colonists will not fight against their mother country. So, how can so few men win against so many?"

"It will not be easy but the Colonists are determined. It will not end until they are free from oppression."

Benny's use of the word oppression confused the interpreter. He watched him struggle as he tried to explain. "Think of it this way," Benny added. "The wolf prowls these woods. He is a fearsome animal that each man here respects as a beast that is vicious. His mere presence in the woods scares each of us. Yet, when the wolf stumbles into the bees' hive, the bees have no fear of him. They attack from all sides and yes, they die once they have delivered their stingers into him. They have enormous courage for their home has been invaded. The small group of bees will drive the fearful beast away." He stopped talking and when the interpreter finished, Benny still remained silent.

Another Chief, to the right side of the horseshoe raised his hand. Obviously, he was less powerful than the previous Chief, who sat in the center. As this Chief rose to speak, Benny realized he had met him before. Through the interpreter, the Chief said,

Creative Ideas & Heroes

"I know this man." That brought more than a few mumbles among the crowd but the Chief spoke over them. "More than him, I know his father. As a Chief I count more enemies among my acquaintances than friends. But this man's father is a friend. He has traded *wampum* for pelts with my people for years but more than that, when we needed help he was there and never asked for anything in return. When the fever struck my people, this man's father went to the white man's village and got us medicine. He also brought the white man's medicine man. In fact, I think his father may have used a long gun to urge the medicine man to come to our sickened camp."

"When the forests burned and animals were scarce and we were without food, his father gave us *wampum*. We then traded the *wampum* with some of you, my fellow Chiefs, so we could feed our people. For this man's father, I will offer him my support."

Another Chief stood and also offered his voice of support for Benny. And to Benny's surprise and delight, still other Chiefs offered their support.

The Chief of Chiefs stood and looked to the first Chief at the left side of the shoe. This Chief nodded in agreement even though no question was verbally asked. The next nodded and so on until the last Chief voted. "On this journey no harm will come to you and your Colonists," said the Chief of Chiefs. "But before you go we must speak of the two braves who accompanied you. Who gave them permission and why?"

"Chief Stillwater of Saratoga," Benny said, caution in his voice.

"Why? He knows only this council decides how each tribe will conduct affairs concerning the Red Coats and the Colonists."

"Chief ..." Benny took a long pause before continuing. "... I don't know the rules you as Chief have established. But I do know sadness when I see it. Chief Stillwater's people are sick, hungry and in a great deal of pain. They have been invaded by both the British soldiers and us Colonists. And nobody has treated them

fairly. Chief Stillwater's problems have mostly been caused by us white men."

Benny took another deep breath, "I didn't go to see Chief Stillwater alone. With me was Colonel Knox. He is the overall commander of this mission. Before we left the Chief, he agreed to help us and the Colonel made a promise. If this mission is a success, he will repay the Chief and his people by sending them a great deal of aid. Food, blankets, medicine and people to help administer the aid will be sent too. I tell you in truth, Chief Stillwater and his people will receive all of this help, even before the Colonial Army gets help. And, you may not know this but the Colonial Army is desperate for such supplies."

"So, if you ask me why Chief Stillwater has sent two of his braves to help us, I would say it's because he is desperate and we made him an offer of hope."

The Chief looked sad and his eyes fell to the ground. "You are wrong," he softly said. "The Colonists, the Red Coats, the French ... none of you did this to us. We did it to ourselves. We saw your ways, especially our young and we were anxious to follow them. But as our people moved more toward your ways, they never understood that they could never be a part of your people. No matter how hard they try, the whites and red man will not become one."

"But that's not the saddest part. You see, once our people tasted the ways of your people, they could not return to the old ways. Many of our people are stuck between two worlds and they don't fit into either of them."

The Chief was motionless as he stood with his head drooped down and his overall posture cried out for help. "My brother, Chief Stillwater did the right thing. He is seeking what's best for his people. His desperation is so great that he assigned you his two sons. He had other sons but they died." He raised his head and said sternly, "This council has decreed that no Chief will help either side unless we vote. But Chief Stillwater has seen much hardship, so much that he could not be with us now. I am asking the council to make an exception for him and his people." Again he looked to the first Chief, who nodded assent and all the others followed suit.

Before leaving the camp of the Chiefs, Benny was able to extend personal greetings to the Chiefs he had met in the past. All of them asked how Father was doing and Benny filled them in on Father's medical problems and his progress towards full recovery. The Chiefs all made Benny promise that on his next trip to the North Country he would take Father along. A friend like Father would always be missed when not there and always be welcomed back.

It was too late to travel so Benny was provided with a tent and some warm animal skins for the night. The next morning he and the two braves made their way back to the boat landing. Benny was delighted to find all the cannons and mortar had been loaded on the fleet of boats. Only the hoists remained to be dismantled and loaded, and that work was in progress. The Green Mountain Boys had formed a defensive parameter and Benny was truly thankful that it would not need to be put to use.

At the landing itself, Benny was anxiously greeted by William, with Smitty and the others also rushing to see him. "We've been terribly worried," said William. "I should never have let you go off by yourself. You should have taken the boys with you."

"Thanks for your concern William, but I really don't think it would have worked any other way. A show of force doesn't seem to impress or scare the Indians. When they encounter force, they just draw back and attack from another angle." He paused to emphasize his next point. "Anyway, talking seems to have done us some good, although I can't help but wonder why."

William wanted to know how Benny got the Indians to refrain from attacking and he wanted all of the details. So Benny told them what had happened but, as is his style, he gave a rather bland accounting of what took place, neglecting to mention his

own somewhat heroic but definitely brilliant role in his meeting with the Chiefs. He then abruptly excused himself, saying, he wanted to check on the boat carrying the one solid brass cannon.

The men left were still standing around talking about how fortunate they were that the Indians decided not to join in on the war when one of the braves happened to be walking by. William motioned for the brave to join them. Although reticent and extremely shy, the brave came forth. In sign language William asked if he had seen Benny's meeting with the Chief. The brave nodded yes but then he signed that it was not a meeting with the Chief.

The men were quite confused and were willing to drop the issue, however, Smitty wasn't satisfied. "I know Benny and if he said he talked to the Chief, then I'd wager my life on it."

William didn't like the awkwardness of the moment. He trusted Benny's word and didn't want anyone to think otherwise. Smitty not only trusted Benny's word, he wanted to prove it, so he motioned to the brave that he wanted to speak or know more details about this meeting between Benny and the Chief. With nothing but hand signals and everyone watching, Smitty and the brave carried on an extensive conversation. And, yes Benny didn't meet with one Chief, he met with many Chiefs, including the Chief of Chiefs of the whole Mohawk nation. The brave even drew out the horseshoe in the earth and showed where he was kept captive and how he could see the entire meeting. He even managed to convey that Benny was braver than any man he had ever met or known about in Indian folklore.

"Why are you still standing around?" Benny said as he approached from the launch area. "The weather is turning, and the lake will probably freeze overnight. All the cannons seem to be secure so let's get moving."

No one moved. Benny didn't understand the reason for their delay, and so .he made his way past some of the men and approached William and Smitty.

Creative Ideas & Heroes

"Benny, you didn't tell us the whole story," William said.

Benny at first had no idea what William was talking about. Then he saw the brave's face, which for once was obviously chagrined. The Indian intrinsically knew that Benny would not be pleased that the true tale of Benny's courageous meeting with all of the Chiefs had been told. Benny went to him and put his hand on the Indian's shoulder. This was Benny's gesture of thanks and the Indian understood.

Benny then turned to the rest of the men and said, "You know how the Indians tend to exaggerate. Let's not make anything of it."

William would not accept that degree of modesty. "If this mission succeeds, everyone will give credit to my brother and that's justified. But a few of us in this war as well as history itself will know of one of its greatest heroes. Benny, I for one am honored to serve with you and to call you one of the most courageous heroes of this war of independence.

You see, that's what history does. It tells of such things as Alexander the Great and his conquests, the French invading the English Isles or the Pharaohs building the pyramids. But what it usually doesn't do is tell the stories of the individual people who struggled or sacrificed or even enjoyed the events that melded together to make history. This mission, to bring the cannons from the North Country to Boston, has an untold number of instances that, had they not occurred and been overcome, might have resulted in our country forever being ruled by the British, and therein lies the tale."

Chapter 15

More Heroes

Colonel Henry Knox and Obie were traveling south.
They had made their way along the eastern coastline of the lake to a small community at its southernmost point called Lake George — the destination for the fleet hauling the cannon.

No sooner had the men arrived when snow began to fall. This was no mere flurry. These flakes were small and they covered the ground, unlike earlier light snowfalls which had failed to accumulate. This was not like the heavy, wet, larger flakes that we often experience on the island. The lack of sea air allows the flakes to be dryer, so they don't compact as easily and can accumulate very fast.

The Lake George community is very small and upon arrival Henry began the task of securing sleds and the animals to draw them. Their first stop was the livery stable and there Henry learned two important lessons. When he inquired of the stable's owner about obtaining sleds, the man asked for what they were going to be used. Henry hesitated at first, but then realized, in a few hours there would be no secret about the cannons. He knew that word of their arrival would soon spread throughout the community like wildfire in a barn. "Cannons. We'll be transporting cannons,"

Henry told the man.

The stable man wasn't very tall and he was rather skinny but he had an abundance of hair on all parts of his exposed body. "We got one or two that might do. How far you going?"

He's being a little too inquisitive, Henry thought, but if he was going to get the sleds he had better answer. "To Boston and I'll be buying. Not asking to loan them. And depending on the quantity each sled can hold, we'll need between sixty and seventy of them."

From somewhere beneath the hairy face came the man's response. "Not going to get them here. And how were you planning on pulling these sleds?"

"Horses, of course." Henry thought the question rather was ridiculous.

"Might happen, if you wait 'til after the spring thaw dries up and the ground hardens," the stable man said. Henry gave a quick glance at Obie who merely shrugged his shoulders. "Between now and when the ground hardens, you'll need oxen. More sure-footed and steadier than horses. Also stronger and can pull the weight you're talking about."

So, Henry learned that he needed heavy-duty sleds and oxen instead of horses. Now, where could he get such sleds and the multitude of oxen needed? He posed the question to the stable man, since he seemed to know what he was talking about.

"Albany. It's the only area that has that many farms around it. That's where you'll get the oxen. The sleds ... well it would probably be easier to have them made rather than trying to find them."

Satisfied, but not happy with the answers, Henry was ready to head on to Albany. "We'll waste no time; we'll leave for Albany right away."

"I wouldn't do that 'til you see how the weather is in the morning. Never can tell how much snow we'll get, but this seems to have the makings of a big one."

More Heroes

"Time is of the utmost importance. We'll push on and get as far as we can. Hopefully we'll make it to an inn. If not, a campfire will have to do." Henry then pulled a packet of papers from his carry satchel. Benny had said that Henry kept a meticulous log in which he wrote each evening before retiring.

Henry rummaged through the log until he found what he was looking for. "Ah, here it is." He read aloud, "Judge Robert Harring. The General himself gave me the name and where to find his house. Right on the northern outskirt on the main road. Judge Harring is not only an enthusiastic supporter of the cause, he is also a good personal friend of the General. So, let's be on our way." He then turned to the stable man. "When the boats arrive please tell Sergeant Benny that we'll be back as soon as possible with the sleds and oxen."

"Be pleased to tell him but I really need to warn you. It's one long distance to Albany and the way that snow's blowin' you'd be a lot wiser and safer to hold up and stay outta harm's way."

That's the third lesson taught by the stable man, but unfortunately Henry wasn't ready to learn it. Obie suggested they should listen to the man and be reasonable, but Henry's answer was predictable. "If the snow is too frightening for you, then catch up to me tomorrow or stay with the boats when they arrive." With that, he mounted his horse and headed out of town on to the main road. Of course Obie was right behind him.

In early winter the periods of daylight are short. So, although it was mid afternoon, the combination of the setting sun and the heavy snow falling made for a very dark start to the trip. Then their situation went from bad to worse, as the stable man had predicted. The inches of snow began to deepen and the temperature dropped. The wind also picked up and at times swirled the snow about them so badly, that they had no idea which direction it was coming from. To complicate matters even further, they found it increasingly difficult to stay on the road. More than a few times they found that they had wandered off the road so badly that they

227

ran into the wood line. Then they had to turn and try to find the road again. At last, after a few hours and now in total darkness, Henry said that maybe they should stop for the night and make camp. The answer he received was disheartening.

"Sir, with all due respect, I'd say if we try to do that we'd never survive the night."

"Why is that?"

"No shelter and even using powder, we'd never get a fire started. Everything's too wet. And the kindling is soaked under the snow. Sir ..." Obie felt he had best lay out the facts as plain as possible ... "Sir, it's too far to go back and we can't stop. As I said, the cold would probably kill us. At the very least we'll lose toes, fingers and ears. We have no choice; we have to push on. Let's pray the horses can make it. The snow is getting pretty steep."

"I'm sorry I got you into this pickle Obie ... I should not have been so anxious to leave today." Henry said earnestly.

"Nothing to be sorry about Sir. You're a man with a cause and causes sometimes blind people. That's why Benny sent me with you. Now all I gotta do is save you and that should help to save your cause."

But this winter storm proved relentless. The flakes just kept coming and coming. They gathered in drifts and piled up everywhere. Where there wasn't a drift, they stacked up well above a tall man's knees. Where they accumulated, by winds into drifts, they were well above a man's head. In one way, however, Henry and Obie were fortunate, because it was so dark they could barely see. Had there been better light, which would have allowed them to see their surroundings, they surely would have given up.

Just when they thought their situation could not get any bleaker, it did. Almost simultaneously each of their horses stopped dead in their tracks, obviously exhausted. With the weight of the men on their backs and the depth of the snow, the horses simply could not move any further. Obie dismounted and gently patted his horse on its neck. "Looks like we'll be walking the rest of the way."

More Heroes

And so, with the horses trailing behind them, they began trekking through the snow. During this second part of the journey both men realized their moment of truth had arrived. Each man spoke to his maker, reflecting on his past deeds. The scale of justice was vividly before them, and they each emphasized the good deeds needed to tip the scale's balance in their favor. They also felt sorrow and regret for their unkind and bad deeds.

The first to fall face down into the snow was Henry. Even Obie, being a woodcutter by trade and therefore extremely muscular, had great difficulty getting the massive Colonel to his feet.

"Obie, I would find no fault if you wished to go on alone."

"I could say Benny gave me an assignment to complete, but truth is we're in this together now. Together we might have a chance at surviving. Alone probably means that our bodies will be frozen and not found until next spring."

"But not before the wolves have made a meal on our remains. So let's push on." Needless to say, there were many more falls and with each one it became more and more difficult for the men to pull themselves up once again.

Ironically, as the hours passed they were getting closer and closer to Albany, their destination. So close that they actually passed by several farms—places where shelter and warmth could have been secured. But it was so dark and the snow was so intense that they were unable to see or smell the smoke emanating from the farmhouse chimneys or see the candles' light flickering through the windows. Had the farmhouses been built closer to the road, Henry or Obie might have spotted one of them, but farmers tend to set their dwellings well back into the property. Privacy is always a concern and a road, no matter how lightly traveled, meant a violation of one's serenity, as well as one's security. As a consequence, Henry and Obie were like ships in a dense fog, sailing past the warning lighthouses and directly into danger.

It was Obie, whose next fall was to be his last. He neither lost his footing nor did he slip. The snow cushioned his downward

spiral as he lost consciousness.

Henry knew his companion was no longer struggling to regain control of his body—he had succumbed to the elements and the exhaustion of the struggle. Henry dropped to his knees and tugged at Obie's body until he could raise his head from the snow. He begged the Lord that Obie's life would be spared. He coaxed Obie to speak, "Open an eye; move your fingers." Then in an almost inaudible whisper, he pleaded "Show any a sign of life." But nothing came forth. Henry was not even sure if Obie was still breathing. He wanted to touch Obie's neck and check to see if his blood was still flowing, but when he tried to get his glove off he couldn't. His fingers wouldn't bend, so the one hand could not grasp the glove of the other hand. Then he realized, it wouldn't help even if he could get the glove off. His fingers were too frozen to sense anything, no less a pulse.

Getting to his feet and with all the strength his large frame could muster, Henry lifted Obie and heaved him over his shoulder. The first step was hard but those that followed were even harder. Then a strange metamorphous occurred. His progress was slow but soon he developed a rhythm to his walk. His mind seemed to go blank and nothing but sheer determination moved him forward. Even the horses stepped in single file behind him. Time had no meaning. Henry didn't even feel the motion of his legs and body. The weight he was carrying didn't exist. He must have walked in this way for hours. He even missed the first rays of sunlight. Daybreak, or what was left of the sun's beams as they pierced through the continuous fall of snow, melded into midday. He continued on in this fashion until miraculously the snow-formed clouds parted just long enough for Henry to see. And there it was, a house. Seeing this house, Henry snapped out of his trance, suddenly realizing he was carrying a substantial weight. His legs were about to buckle. He was exhausted, terribly cold and in a great deal of pain. Nearing the front steps of the house, he couldn't see anyone at all, but the sound of dogs barking was music to his ears. In fact, those were the last sounds he heard for quite a while, for, as he tried to lower Obie, his legs gave way and he, too, passed out.

Chapter 16

Miracles
&
Love

It was that moment between sleeping and awakening, that
usually occurs early in the morning, when the body is loving the
feeling of sheets and blankets and wants to cling to the comfort
of the bed. The brain, on the other hand, is yearning for a new
day and wants the eyes and other senses to come alive. It was a
moment such as this when Obie felt the object on his forehead. He
had been lying on his side in a state almost of euphoria, when he
was disrupted by what he was sure, was a gun placed against his
head. He was right.

"Mister, I'm a Colonist. Hands up! You're my prisoner."

With both eyes now wide open, Obie could see the gun. It
was carved out of wood. The location on his forehead, where the
barrel of the toy gun was placed, made his vision quite cockeyed.
Nevertheless, he found himself looking down the long barrel to
the blue eyes, red cheeks and floppy blond hair of a young boy.
"Hello," was the only word he could say before the toy gun was
whisked away by a woman. And it was done in such a manner that
it had to be the boy's mother.

"Now Tommy. I told you not to come in here and certainly,
you know better than to disturb our guest." She was trying to

whisper, but it didn't work. Obie looked up and was astonished by how much she looked like the little boy. Of course, her hair wasn't floppy but was rather neatly pulled back and tied into a knot at the back of her head, but it was the same golden yellow of the boy's.

When I first heard about Obie's looking at this young woman. or should I more correctly say, ogling at her, I was upset. But then I realized he is not married, and not even intended and certainly eligible. Not that it justifies looking at a married woman in that ... well, in that way. But then an explanation was offered that does excuse or at least make more acceptable that kind of behavior.

So Obie was lying there in bed, looking at this lovely young woman. She too, most probably, couldn't avoid seeing his facial expression. "My son. You know, I guess it's typical. At four years of age he is curious about everything. But he's usually pretty good, except when he's feeling mischievous."

Obie was not really listening, just looking, when it hit him that he had gone from sleeping to dreaming. That's it ... he must be dreaming, but then it dawned on him that he had completely forgotten his assignment. This realization not only jarred him but also jolted him out of bed. "The Colonel! I have to take care of the Colonel." There he stood, ranting about the Colonel, with nothing but his long skivvies on and in front of a woman. "Oh!" He dove back under the covers. "My clothes. Where are my clothes? And where is the Colonel? Is he all right?"

"For heaven's sake. Please stay under the covers. Yes, the Colonel is all right. He slept from yesterday afternoon 'til early this morning. You on the other hand, well ... we're waiting for the storm to subside, so Charles, our farm manager, can go and fetch the doctor."

"Thanks, but I don't need a doctor. I need to be with the Colonel, to see how he is."

"Soon enough you'll see your Colonel, but for now we need to be certain your feet and legs are working. I've been passing the bed warmer, with hot cinders in it, beneath your legs for hours, but the last time I looked they were still somewhat blue."

"You've been looking at my legs?"

"Of course," the woman said as calmly as possible "How else could I tell if they were getting better or needed to be cut off?"

Obie sat up and reached for his legs and feet. Yes, he could feel them. Well, maybe not his toes. Then again his feet weren't too sensitive either. His legs ... oh yes, he definitely could feel his legs. "Yep, everything's just fine," he said after all his probing. He then looked about, "Would you know where my clothes went to?"

"Yes, I have them on the rack drying in front of the fireplace. They were pretty wet and frozen stiff, you know."

"I'm sure they'll be good enough."

"As I say, not until they are dry," she said cutting him off and letting him know that she was making the rules. "And what, may I ask is the name Obie short for?" she said changing the subject.

"It's not my real name. When the Hawkins family adopted me, they didn't like my given name, Edward. They said they had a relative named Edward and they detested him. Funny how people can get to like a name if they like a person and despise it if they don't. So they renamed me, Obedia, and that became Obie for short."

"Sounds comical but ..." Her smile softened. "If you say it enough, it has a nice ring to it."

She started to leave the room but then the master of the house and the Colonel walked in.

"Good to see you in an upright position," said Judge Harring.

Obie spotted Henry and nearly bounced out of the bed but then he recalled the last time he did that, and she was still in the room.

"Sit tight Obie," Henry said sternly.

"Sir, where are we and how did we get here and most importantly, how are you?"

"A miracle, nothing short of a miracle. That's what happened."

"But I don't remember getting here."

"Obie, if you were alone, you would have died. If I were alone, I would have died. We saved each other, and I will be eternally grateful to you. And, by the way, I plan to thank Benny too. He sent you to protect me and you did, and what's even more amazing, in fact another miracle, the Lord delivered us to the very house we were seeking. This is Judge Harring. And I see you've already met his daughter, Marion. She's the lady of the house and she's very much like Benny, not someone to argue with."

"Now young man," the Judge addressed Obie. "Your Colonel and I were about to retire to the study, so we can map a strategy for getting the sleds and oxen you'll need. So, if you'll excuse us, I'm sure Marion will attend to your needs."

As the Judge and the Colonel started to walk out of the room Marion became a bit patronizing. "Father, it would be wonderful if your strategy session didn't require too much rum."

"No. No. No indeed. Just enough to help clear the mind."

No sooner had they left the room when Marion turned to Obie. "His mind will be clear and then blank before supper. So let's get on with it. Up and out of bed and take those skivvies off. I can smell them from here and I only caught a quick glance but it seems to me, they could use some mending as well as a washing."

"Huh?" he said, turning beet red from mortification.

"Oh don't be so embarrassed. Get a sheet around you and get them off. Or if you'd be more comfortable, I'll step out and you can hand them out to me. Then you can come down to the kitchen for your bath. Our girl already has the hot water up."

Obie couldn't believe what he was hearing. "A bath! But it's not spring. Just because I didn't die from the snow doesn't mean I'm ready to die from a chill."

"There's not a grain of truth to that old wives' tale. Why I've read about countries where they go into a room that has stones in a fire, then they throw water on top. The room fills with water vapors and they stay in there filling their innards with the vapor until they can't take it anymore. Then they run outside and roll around in the snow."

"Then do they die?" Obie asked with a disbelieving look.

"Well, you're taking a bath. If you die, I'll apologize. So you don't think I'm handing out medicine without trying it myself, you should know that I take two baths a week and more in the summer."

"I'd venture to say, your husband doesn't take that many baths."

"Quite right."

"See! I knew it!" Obie felt a twinge of victory.

"He died," she said so sadly that Obie's victorious feeling quickly vanished.

"I'm sorry," he said softly.

"When he was alive he frequently took baths." She paused, regretting the conversation had taken this sort of turn. "And, no he didn't die from the chill. He got kicked by a mule. Just below the knee. Doctor said the leg wasn't broken, just swollen. The next day he died."

"That's terrible," Obie commiserated.

"It's okay. I only regret one thing, he died before our son was born." She paused a moment to reflect, "Now, you are going to get out of those skivvies or else ..." she said abruptly changing the topic.

In a move that was completely out of character for Obie, he started to get up. "Well, if those are my options then I think I'd like to check out the or else. So ..."

"Oh no! I didn't mean it that way." She could hardly speak, then blushed and bolted for the door.

"I figured as much."

After a bath, some clean and mended clothes and a hot tea with rum, Obie was ready to join Henry and the Judge. Henry reviewed the strategy he and the Judge had come up with. The next day was Sunday and with some good fortune, the snow would stop and the farmers as well as the craftsmen would be in church. The Judge would make a plea and hopefully a number of sleds and oxen, along with their owners to drive them, would become available. The Judge didn't think enough sleds would be on hand to carry all of the cannons and mortar, so some sleds would have to be quickly constructed. Henry would lead the available teams north to Lake George and Obie would wait for the newly constructed sleds to be ready, then he would lead those north. The barn on the Judge's homestead would be used to construct the sleds and also serve as a staging area.

As they were reviewing the plan, a large black man knocked and entered the room. "Snow's let up," he said, walking to the fireplace and warming his hands. His hands were in direct proportion to his enormous build. The Judge introduced Obie to Charles. "How soon do you think you'll be able to go?" the Judge asked Charles.

Despite his size Charles was surprisingly soft spoken. "I'm about ready and if the sawmill isn't open, I'll go to the miller's house. Considering how much money he's about to make, I don't think he'll mind being disturbed."

"Good," the Judge said. "But try to get back before dark. I don't want to be worrying about you all night."

After Charles left, Obie felt free to speak.

"Judge, that's a mighty thoughtful way of speaking to a servant and a slave at that."

"Slave? I'll have you know, Charles is a free man," the Judge said indignantly. "And as far as a servant's status, he's not that either. He and I are friends. He lives here as a free-willed person and in exchange for room and board, he manages the house and farm, especially when I'm away in the city presiding at court. In addition, I pay him a small stipend."

"Sorry Sir. No offense intended. It's just that, anytime I've seen a Negro—not that I've seen that many—they've always been slaves." Obie's tone conveyed his apology.

Miracles & Love

"It's a crime and sin against humanity. It's also the main reason I'm putting effort into this revolution. If the revolution succeeds, we Colonists will be a free people. Once that happens I'm sure we will see the injustice of keeping other people as slaves. It may take time, but freedom for all mankind is essential, especially if we are to call ourselves civilized."

"Obie, I asked the same question earlier and I would make two points," said Henry "First and foremost, the Judge is a man who places his money behind his convictions. Marion said that when Charles was placed at auction, in Virginia, the Judge outbid all the others who wanted to buy him. Just look at the man's size. Any tobacco farmer would want him, especially for breeding purposes. A farm with a number of slaves the size of Charles would be very productive, and he has good temperament for a Negro, as well."

"I may have bought him, but that very day I gave him papers setting him free."

"Yes Judge, but not all men think like you. I'm specifically thinking about our southern colonies, where the very survival of the plantations depends on slavery. In those states it is not a matter of moral belief. Slavery down there is a commodity that underlies the entire financial stability of those colonies. That's a fact Judge. That's the world we live in," Henry said in a matter-of-fact tone.

"It may not happen in my generation, I grant you, or for several generations to come, but eventually man's conscience will outweigh his greed and all men will be set free. At least, I pray that is so."

Henry knew it was time to pursue another topic of conversation.

"Well Obie, you now see that our revolution has many aspects to it. So, those sleds ... you'll be in charge of the construction of them. Just make sure they can handle the weight of the cannons. Charles went to buy all the oak lumber you'll need to start. And we should know by tomorrow, just how many sleds we'll need.

While you're building the sleds, I'll start the first of what I suspect will be several round trips."

The Judge awkwardly cleared his throat. "About that being in charge stuff, with Marion around it would be refreshing to see somebody actually succeed in taking charge."

"I think I can handle that situation," Obie said, puffing out his chest.

Henry laughed. "We'll see about that when I get back. If your voice becomes high pitched, we'll know who took charge."

As I listened to the story, it became apparent to me that a very loving romance was in the making. So, at this point I will refrain from writing anymore on the subject.

Chapter 17

Preparations
&
Waiting

Contrary to current scientific opinion, Benny was
convinced that weather conditions just don't change direction
over one area. His belief was that weather moves from one place
to another. The fleet of boats he was commanding didn't meet with
any snow until they were more than halfway to the shoreline of the
community of Lake George. And yet, the community itself already
had quite an abundance of snow.

They had covered almost twenty miles before the tiny flakes
began to fall. Along with the snow, the winds kicked up from
all directions. Benny was grateful that Henry had negotiated
for the boat owners to command their own vessels. Somehow
they managed to stay fairly close together and yet they avoided
colliding.

The only mishap, which could have become a real catastrophe,
occurred when an unusually strong gust of wind blew the scow off
course. It glided onto a partially submerged boulder and got hung
up. This could have been a catastrophe, because the largest of the
cannons, the one made of brass, was aboard that vessel. To add
to the problem, many of the other vessels had been ahead of the
scow. The snow had become so dense that the crews never realized

that the scow was in trouble. Only the Bateau, the flat-bottomed, French styled boat that had a raked bow and sides, was behind the scow. In fact the Bateau almost ran into the scow from behind. If that had happened it would have pushed the scow further onto the rock.

Patrick was a crew member on the Bateau. At first he didn't see the problem, but then he and the others on the Bateau slowed their vessel and steered toward the cries for help. That's when they saw the situation. Patrick stood on the bow and tossed a line to the crew on the scow. The crew of the Bateau then rowed as hard as they could, while the scow's crew used their oars to shove off the boulder. The teamwork proved to be successful, but not without a price. As the scow came off the boulder, it tilted severely over on its side. The large brass cannon broke loose and quickly slid overboard. It sank in a flash, its only trace a whirlpool that spread across the water.

Without hesitation, Patrick grabbed a line, took off his boots and dove into the icy water. He surfaced once, filled his lungs with air and re-submerged. Moments later he resurfaced and handed the free end of the line to the men on the scow who immediately turned the boat around and headed for shore.

Patrick was hoisted back onto the Bateau. Some of the men quickly helped him get out of his soaking wet clothes and covered him up with coats offered by others. Both boats landed and the crews joined together to pull the cannon ashore. It was a miracle that the big cannon was able to be moved so smoothly. Luckily, it didn't get stuck on any rocks or submerged tree trunks. Because of the scow's front-end design, the crews were able to tip the boat and at the same time lift the cannon onto the deck. It took a great deal of coordination and manpower but they did it. Patrick made nothing of his courage but the men on this mission would never forget his deeds or him. Both crews gave him a rousing cheer and then hurried to catch up to the rest of the fleet.

Landing at the Lake George community brought another

Preparations & Waiting

cheer from the crews. Benny told me that he was never happier to get off a boat in his entire life. As quickly as possible the men assembled the hoists, and the first part of the cargo to be removed from the vessels was the munitions. There was some fear that the powder would get wet. As luck would have it, William and Smitty pulled up with the wagon just in time to help offload all the munitions. The men were so happy to see each other that they began to hug. Benny said the stableman, who was standing nearby, must have thought they were all crazy. After hoisting the cannons to shore, the men dragged the boats ashore. It wasn't a difficult task given how easily the boats slid over the snow. Knowing for sure that the lake would freeze over that night, the men turned over the smaller boats and covered the larger ones with old sails.

The men worked as fast as possible. Between the mounting snow and the stableman's offer to use the barn for shelter, they had plenty of motivation. Once their tasks were done and the men were warm and snug in the barn, they received yet another treat. The two braves had been very successful in their hunt that afternoon. Dinner, cooked over a smelter's pit, featured roasted Canadian goose. The stableman contributed a large fungus that he said grows only on the north side of trees. He guaranteed it was safe to eat. William and Smitty noticed the loose chickens running about the stable, so Smitty went on a search and collected several eggs. He cooked the eggs, mixing them together with some of the corn meal he had bought at the fort gate. Another item William had bought at the gate was a small barrel of rum that he kept under a tarp. To say the least, a feast was consumed and enjoyed by all.

Benny found it impossible to rest. He had become concerned when they arrived at the landing and the stableman told him of the Colonel's insistence on traveling through the snowstorm. Benny knew there was nothing he could do. He couldn't send men to find them; the conditions were too treacherous. The odds were greater that a rescue party, if it could catch up, would pass right by rather than meet up with them, since the visibility was so poor.

Benny appreciated the warmth of the barn and the comfort of the straw bedding but he was disturbed by his restlessness and couldn't sleep a wink. Finding it impossible to lie down any longer, he got up and walked quietly past the men. He realized his attempts to be quiet were almost laughable. The snoring and snorting emanating from the men would have drowned out a rousing tune played by our town's fife and drum boys group.

He made it to the smelter's pit only to find William placing kindling under a kettle of water. "Can't sleep?"

"No. But I figure a cup of tea might help. Shall I make it two cups?"

"You fussing over Henry and Obie too?"

"Yes." William stopped speaking to reflect. "You know, most people don't really understand Henry. I'm younger than he is but somehow, I've always been the one who has had to look out for him. He's very big and he has a commanding way of speaking, but what few people know, is that those attributes have often caused him great difficulty. Sometimes he gets an idea and he doesn't think it through all the way. And then he can also get mighty stubborn."

William stopped fiddling with the kindling and looked right at Benny. "That's why he needs people like you. He needs help with reasoning, to think ahead and to consider the unanticipated. Since you two have teamed up, I've seen you help him with those things and yet, you do it so he doesn't feel you're trying to upstage his authority." William put his head down. "I just wish you were here to talk him out of taking off in this storm."

Benny knew there were no truthful words that could be said that would relieve William's worries. In fact, he shared the same concerns and yet he tried to offer some assurance. "In time Henry will learn how to think about actions and consequences. He will surround himself with good advisers. For now, I'm also worried about his, as well as Obie's safety. But God has a way of taking care of little children and grown men who still have the heart of a child. I've been asking God to help both Henry and Obie and the more voices who ask for help, the more God tends to listen."

William looked up. "Then I'll raise up my voice and ask for a miracle to get them safely through this storm."

Days passed while Henry was waiting for the sleds to be delivered to Judge Harring's farm. Likewise, Benny was waiting for Henry to return to the lake. It had been too long since Henry and Obie had left the landing in the midst of the storm. Benny had no way of knowing where the two of them were or even if they were still alive.

While waiting, Benny wasted no time in organizing the men so that they could work to restore the cannons. Of prime concern was the amount of rust inside the barrels of the guns. There was an abundance of rust on the exterior of the weapons, but that wasn't necessarily problematic. That rust wouldn't impede a shot but the rust in the tube could cause a shot's direction to go astray. Also, a shot's distance could be drastically affected, and it could also cause a misfire or worse yet, it could cause the entire cannon to blow itself up.

Benny also examined the cannon balls or, the shots, as most of the men called them. They had been stored with the powder, so they were in good shape. What surprised Benny was the variety of shots. There was a good supply of the twelve pound solid shot. These were the balls the army would need most and they would be fired from the smaller cannons. The combination of the smaller cannons and the twelve pound solid shot meant that the army would have very good accuracy within a one mile distance.

There were also several other types of shots. The one that causes the most damage, and therefore is considered to be the most deadly, is the hollow ball. This shot is typically rigged with a fuse and filled with gunpowder which explodes after it lands. Just imagine the damage it can inflict if it lands on a ship or the roof of a building.

That one giant brass cannon they were transporting had the

same array of shots, but in addition, it had one particular kind of shot that was very different. It looked like it had two smaller cannon balls attached to each other by a three-inch bar. The way it works is that the entire contraption is wrapped in cloth and soaked in oil. Just before it's fired off, a flame is dropped down the barrel igniting the double spheres. Once fired and airborne, the shot spins. Its target is usually a boat's sail. If it hits the sail, it sets the entire mast and subsequently the rest of the ship on fire.

Benny marveled at the various forms of cannon balls. Well ... maybe marvel isn't quite the right word to use. In fact, he was in the midst of conflict within himself. Benny has always detested war and conflict between men. He believes war is extraordinarily uncivilized and represents man's greatest injustice against his fellow man. On the other hand he was intrigued by the ingenuity and creativity it took to conceive of the various kinds of cannon balls. It greatly troubled him, however, when he considered the havoc these weapons could wreak on living, breathing men.

Benny was completely focused on one of the shots when one of the Indians appeared next to him. The brave was so quiet, almost motionless, that Benny wasn't sure if he had just arrived or if he had been standing there for a long period of time. Although the two Indians were supposedly attached to the troop and should have been under the same supervision as the other men, in reality they were more like free spirits. They knew their duties and went about accomplishing them without anyone having direct command over them. Benny realized they had been missing for a long time and he had no idea where they had gone. He pointed to the Indian and then to himself. It was his way of asking the Indian if he wanted to talk to him. Indeed, that was precisely what the Indian wanted, so the two men left the others and walked out into the snow. As they did the Indian used hand motions, such as pointing to his legs while making a lot of noises, obviously words, which Benny did not understand. Benny caught one word, however, and put it together with the hand motions. "You mean you saw the

Preparations & Waiting

Colonel?"

The Indian understood Benny's meaning, and nodded an excited affirmation. Through further signing the brave indicated that the Colonel would arrive there in a couple of hours. Benny easily interpreted the rest of the signs, learning that the Colonel was traveling on a sled, being pulled by a great horned beast— obviously an oxen.

Relief and excitement commingled and swelled up in Benny as he rushed back to the landing area and told the men that were working on the cannons that the Colonel was safe and would be returning to them. He then sprinted for the barn to find William.

Upon hearing the news, William became overjoyed, but true to form, he didn't show it by jumping up and down or shouting in glee. Instead he lowered his head and said something inaudible, tears flowing down his cheeks. Using his sleeves to wipe away the flowing tears, he said a fervent "Thank God."

Benny grasped his shoulders and gave him a warm hug. "We're all brothers in this war. Some of us are more brotherly than others. I'm just relieved your brother is alive and well. And he'll be here pretty soon."

"How did you find out?"

"The two braves. They seem to understand our needs and then they go and do things we aren't even aware of. I guess they went out looking for them. Wait! Them? The braves didn't say anything about Obie." Benny went back to the landing area to find the Indian who had brought the news. No luck. The brave was gone again. Little choice remained but to wait for the Colonel, and hopefully Obie, to arrive.

As the old saying goes, when you're waiting for something to happen, time flows like molasses during a winter's freeze. Benny and William were joined by Patrick, Doc and Smitty as they sat near the pit fire. Soon the other men started to drift into the barn. They had finished working on the cannons and it was nearing mealtime. Two of the men came in carrying a round pole, about four feet long and three inches in diameter. Each man carried the pole from one of its ends. Hanging in the middle was a cauldron filled with venison stew, cooked over an outdoor fire for hours. The cauldron swung by its handle as it was brought into the stable, the aroma from the cauldron's contents spreading about the barn even before it was lifted and placed on the pit fire to keep warm. Biscuits were also on hand and as quick as a wink, the men lined up with their plates.

After working hard for the better part of the day, a good hot meal was more than welcome. It was so good that for a while there was very little talking. But then, a simple comment was made by one of the men that got everyone stirred up. "Nothing like good cooking from Massachusetts folks. Best cooks in the land."

"You're right. It is good cooking, but that's because we guys from New York cooked it!" said one of the former prisoners.

"Yeah, but our folks from Boston supervised and told you New Yorkers what to put into it."

"Don't get so high and mighty Mister Massachusetts. Remember, a couple of us are from Connecticut and if it wasn't for us, you might be in a hot pot and not supervising it."

"Bull! We're the Sons of Liberty and we don't need any of you from the other colonies to settle this matter with the King. We can do it ourselves."

Now Benny hadn't spoken up to this point but he really couldn't contain himself any longer. "Listen up," he interrupted. "This local bickering has got to stop. It can undo us faster than the Red Coats can. We've got to put aside the idea that the whole movement is about a colony or a bunch of colonies. It's time to think of ourselves as one people. I think the man from Virginia said it best: we've got to think of ourselves as Americans. We're Americans first and the colony in which you live is secondary."

"Well said and never were words more true!" beamed out a voice from behind him. It was Henry Knox.

Everyone jumped to his feet. They didn't greet Henry army

style, with a salute, and standing at attention. Instead, they let the joy of the moment take control and rushed to him, shaking his hand and patting him on the back. Their voices escalated with the joy they felt upon seeing him safe.

Benny had clasped Henry's hand, but the big fellow, being so pleased with his second in command, reached out and hugged ... well, more like squashed him.

"Where is Obie?" Benny asked when the roar settled down.

"Oh, he's fine," Henry quickly said. But then Henry saw Benny's look. In truth, when Benny is dissatisfied with something his face can't hide his feelings. Henry quickly dispatched the well-wisher and addressed Benny.

"At first I was angry that you had ordered someone to watch over me, but then he saved my life. Actually, since I can't testify as to my state of consciousness for long periods of time during that trip, I think he saved my life many times. Together, he and I lived through a miracle. I can't tell you how much I appreciate him and how grateful I am to you for insisting he accompany me."

"So where is he now? And, why isn't he at your side?"

"That's my doing. I knew I'd be traveling with several other men." Henry waved his hand about the barn at the men milling about, most of them with plates of food in their hands already. "So I gave him another assignment. I'm sorry if I countermanded your orders but it seemed like the logical thing to do."

"What's he doing?"

"Right now he's supervising the construction of our new sleds. I'm going to take the first load back to Albany in the morning, and depending on how many cannons we can fit onto these sleds, we'll know how many new ones to build." He looked straight into Benny's eyes. "And don't worry, I'm really safe now. Besides," he said in a whimsical voice, with a twinkle in his eye, "there's a certain young lady, the Judge's daughter, who has truly caught Obie's attention. I suspect, we might be hearing bells in the future — and I don't mean sleigh bells." Then Henry decided that a very important situation needed his attention. He had spotted his brother William standing by the smelting pit just staring at him, so Henry quickly broke off his conversation with Benny and went to embrace his brother.

The next morning all of the men were up and at work early. Even before dawn they were hoisting the newly cleaned and restored cannons onto the sleds. By the time Henry arrived at the landing Benny had seen to it that each sled had just the right number of cannons aboard. He had also made certain that the cannons were secured and well balanced.

"Am I ready to move out or should I say glide out?" Henry quipped.

"You're all set and while you're gone we'll get to work on the rest of the cannons."

"Good, because I'm hoping to make the next trip our last trip from here." Both men walked around, counting the remaining cannons and the carriages they were hoping to replicate. "I figure we'll need a total of thirty more sleds. Of course, that depends on how many cannons each of the newly designed sleds will hold. I sure hope Obie's working on them," he grinned, "though I'd understand if he got a bit distracted ..." Henry added with a laugh.

"Henry, I know Obie. Don't even have the slightest worry. He'll get the job done," Benny reassured him. Then, he too grinned. "But if she's as nice as you say, then he's probably working double time to catch up on work." Both men laughed but then Benny's face turned somber. "I have something else I'd like to discuss before you leave."

Henry's facial expression also changed. "That tone scares me. I hope you're not going to tell me that you found something wrong with the cannons and they won't fire off."

"No, no. Nothing like that. I just want to make a plea for our two Indian braves. Their job is done once we cross the Hudson, and I'd like to offer them and their tribe some help for all they did."

Preparations & Waiting

"I know what they've done. I even know about how they helped stop us from being attacked. William and I talked for most of the night. He really respects you and he told me in great detail what you and the two Indians did." Henry paused. "I am forever in debt to you," he continued solemnly. "I'm alive because of your foresight. We have the cannons because of your courage and bravery ..."

Benny tried to interrupt but Henry put up a hand, signaling he wanted to finish his statement, and that Benny should listen to him, no matter how embarrassed he was getting. "I know of no other man who would have walked into an Indian war council and lived to tell about it. Which of course, you didn't tell anyone you did. Okay, I'll embarrass you no more. Suffice to say, you are a true hero of this revolution and I'm sure one day you'll be a legend."

"Henry. Sir ... if I may, there will be many heroes and people turned to legends before this war is over. I didn't do anything heroic and as far as a legend goes, heck, the Indians wanted no part in this war. It was easy to talk them out of attacking. They're just trying to survive and hang onto what they have. They really don't want to be caught in the middle. And if there are any heroes, it's those two braves. They knew that the penalty for helping us would be death. They took a life and death chance by doing something that was outlawed by the war council. The odds were that they were going to die for what they did."

"And you don't think your marching before the council of war was any less a death-seeking stunt?" Henry asked with raised eyebrows.

"Henry, please. This is not about me. It's about two braves and their people, their tribe, who are mostly sick, underfed and trodden down by settlers." Benny paused, and clasped his hands as though he were praying. "This is my plea ... the braves don't cross the river. That we knew from the start. They were to help up here in the North Country and they did a good job. So they'll be going back to the compound. I'd like to send Doc with them. Let Doc go and help that tribe. He can help with the sickness and then he can catch up to us on the mountain trail."

Henry nodded affirmatively, giving Benny the feeling that he was very much in favor of the idea. Then Benny presented the second part of his request.

"I'd also like Doc to drive the wagon to the Indian camp and leave it with them. We won't need it anymore. Once we hit the mountains, the wagon will be more trouble than help, so I'd like to give the tribe the wagon and the team of horses."

Henry was quiet but kept nodding yes. Benny took Henry's head nods to mean that he was in complete agreement.

"So, may I ask Doc to go to the compound?"

Henry kept nodding yes. "No," he said after a prolonged period.

"No!" Benny was stunned.

"That's correct. No!"

"But! I ..." Benny started to argue. Then he stopped himself. He understood the rules. This was the military. Argument has no place there. Command, obedience, orders, duty and honor were the only acceptable behaviors. Discouraged, Benny forced himself to stop speaking.

"No, Benny. I'm not going to authorize your request." Henry looked down and moved some snow into a mound with his boot. "That is, not without certain added provisions. I would like William to go with Doc. They've developed a really great working relationship and I'd like Will to learn more than just military life. Second ..." He was still looking down at his foot and shuffling the snow into a bigger mound. "I'd also like to have them stop at that general store in Saratoga and fill up the wagon with supplies for the tribe. And ..." he looked up at Benny, "I know I've said it before but if it weren't for those two braves, we'd have no mission right now and we'd be lucky to be alive. The only thing that saddens me is that I just don't know how to thank you enough."

Preparations & Waiting

"Colonel, you just did," Benny said gratefully.

"Mister Young. Mister Young." He must have fallen asleep as I was reading to him.

"Heard you the first time. What is it?"

"I thought you might have dozed off, I mean, your eyes being closed and all."

"No I was just closin' my eyes. At my age they get tired you know. But heard every word you read."

"Well, anyway, it might be a good time to stop for the day. I've been reading for a couple of hours and we only took those few minutes out for that great sandwich you made. Thanks again for that. For now, I think I'll head for home but I'll be back in the morning. Same time."

"I'll be waiting for you and I'll have the coffee ready."

"I'll probably stay a while longer tomorrow. Seems to me that I can probably finish it. Rachael writes in such a flowing way that she makes it easy to read."

"Just want you to know, I appreciate your readin' her diary to me. Learnin' a lot about my relatives."

Now that was the nicest thing Mr. Young has said to me. For sure I was coming back in the morning.

The next day, with coffee on a snack tray, a fire simmering, and Mr. Young as attentive as I had ever seen him, I once again began to read Rachael's diary.

Chapter 18

No Way to
Treat Guests

There is an old adage, "absence makes the heart grow fonder." I can't begin to describe how true those words are. Every day Benny was gone my heart yearned more and more to be near him. I would have slept in snowdrifts, ridden in the back of a manure wagon, or gone to the end of the earth if I could only be next to him. And, intuitively, I know he was experiencing the same pangs of separation. I knew that his mission duties might distract him but I also knew that once an emergent situation was over or a task he was working on was completed, he would once again think about our loving relationship.

The only time I was somewhat distracted from thinking about him happened early on a bitterly cold morning. It had been so cold the night before that all of us, including Mother and Father, had abandoned our bedrooms for the warm comfort by the fireplace. We moved the table away from the hearth and set our bedding right down on the floor. Father kept the fire well stacked with wood through out the night. He had the fire roaring so the crackling sounds were really quite loud, so loud that even the dog never heard the patrol of Red Coats nearing our house. It was only when we heard a startling loud rap on the door that we realized someone was outside. My youngest sister, Elizabeth opened the door and in marched an officer with two junior officers.

"Greetings on behalf of His Majesty," said the officer as he quickly passed by my sister and moved to the fireplace, stepping on the bedding that was on the floor. None of us returned the greeting.

"I'll get right to the point," he said as he whirled around to face us, and at the same time carefully scanned the room. "Quite a nice home. Of course you are aware of His Majesty's rules concerning the housing of our troops." He moved past Mother to one of the bedroom doors, opened the door and glanced inside. "Perfect," he said. Then he moved to the other bedroom door and after inspecting the room he uttered the same approving phase. "I had planned to have you house one of our officers, but since you apparently are not using these three rooms, we can station three of our officers here."

"I don't like sharing my bedroom." Father's tone was very stern.

"I'm not suggesting you share it. A British officer will need to use it by himself," the officer said in an equally stern tone. "You will continue to sleep here on the floor. Is that clear?"

"Oh, that would be fine," Mother responded quickly before Father could answer, placing her hand on his arm.

Father looked at Mother. He seemed to know she was trying to prevent him from speaking to save him from getting into trouble. The frown she gave him when their eyes met drove home the point. "Yeah ..." he said, but then thinking better of it he stopped speaking, and tilted his head without moving the rest of his body, until the officer came back into view. "Yeah, your officer can use it but just give him a warning. We do have a critter problem, so I hope he's not gonna be the type who gets scared."

"What in the world ..." Mother mumbled.

"What kind of critters?" asked the officer.

"Darned if I know. They only come out at night, so I've never

No Way to Treat Guests

seen 'em. But I do hear 'em crawling and slithering about. Haven't had one bite me ... yet. Though I keep myself covered, head to toe."

The officer took a moment to digest Father's warning. "Hear me clear," he said in a forthright manner. "You'll not be dreaming up stories to scare my men off. If you do, I'll consider it an act of treason and I'll have you shackled and stored in the bottom of a ship in the harbor, down in such a hell hole you'll be in the company of real critters. I've been assured that some are slimy, some are hairy, and some have never been observed. But all crave flesh, especially human flesh. Now, have I made myself clear?"

"Oh yes. Very clear. But Sir, you malign me in error. I only spoke so no one can say they weren't warned."

"Then let us consider each other warned," the officer said as he marched to the door and left with his men. Mother trailed behind them, obviously hoping to smooth things out with them.

After the troops vanished down the road toward Mattituck, Mother came back inside and we all gathered around the fireplace. A pall of deadly silence engulfed us, with Father pensive and Mother seething with anger. If my sisters and I could have gone someplace that wasn't freezing cold, we would have quickly vanished. We knew that Mother was going to erupt and that it was going to happen real soon. Within seconds our prediction came true.

Mother's face was beet red and it wasn't from the heat of the fireplace. The eruption came in the form of utterances flowing from her mouth. They resembled, if one could imagine, what Indian war cries would sound like. After a string of these strange and highly ear piercing cries, Mother calmed down enough to once again use words. Although, they weren't said in sentence structure, they sounded more like ranting than anything else. But we got the idea and while Mother would never curse she surely came close.

Even though Father was the object of her ranting, he stayed very calm, although, with that twinkle in his eyes and grin, it

seemed that his expression could be better described as one that was contemplating mischief.

Mother paid no attention to his look. She was simply seething. "I know you've had a long bout with the vibes and your thinking has been confused but ..." she said exhibiting a great amount of restraint. "But, my dear husband, what you did was calculated and not because of your illness. I could see it. You actually baited that officer. What's wrong with you? Do you want to end up in a ship's dungeon?"

Mother's logic seemed pretty solid to me. On the other hand, Father was reacting very strangely to the entire episode.

"When you chased after him, what did you say?"

"Well ..." She started with a huff. "What could I say? I told him the truth. I told him about your illness and rather poor ability to think like a normal person."

"My dear wife ..." Father stopped speaking for a second so that Mother could appreciate his sardonic use of the phrase. "You did well." He paused and this strange grin once again came over his face. "Now, let's set out the rest of the plan."

"The rest of the plan?" Mother was confused. For that matter, so were the rest of us.

"Right ..." he acted somewhat surprised. "What did you think I was doing? You see, that officer was convinced I was giving him a difficult time. But now, after you, my dear wife have talked to him, he's not so sure. He must be wondering if I'm just against the Crown or as daft as a bell clangor." His grin grew wider and with all due respect, at that moment I had to believe that his last description of himself was on target. But then the grin dissipated and he began to lay out his plan. Gosh, but it sounded crazy ... so crazy that it just might work.

When he finished detailing his plan, Mother stared at him. "It's so wonderful to have you back, full of mischief and as normal as ever. Oh, my dear husband, I do love you so."

Father's grin was back. "Well I can't tell if I'm still nuts or back to normal, either." He searched for Mother's hand. "I've always loved you. Never stopped and never will." As proper as ever he kissed her forehead. "Now! Let's go to work. We have a lot to do before those officers come back."

The rap on the door was so forceful it rattled the walls and startled us so that we nearly did jump out of our skins. Mother composed herself and answered the door. In strutted the brash officer and his two junior officers. I was surprised to see him but Mother was indeed very shocked. "Why are you here?" she said. "I thought you said three of your subordinates would be staying here?"

"My good lady, you almost sound as though you'd rather I not be here." He smiled and I swear it was an evil smile, "Am I not welcome here?" His inflection was laced with sarcasm.

Mother was always good at regaining her composure. "Oh, but my surprise is because I'm so pleased. It's a real honor to have you stay in our humble home. And ..."

She was interrupted ... no, make that rudely cut off by Father. He belched! It was one disgusting and totally impolite sound that started in the pit of his stomach and worked its way up his throat. He didn't even cover his mouth as the guttural roar came out.

"Excuse me, I meant to puke!" he said looking straight at the officer.

"Oh no! If you're going to start puking again, just go outside. On second thought, don't do that, it's much too cold out there. Just go stand in the corner and puke." Mother then turned to the officer and started to offer an apology, "I'm sorry about ..."

"No. No," the officer chimed in. "Considering from whence it came, it's quite all right. When I got to town, I spoke to a number of Loyalists, all of whom assured me that his bout with the vibes has left him ... shall I say, different."

"Nevertheless, I beg your patience and indulgence."

"Considering the circumstances, your request is easily granted."

"I thank you and now that we've gotten past a most awkward moment, won't you ..." Mother looked at the rest of us, "please join us for supper. Father, please take your seat at the head of the table."

Once everyone was seated, the officer said, "My, the table is so nicely set. And, am I presuming correctly that you young ladies helped with the table and other chores?" he said addressing us, the children of the house. I said yes and my sisters nodded in agreement. "And I'm also presuming that you're getting to that age — and each of you look so pretty — that many suitors have been knocking at the door?"

"Oh no, no Sir. I'm engaged to be married," I bluntly said.

Mother rolled her eyes and excused herself to get the food on the table. My sister, Sarah said she was missing a plate, so she too got up.

"So, may I ask, who the lucky young man might be?"

"My brother."

"No, I meant, who are you marrying?"

"She's marrying her brother. You got something wrong with your hearing?" Father asked truculently.

"Hmmm. Guess not," the officer said in a subdued tone.

Simultaneously, Mother and my sister returned to the table with a pot of stew. "Look at all the mouse drippings on this plate. It must have been sitting on the shelf where they have a nest."

"Let me see that plate. No! They're not mice droppings, they're too big. They have to be rat, sh...er."

"Shit! She doesn't use such words, but its rat shit." Father looked closer, "You bet, rat shit for sure."

Mother then picked up a knife and scraped the drippings off the plate and into the pot. "I just hate letting things go to waste."

The officer was horrified and his two subordinates were beyond that stage.

"Oh, we forgot the bread," my other sister, Elizabeth said as she quickly got up and went to the cupboard. She lifted up a loaf

No Way to Treat Guests

of round bread that was blotched with green looking fungus. We watched her making a loud fuss over getting out a knife to cut the loaf of bread, Father unobtrusively stepped on a little sack that he had placed under the table. It contained dung that was loaded with "odor."

"Gotta make room for more food," he exclaimed as he moved his chair back, and put both hands to his lower stomach. The three other men were literally gasping for air and didn't notice Elizabeth grasp a string that was tied to several objects in the bedroom, behind the cupboard. As she retrieved the bread and turned to face the table she tugged on the string.

The sound coming from the bedroom was thunderous. And, as though on cue (which of course it was), Father jumped up and ran to get the fireplace poker.

"Don't move! I'll get the critter!" he yelled. With the poker in hand, Father ran to the bedroom door, opened it and lunged inside. Screeches and horrific wild animal sounds coming from behind the door were so loud and scary that all of us at the table cringed in fright.

The officer moved to get up but Mother reached over and grasped his arm.

"Please don't," she said, "Father has had to deal with them before. The fewer people in there mean they'll have fewer targets to attack."

"But madam, he may need help." The officer was adamant, but no sooner had he finished his sentence, when the noise stopped. Several suspense-filled moments passed as we remained motionless and silent. We waited and waited … and finally the bedroom door creaked open. It didn't creak open all the way, but only an inch … then another. It remained in this position for quite a while, building suspense, when, with a burst, the door bounced open all the way. It actually banged against the opposite wall and was quickly on its way to closing again when Father reached out and stopped its motion. With much flare and drama, he stepped into the doorway. He was saturated with sweat and blood and looked exhausted. With one hand he barely clung to the poker. Blood dripped from its downward pointed tip. In his other hand, he held up a long snake-like piece of flesh. It was several feet long and the blood from it had splattered all over Father's hands and arms. "I couldn't kill it but at least, this time, I got a piece of it. This is its tail."

"My good God!" exclaimed the officer. "If that's the tail, where's the rest of it?"

"Got away," Father said with disappointment in his voice. "But one day I'll kill it for sure."

One of the junior officers could no longer contain himself. He jumped up from the table and ran to the door of the bedroom. "But where did it go? I don't see the rest of its body."

"Well, that's what makes it so hard to kill. It can shrink to nothing and slither out through the thinnest crack. Then, in a flash, it can just grow to a giant size. This here is the tail. Go figure how big the body of this critter grew to." He waved what was supposedly the tail and made certain he splashed the officer with some blood. "Dang but I was sure I had it this time. Of course it won't take it any time to grow a new tail."

"Nonsense! Pure nonsense!" shouted the officer. "You expect us to believe all this nonsense?" he ranted. "And that can't be a tail. It looks like ... It looks like a sausage, that's missing the string. That's what it is!"

Father cut him off by throwing the thing to the floor. Then it happened. The "supposed" tail began to move about. It squirmed around the floor and actually vibrated. "When was the last time you saw a sausage do that?" shouted Father.

The junior officer, who had remained behind his chair, abruptly bolted for the door. Hot on his heels was the junior officer who had searched out the bedroom. The officer in charge started to order his men to stand their ground, but the tail became even more energized and started to flail about. It hit the officer's leg and

No Way to Treat Guests

that was enough for him. He, too, headed for the door, lunging through it. Then he stopped and reentered the house cursing. "I don't know how you did it, but I know this is all a hoax. But it doesn't matter. You're crazy people and I want to get as far away from you as possible. I don't want my men near you." He then pointed to me. "And you! Marrying your brother is really the sickest thing I've ever heard."

"But you ..." He pointed at Father. "You're really crazy. But I wouldn't stow you in the bulge of a ship because you'd drive the entire crew completely crazy. I hope never to see any of you again!" He left, slamming the door shut.

The blast of cold air had chilled the house and maybe that's why we stood frozen in place for so long. Then Mother began to laugh and we all knew that the moment had turned joyous. We had won. We had just scared off the British officers and we felt like we had scared off the entire empire.

"To think, some green mold smeared on bread, chicken blood, a skinned, headless eel and great acting scared them off," Mother continued to laugh.

And as for Father, it was so good to see him laugh again. Mother even suggested he try out for a Shakespearean part in one of the New York theaters. Even my sisters, Sarah and Elizabeth, were laughing and congratulating each other on a well-carried-out plan.

"How come you're not smiling?" Father said turning to me. "Aren't you happy we scared them off?"

It was true. I wasn't smiling. To me the issue was simple. At first I hesitated, but then I just had to share my feelings. "You see, a skinned eel for a tail, caraway seeds for mouse droppings, chicken blood and even moss ... it was all fake. But that officer thought the sickest part was my planned marriage to my brother." I was on the verge of tears.

"Pay him no attention. He just doesn't appreciate your idea of brotherly love." Father's own sentence struck him as funny and

263

he got really carried away by his own humor. Well, that did it! Mother started laughing again, my sisters were already rolling in laughter and soon we were all hysterical.

Chapter 19

The Path to Success

Just a couple of days had elapsed when the Colonel returned

to Lake George, with another batch of sleds and oxen, enough to handle the remaining cannons. The camp was filled with excitement as the men knew a giant step in the mission was drawing to a close. They had successfully retrieved the cannons from the fort and were now moving on to the next challenge of heading south and then east to cross the Hudson River. This could be the part of the mission that was most treacherous. The degree of danger largely depended on where the crossing would be attempted. There are locations along this mighty river where crossing would be totally foolhardy. This is especially true at its southernmost points where it merges with other rapidly moving bodies of water. Such confluences tend to generate rough waters and currents that are very hard to navigate, even under tranquil conditions. Given the exceptionally heavy load posed by the cannons, and the inherent balance problems of such a load, the odds of capsizing were greatly increased, especially in rough waters.

After much discussion with Benny, Henry had selected several potential sites for the launching point. The opposite side of the river had a similar landing area. The locations shared other favorable traits. At each location selected, the river was fairly narrow and at this time of year the currents weren't usually too rapid, which could help with a solid freeze. Also, obstacles were well noted and easily avoidable. For the most part those engaged in this mission were not seamen, so part of the excitement was due to a sense of relief that they were facing the last water obstacle that had to be negotiated. Once beyond the river they would have to deal with mountains and valleys, terrain they all had previously experienced.

Benny was the last officer to leave the camp. He went to extend his gratitude to the stable owner for all the help he had given to the men and the cause. "You know, by offering us your warm stable in a blizzard, you not only saved many of our lives, but you also helped boost our fledgling colonies' battle for freedom."

"Didn't know I was being a hero. Just saw men who needed shelter and heck ... got a big barn here, why not share it?" the stable owner said in short, matter-of-fact bursts, typical of a New Englander.

"All the same, you have our gratitude."

"Good luck and test the ice. Oh, and make sure you unhitch."

"What do you mean, unhitch?"

"The oxen. Unless you got a couple of feet of solid ice under you, they'll break right through. Ya know, they don't step lightly on ice. They pound down on it, probably thinking they'll get a better footing. But, without thick ice, they'll bust through and sink the cannons and probably also drown themselves. And you'd best be prepared to sit a while before trying to cross."

"Why? Why, should we sit and not get across as fast as possible?"

"The thaw."

"But, it's freezing now and it can't get much colder. What thaw?"

"See ya never been up here in winter. Usually, right after a

The Path to Success

big snow storm we get a time of thaw."

"For how long?"

"Hard to say. But I've seen that river flow pretty strong a couple of days after a good snow. Don't know why, but it happens. May not happen this time; but don't be surprised if it does."

As the last of the sleds pulled out, Benny mounted his horse and caught up to Henry who had moved on ahead with several of the oxen-drawn sleds. Benny shared the stable owner's advice.

"Tell me this is a joke. I'm so cold, even my rear end is frozen." Henry responded.

On their way south they once again stopped at the Judge's farm. Arriving at Judge Harring's house, Henry was both relieve and delighted to have all of his men together again.

The reunion of the Mattituck men folk was more than just a round of greetings. The men had been through a lot together and they had formed a bond that would last forever. Obie, having become accustomed to the area, ran off to the General Store and brought back a bottle of applejack. He handed it to Benny, Doc, Smitty and then it came back again to Obie. The barn, now a woodwork shop, was warm and served as a nice place to share stories and thoughts of home. Doc was the first to share his future plans, which included asking the Penny girl to marry him. She and Doc had gone all through school together and he confessed, every time he sees her he feels a romantic twinge. Yet he never overtly expressed his feeling to her. "See, it's like this ..., she's very pretty, with her dark eyes and long flowing brown hair and she's quite a perky gal, but there's a problem. You guys know her family. Saying they're prominent is an understatement and here I am, not much to really offer. Oh, I do a lot of healing and I think our neighbors appreciate what I do. For my services, I often receive sacks of corn and potatoes but ... heck ... I don't have many pennies tucked away."

"Pennies for the Penny girl!" Benny laughed as he continued, "You don't really think finances matter to her, do you?" He didn't

267

wait for an answer. "She's a fine Christian woman and I'd wager she'll even help with all of the doctoring you do."

All of the men from Mattituck who were in that barn knew her well and they shared their belief that she would make a wonderful wife. Benny then told Doc of the plan he and Knox developed: to have him and William help the Indians at Saratoga Springs. When Doc heard the assignment he readily accepted it.

As Henry predicted, Obie announced he would be returning to Albany after the mission was completed. He shyly admitted, that he, too, would be getting married. The Judge's daughter and her son would make a fine ready-made family. Both Doc and Obie were congratulated and wished many blessings.

"There's something I'd like to share," said Benny, "but before I do, let me just say, it's not as crazy as it sounds. I mean, we've given it a great deal of thought and there really isn't a blood problem and ..."

"Sounds like you've decided to become a vampire. What's with this talk of blood and all ...?" Doc said, drawing a laugh from the others.

"Okay. Here it is ... but mind you, this is not just a snap decision. We've really talked it out and ..."

"Benny!! For crying out loud! Tell us before you drive us crazy!" Obie shouted.

"Rachael and I are going to be married."

Talk about a long period of silence ... it seemed like an eternity to Benny. Finally, he couldn't take any more of their nail-biting silence and defiantly asked, "Well?"

"Well, what?" asked Doc.

"Well, isn't anyone going to tell me how crazy I am?"

"Benny, we've been friends for a long time, all of us, since we were kids." Obie paused while the others nodded in agreement. "So let me be the first to say congratulations and many blessings. But why would you think this comes as a surprise to any of us? We've known for many years that you and Rachael would someday marry."

The Path to Success

"Yeah. Why do you think none of us ever came by to court her? We always knew she was spoken for," Smitty added.

"If I think about it, it seems to me that we were just finishing the first grammar book in school, when we all figured it out," Doc chimed in. "Maybe you didn't notice, but we sure talked about how she looked at you."

"Yeah, and it wasn't very sister-like! More importantly, when's the wedding?" asked Smitty.

Benny was perplexed, in fact, completely stupefied. He was actually shocked that our friends had figured out how we felt about each other and already knew that we would ultimately get married.

"Rachael's at home planning the date and whatever."

"Great. We'll need a good party after this mission," Smitty said, lifting the bottle of applejack. "To you my best friend, I wish you much happiness in your marriage. And Benny, I'm sorry you didn't surprise us like you thought you would with your big news. We only have one question. What took you so long to decide?"

The applejack went down smoothly, the talk became a little more somber, the hours faded away and a red rooster hopped down from his roost to get ready to greet and announce a new day.

Henry Knox was so excited that they were finally going to cross the great Hudson River with all of the cannons that he couldn't sleep. He had tried several positions and had even gotten out of bed to tighten its supporting ropes, all to no avail. He was wide awake and while he didn't want to disturb the Judge's household by leaving his bedroom, and wandering down the stairs, he finally gave in and got dressed. He carried his boots and a newly acquired sword, hoping to make as little noise as possible. The creaking stairway, especially because of his weight, didn't cooperate. Each step grunted and sang out loud, so loud that everyone else in the house rose from their slumber.

To Henry's surprise, Benny was sitting in the kitchen, at the table, studying a map.

269

"I thought I was the only one who couldn't sleep. Are you excited about getting across the river, too?"

"To tell the truth, I'll be a happy soul when the last cannon gets to the other side."

"Have you figured out where it will be best to cross?"

"Last night Obie said you and the Judge decided on a spot called Half Moon Ferry. I haven't found it on the map, but I need to let Doc and William know where it is, so they can catch up to us."

"It may not be on that map. I hear tell the landing there is pretty small, but I suspect all the folks around here know where it is. They'll just have to ask someone for directions. Oh, be sure to tell them, once on the other side of the Hudson, we'll travel on the Old Post Road. Pretty much, it's the straightest route to Boston."

"What about the hills or even mountains?"

"Judge says there are some but unless we go way south, it's about the most level road going east. Cuts through a number of valleys. It'll take us eight or nine days to get to Boston. Of course, that's once we get to the other side of the river."

"That sure sounds good. And Henry ..." Benny became serious. "Please remember once we get the cannons to Boston, those of us from Mattituck will have done our job. We're heading home."

"Benny, that's what we agreed to but I'm asking you to reconsider. You'd have a great future in this army."

"Thanks, but I'd prefer spending the future at home. All I want to do is take care of my family and be a farmer."

"Okay, then let's get those cannons rolling ... I guess I mean sledding. Anyway, if you change your mind you're more than welcome to join us and I'm sure the General would agree to promote you to an even higher rank."

Bundled up for the cold, the two men stepped out of the back door and with lit lanterns in their hands, they headed for the barn. The element of surprise stopped Benny first. Then the same sensation struck Henry. They both realized that they were far too warm in their winter coats. As the stable owner in the town of Lake George had predicted, a thaw had set in.

"How damnably cruel ..." Henry said and added even more blasphemous. words to his exclamation.

Once in the barn, Benny went to saddle up the horses. He tried to be quiet, but it really wasn't necessary. Most of the men who had spent the night sleeping on hay bundles were already beginning to stir. Doc spotted Benny and rolled out of a hay bundle. "Great night of sleep. Nothing beats a hay bundle."

"Right now you look like half the bundle's stuck to you. Don't know how attractive that would look to that Penny gal I expect you'll be courtin'."

"I just hope some other guy doesn't get to her before I do."

"I could ask you why you didn't think to approach her when you were roaming around Mattituck. Doc, you're one of the most educated and well-spoken people I know. How could you not have approached her years ago?"

"Tongue tied when it comes to her, I suppose. But now, I'm determined to do it as soon as I get home. I mean ... you know, with the war and all."

"Doc, I've already had that conversation with Colonel Knox, and he agrees. After this mission is done we're both homeward bound. And speaking of that, I figure we'll be leaving Boston in about two weeks. We're taking the Old Post Road, probably out of Rensselaer, so you catch up to us when you're done caring for the Indians. I'm telling you the time frame because I know once you get involved with a patient; it's hard for you to pull away."

It was just prior to dawn when they left the barn. It was that time of day when the moon provided the last rays of its light and the sun was peeking up over the eastern horizon. The cloudless sky let enough light shine so that they could make their way to the water front. Henry was well ahead, in fact for most of the short trip, he was out of Benny's sight. As Benny made his way down the slope to the riverbank, he went straight past the ferry station, which was

closed for the season. He arrived at the riverbank when he saw that Henry had already dismounted and was walking around on the ice covered river. He was about two hundred feet from shore. Falling through the ice out there would have meant almost certain death. Benny hopped over the watery edge and started to walk towards Henry when he heard the first ominous cracking sound.

"It's giving way under my weight. Henry! Start back!"

Within moments the thicker ice started to give way. "Henry! This is crazy ... Damn ... You're going to break through ... Get back to shore!"

Well, of course it was too late. If Henry stood still, it would be bad enough, but he was so outraged at the mission's misfortunes of weather, that he was ranting, raving, cursing, and worst of all, stomping his feet. Benny could not believe his eyes. Henry was stomping his feet while standing on ice that was breaking up. In complete disregard for where he was, Henry was having a temper tantrum. Furiously, Henry stamped his foot down once more and that was one too many times. The ice gave way beneath him and down he went into the icy water.

Benny looked across and saw that the first time Henry dropped below the ice he plummeted straight down, right up to his neck. Then Henry bobbed up and on the second downward plunge he only went down to his waist. But then the river's current took control and swirled him in a circle, as he flared out his arms trying to grab onto the ice's surface.

Benny watched, in anguish, searching his brain for a way to help. At this point, even a few more steps out onto the fractured ice would have meant he, too, would break through and probably drown. With all of his might, Henry turned so that the current beneath the ice was to his back, allowing the front of his torso, instead of his back, to face the frozen ice surface. Although his legs were being dragged forward, at least his arms and upper body were at an angle that allowed him to try and pull himself out of the water.

The Path to Success

Benny knew he had to act immediately before Henry went under and drowned. He sprinted back to the shoreline and rummaged around for a long branch, but each one he tugged either broke or was too firmly attached to a tree. He could break one free, but that would take more time and time was what he didn't have. Finally he found a branch that was too long, too wide and too heavy, but given the circumstances, he figured, it would have to do. Once more on the ice, he was able to move it fairly easily. The ice was too fragile for Benny to stand on, so he more evenly distributed his weight by lying flat on his stomach. Tugging the limb, he crawled, squirmed, pulled with his hand and pushed with his feet until he got as close as he could to his commanding officer. He then twirled the big branch in an arc and the tip stopped right in front of its target.

"Thank God!" Henry shouted as he grasped the branch and started to pull himself out.

Henry was smart enough to lay as flat as he could and let Benny pull him to the shoreline and safety. Once he got him on shore, Benny knew Henry had to be half-frozen. He had to get him warm and it had to happen immediately. There was simply no time to waste. They couldn't head back to the Judge's house, because it would take too long. Benny grabbed the weakened Colonel by the arm and led and pulled him to the Ferry Station building. Stumbling up the porch steps, they approached the front door. It was padlocked but Benny didn't give the lock or the sturdiness of the door any consideration. He merely raised his leg and kicked the door near its handle. That first kick weakened the door lock and the second kick made the whole frame give way.

"Get yourself warm and dry your clothes. I'm heading back to the Judge's house. I want to head off the men from bringing the cannons here."

"Don't be in such a hurry. It'll freeze again, probably later today. Then we can try another crossover." Henry would not be deterred, even by the weather. Nor would he be flexible about his

decision.

"Henry, I'm just ..." Benny tried to share a new plan, but the Colonel wouldn't let him speak.

"No! No! No! The ice will be fine. We'll just be more careful."

"Colonel, being more careful means we have to change plans."

"I'll not hear of a delay. In fact, I have an idea that should solve the problem."

Benny refrained from speaking thinking that maybe the Colonel had come to the same conclusion — an alternate departure point, with less rapidly moving water and maybe a shallower crossing, could be found. Obviously, the river is shallower further north, so maybe they would have to travel north again, Benny thought

But Henry had another plan in mind. "Don't stop or slow the cannons from getting here. As soon as they arrive, have the men gather all of the buckets they can find. It's scientifically well known that ice makes ice." As Henry spoke his bulbous belly bounced and since he was wearing only his winter long johns, the gyrations were a humorous sight. "Yes! Yes! Yes! We shall take a misfortune of weather and turn it completely around." The Colonel was raising his voice and to emphasize his point he also raised his right hand, extending his index finger upward toward the shack's ceiling. The pose was an incredible sight. There he was, in his winter skivvies, his skinny legs supporting his huge frame, theatrically pointing his finger to the heavens.

Benny could no longer contain himself. He burst out laughing. At first, Henry was perplexed. He couldn't figure out what had caused this silly reaction Benny was displaying. Then, with his hand still raised high above his head, his eyes glanced down at his own torso or, at least those parts he could see. In fact, except for a mirror view, he hadn't seen any parts south of his stomach for years. This glance at himself allowed him to understand why

The Path to Success

Benny had broken into a fit of laughter. Still posing, he knew that he presented quite a funny image. Soon he joined Benny in laughter and together the men enjoyed a lighter moment.

And so, Benny carried out the orders he was given. As the men arrived with the oxen and cannon-laden sleds in tow, they scattered to nearby villages and farms to gather together as many buckets and pails as they could buy, borrow or be given. They then carried out their Colonel's instructions. Selecting a projected path across the river, they poured water into every crack they could find. They cautiously moved out onto the ice, lighter men in the lead. When the cracks didn't mend into solid ice, they poured more water into them. They continued this process for hours but, as early morning became midday, they came to realize their efforts were useless. Along with the day's progress of time, had come an increase in temperature. The warmer temperature, although not drastic, was enough to cause greater fractures in the ice and not as Henry had projected, a mending of the cracks.

But Henry deemed these to be surface fractures and he was convinced that the ice underneath was now strong enough to hold heavy weights, especially if the weight was moved quickly across the ice surface. Based on his conviction, a sled, holding a sixteen-pound shot cannon, weighing more than a ton, was brought to the river's edge. The ox was then released from the sled and several men stood behind the transporter, ready to exert the energy needed to glide it across the ice. On Henry's command they shoved off and the sled moved forward. As the men pushed, the sled picked up momentum. It looked like a successful crossing was well under way but the strength of the ice, where the water runs deep and the current moves rapidly was yet to be tested. That test came when the sled and men were nearing the midway point of the crossing, about the same distance from shore where Henry had almost drowned. Unfortunately, as with Henry's previous attempt, this try also failed. The ice cracked and heaved beneath the sled and it was only because of the quick reactions of the men, not to mention their bravery, that all was not lost. The sled tipped and the men grabbed onto the harness rigs. They righted it, but not before it lost its cargo to the river. The cannon slipped from its bindings and plunged through the cracked ice to the river bottom.

Dragging the sled, the men made a hasty retreat for the shoreline. However, despite their rush to the safety of land, they were cautious not to step into any of the so-called surface cracks. When they made it to shore, their companions gave them a warm welcome. Even the Colonel complimented them for a valiant attempt and their safe return. However, not everyone on the mission was there. Benny was notably missing and his absence got everyone's attention, especially the Colonel's. Midday turned to afternoon when Benny finally reentered the Half Moon Ferry Station. There, he found his commanding officer seated on a stool with his logbook perched on a lamp table. As was his normal activity, the Colonel was copiously writing in his log. He looked up and at first he smiled—a sign that Benny took to mean the Colonel was glad to see him but that clearly wasn't the case.

"It is against every army's regulations for any man to leave his duty station without permission. Are you aware of that regulation?" the Colonel barked out.

Benny was caught by surprise. He hadn't seen or been the focal point of Henry's regimental dogma before. He answered with as much military jargon as he could muster, "Yes Sir, I did leave without first asking permission but with good cause. May I share that cause with you, Sir?" Henry's anger wasn't about to vanish. He merely nodded his head.

"Sir, I was on a quest to find a safe means of crossing this river." There was still no response from the Colonel. "I've met with some local people, and I was even able to get a map."

"So?" Henry asked in a tone that implied, "Why would I care?"

"Sir. It's a map of where the Mohawk River meets the Hudson River."

The Path to Success

"Again, so what?"

"It's the spot where the Hudson is very shallow. The locals think we're crazy to try and cross here at Half Moon. They say we should go a bit north, right near the town of Troy. There's a spot called Sloss' Ferry. It's really on the Mohawk River. The shallowness of the spot means that there is no rapidly moving current. They say the ice is always stronger there. We should be able to cross safely."

"So ... now I care." The Colonel said, speaking slowly. Then he stood up and faced Benny. "Sometimes I let rules get in the way of good judgment. For my sake, thank heavens you have good judgment."

The next day the Colonel ordered his men to follow Benny's suggestion. At Sloss' Ferry, the river crossing took more time than anticipated, but it went without further incident. The problems of weather continued to plague the mission. The snow and slush turned into mud. It got so bad that the oxen could not pull the sleds. The men had to join the animals in the struggle. The men became beasts of burden. They pushed and tugged the sleds, not only up the slopes but also down the hills, as rocks and boulders became cogs not in wheels but of rails.

As they approached the border of New York and Massachusetts, they also began their ascent into the Berkshire Mountains. Henry knew that the road they were taking, the southern route, had far fewer steep mountains than either the middle or the northern passageways. Still, he wished he didn't have to deal with any mountains at all, but that would have meant going straight south until they approached the lower Connecticut tier. That approach would have consumed many more days of travel and once again, he reminded himself time was of the essence. Due east, over hills and mountains and down valleys was the only logical choice.

The pathway they were following was the most commonly used east-west route in the New England colonies. From its very

beginning at the New York border to its end in Boston, the route is an obstacle course. Not only is it grooved with ruts and holes, the size of craters, but it also is littered with rocks. Avalanches and landslides continuously poured debris, in the form of rocks, big and small, all over the road. Even rain washouts and snow melts deposited rocks and earth onto the road, so much so, that using the term roadway to describe it is ambiguous.

Travelers took to this byway on foot, horseback, wagon, stagecoach and every other type of transporter that could roll or be dragged along its surface. The heavy traffic meant that the path was a clearly visible roadway, with no trees or brush to hinder movement. But still the surface was marred with ruts and holes. Also, it's actually a one-lane road. When travelers approach each other from opposite directions, one party must find an area to pull off the road and yield to the other side. As a rule of thumb, travel along this route, especially in winter, is problematic, foolhardy, and especially exhausting. The men on the mission felt no exception to this rule. The Colonel, who was mainly being propelled forward by nervous energy, often felt his body yearning for a long winter's nap. His men never complained, but he knew if he were tired to the point of exhaustion, they had to be even more fatigued. After all, for most of the day he was on horseback, while his men were on foot, tugging, pulling and at times even restraining oxen and sleds.

With all of this in mind, with the knowledge that winter meant days with brief periods of light, Henry established a schedule, which stopped the mission's movement by mid afternoon. As that time approached, Henry would ride ahead to find a suitable area to pull the sleds off the road and make camp. Once the sleds arrived at the selected location, some of the men cared for the animals, others set up camp and still others prepared the evening meal.

After spending the day engaged in strenuous labor, then setting up camp, the men usually ate quickly and went straight off to sleep. On one such evening Henry decided to walk around the camp before retiring himself. Light rain was falling as he made his way around the bedrolls. Most of the campfires were well stacked with wood and men were scattered about them trying to keep warm. Almost all of the men were buried beneath their winter gear and the only snaps to attention and military greeting came from the sentries who were on duty. Then the Colonel came upon one person who was so busy with something that he hadn't noticed his commanding officer approaching. It was Benny; he was leaning back against a sled. Before him was a roaring fire. It gave him plenty of heat to ward off the damp drizzle and also provided light to write. Benny was startled by the approaching man, but then he realized it was Henry. Benny started to get up to properly greet the Colonel.

"Sit, sit, sit. In fact, if you don't mind, I'll join you," Henry said as he squatted next to Benny.

"Ah, the fire feels good. This drizzle and fog makes everything so damp, it just makes your bones ache." As Henry made himself more comfortable on the ground he glanced over and saw that Benny had written quite a bit on a piece of paper. "Hard to keep the paper dry. If you don't mind my asking, what are you writing?"

"A letter to my wife to be." Benny paused. He's a very private person but once he gets to know someone he tends to drop his guard, and that's something of a contradiction in his character. He can be rigid, very rigid, but once he knows and trusts someone, he'll share his deepest emotions. Such was the case on this particular night.

"I just haven't been diligent enough with Rachael. I mean, I haven't written as often as I should have," Benny told Henry.

"So, are you writing that to her?"

"Yes. And I'm trying to express to her that my love will never wane. And, yes, being in these mountains working, but being alone and away from her, does make me want to be home and with her. But, absence isn't why my love for her is so powerful. I would feel the same way if we were together on the front porch swing. It's an emotional feeling. A powerful emotional feeling. I love her with all

my heart, here, there or anywhere."

Henry was entranced with Benny's honesty.

"I've just learned a whole new aspect of your personality. You always present the image of a strong man who has convictions and no fear of standing up for those convictions. But I hadn't realized the depth of your emotions and I'm surprised by your willingness to talk about them. A lot of men hesitate to think about such emotions, and most men would never openly discuss them." He hesitated. "You know Benny, I think such an open display of honesty makes you even more of a man."

"I don't see how speaking about the things that influence your life can make you more or less of a man," Benny said, looking at the flickering flames as he spoke. "I know for sure that what's in my heart, sways the way I think, and the way I think is the way I speak."

"Well, I've never shared any part of my private life with the men I've worked with, either in business or here in the army. I have it in my head that if other men know about my personal life, they'll respect me a lot less."

"Henry, they may respect you more."

"I don't know about that. Hearing words like love ... well, that just doesn't sit right with a lot of men, especially men who do the work of war."

"Maybe so, but I don't see it. I think a moment like this could mean a difference between winning or losing the war. See, I believe honesty is the stuff that makes us human." Benny then decided to show the Colonel what he meant. "Are you married?"

"Sure am. About two years ago I married the nicest girl in all of Boston, Lucy Fluker. She's a good woman. It takes a lot of fortitude to put up with me. I mean, most husbands are by their wife's side. They may be farming or working in a town, but at least they're home. In my case, we weren't married but a wee amount of time when I took off to join the fight at Bunker Hill. I even left her when we were courting." Before going on, he turned to look at

The Path to Success

Benny's face. "Swear I did. Heard there was going to be a bit of a showdown right at the Boston waterfront. I didn't plan on getting involved, but once the shooting started, well ... I had no choice. We lost a few men that day. Good men, God rest their souls." He turned to look at the dancing flames. "Yeah, now they call that the Boston Massacre."

Benny stayed silent. Somehow, he knew that would encourage the Colonel to keep on talking, and it did.

"Yep, married Lucy in '74. Her parents never approved; they're strong Loyalists. They call me the enemy. They think I'm in uniform because I can't get a real job." Henry clenched a fist and brought it to his chest. "They know damn well that I owned a bookstore before joining up." He stopped to reflect. "It's true. I didn't pay a whole lot of attention to the business' finances. I did a lot of reading, almost, all of it on military stuff, mostly artillery. That's really why the General made me a Colonel of the Continental Regiment of Artillery." He stopped speaking for a moment to appreciate his own title. "Not bad for a kid who had to leave school at the age of twelve," Henry added with pride in his voice. "That wasn't my choice. My father died at sea. You know, he was a ship's captain. When he died in '59, I had to help support Mother and my brothers. I never thought things would turn in this direction." Then he abruptly stopped talking and faced Benny again. "Once I start talking I just don't know when to stop."

"Not true. But you made my point. Now that I know all of those things about you, I know your real human side, one that makes me want to protect you and guard you from any enemy that wants to hurt you. That's an advantage of men getting to know their fellow soldiers."

Henry got up off the ground and brushed off his uniform.

"I still have to think about that. Anyway, enjoy writing to your wife-to-be." He started to walk away; then stopped. "I haven't told many men my story, but I shared it with you. So you might as well know one more thing." He looked at the fire; then back at

Benny. "I write to my wife almost every night, and I always tell her I love her."

By the next morning, the drizzle that had soaked everything had stopped. It didn't turn to snow as the Colonel had hoped. It just stopped. And so, the men and oxen labored at moving the sleds through an even wetter and sloppier roadway. The road's wheel ruts were so deep that sometimes the sleds' rails didn't even touch the bottom. This caused the base of the sleds to get hung up on the roadway's center. Such hang-ups required even more effort and progress was made even slower.

Day after day passed in this way. As a consequence, many more days were added to the trip and Henry became more and more anxious. On the brighter side, the route they were on passed through a number of villages and towns, not that the road got any better, but in most cases, the townspeople turned out to see the many cannons heading for the army surrounding Boston. Word of the caravan usually got to the towns long before the men of the mission and their cannons arrived. To their delight the men were usually cheered as they made their way through the town.

Great Barrington was the first of the larger towns in their path. Although Benny had routinely assigned men to an advance patrol, with some to serve as rear sentries, the Colonel had ridden ahead to check out the town for himself. Once he was satisfied that it was safe he returned to the men.

"Look sharp! Look sharp! You're the men of this revolution. They call us Continentals. Be proud of it and look sharp!" he told his men.

Benny was well aware of the Colonel's concern about the towns they would be moving through. He just didn't like the Colonel's strategy for determining the safety of venturing into a town. The concern was simple. Throughout the region many towns had, so to speak, en mass, decided to align themselves with the King. They were Loyalists and you might say that some towns were completely occupied by these Loyalists. The Colonel

The Path to Success

and Benny, for that matter, weren't terribly concerned about running into a small British army patrol. Such a force would be easy for Benny's advanced units to spot, and they could marshal a considerable defense against a small British force. The cannons they were hauling could easily be activated. Such formidable weapons were not likely to be challenged, especially by a foot soldier patrol that might be wandering the mountains.

The real concern comes from the Loyalist residents. A foolhardy group of them might decide to make a stand for His Royal Majesty. Unlike the King's regular forces, the Loyalists wouldn't hesitate to use tactics such as sniper fire or the planting of a roadway explosive. In that regard, the Continental Loyalists and the Patriots weren't much different. From previous wars and skirmishes with the Indians, they had learned not to stand in rows, shoulder to shoulder, and exchange shots.

The Colonel could not take the chance that his men and their critical cargo would push their way into a trap. Riding alone into a town allowed him an opportunity to investigate the safety of the town. He would ride, sitting as erect as possible in his saddle, making himself a worthy target—a prize for the Loyalist sniper who could brag that he shot a Patriot officer, right in the middle of the road, easy as hitting a sitting duck. All the while, Henry knew the echoing sound of a shot would serve to warn Benny and the other men of the mission. And Henry didn't just pompously ride through the towns. His eyes and ears were perked up for signs of danger. He looked for subtle signs everywhere. Although he stuck out like a sore thumb, he considered what he was doing to be a good strategy.

Benny thought otherwise. He told the Colonel, his strategy was suicidal behavior and if it worked and he got himself killed, the entire mission would be in jeopardy. Colonel Knox paid no mind to Benny's concerns and town after town he promenaded his horse as though he were in a parade.

Doc and William caught up to the column just before it entered

Springfield. The Colonel and Benny happened to be together, discussing the weariness of the men and the slow progress they were making, when Doc and William rode into camp. There were lots of warm greetings and immediately after hugging his brother, Henry asked if he and Doc had seen any British troops moving in from the rear of the column. William assured Henry that there was absolutely no danger of being attacked from the rear. That news made Henry feel a little more comfortable and he told Benny that the rear sentries should be pulled into the main column to help move the sleds. The extra hands were certainly needed. Doc and Benny ended the evening by having supper together and talking. They were soon joined by Smitty, Patrick and Obie. The rain started again, so eating next to a roaring fire felt even better. Although, to be fair, Doc's description of his encounters in the Indian village did put a damper on the meal. Suffice to say, he described a whole village of people in dire need and at the end of his discourse, he added his intention to make the rehabilitation of that village his life's mission.

Before leaving Albany Colonel Knox had sent two of the former prisoners, who were now regulars in the army, ahead to the Continental Army camp near Boston. Their mission was to get word to the General that the cannon moving mission was progressing successfully. Of equal importance, replacements were an absolute necessity, so they were to give the General a sample of the wooden cannon carriages and mounts. Also, they were to supply the number of each type of cannon, so the General's men in charge of heavy weapons could set the new carriages in the locations where the cannons would be most effective. Once the cannons arrived in the area, the artillery division would take over placing them on location. Upon entering the town of Brookfield, the two men rejoined the mission forces. Colonel Knox was delighted to hear about their successful trip. He was even more delighted to receive a hand-delivered, sealed letter addressed to him written by the General. While this is not verbatim, the following is the gist of

The Path to Success

the General's message:

Dear Colonel Knox:

Work will begin immediately to construct the carriages. Many men in camp are former carpenters. Unless your sleds begin to fly like crows, all of the frames will be completed and in place before you arrive. With reference to the placement of the cannons, I wish you were present to oversee that task. You are a recognized expert in matters of artillery strategies. I will give much consideration to the target alignments.

Signed by General Washington
Commanding Officer of The Army of the Congress

The letter gave Henry even more incentive to push on. He exhorted his men to push and pull harder. To the men who handled the oxen he urged them to feed the animals more oats and less hay, reasoning that the oats would give the animals more energy so they could pull harder. It's hard to tell if Henry's idea worked. Generally speaking, when beasts of burden consume more oats, it's like giving more wine to men. A little helps them feel perky but a lot tends to make them drunk. And although a drunk may be stronger, self control becomes a big issue. Following orders, the oxen handlers did as requested. The end result was quicker movement and more hustle and bustle, but there were also frequent tipping of sleds, animals refusing to budge and in some instances, oxen becoming belligerent and trying to gouge their handlers. All of this added up to loss of time. Sleds had to be righted, cannons re-secured and animals had to be calmed down. In more than one case a belligerent and out of control drunk, had to be sidelined. All in all, the increased pressure tactics didn't work. Benny's only comment was that everyone should learn a lesson from the experience.

"We should strive not to work harder but smarter," he said. Funny how often that line was quoted.

As town after town came and went, Henry continued to do his sore thumb impression. He did, however, stop urging the men to look sharp as he returned to the column.

Something interesting began to happen in the towns they moved through, starting with the town of Worcester. When the men passed the village square, which usually had a church as its centerpiece, the men saw people praying on the church's front steps. As the column struggled forward the prayers seemed to get louder. Finally, Benny rode close enough to hear and when he returned he told the men what the townspeople were doing.

"They're praying for snow. They know, even a little bit of snow, would lighten our burden."

"You'd think God would be on our side in this fight, so why is He punishing us like this. A winter without snow in these mountains ... why, it's unheard of. So why is He punishing us?" one of the men asked. He got a lot of grunts of agreement from the other men.

"Careful now," Benny cautioned. "When God does things, He always has a reason. Besides, there have been hundreds of wars and the Bible doesn't always talk of God taking sides."

"But He is taking sides. He stopped it from snowing, didn't He? So that must mean He's siding up with the Red Coats."

"Maybe," Benny casually said as he looked over at the people praying at the church. "Then again, maybe this is the weather He had planned and we just happened to walk into it. See, maybe He decided to stop a flood from happening and therefore he saved many lives and whole villages. Point is ... we just don't know how God thinks or why He does the things He does. We just don't understand and probably never will understand Him. Maybe that's why we say, 'Thy will be done.'"

"So what are you suggesting?"

Benny chuckled. "That's simple. Do what the people at the

The Path to Success

church are doing. Pray. But don't ask for snow, because you may have your prayers answered and then some. I say, pray for help and let God figure out the best way to help." And so the men prayed for God's mercy. That night the temperature dropped and three inches of snow fell.

The column made its way through the towns of Shrewsbury, Marlborough and Framingham. The blessing of snow disappeared as they got to lower altitudes. Although it helped that they were on a declining slope, nonetheless, it once again became a struggle to keep the sleds moving forward.

Somehow, though, the struggle didn't seem to be as daunting as before. The knowledge that they were getting close to delivering the cannons bolstered their spirits. Henry was becoming more and more excited. When they reached the town of Waltham, Henry knew they were but a short distance to the procession's final town of Cambridge. He got so excited in fact, that he abandoned his normal procedure of returning to his troops and giving them the all clear sign to enter. Instead he rode straight on to Cambridge. There he was more than surprised and delighted by the awaiting crowd. People had come to the town from all over the region. They had come to see the many cannons that were on their way to set Boston free.

As Henry rode into town, people shouted at him, wanting to know how long it would be before the cannons would arrive. After Henry told them it would be several hours, he expected the crowd to disperse and head for more comfortable environs. To his surprise, people were not giving up their spots along the route. They weren't about to give up an opportunity to be among the first people to see the cannons enter their town. Bragging rights are important.

Their wait wasn't as long as the Colonel had predicted. The column's speed and progress was aided by both the desire of the men to reach the finish line and the fact that many of the men of Cambridge decided to help move the sleds forward. Within a

short time, the long train of sleds, carrying the precious cargo of cannons, could be seen just outside of the town. That's when the unofficial, but often heard, town's fife and drum band sounded a regal tune and marched out to greet the column. Henry had rejoined his men and led the caravan into the town. The music blared and the crowd roared. Colonel Henry Knox and his men were heroes.

When the shouting calmed down and the musicians took a break, Benny rode up next to Henry "Mission accomplished, Sir. Congratulations! Your vision has come true."

"It was a vision but it only came true because of you and the men. I would ..." Henry was interrupted by movement of men — more precisely, approaching troops, coming from the other end of town. The General had sent his artillery brigade to relieve the Colonel of the cannons. From here the brigade would take the cannons to their newly constructed carriages and designated locations. They were to be immediately deployed for action.

At the head of the brigade was a very young officer who approached Henry and saluted.

"Sir, the General sends his regards and congratulations. The General asked that you and your men rest. I am to relieve you and your men. He said to be sure to tell you, that you deserve a rest. However, you are to report to him at first light tomorrow."

After all of the toil, worry and anguish, the mission had ended with a brief but courteous message from the General. Henry should have felt overjoyed with the knowledge that he had masterminded and completed an incredible feat. He wasn't; in fact he became somewhat depressed. Henry couldn't explain it either but he knew he needed to go someplace to sulk. His only response to the young officer was a salute.

"I know an inn on the eastern outskirts of town. Care to join me for a couple of rounds of rum?" he asked Benny.

"Somehow the music and the cheers didn't do it for me either. But the problem is that our men may have the same feelings."

The Path to Success

"You make a valid point." Henry took a moment to think.

"This mission didn't cost half as much as we initially thought, mainly because our troops were both men and beasts of burden. We didn't need to hire many more animals. Yes indeed. The men are deserving. Have them all meet us at the Cambridge Arms. Dinner and drink will be provided. It's the best bargain the Continental Congress will ever get."

As the evening progressed the Colonel's sullen mood seemed to change. Good rum tends to help one's disposition, at least on a superficial basis. But, also Henry's wisdom prevailed and he didn't consume much anyway. He knew his brain needed to be sharp for the morning meeting.

Benny, too, did not drunk much. Not that he had an excuse. It just wasn't his nature to over indulge. Nonetheless, the evening was a wonderful treat. The food was hearty and delightful. As promised, the rum was excellent and the men really enjoyed Henry's spirited speech, mostly because the speech was very short, and the toast offered by Benny was equally brief and very meaningful.

Chapter 20

The Spy Business

As mentioned before, good rum, hearty food and a real

reason to celebrate always seems to lead to a memorable time. Only one person seemed not to be having a good time and it was Benny. He was looking at but not really considering the cup of rum that was before him on the bar top.

Henry came up from behind. "You're mighty quiet and all by yourself, Sergeant Benny. Rum's not working? Or perhaps, there's not enough of it?"

"No. I've had more than enough rum." Benny looked down at his half filled cup.

"I've gotten to know you and I can tell when something's on your mind. What's the problem?"

"It's probably not the best time to say this, but I'm confused. And, I've got to be honest. There really is something bothering me and it should be bothering you and the General as well."

"This sounds big. What have I missed? Let's hear it. Then I'll tell you if it's a good time to discuss it."

"Don't you think it's odd that the most powerful army in the world is sitting only a couple of miles from here and they let us drag those cannons right up to them and didn't do a thing about it? It's like, they're letting a firing squad set up and shoot at them, when they could have prevented it. They could have attacked us anywhere on the road and we would not have been able to stop them. And don't rationalize that we could have fired the cannons at them if they attacked. That's utter nonsense. We could never maneuver those things, at least not quickly enough, and because they were on sleds, we surely couldn't fire them accurately. So I ask again: Don't you think all of this is odd?"

It took a long time for Henry to consider the question. "Benny, you're right. I'm as puzzled as you. But who cares? We did it."

"Did we really do it? Did we drag the cannons all the way from the North Country to Boston, with every town having at least half of its people being Loyalist and none of them telling the Red Coats what was happening? I'm telling you, the British knew what we were doing from the second we left the fort, so why didn't they do something to stop us? Henry ... the pieces don't fit," Benny exclaimed.

"You're like a dog with a bone. Let it go! Just tell yourself we were successful." Henry put his arm around Benny's shoulders. "You did a great job. I'm proud of you. Now drink up and come back to the table."

Alone again, Benny reconsidered his drink, left it at the bar, and walked out of the pub. He knew what had to be done. It was still light outside and he decided to walk. For obvious reasons, he didn't want to ride or take his long gun. He figured he could walk to Boston Center before sunset. His biggest concern was getting past the road blocks. On foot he might be able to walk around them. He set a quick pace and didn't need directions. In Europe there is a saying, "All roads lead to Rome." In this area, all roads lead to Boston.

The first road block came into view. It was manned by what he figured to be Continental troops, since they didn't have on any specific uniforms or even have a flag hanging. To his amazement, there seemed to be a lot of people passing by the blockade. The

The Spy Business

people passing through weren't even being stopped for questioning. He decided to join the others and managed to walk with the crowd right past the guards. This was more than strange. and curiosity got the best of him.

"How come the guards just let us pass?" he asked a man walking near him. "I thought they were stopping people from getting in and out of the city. You know, like in a siege."

"They stopped us for the first couple of days, but then, a lot of us got really angry. We work or some of us have businesses in the city, and a lot of Colonists have relatives in town. We need to earn a living, or see our family, and this blockade could go on for a long time. Even with those cannons arriving, nothing will probably happen until next spring. So the guard and the make believe officers decided to pay us no attention. If shooting ever starts ... and most of us don't think it'll come to that, then we will probably be stopped again."

It seems not everybody took this "ruckus for a cause" to heart. Most thought it was going to go away. And to Benny's further amazement, the Red Coat blockade was even more lenient. In fact, it was practically nonexistent.

"And the Brits ... they're begging for people to come to the city," his walking companion offered. "They lost a lot of help because of all this war talk. And the British army is sure spoiled. They may be fighters but they sure don't like washing their own clothes or cooking for themselves. And that goes for the foot soldiers as well as the officers."

Benny made his way to Faneuil Hall and quickly spotted what he was looking for—the British Army Headquarters. It wasn't easy to miss, this fairly new mansion, overlooking the harbor with flags flying and sentries posted. Benny stood on a side street about a block away from the headquarters. For a while he watched a lot officers coming and going, most of the officers were driven up by horse-drawn carriages. Benny continued to watch for quite a while and as he did he contemplated how he might get his hands on a British uniform and enter the building. He also was considering what reasons he would give for being there once he got into the building. That's when he saw a large number of civilian types of people exiting the building from what must have been the servants' door. He made straight away for that servants' door and along with several other people walked up a short stairway. It was crowded and a lady at the top of the landing was directing people to their assigned posts. Most of the people were familiar with the routine and merely greeted the lady as they moved through various doorways to their respective jobs. When Benny got to the landing he was ready with his line. "I'm new but I'm a pretty good waiter," he told the lady.

"We surely need help, but new people get barn duty. That way ..." She pointed to a door at the back of the hallway. Benny moved according to her direction and started to walk down the hall.

"Say you!" he heard from behind. "You might be in luck. Not enough wait service has been showing up and tonight the General's staff is dining here."

"Thank you, I appreciate that." Benny made his way to the kitchen. "Thank you Lord, I know it had nothing to do with luck," he mumbled as he pushed open the door.

Benny found the uniform closet, put on a jacket, shirt and tie and made his way to the kitchen. There, on the table and counters, trays were loaded with glasses of drinks such as champagne, rum and bourbon. Food trays were neatly arranged with the British royalty and officers' favorite appetizers, French hors d'oeuvres. With a tray of beverages in hand Benny made his way to the parlor; it was truly a grand room, with a very high ceiling, crystal chandeliers and a gigantic fireplace that was roaring with flames.

The General's staff was larger than Benny had initially thought. The room was quite crowded, with one obvious deficit. There were no females. He knew that many of the officers had taken local young ladies for wives, but this was obviously an "officer's only" function. Benny's first tray of drinks was depleted

The Spy Business

in seconds. Along with other waiters, he brought out more drinks. As Benny circulated through the party, his ears were perked for bits of information that might help him understand the logic behind this side's war strategies. Soon his diligence paid off. Loose tongues began to wag, especially since the General hadn't arrived as yet.

The officers were apparently talking about General Howe, the Commander of all British troops in the colonies. "Hard to lead us and organize a war effort when you're flat on your back most of the time," one of the officers said sneeringly.

"You're just jealous of the peacock. He just spreads his feathers and attracts women. The two he's bedding now are real beauties. Shame they come from the wrong side of the canal in New York."

Benny had to move on or risk suspicion. As he circulated among the officers, he realized that a group of three men seemed to be more lucid and vocal about what was going on than anyone else at the function. With his back to the three men he approached another group. These men were speaking about the lack of snow and how much easier this winter had been on the ranks. But Benny was more interested in the gabby threesome. Because his back was to them he couldn't tell which of them was speaking. In part he heard, "... for weeks they were sitting ducks. Just one squadron could have wiped them out and we could have added a nice stock of cannons to our artillery. They were our guns anyway. Why he ..."

That discussion as well as all chatting was stopped by the stomping down of the caller's cane. He announced it was time for dinner and all were to enter the dining room.

Benny returned to the kitchen for his next assignment. He was to man a carving cart. This cart was on wheels and it was somewhat unique. Its top surface was made of metal, probably sterling silver, and underneath it was an oil-lit pan, which provided a flame to keep the top warm. The top was a serving tray that had

a host of roasts on it. Beef, ham, and wild fowl were among the offerings. Benny's job was to carve for the officers at table side. He was admonished to always cut portions that were larger, much larger, than requested. Because of the shorthanded kitchen staff the soup had not been served as yet. Benny was then told to place a tureen of soup on another cart and help with that serving first. He entered the dining room and heard General Howe giving a toast. Some of the toast remarks were humorous, at least the officers thought so, or were they laughing because it was the expected reaction? No matter, thought Benny.

One comment caught his attention.

"And, their so called General Washington—I say so called because, to his misfortune, he's never led men in a single military victory—his history shows that he was beaten in all seven battles he led during the French and Indian War." Howe went on with his toast, which was sounding to Benny much more like a speech. "But, to George's credit, here's a little known secret. He makes the best bourbon in the colonies. His still is mass producing and gentlemen, I tell you, a bottle of his bourbon and a fine damsel and you'd know what heaven is all about."

There was a little too much wine for some and certainly way too much for one of the threesome Benny had heard in the parlor. As the discussions grew louder the one individual became even louder.

"... if we wanted to and no cog on our side got in the way, we could kick them and the cannons back to the lake where they got them!" the man said much too loudly, although Benny couldn't figure out to whom he was speaking. The room became silent. The loudmouthed officer knew that he had just committed a major faux pas, but he had drunk too much alcohol to know that his mistake would probably end his military career, at least as an officer. The real problem was that he made the statement so loudly that even General Howe heard him. And the General is famous for never taking kindly to criticism from either the newsprint or

The Spy Business

his subordinates.

The General slowly rose to his feet and everyone in the room knew he was about to explode.

"So now I'm considered to be a cog. I'm stopping the wheels of the war effort. Is that it?!" he bellowed. The General didn't expect an answer and didn't get one. He lowered his voice. "Let me remind all of you of some military history — history that is based on good military strategy. Napoleon ravaged Europe but he and his army collapsed at Waterloo. Why? I'll tell you why. Because he fell for the bait. He saw a victory ahead and all he had to do was bring all of his forces together and charge forward. He never realized that he would be smashed from all sides at one time and he didn't leave any troops behind to guard his flanks or rear."

Before continuing Howe moved his chair back and started to walk behind the seated officers. "And we, much like what occurred at Waterloo, will do the same. Let General Washington gather all of his troops and have them in one place; then, we will destroy all of them in one major battle, leaving none behind to annoy us and disrespect the King again."

As he finished his sentence he moved behind the loud-speaking officer, and placed his hands on the man's shoulders. "So now to your next question. What do we do about the cannons? The answer is simple, we move. Yes, we move. You see, they still don't have all of their supporters together in one spot. There are many on the fringe. We want them to join up and gather together." His voice got more intense and stronger, "Yes! We want them to all join together, in one place ... Then we will swat them like an ant on a tabletop," said General Howe as he raised his hand and forcefully slammed it down on the officer's shoulder.

It was at this moment that one of the other waiters dropped a serving spoon and got everyone's attention. The General then realized that he was divulging information in front of civilians.

"You! All of you servants! Out! Get out!" he bellowed.

Benny left his assigned cart along with the other waiters, but

297

unlike the other servants he didn't stop. He walked through the kitchen, to the uniform closet, changed back into his own clothes, walked down the hall steps and headed straight for the outskirts of town. First he came to the British blockade and as with his entry to the town, nobody stopped him. Soon he came to the Continental blockade and to his surprise and amazement there he was stopped. The guards asked him several questions, including if he was a soldier, to which he responded that he had been but had completed his assignment and was therefore now a civilian again. They didn't believe him because the war had hardly begun. Based on this, it was not reasonable to think that someone had fulfilled their obligation already. Without further discussion, Benny was taken as a prisoner. He spent the rest of the night shackled around a tree with his hands behind him.

His protests and claims that he needed to see Colonel Knox right away were ignored. It wasn't until dawn, when the changing of the guard took place that Benny was unshackled from the tree and placed in leg irons. He was then marched to the main camp.

The march depleted his energy and he told himself that he didn't care if they were taking him before a court martial for further punishment. One of the guards told him, at the very least, he would be charged with desertion and depending on where he went in Boston, maybe treason. As Benny and his escorts entered the army's main camp he was paraded before many soldiers all of whom looked upon him as dirt. Amazing how the word traitor gets around. Benny tried to keep his head up, but the shackles and leg irons dragged his stature down. Then he saw Henry about to ride out of camp.

Henry heeled his horse and rode straight towards Benny.

"What in the world! Release this man!"

"But Sir, we caught him sneaking behind our lines."

"Colonel, I didn't sneak anywhere ... well at least not then. I walked right up to the guard blockade and told them who I was and that I needed to see you right away."

The Spy Business

The commotion caught the attention of General Washington, who had come out of his field tent to greet Henry. The General approached the group and recognizing Benny he said to him, "So, as I recall, the last time we met you questioned my wandering away from my post. It seems I now have an opportunity to ask you the same question."

Benny started to tell both men about his decision to venture into Boston and what he did there, when the General stopped him by raising his hand.

"Time for something hot to drink—in private. Besides, your father would never forgive me if I didn't take better care of you than this." He turned to lead the way to the tent but then stopped, and looked at Benny. "You must often be told that your resemblance to your father is striking."

For a moment Benny was confused. "Which father?" he mumbled in what he thought was below hearing level.

Washington heard Benny's quip and instantly said, "That's right. I guess I'm one of the few who happens to be fortunate to know both of your fathers. And yes, I was referring to your birth father and yes, Benny you very much resemble our senior statesman."

With that the topic was dropped and they returned to the business of war.

Benny shared what he had heard during his short career as a waiter in the enemy camp. Neither the Colonel nor the General could believe that Benny had the nerve to walk right into the Red Coat's headquarters and literally spy on General Howe. The information he presented would be key to Washington's planning. The General called for an orderly and asked him to see if Major Green had left for Philadelphia as yet. If not, the General asked that he report to the field tent. Within moments, Major Green requested permission to enter.

The General spoke first. "Glad to have caught you before you left. That correspondence I wrote to the Congress, the one

that recommends the establishment of a new post. Do you still have it?"

"It will not leave my pouch until it's delivered to Congress. Even if we are intercepted, it will stay in my pouch, except it and all the other documents would then be blacked out with a bottle of ink poured over them."

"Such precautions are necessary and I thank you for taking them. But I would like to add a recommendation to that correspondence."

The General took the document in hand and then asked the Major and the Colonel if he could have a few moments alone with Benny. It was a lengthy document and the General placed it on his field desk. He then wrote some additional comments in it. In particular, he added Benny's name — his birth name. When the General was satisfied with the document's contents, he turned to Benny. "I think you should read this. However, before you do, first understand one thing. This position is answerable only to Congress. No one else will have authority over the post. And since Congress has followed most of my recommendations, I see no reason why they would reject this one. Decide now, if you accept."

Benny was perplexed but he did as the General ordered. He read in silence and the General was gracious enough not to glare at Benny as he read. In fact the General went about examining other papers on his desk. The contents of the document Benny was reading were quite detailed. In fact it was a description or job description of a proposed governmental post, a most unusual position that really intrigued and at the same time puzzled Benny. Without going into all of the details, only because Benny felt he would be breeching a confidential communication, he did say that its intent was to establish a position to develop a system of international espionage, a position that the public would be unaware of and it was to be so secretive that only the members of Congress would know about the job and the person whom they appointed to fill it.

The document was neatly written, probably copied from Washington's notes by his secretary. Benny surmised this because at the very bottom, just above his signature Washington, in scribbled hand writing wrote, "It is with great confidence that I recommend Benny Tallock ..." And there it was. General Washington wrote Benny's birth name.

After reading the document Benny handed it back to the General saying, "Thank you for such a degree of confidence but I don't have the knowledge or skills this post would require. I'm a farmer; I love it and that's what I'll always be."

"We'll see."

Chapter 21

Homeward Bound

It was mid morning when Henry and Benny left the army's headquarters. They decided to ride out to Dorchester Heights, the steep hilly area that overlooked Boston and the harbor. The cannons had been strategically placed along this high vantage point. At one point they stopped their horses and sat motionless. Both men knew that the discussion Benny and the General had would always remain highly confidential and therefore would not even be brought up. It is the military way.

They decided to inspect the cannons. Henry liked what he was seeing. "Judging by where these first few are placed, I'd say the General has a good command of artillery usage."

"If my eye is aligning them right, it looks to me that that one and that one ..." Benny pointed to several cannons before continuing. "are taking dead aim at Faneuil Hall and Howe's headquarters. And those over there are targeting the ships in the harbor."

"Yes, yes, and from the other ridges the trajectories divide the city into quarters."

"So Colonel, are you at liberty to say when the bombardment will begin?" Henry thought for a long moment—so long that

Benny interrupted.

"Sir, sorry, that was an inappropriate question for me to ask. I was just hoping that somehow we could tell the people down there when we would start the bombing. I'd just like to see the people ... well, get out of harm's way."

"That's not a very good war strategy," Henry sternly said.

"I know but you also know my belief about war. It's unnecessary and a waste of lives."

"Good or bad, you have a lot of others agreeing with you. And Benny, let me share something with you in confidence. We may never see a shot fired. Our General may be the commander of all our military, but he has to answer to Congress. And they are so political that I sometimes wonder whose side they're on. Pack of talking fools, they are. Right now we could strike a blow that would damn well end this war. We shouldn't let Howe and his men just move away. We've got him in our sights. We've caught him with his britches down. It would take us less than a day to blow up all their ships in the harbor and nail down their ground forces. At the end of that day, they'd surrender for sure. I know what you heard at their headquarters, but I feel certain that we could cut him off from escape. But politics gets in the way. The Congress wants to wait. I tell you, the General's a better man than me. I'd just make like I never got the order to refrain and I would start bombing."

By the time the Colonel and Benny got back to camp, the word had gone out that General Howe had ordered an immediate evacuation of Boston. According to Howe's order, all troops and every Loyalist citizen who wished to leave would be provided with passage aboard one of the ships. At that time Henry had no idea but even his in-laws, loyal as ever to the Crown, would leave Boston and never see their daughter or their grandchildren again.

So it was over. The cannon mission had been successful beyond anyone's wildest imagination. The British troops and their leadership had gone into full retreat. The Patriots claimed their

Homeward Bound

first victory. Before he boarded an escape vessel, General Howe even sent a letter of congratulations to General Washington. And, always the gentleman, Washington held back his troops for an extra day, before marching in and claiming Boston for the Continental Congress. This stalling allowed the Loyalists enough time to gather their valuables and say goodbye to their friends and family who had aligned themselves with the Patriots.

Benny was happier than most of the other men that a potentially major conflict had been avoided. However, some of the other men were actually disappointed; indeed they were spoiling for war. They wanted revenge for the Minutemen who lost their lives, revenge for the Patriots who died at Lexington and Concord and revenge for the citizens who were gunned down during the Boston Massacre. Revenge, revenge, revenge ... which always begets more revenge.

For Benny, it was time to go home. He refused to even think about his discussion with General Washington. What was it anyway? It wasn't an offer. He couldn't make an offer. The way he wrote that document, even General Washington didn't have any authority or say in the job description. Besides, Benny thought, what a ridiculous idea for a position. He would be in charge of a bunch of people who ran around the colonies and other countries spying on other people and foreign governments. Talk about a suicide position. And to really complicate matters, Benny didn't even want the job. It was time to get married, raise children and live as a Continental and contented farmer.

When Benny rejoined the men, he found Obie anxious to head back to Albany. Obie said news of the British retreat would travel fast and the Judge's daughter wouldn't be tolerant of somebody who just lingered about.

"Nope," said Obie, "she would want him back there and he'd better be quick about getting there." Doc and Smitty were delighted to be going home, although, Doc said his visit would be just long enough to ask Penny to marry him, then he'd be heading

back to the Indian encampment.

Patrick said he'd like to ride with them to Mystic, Connecticut. He would then take the shoreline route to New Haven, while they went across the Sound.

"If I don't get back to law school, I'll probably fail for the term. How would I explain that to my father?"

"You mean he doesn't know that you left school to join the mission?" Benny was astonished.

"Of course not. He'd never give me permission to leave school … no matter what the cause. Besides, he's a devout Loyalist."

"If I had known …"

"Then I'm glad you didn't know. If you had known, then I may never have had the chance to serve my new country. And these colonies are my country."

"Patrick, don't get angry, but if something had gone wrong, what would I have said to your father?"

"I know what I would like to have had you say to him."

"What?"

"The same thing I would tell anyone. If I were to die for this cause, I would say that my only regret is that I had but one life to give to my country."

"Well, we're all thankful you didn't die but …" Doc smiled, "The war isn't over yet. By the way, I never did get your full name … I mean just in case."

"Nathan Hale. But my nickname is Patrick."

Benny had hoped to leave just after daybreak. With no snow on the ground and no refreshed horses to carry them, Benny figured it would take a couple of days to make it to Mystic. From there they would board a ferry and if good weather continued, it would take less than another day to arrive at Mattituck Harbor.

As with many plans, this one didn't go off on schedule. The next morning, just before departure, Henry showed up. At first he tried to persuade them to stay on with the artillery brigade. He offered the men everything from more comfortable tenting facilities

Homeward Bound

to promotions and raises. Of course, Henry stipulated, the latter two offerings would have to meet with the approval of the upper command. He finally realized the men believed that they had fulfilled their promised duty and no bribes would entice them to stay longer. He insisted on having them served a hearty breakfast and then sent them off with formal gratitude and ceremony.

The General couldn't be present but most of his headquarters' staff came to the sendoff. They made certain that everyone knew that thanks were extended on behalf of the General and the Continental Congress. On behalf of the others, Benny accepted the gratitude and expressed appreciation of Colonel Knox, citing him as an outstanding, dedicated officer and a visionary. "Colonel Henry Knox is a true hero of this war," said Benny, finishing his statement, and all of the men gave a roaring cheer.

The Colonel hugged each of the men, including Benny. Then he assured them that their trip south would be safe. Henry said that all reports indicated that British troops, right down to the Connecticut waterfront, had been ordered into Boston before the cannons arrived. Benny was relieved to hear Henry say that all the British troops were sailing north.

Benny headed the small group south on the Boston-Hartford Road. Traffic heading into Boston was so heavy that Benny led the way and the others followed in single file. They passed hundreds of wagons and carts and people on foot, all heading in the opposite direction. When the battle of Boston was imminent and the city itself could have been a battle ground, they had left the city, journeying to safer areas. Now, the returning Bostonians formed a lengthy column of refugees returning home.

"I'd say most of them were Patriots," Benny said to Doc, who was just behind him.

"Probably right but I don't think you'll see many Loyalists take to the roads. I'd guess most of them boarded those ships with the Red Coats and headed north. I'd also wager, no one will ever see this much traffic traveling into Boston again."

The Legend of Benny

Although the breakfast banquet was more than substantial and most of God's creatures could survive nicely on that much food for days, man's eating habits are set by the clock and not necessarily the need to exist. Therefore Benny's wishes to continue to travel were altered by cries of hunger. A light meal and good night's rest would make the morrow's trip easier to handle, Benny reasoned. The stable hand was backed up, because there were many wagons and carriages whose horses were first on line to receive care. The stable promised to care for their horses as soon as possible. The innkeeper, frantic and cranky from a long day's work of serving Boston-bound customers, asked for their patience, as the men scattered in pairs about the lobby.

While waiting, Benny looked around the interior of the inn. He couldn't help but feel that most inns came out of a mold. Most had a dining room located to one side, with a bar along with small tables usually located on the other side. Directly ahead would be the inn's registration desk. A stairway always led to the upstairs rooms on one side of the desk. On the other side of the desk there was a closed door that inevitably lead to the innkeeper's quarters. The restaurant was normally dimly lit with aromas of foods that were subdued by the noxious layers of tobacco smoke that hung from the ceiling. The noise level was high, mostly caused by the boisterous patrons at the bar, but also in part because of the low ceilings. Benny couldn't help but reflect that despite all these negative features, the atmosphere of most inns was very comforting and inviting. He was about to share his thoughts with Smitty when a British soldier suddenly stepped out of the bar area with a pistol in hand.

"Stand your ground!"

The men did as ordered and within seconds more Red Coats appeared in the doorway. It was then that Patrick, knowing they were about to become prisoners of war, displayed his youthful impulsiveness and swatted a vase off the entryway table, right at the lead Red Coat. After that, the only way I can describe what

Homeward Bound

happened is that "all hell broke out."

When the lead soldier with the pistol turned to face and presumably shoot Patrick, Doc lunged at the gun forcing the shot to strike one of the oncoming Red Coats in the leg. Usually people run from gunfire, but that didn't happen this time. Instead, patrons from the dining area poured into the little lobby. It was hard to figure out who was on whose side. The innkeeper grabbed Doc from behind, but Smitty changed that circumstance by using the butt of his long gun to alter the hotelier's head.

"Hey thanks. By the way, I think there's a table freed up for us now," Doc joked.

Benny swung his long gun at the troops in the doorway. That drove them back into the bar.

"Get out of here!" he yelled to his friends.

Before heading for the door, Smitty fired a shot into the bar. Those in the bar scrambled to get away from the doorway for fear more shots would be coming.

"Go! Go! Go!" Benny yelled.

Thank goodness the stablehand had not yet gotten to care for their horses. Doc got onto his horse and pulled Benny's along, while Smitty climbed aboard his and pulled Patrick's toward the inn's entrance.

Just to make sure that no one was foolhardy or brave enough to come out of the front door and chase after them, Doc lifted his long gun and let a volley fly. Long guns are not very accurate to begin with and trying to hit a door from a distance while galloping on a horse is nearly impossible. But the concept worked, the front door remained closed.

That however, was not to be the end of their encounter with the Red Coats. As they rounded the front of the inn and headed towards the long pathway to the road, they were shocked by what they saw: two lines of Red Coats, long guns raised and awaiting the order to fire. Patrick was in the lead and without hesitation he lashed at his horse and bolted down the path. It was split-

second thinking but Benny felt that Patrick had made an error. The Red Coats must have made their way out of the inn through the innkeeper's quarters. They were lined up parallel to the road, in two lines. After the first line fired they would kneel down so the second line could take aim and fire. They stood motionless with total concentration on the road before them. A rider moving along the road would have a volley of iron balls to dodge.

Benny felt surrender would be preferable to being shot like ducks in a row, but Patrick's quick movements stopped any opportunity to think. Benny had no choice. He, too, lashed at his horse's hindquarter and heeled the beast to move as fast as it could. Patrick once again did the unanticipated. He was riding straight down the pathway, about to cross in front of the motionless but ready to fire enemy, then suddenly he bolted off the path and rode directly to the side of the front-facing troops. He plowed into them while he kept lashing his horse. The three men rode at full speed, right past the crumbled Red Coat lines. Patrick had been temporarily slowed but he too was now moving away from what nearly amounted to a firing squad.

They were moving swiftly down the path when the Red Coats finally set off their volley of shots. Most whizzed by the four escaping Patriots, but two shots hit their marks.

Chapter 22

Revenge

Tragedy had struck our four men. Tragedy also struck

back home — a tragedy born out of revenge. That is the worst kind of tragedy, because it could have been avoided.

Mother was working at the hearth with my sisters and I was helping her with the cleaning. Later I was going to roast some root vegetables we had stored away for days like this. Our dog began barking. That's when I heard the shot. I opened the door and there was Mr. Rivers, pistol in hand, walking away from the barn. He was walking slowly and made no effort to hide the handgun. I called out his name but he never stopped walking toward his horse.

We heard Mother scream Father's name over and over again. Before getting to the barn we found Father. He was sitting on the ground, propped up against the corral's fence. Even from a distance, I knew he was dead. I rushed to him and dropped to my knees next to Mother. She was pleading for him to open his eyes but I could see the wound, a single shot to his chest. He was shot at close range. He must have died instantly.

I know I sound very analytical, but even now, I have to try hard not to let myself become prostrate with grief. If I let even a

little emotion seep into my thinking, I know I'll become frantic. Mother was so distraught that she never even noticed me get up from the ground and go into the barn to saddle up. I took the long gun from its rack and told my sisters to go and help Mother.

When I got to the Rivers' house, I tied up the horse, checked the load in the gun and made my way to the front door. I turned the doorknob and gradually nudged the door open with the gun. What I saw was so vivid and traumatic that I was at once mesmerized, revolted and sickened to the point of vomiting. I felt as if I were going to faint. I forced myself to regain control, especially over my bodily functions. Lowering the gun I walked all the way in. There at the kitchen table was Mrs. Rivers. Her face was lying flat on the table with her arms stretched out. Fluids, especially blood, was dripping from her mouth and nostrils and pooling on the table. An apothecary jar was lying empty on its side, on the table. Whatever poison she took must have killed her in a very painful way.

Mr. Rivers had obviously been sitting in a chair opposite his wife. He and the chair were no longer in an upright position. He, too, was dead. Like his wife, he, too, had committed suicide but his method was quicker and much more violent and probably less painful. He had shot himself through the temple. In truth, there was very little left of his head and face that could be recognized. I turned to leave and couldn't help but notice something about Mrs. Rivers' face. Despite the flow of blood from her lips and nostrils, she looked like a person at peace. She was always very pretty. Her form of suicide hadn't diminished her fine looks.

I needed to see someone who could help. How I wished Benny was here. He always seems to know how to handle a crisis. It wasn't until I got to the parsonage and was with Pastor Timothy and Grace that I collapsed from emotional exhaustion.

Chapter 23

Wounded

Benny and his companions didn't die, but for two of them
the little round iron balls did so much damage that their lives would never be the same. Benny was struck by the first ball. It entered the back of his right knee, went through the right side of it and exited next to the kneecap.

In Smitty's case, the ball entered his back on the right side. The shot entered just above the hip and lodged itself somewhere near his stomach.

Incredible as this may sound; neither man fell off his horse. In fact, while they couldn't keep up with Patrick, they did clip along at a strong pace. They made it to the roadway and turned south. With every stride his horse took, Benny wanted to scream, because the pain was so excruciating. On the other hand, Smitty felt no pain. He didn't even feel the wetness on his right side. Blood had spurted from his wound and flowed down past his waist. His pant legs were saturated and his boots were filling up fast. It was probably the loss of blood that numbed the pain and all the other feelings. Smitty had no way of knowing but the blood loss made him lightheaded and he was entering a very tranquil state. He tried to sit up tall in his saddle but soon he began to weave about.

313

Doc was in the rear of the group and was the first to see Smitty swaying. He moved quickly to Smitty's side and grabbed hold of the reins, stopping the horse. Likewise, Benny halted his horse but he had no control of his body and he slid from the saddle. Hitting the ground was so painful that his brain could no longer cope with the intensity and he thankfully passed out.

Doc lowered Smitty to the ground, while Patrick went to help Benny.

"We can't stay on the road. The Red Coats have to be right behind us."

"They were infantry. They won't be coming after us," Doc told him.

While Doc tended to Smitty, Patrick checked on Benny. He dropped to his knees and discovered that Benny's right leg was actually folded in an impossible position under his torso. It was gruesome and Patrick's stomach flipped at the sight.

"Doc, you need to see this."

"Okay. But first grab a piece of cloth from my medicine bag on my horse." Patrick did as requested and when Doc asked him to place the cloth over Smitty's wound and put pressure on it; he complied, but he kept his eyes closed.

Doc checked Benny's eyelids. They were flickering but he was still unconscious. Doc knew that he could never straighten out the leg if Benny were awake, the pain would be intolerable. Doc maneuvered both Benny's torso and his leg, struggling to pull the leg into a straight position.

"We've got to get off the road. We've been lucky so far ..." said Patrick letting go of the cloth.

"I'll work on Benny's leg. Best it's done while he's unconscious. You find us a safe area that's not too far from here." Luckily Patrick didn't need to go far. Even though both sides of the road were heavily wooded, Patrick had walked only a few paces when he spotted an animal path—not a clearing but one that could accommodate him and the horses. They decided to move Benny

Wounded

first. Doc had used tree twine and a couple of branches to splint the leg. They lifted Benny and draped him over a horse, left him in the clearing and then fetched Smitty. They planned to wait until dark to light a fire. No one would be on the road after dark. They covered their wounded and then Doc and Patrick sat and shared some dried beef strips that Patrick had tucked away in his saddlebag.

"Are they going to be all right?" Patrick asked Doc.

When Doc responded his voice was filled with emotion.

"I just don't know. If a fever sets in, it'll be a bad sign. Smitty lost a lot of blood. This in itself isn't that bad, from everything I've learned you have to blood-let a wound. It gets rid of all the bad blood. But too much can kill a person. Like everything else, there is a fine balance."

That's when they heard the troubling noise. It came from an area just opposite them, at the clearing's wood line.

"That wasn't from a four legged critter," Patrick said softly. He cocked his long gun. Doc had dropped and lost his gun when they escaped from the inn so he picked up a hardy branch from the woodpile they had gathered for the fire. Both men intensely studied the wood line. Then they heard another cracking sound but Patrick still didn't fire. Patrick aimed his long gun in the direction of the sound but suddenly he felt the barrel tip of a long gun jabbed into his back. Doc, too, felt a gun point in his back. He dropped the branch and Patrick knew that they had been tricked into an impossible situation. Self-defense or escape was impossible, and so Patrick lowered his long gun.

From the wood line two Indian braves appeared. Doc turned around only to find his sudden movement was treated with a hard jab of the gun. However, he did get his answer. They had been captured by Indians, a circumstance that Colonel Knox had warned them about. Doc realized that they should not have sat and chatted while eating their dry beef. They really should have stood guard.

Then more Indians came through the woods and Patrick and Doc were tied up. Their hands were secured behind their backs and then the Indian in charge of securing them went to check on Benny and Smitty.

"Hey! Those men are injured!" yelled Doc.

There was no response, but then another Indian went over and squatted between the two wounded men. He didn't touch either man but ran his hands slightly above their wounds.

Still another Indian entered from the woods.

"Get a look at this one," Patrick whispered to Doc.

Doc looked over at the Indian who was entering the area. Oddly enough he wore a hat and coat.

"He can't decide if he's Indian or if he wants to be one of us. Probably stole the hat and coat from some settler."

"He probably killed the settler first."

"Afraid to say, but we may be in for the same treatment."

Patrick didn't like that. "Let's not give them an easy chance at it. Let's make a run for it. Maybe one of us will have luck and get away."

"Not yet. Let's see what they're up to first."

"Okay, but let's not let chances go by or what they're up to may be slicing our necks."

The Indian who was squatting between Smitty and Benny said something to the Indian in the hat and coat. That, in turn, led to this oddly dressed man shouting something. Whatever he said had to be some pretty strong words because Indians moved in all directions. The gun wielders forced Patrick and Doc to the ground. They both realized there was no chance of escape anymore, at least for now.

Other Indians rummaged through the woods and came back with long skinny tree trunks, vines and long grasses. They quickly rigged together stretchers and carefully, very carefully moved Smitty onto one and Benny onto the other. The movement partially woke up both of the injured men. Once Smitty was

Wounded

placed on the soft grass bedding of the stretcher, he fortunately passed out again. He woke and the pain that set in was unbearable, causing him to cry out in anguish. To Doc and Patrick, the cries were heart wrenching. Even if they weren't prisoners Doc knew there was nothing that he could do. He had seen enough injured people to know that when they pass out the pain is subdued, but if they survive, they would eventually wake up to face pain beyond description.

Smitty's cries may have accelerated the Indians need to get back to camp with their captured prisoners, because in seconds the entire party was quickly moving through the woods. Doc had no idea how long they had traveled, but it became apparent the leader wanted to get to their destination before dark. They took no breaks and the paths they traveled were not much more than deer trails. The trail became thicker and thicker, then all at once it opened to a vast clearing, which housed an Indian village.

Darkness had just set in, so their visibility was quite obscured. Still, Doc could see that the village was thriving. Of course, the children came running to see the prisoners that had been taken by their war party. But beyond the immediate ruckus and attention they were drawing, he could see many huts with pelts hanging on sticklike contraptions around them. Pelts meant warm clothes, food and trade for other goods. Pelts also meant good nourishment and self-sufficiency for the Indians. Yes, he thought, this is a thriving community.

Doc and Patrick were delivered to an empty hut. Their hands were set free and within moments they were given a hot brew to drink. A little while later, several tree branches that served as skewers were brought to them. The skewers were loaded with venison. Doc tried to communicate with the Indian women who had delivered the food.

"Where are our friends?" he asked. The two squaws were very kind. They obviously didn't understand him but at least he received their smiles.

Patrick decided to try. "Where are they?" he asked loudly.

"Patrick, just because they don't understand our language, it doesn't mean they're deaf."

Patrick knew Doc was right and he was about to say so when the hut's apron opened. In came the Indian who dressed funny. In English that sometimes sounded backward and other times was missing key phases, he carried on a one-sided conversation. "It is right. My people are not ready to talk like you. Change will come. As always change comes. For now I teach the young. They learn your tongue best. Then someday all my people will talk to your people." He stopped speaking when Patrick interrupted and asked where the other two men were. "Come," was the Indian's only response.

Doc and Nat placed their food on woven mats and followed the Indian. They were led to another hut and upon entering they saw Benny and Smitty, once again lying next to each other. This time they were being attended to by an elderly woman and two younger women who appeared to be her assistants.

Upon seeing Benny, Doc moved past the Indian man and knelt on the ground next to his friend and leader. The elderly squaw smiled but continued to work. She lifted Benny's head up and pressed a bowl containing liquid to his lips.

"What is it?" asked Doc.

"Grasses boiled with tree bark. It will stop the pain."

Now Doc knew more than a bit about medicine and what he had just heard was not possible.

"Only sleep stops pain," he said. He wanted to continue to explain the findings of modern medicine, when a groan from Benny stopped him.

Benny mustered all the strength he could and forced his eyes open. At first, he saw nothing but then he began to focus. Slowly he recognized Doc's face. He tried to speak but his thoughts and words were not coordinated.

"Where are we?" The words were spread apart and slowly

Wounded

spoken. Even Benny felt as if he was speaking in slow motion.

Before Doc answered, Benny spotted the Indian with the funny clothes and again he forced words out. "Chief." Anyway, calling the Indian Chief by name got Doc and Patrick's attention.

"You're the Chief?" exclaimed Doc and then he realized he probably sounded very insulting.

"Yes. Well you see, we Indian Chief are not at all like your King. We don't put on our crown or wear our robes all the time. Mine are stored in the palace."

"I deserve that. I'm sorry."

"You feeling better?" Patrick asked Benny.

"I don't know that better is it. I feel very groggy?"

"That is from the medicine the squaw gave him," said the Chief.

"You mean it really stops pain?" Doc really didn't believe what he had just heard.

"For many moons, many braves have not had bad pain. Our medicine squaw, the one caring for them ..." He looked at Benny and Smitty. "She was taught the use of medicine by her father. And he by his father. She has now taught her son, the brave who first cared for them."

Patrick spoke up, "You mean the man who ran his hand over both of them but never touched them?"

"It is he. That is another thing she has taught him. He can feel inside, past the skin. He can tell if the heart is broken or a bone is broken. He told me the knee will bend no more and that one ..." He pointed to Smitty as he spoke, "has lost blood but inside everything is still fine."

"I don't believe it!" Doc spoke not in a negative tone but in one that suggested how incredulous the concept was.

"Doc, Doc," Benny called out.

"I'm here Benny."

"What were they?"

"What were who?"

"The Red Coats. There were so many of them." Benny was still struggling to speak but his voice was becoming clearer.

"They were regulars, infantry. That's why they couldn't chase us."

"How many?"

"Hard to tell. I mean, we were all moving so fast and things just seemed to explode around us."

"We took no count but they passed us yesterday, on their way north."

"Chief, take a guess. How many?" Benny pressed despite his state of health.

"Maybe ten hands."

"You mean fifty?" Doc asked.

"Yes."

"Maybe they don't know that Howe has left the Boston area," Patrick said.

"Not so," the Chief said in a raised voice. "Two days ago, we heard at the Toll House about the cannons and how Howe and all his men ran to the boats to escape."

"So that infantry group, which is probably a platoon, also knew about what had happened in Boston."

Benny was forcing his eyes to focus. He shook his head to try and brush off the effects of the Indian woman's medicine.

"Yes. Talk at the Toll House is free. The more grog, the more free. The Red Coats talk of revenge. They say they will take the guns away like taking toy guns from children. The Colonists just talk of taking the cannons away from the King."

"Ha! Now we're reduced to being spoiled children."

"How will they take the cannons away from us?" Benny asked.

"Not a problem they say. Many troops heading north." The Chief shrugged his shoulders. "Surprise attack, it works."

"Many? How many?" Benny pressed.

"The men who hurt you were first. Many more are following.

Wounded

They come from across the water and along the coast road."

Benny raised his head and tried to gather his thoughts.

"We've got to warn our men," he said after a moment. "Doc and Patrick, I need you to do something. It will be very dangerous, so if you say no, I'll understand." He hesitated but only for a second to catch his breath. "Go back to Boston. Find Colonel Knox and warn him. He and the cannons are going to be attacked from the rear. Hundreds of troops. Also, tell him ..." Benny tried to sit up as he spoke. The medicine squaw helped him. "Tell him, the ships the Red Coats were on may turn around. It could be a coordinated counter attack." He paused as a flash of pain shot up his leg. "Don't travel together and stay off the main road until you get around that platoon we ran into."

Both men nodded their heads; they would do it.

"I will send my scouts to guide you," said the Chief. "No need to use the road. And it is best if you travel now, at night." Without any further discussion the plan was put into action. Doc and Patrick left separately, with their escorts. Benny wanted to be more involved but the need for sleep overtook him.

It wasn't until the next day, around the noon hour, when Benny was awakened by the medicine squaw that he realized he had slept for so long. He looked over at Smitty who smiled back at him.

"How you coming along?" Benny asked.

"I've felt better, but considering I got a hole in front and one in back and I'm still talking about it, I guess I'm doing all right." Smitty then motioned towards Benny's leg. "How's it feel?"

"Hurts like crazy. More today than yesterday. And somebody put my whole leg between some straight branches."

"Medicine squaw," as Smitty spoke he motioned toward the lady. "She also gave us something for the pain but I think she decided to let us tough it out from here on."

"Smitty, I don't know about you, but whatever she gave me worked just fine."

"Yeah, but it also made me real sleepy."

The hut's flap was raised and the Chief came in. He wasn't his normally relaxed self. "I hear you speak of sleep. That would not be good for now. Red Coats attacked a village near here. Our people tell them we are friends. Allies … but the Red Coats attack anyway. Braves from there say the Blue Coats, you call them Hessian, they led attack. They take guns, furs and anything they can sell. They say it is our price for them to war on you for us. Also say they will come here. They cannot find you here. It would be death for you and us."

"We understand, you have already helped us and one day we will repay the favor," Benny said.

"What our people do for you is not for repay. You and your father have always been good to us. It is from the heart that we help each other." The Chief put his hand on Benny's shoulder. "Now we must move you and quickly."

"Chief, do you think we can make it to a ferry or another boat, so we can get across the Sound?"

"Not safe. Many Red Coats along the waterfront. All around us they are gathering. Must move away from here."

"Benny ..." Smitty started to say something, and then withdrew the idea.

"Smitty, if you've got an idea, now's the time to share it."

This time, Smitty didn't hesitate. "What about that inn your friend the Rabbi owns?"

Benny thought out loud about the idea. "He's helped us before and somehow I think hiding a couple of fugitive Patriots is something he would enjoy. Problem is, it's far from here and I don't know if we would be able to make it."

"Listen tree branch leg, if you can make it, I'll put my fingers in these holes and keep up with you," Smitty said, chuckling.

Benny knew it would be up to the Chief. They really couldn't travel without the help of his braves. "Would it be safe enough for your braves?" he asked the Chief. "And would it be too far? The

Wounded

inn Smitty is talking about is in New Haven. It's a long ride from here."

The Chief reflected for a moment. "Our braves can help, but they can only help if you are able to ride the distance you speak of. Can you ride?"

Benny looked at Smitty. "From here to London if I have to."

They were hoisted onto horses and both men fought to hold back tears. The pain was that intense and yet the medicine squaw could not help because her medicine would severely interfere with their riding abilities. So thanks and farewells were exchanged and they were on their way. Benny was pleased to have two braves guiding them. He was even more pleased to discover that another brave was serving as an advanced scout and still another as a rear guard.

Smitty was hunched over in his saddle for practically the entire trip. Yet he fared well compared to Benny, whose leg throbbed not only from the wound, but also from the long branches that braced and held it straight. It was well after dark, on a moonless night, when they arrived at the inn. Rabbi Saul unlatched the door and even though he held a candlestick, he didn't recognize Benny or Smitty. At first all he saw were the Indian braves and that sent him into a panic.

"It's me Rabbi ... Benny."

Less alarmed but still befuddled the Rabbi waved them in and shuffled over to the registration desk. There he used his candle to light several other candles on the desk top.

The Indians didn't follow Benny and Smitty through the doorway. Instead they quietly disappeared into the night. When Benny turned around he saw they were gone. He regretted not having had an opportunity to thank them.

The Rabbi knew the men needed shelter and considering their battered condition he also knew they were, so to speak, escaping and hiding. Considering his past experiences with Benny it wasn't hard for him to figure out the circumstances. But the details could

wait until morning. For now, he decided, he would accommodate these men and let them have the rest they desperately needed. He helped them into the lobby and one at a time he managed to get them up the stairs and to a room.

The next morning Rabbi Saul and his wife Ruth had tea brought to Benny and Smitty's rooms. Both men were awake. They had woken earlier and from their window they could see horses in the stable area. The horses were not theirs; they hoped theirs would have been cared for earlier and perhaps hidden. These horses were adorned with military reins and saddles. Benny and Smitty stayed in their room and out of sight.

Benny was forthright and honest with the kindly Rabbi. He told their entire story and ended with how they chose to come to the inn. "I know this is very dangerous for you. We've already put you in harm's way. If you want we'll leave right away," he told Rabbi Saul.

The Rabbi's short and chubby frame seemed to shrink even more as he stood in front of the room's beds. His bald head grew more lines from frowns and his blue eyes were sunken. He remained in this pose for what seemed like an eternity to Benny. Then he started to speak. As he did, his body stature seemed to grow, his frown disappeared and his blue eyes transformed to look like sapphire stones. "Do I look like a menche to you?" he said with a heavy Yiddish accent and as he spoke his tone became fiery. He was now preaching to his substitute congregation. "Are we not brothers in this fight?" He even mocked himself. "Do you think because I look like this," he deliberately forced his stomach forward, "I am not a worthy adversary of the Red Coats?"

Like all good sermons, the speech went on. Also, as with all sermons, it was a bit too long. But, the point was made and Ruth assured both men, she would heal their wounds with her good food.

A few days later, both men were feeling much better. The pain was still there for both of them, but it went from sharp and excruciating to constant and somewhat tolerable. What helped

Wounded

them forget their pain, at least for a brief period, was the arrival of Doc and Patrick. It was Patrick who came in first.

"Mission accomplished, Sir," he said as he saluted the men.

"We followed orders and traveled separately until we met again at the Indian camp," Doc told them. He, too, saluted the men, but then he walked to the side of the bed and embraced each of his friends. "Oh, before I forget the exact words, Colonel Knox wanted me to tell you, 'The seed and the apple are the same. Service above self.' He also said to tell you how much he appreciated the warning. They'll be well prepared."

Within a few days the group was ready to travel. Benny however, felt caution had to be taken, and since Smitty's wounds had healed quicker than his own, he decided Doc and Smitty should make their way back to the island first. He also sent Patrick back to Yale and insisted he visit Mattituck during his summer break. Before leaving Doc said he would first get Smitty safely home, then he'd return to help Benny get back to the island.

Chapter 24

Wedding, Spying
&
Recognition

The snow and the cold had culminated in an otherwise
mild winter. Then one morning Pastor Timothy came to visit. At
first my heart sank. I was so afraid that our Pastor was bringing us
horrible news. As soon as he walked through the door he grasped
my shoulders and told me that everything was all right. He said
that Benny was alive—wounded but alive. I have no idea how
long Mother and I hugged and cried together. My sisters, Sarah
and Elizabeth also joined in.

It seems that Doc had heard from the ferryman that British
troops were occupying Mattituck and other nearby villages.
Doc didn't want to chance leaving Smitty at his house so he had
delivered him to the church where the Pastor's wife was now
tending to his wounds. Pastor Timothy also said that with so many
troops gathering on the Island's North Fork, it was too risky for
Doc to return to New Haven. He said that he, himself, would be
going to Connecticut.

"Not without me," I said, more forcefully than I should have,
especially since I was speaking to a clergyman.

"Not a bad idea, a clergyman traveling with his daughter to
the New Haven Presbytery."

Early the next morning, we were on our way when things began to unravel. Most people become seasick when they're out at sea. That's logical. In my case, though, we hadn't even left the dock. We had hardly made it out of the harbor when the urge to regurgitate took over. I made it to the ship's side rail and heaved over and over again. And to add to my misery, I heard the captain. "'Tis a real shame to waste good chum. We ain't fishin'. For a thin filly, she's sure layin' out a sizable slick."

With my head drooped over the side of the boat and the wind making sure most of my vomit returned to decorate my coat and dress, all I could think about was Benny. Oh, I love him so. Even in my state of total disaster, all that flashed in my mind was his wound, his pain and how I desperately wanted to be with him. I'm not sure if it was my focus on Benny or my determination to be tough in front of this captain who was so amused, but I was able to straighten myself out. Though I was still really sick, I managed to get to the side of the cabin where I sat down behind a barrel. At least I was out of the wind.

What seemed like a never-ending voyage was finally coming to an end, though. At last we sailed along the Connecticut coast to the New Haven harbor. We made it to the dock and as we had expected, when we disembarked we were stopped by both the Red Coats and the Hessian forces—not once but several times. Unlike many other travelers, we were questioned but not detained, or taken into custody. It may have been because Pastor Timothy wore his clerical collar or perhaps it was my deplorable looks and foul smelling clothes, due to my "illness."

When we got to the inn, we found ourselves in an awkward position. There were so many British officers dining at the inn, that we dared not say who we were looking for, especially since the Rabbi or his wife, as Doc had described them, did not appear to be present. Pastor Timothy requested two rooms. According to the hostess, there was only one room available—with a single small bed. It usually cost more but since a clergyman and his daughter were renting it, she gave us a discount. She explained it was the innkeeper's policy.

Pastor Timothy was thirsty and hungry. I was too, but I was so embarrassed by my appearance that I had to go to the room to freshen up. The receptionist assured me that a pitcher of fresh water and a bowl had already been placed in the room. I took the key and my travel bag and started up the stairs and enroute I met a strikingly handsome woman. She had beautiful blond hair. We greeted each other and she stood to one side so I could pass by. When we were on the same step together, I realized how tall she was. That's when it dawned on me. I knew who she was from Doc's description.

"Are you the Rabbi's wife?" I awkwardly asked.

"Why, yes I am. And who might you be?" She wasn't whispering but her voice was very soft and so incredibly gentle.

"I'm Rachael, Benny's betrothed."

"Oh! Benny spoke of you but he didn't mention you would be coming." Even her surprise didn't change her gentleness. "Well, well, well ... let's see ... I don't mean to interfere, but he really shouldn't see you like ... well ..."

"Oh I know. I look frightful. I probably could scare away witches. I was just on my way to the room." I showed her the key.

"Fine. Fine. Let me help you a bit." Before I knew what was happening she took my travel bag from my hand, turned and led the way to the room.

By the time I got down to the dining room, the Rabbi's wife had helped get the wrinkles out of my Sunday church dress and had taken away my soiled clothes for cleaning. As we left the room she took on a motherly attitude.

"No matter how long you're married, never let your husband see you in an undignified state" she admonished. "If a wife cares for herself, then her husband will also care for her. Am I being too blunt?"

"Oh, no. I appreciate the advice."

The Legend of Benny

In the dining room I sat with Pastor Timothy and as the Rabbi's wife had recommended, we waited. "Once the officers have had their midday tea, they tend to return to duty," she said. She followed this by telling me that if it seemed safe, she'd then ask Benny to join us.

Why in the world would I have to wait to see him? I didn't say that out loud, but I wondered. I also thought, for gosh sakes, we grew up together, in a one room house. We had some unwritten and unspoken privacy rules, but realistically, there is very little about each other that we don't know. No matter. I've waited this long to see him, I figured a few more moments shouldn't be that hard to bear. Pastor Timothy was enjoying the honey biscuits and tea. I felt sure that eternity was shorter than the wait I had to endure.

The midday crowd dwindled and when the last of the patrons departed, Ruth went to get Benny. I couldn't sit still any longer, and so anxiously I went to the reception area. Then I heard a door close upstairs and an odd set of footsteps that sounded more like a thump and then something being dragged. There was no doubt in my mind that it was the sound of a lame person, dragging a leg. It had to be Benny. And then, still out of sight, he started down the stairs, but once he came into view, I could no longer contain myself. I raced up the stairs to meet him. At last I was where I had wanted to be, now and forever more — I was in Benny's arms. I forgot all the rules of proper etiquette. Benny and I hugged and kissed. I cried. He wiped away my tears. He smiled. I ran my fingers over his face. At last it was our moment of togetherness. It must have looked as passionate as it was. When we finally stopped embracing and looked around, everyone was gone, that is everyone except a little round man with a bald head, who was standing at the top of the stairs. He smiled at us.

"You know," he said, "vhere I come from ve throw buckets of cold vater on dogs that are locked together like that."

In the dining room Benny and I were once again given some

time alone to talk. After exchanging greetings, Pastor Timothy went off to speak with Rabbi Saul. After promising us an unforgettable evening meal, Ruth went to resume her kitchen duties. The news of Father's death overwhelmed Benny; I had never before seen him cry. Then he fretted over Mother. How was she doing without Father? They were inseparable. He cried again and then we prayed together. Father was a different kind of man, but we were sure that Jesus, as he promised, had prepared a room for him in heaven. I was equally distressed at seeing Benny's leg. He did say that Ruth had nursed him well. He even joked that her chicken soup with matzo balls was helping to make the knee bend better. Given the degree of damage of the area around the kneecap, he'd been well advised that it would probably never bend again.

It wasn't until the others rejoined us that I learned why Benny's room had been off limits to me. Apparently when Patrick and Doc returned from their mission to warn Colonel Knox, they brought back a letter for Benny. That letter contained some information that Benny could share, but the rest was for his eyes only. It originated in Philadelphia and was directed to General Washington. When it was handed to Doc, he was told it was to be destroyed if there were any possibility it could be read by anyone other than Benny. Benny was able to share, however, that Colonel Knox appreciated the warning and discussed the information with the General. Benny was instructed to provide some additional information concerning British troop movements, and that was all he could tell us.

"Well, now that Rachael and I will be taking you home, I'm sure you're delighted to know all of this war stuff is over, at least for you," said Pastor Timothy. "From now on you can sit on your home porch and talk about which side made good moves, and which Generals should be tarred and feathered for blunders."

"And from now on you'll be a farm manager. We'll hire help so you can get off that leg. Hopefully you're well enough to travel, so we can head for home tomorrow," I said with great anticipation.

"If the weather holds, we'll have you home by tomorrow night," said the Pastor.

That's when I looked across the table and saw a downcast expression on the Rabbi's face. In fact, he wasn't looking at anyone. His eyes were unfocused but he was staring at the tabletop. I knew something was wrong. Benny and I were sitting next to each other, holding hands. I let go and spun around to face him.

"I can't go home," Benny said. "That's why I had to share some of the letter with you."

"When can you ... come home?"

Before answering Benny took a moment to think but I knew he'd already rehearsed every possible angle of this discussion. "I just don't know. And if I were to say anything other than that, I'd be saying something I can't justify. I've been assigned ... well; let me leave it at that. I've been assigned."

"But you're hurt," I said, fighting back tears.

"It's not that kind of assignment."

"So ... Benny," Pastor Timothy was trying to get a better perspective on what was being said. "Are you saying, Rachael and I should go back home ... alone, without you?"

"Yes," Benny spoke very softly and slowly. "I'm sorry but I can't go home yet. Not right now. When Doc said he would come back to get me ... well, things were different then. There have been new developments. I may be leaving here but I'm not heading for the Island. Not yet."

"Then I'm staying with you!" I snapped. "Where you go I go!" My voice was strong and my urge to cry was completely gone.

That raised a few eyebrows. "Why you're not even married. That would be scandalous," the Rabbi's wife sternly said. "Now, listen here you two and I mean both of you. Your mothers aren't here so I am speaking for them. No! You simply cannot live together. Why, it's immoral and sinful. You don't just act like you're married."

Wedding, Spying & Recognition

"Okay, okay. If that's the way you want it." I then looked Benny straight in the eyes. "Benny will you marry me?"

"You know I can't wait for the day when we can get married."

"Are you sure?" I asked ever so softly.

"Of course I'm sure."

"Good! Then today's the day! Pastor Timothy will you marry us?" After I said it, I couldn't believe I had the nerve to be so brazen.

"When?" Our Pastor doesn't usually rattle that easily but he was obviously rattled now.

"Now!" I sounded even more brazen, but at least I was calm.

I don't know if it was my answer or my calm forcefulness, but the four of them were unnerved. They became very quiet. Then, after what seemed like forever, Benny, who was just staring at me, broke the silence. His voice was still filled with romantic charm.

"There are so many reasons I love you. Your quick solutions, no matter how crazy they may sound at first, are usually so fitting. Yes, no time would be better to marry than now."

He then spoke to Pastor Timothy and Rabbi Saul. "Would you both honor us by performing the nuptials?"

"It would be my pleasure."

"There's a lot of history between your parents and me," said Pastor Timothy "If your dad were alive, he would be delighted and I know your mother will be happy to hear of the wedding. I'm sure she would have loved to be here but she knows these are extraordinary times demanding extraordinary actions. She will understand."

The Rabbi and Ruth were confused. "Whose parents are you talking about?" Ruth's facial expression and her tone betrayed her confusion.

"Oh! I'm sorry. I should have been clear. They're brother and sister and have the same mother and father."

Ruth's display of confusion got more intense as she turned

to the Rabbi. Together, their expressions went from confusion to shock. Our Pastor looked at them and knew he had a lot of explaining to do. Benny just looked at me, "Here we go again." He motioned for me to get up and together we left our Pastor to explain the true nature of one sibling marrying another.

"I know when someone is just joking but forgive me Pastor Timothy, you just don't seem to have that type of personality," said Ruth. She then turned to me. "Before you two run off, can I just ask one thing. Can the wedding wait until tomorrow? There are some things, like a proper wedding dress, and a well-prepared celebration meal, not to mention befitting sleeping arrangements that need to be organized."

I smiled at Benny. "Tomorrow will be a fine day for a wedding," he told her.

The wedding was beautiful! Not many people attended. Actually, if you consider the fact that both Pastor Timothy and Rabbi Saul were officiating, then there was only one person in the audience, Ruth. Oh, not quite true, because she became my maid of honor. So, does she count as an attendee or as a member of the audience? No matter. The only thing that mattered was that Benny and I were together and professed our everlasting love and commitment, before God, to each other. The ceremony was held in the same dining room we sat in the day before. The Rabbi closed the room to the public, between lunch and midday tea, by placing a sign on the door that read, "Closed for Religious Observances."

When I arrived, escorted by Pastor Timothy, who also served to give me, the bride, away, the room was nicely lit with extra candles and Ruth had also made bouquets of winter plant branches which adorned the makeshift altar.

The night before Ruth had come to my room with a lovely dress for me to wear to the wedding. It was large on me but the very talented Ruth took out her sewing box and in no time at all had altered it to fit me perfectly. Not to flatter myself, but I must have looked beautiful, for when I entered the room, Benny actually seemed stunned. His eyes were so fixed on me that I turned beet red with embarrassment. I can just imagine my red face with the white dress. What a sight! Benny also looked different. Someone had lent him a new white shirt that was ruffled in the front and at the wrists. He looked dashing in his blue long length jacket.

"I've known you all my life but I've never seen you look more beautiful," he told me. That darkened my red face a couple more degrees. And, to tell the truth, I had never before seen that lustful look in his eyes. I turned even redder!

I suspect I wasn't the only one who saw the look. Pastor Timothy put his Bible down on the makeshift altar in much the same way a judge slams the gavel down to regain order in the courtroom. It got our attention, at least for the moment. The manner in which the Pastor and the Rabbi conducted the ceremony made me believe they'd done this as a team before. If I didn't know better I would have suspected they'd spent hours rehearsing. The only part that seemed strange was when Benny was asked by the Rabbi to step down and crush the wine glass. Benny had a hard time bringing himself to crush a perfectly good glass.

After we exchanged our vows, no one said that Benny could kiss me. Somehow it seemed like the most logical way we could celebrate our union and so we embraced. Yes, we embraced and kissed in public. And if it wasn't for the banging and slamming of fists on the door we would have stayed embraced for a whole lot longer. We stopped when the Rabbi went to open the door. In rushed a young man who sped quickly to Benny. He saluted. "Sir, my apologies for interrupting but it is important that we speak privately."

Benny nodded his head and motioned for the young man to lead the way to the kitchen.

"Remember, we don't salute." Benny said as he closed the door. Within moments Benny came rushing out of the kitchen. "Everything is back to normal. Pastor, pack up and head for the ferry. Take Rachael with you. Rachael, go and change into your

traveling clothes." He then turned to the young man. "Go up to my room," he ordered "Get the maps and charts off the walls and bring them down. Burn them in the fireplace. All right, everybody, let's move."

"I'm not going. I'm staying with you," I said adamantly.

"Rachael, I don't have time to argue." As he spoke, he looked at my face and realized I wasn't about to change my mind. "Fine! But we must move quickly. Get changed and wait by the stable."

Within seconds goodbyes were said, maps and papers were burned and the inn was restored to normal. Pastor Timothy was on his way home and Benny and I were in a single horse wagon heading away from the inn. It was quite a surprising turn of events and to add to my surprise, when Benny met me at the buggy, he was wearing a clerical collar—he had borrowed one of Pastor Timothy's. I was more than bewildered as we left the inn and headed west instead of southeast. But then again, I didn't care. I was as happy as any new bride could be, I was seated next to my new husband.

Honeymoon. It's a wonderful-sounding word. I read somewhere that the term honeymoon first came into use in the mid fifteen hundreds. The idea was that the first moon or month of marriage is supposed to be the sweetest of all—a taste of honey. That being said, I can honestly say, I can attest to its validity. And if done right, every month thereafter can be a honeymoon. Maybe not every moment of each passing month, but certain segments can be blissful enough to make the overall month feel as if it were filled with honey.

Our honeymoon began as we left the inn and started to make our way west. We had gone only a few hundred yards when a platoon of Red Coats came rambling toward us. Most of them passed us and turned into the inn's entry, but one officer at the end broke ranks and came over to our wagon.

"Have you been at the inn?" he demanded.

Benny spoke softly with his head half down. "Not many

a religious man can afford a place like that and I cannot say I condone the beverages that are served in such establishments."

The officer didn't seem to pay much attention to what Benny was saying. He was staring so intensely at Benny that you might think they were long lost brothers. "Do I know you from somewhere?"

"If you're going to the inn, then I don't believe we've had the pleasure. As I just said, libations of the kind served there are not for members of the clergy. But if you attend any of the churches around here, then we may have met. I like to serve the Lord in different locations. That way I can tell more people, like you, that it's not too late to repent. My wife and I are heading for a nearby church. Why not forgo the way of the inn and come join us. Living the life of a military person is very dangerous and one never knows when the end will come."

"Thank you Reverend, but I'm on duty now; maybe some other time."

"Thank goodness he wasn't too sober the last time we met or he would surely have remembered me," Benny said as we rode off.

"You know him?"

"Not really. The last time we met we were at the inn and I was pointing a long gun at him. As I recall he promised to get me someday. As I say, it's a good thing he was drunk that night."

"I'm sure that collar helped to throw him off." Then I thought of something. "You know, I think that's the first time I've heard you lie."

"Oh, but I didn't lie. All I said was the clergy shouldn't indulge. There is a difference."

"Well I think that's just playing games with words but I suspect it did save our lives, so it's all right." That was the first thing I learned on our honeymoon. I should never ask Benny anything that concerns this mysterious stuff he's doing. He may not lie but I'd never hear the whole and real truth.

When we left the inn Benny had not made a mistake by

turning west, as I thought perhaps he had. He knew where he was going—to New York. We would reach it by tomorrow but this night we would spend in an inn on the New Jersey side of the river. That establishment, known as The Land's End Inn was incredibly beautiful, sitting high on a cliff overlooking the Hudson. The island of Manhattan is just across the river and when the sun set in the west the city came alive in the winter sky. It was so romantic to just stand on the back porch, holding Benny's hand and reveling in God's magnificent painting of pink, purples and gold.

"Are you feeling calmer now?" he asked with a smile.

"Oh yes." But in truth I wasn't. I was still nervous and for many reasons. It started when we first approached the inn's entryway. The only inn I'd ever stayed at was the Rabbi's and that was small and quaint. This inn reeked of grandeur. When we entered the circle in front of the main entry a footman came to assist me off the wagon.

The building has these huge columns and a portico extended out from the front door. In school I'd heard about such places but never thought I'd ever see one. Then Benny escorted me inside. That's when I became nervous to the point that he knew there was a problem.

"Are you all right? You look terribly flushed."

"Benny, look at this place. The chandelier is burning more candles right now than we light all winter. And I've never stepped on a rug that's so thick I can't see my boot. How can we afford this?"

Benny didn't answer me at first. He registered us and was given a key to the room but before going up and getting ready for dinner he wanted to see the river, and while we were looking at it he finally gave me my answer.

"Yes, this inn is very expensive," he told me "It's so expensive that the Red Coats would never think to look for me here." Then he smiled and whispered the rest of his answer. "It's a business expense and in the letter I received, Congress said, no expense is too high, if what I'm supposed to create really does happen. Now before you go asking any more questions, that's all I can tell you."

Now, about my wedding night. I was raised on a farm. I know what happens when we put a bull in with the cows — I've seen it myself. I've also seen it happen with goats, sheep, pigs and even chickens. No mystery. Once the male is in the coral, pen or coop, there's a bit of strutting on his part and some coyness exhibited by the female. Then he mounts her. As they say, that's the whole ball of wax. Somehow, I'd always believed it would be different with people. Well, at least for me. And it was! What Benny lacked in experience, he made up for with compassion and love.

The next morning I felt radiant and happier than ever before. I was also starving. Benny had gotten up earlier. He said his leg had stiffened up during the night and when I smiled and said I know ... well ... that postponed breakfast for a while longer. Leaving the inn, I looked back at it one more time. It was truly a memory, never to be forgotten.

We traveled to a little riverside town called Secaucus, which had many ferries going to Manhattan. Benny got us and our horse and wagon aboard a barge-like vessel. The river at this juncture was very narrow but it could be rough. Fortunately we had no problems crossing and we landed at the end of Wall Street. I had never been to the city before and the number and height of the buildings was astonishing. They were literally right next to each other. Benny knew his way around the city and was looking for a specific street. In fact, he was looking for a specific house. It wasn't long before he found it.

Then he rode past it.

"If that's it, why aren't we stopping?" I asked him.

"Not yet," was his only response, as he maneuvered around the block and passed it again. Then he drove the wagon around yet another road and once again we passed by the building. Finally he stopped the wagon around the corner from the building. "Here, take the reins and keep the wagon moving. Don't pass the building I'm going into but meet me on this corner. I shouldn't be long." He then got off the wagon, though it was not an easy feat. I could see his leg was really bothering him. He even got the crutch from the back of the wagon. "Now listen. This is important. If you see any Red Coat activity near that building, I want you to head for home. Real quick." He started to walk away then added, "I love you."

"Benny. Wait!" I half shouted in a whisper voice. I certainly didn't want to draw anyone's attention. He turned and came back to the wagon, "I don't like what you just said. It seems dangerous. And, how am I supposed to get home? I've never been here before. I don't even know where I am."

"Rachael, if you talk any louder, it will become very dangerous and remember I didn't want you to come along. Now, if anything even remotely suspicious happens, go to the end of the road and turn left. You'll be along the East River. Take a ferry across and head east. Keep going until you get home." He looked up and down the street. "Now that you've drawn me back, let me loosen this right here." He took his crutch and placed the arm cross bar between a couple of wheel spokes and twisted it. The arm support popped off revealing a hole in the top of the shaft.

"What's that?" I couldn't resist being inquisitive.

"I've hidden a letter from the General in it. I figure it might be awkward trying to pry the crutch apart in the building." After removing the letter and placing it in his pocket, he placed the armrest back onto the shaft and started off again.

I did as he instructed. I maneuvered the wagon up and down several streets and tried to look nonchalant but I stayed keenly alert for any sign of trouble. Since it was about midday, there were many people moving about the streets, but at last I saw Benny heading for the corner. Since there were no Red Coats around I figured it was safe to pick him up.

"Hi stranger. Care for a ride?"

In no time at all, the crutch was in the back and Benny had climbed aboard.

"Thanks miss but what is your husband going to say?"

Wedding, Spying & Recognition

"He's going to confess that he was a little too cautious. That place was as safe as could be. There weren't any Red Coats in sight. You're being so overly careful that you're going to drive us both crazy."

"Maybe, but just remember it only takes one slip-up or careless move." Benny wasn't smiling as he took the reins.

We made it to the corner and turned left when the British foot soldiers came from the opposite direction and turned into the road we had just left.

"Benny, are they going to the building you just left?" I quietly asked.

"I'm sure."

"But, whoever you saw in there, is he in trouble?"

"Maybe he is ... then again ..." I could see Benny was trying to think. He probably had the same concern. "Somehow I don't think so," he mumbled. "He's smart and very wealthy. He must have anticipated this kind of situation. But we, on the other hand ... we're dispensable."

He tapped the horse to make it move faster. Without being told, I knew Benny was alarmed that they would soon be coming after us. He weaved in and out of streets and seemed to know exactly where he was heading. Within seconds we were in the carriage yard of the London Mercantile Building, Father's former place of employment. We got off the wagon and took our travel bags. Benny also grabbed his crutch. Upon entering the building, Benny remembered the man that Father used to do business with and we went straight to his office. The gentleman was kind enough to see us and he was even kinder to us when we told him of Father's passing. Benny assured him that we planned to meet all of Father's financial obligations. He told him that we were going to continue the *wampum* for fur trading business. After a brief but mutually acceptable discussion the man said, "If there is anything we could do for you, please don't hesitate to ask."

"No. No. We're fine," said Benny. Then, he acted as though

a thought had just occurred to him. "Oh, there is one thing. We made our way here by wagon and ..."

Well, I'm still amazed at how Benny did it. Within a few moments, we left the Mercantile not with the horse and wagon we came to the city in, but with another horse and a two seat carriage. It was a little too fancy for me and it certainly made heads turn as we rambled through the city, across the river and out onto Long Island. I must admit I felt wicked and prideful to be receiving all that attention.

To disguise us from would-be-followers; Benny once again donned the clerical collar. We were stopped at several checkpoints. Each time Benny explained that we were being sent to the eastern region of Long Island to replace an eccentric Pastor who was promoting the rebellion. Benny slowed down enough to count the British war ships in the river. He even managed to find out how many Red Coats and Hessian troops were in the region.

"I pray we'll be safe where we're going," he said to a guard at one checkpoint. "It's out on the North Fork. Say, do you know, are there many militia out there?"

"Yeah, but we got thousands of men here and we'll be marching east to wipe them out," said the guard, wanting to be more important than he really was.

"But this is Brookline. Where would we get that many regulars from?"

"General Howe. He sent them from Nova Scotia. Figures to move east and trap the rebels or at least push them off the end of the island."

Benny raised his fist and cheered. "A blow for King George!"

The guard also became exuberant, "Here! Here!"

"Oh, but do you think we really have enough troops?"

The guard didn't hesitate to reveal all he knew after looking about so no one else could hear him. "A fellow townsman is assigned to headquarters and he said we have nearly fifteen

Wedding, Spying & Recognition

thousand troops here and eight thousand more on ships heading here right now. He tells me Howe figures to end the rebellion right here." Of course, before we departed, Benny offered a blessing upon the guard.

The trek home seemed like an endless honeymoon. We went back and forth across the island as we progressed east. Benny was particularly interested in seeing the major harbors on each shore. I knew he was on a reconnaissance mission but that didn't matter. What really counted was our being together. It took over a week to make our way out to Mattituck and it was amazing because time passed so incredibly fast.

Along the way we stayed at inns and some nights we even had dinner and bedded down in hotels. It was really glorious and yet I couldn't wait to get home. All I really wanted was to be on our farm, with Benny and our family. I wanted to be his wife. A farmer's wife.

While we were traipsing back and forth, somehow Mother knew our journey would end safely. She and our sisters had completely reorganized the house, giving Benny and me the larger and more private bedroom. Her intuition can be uncanny at times. She even prepared an elaborate meal of rabbit stew with all the trimmings.

As delightful and warming as that night was, though, the next day proved to be troublesome and frightening. When we woke, Benny announced that he would be leaving and he had no idea when he would be coming home again. It shouldn't have come as a surprise. With all the reconnaissance work he was doing, I should have realized that he would have to report the information to someone.

The events of that morning were to be repeated many times. As the months went by Benny devoted less and less time to farming and more and more time to, as I call it, the spy business. Yet Benny still fashioned himself to be a farmer, so we did the most logical thing. We hired a person to manage the farm. Ironically, that helper

turned out to be Smitty. Due to his wound, he could no longer work full time as a blacksmith. The ball that went through him had pierced his lung and the continuous smoke of the smelting pit was too irritating. As a consequence he was out of work. Benny hired him, which led to his being around the farmhouse a lot. This in turn led to his marriage to one of our sisters, Sarah. For a wedding gift, Benny gave him a parcel of land and helped him build a house on the other end of the farm.

It was quite a change but then we witnessed several changes in rapid succession. Doc married Penny and while he practiced medicine in town, he also took time away to spend at the Saratoga Springs Indian encampment. The Mercantile Company went bankrupt, which meant the indentured loan or mortgage was due in its entirety immediately. Somehow that didn't seem to faze Benny. He paid the bill and didn't discuss it. His nonchalant manner of handling the matter troubled me.

"Farming has been good to us but not so good that we could pay off such a large debt so easily," I asked one night as we were going to bed. "Where did you get the money to pay off the loan?"

"I've never asked for a salary but I do get paid for what I do. And it's much more than I can believe. Most of it, I just put in the Riverhead Bank. I know you don't normally like to discuss finances, but since you raised the question ..." He went to his dresser and pulled out a bank ledger sheet and put it in front of me. "Now you know what we have so use it as you please."

Something else changed too. For the most part Benny stopped his erratic traveling. Nowadays he leaves on the first Monday of the month and is only gone for a week. It's the same schedule as our Congressional people and I guess that part he didn't think had to be kept too secret because, on occasion he did mention he was appearing before Congress. He also altered his manner of dress. He went from rough farm wear to businesslike attire.

And while he wasn't traveling that much, other people were coming to the house to see him. They usually arrive at night and leave before dawn. There have been so many visitors and since they all need to talk to him in private, we finally decided to add another room. It has become his office. And, of course, I know those visitors and his monthly trips have to do with the rebellion, so I try to contribute my share. When visitors come I always offer food and refreshments. We also placed a large chair with down feathered cushions in his office. It's used when a visitor needs to rest before moving on to his next assignment.

Life went on like this for almost two years. Then, during the third year of the war effort a memorable event took place. Unfortunately, due to its secretive nature we were never able to share it with others. It happened on Christmas Eve. Most people in the colonies didn't treat Christmas as a day of celebration and merriment but we were different.

"If you don't celebrate the birth of the King of Kings, what should you celebrate?" said Benny. So, on that day I was in the midst of preparing a special meal when a messenger from the church arrived. He said it was important for us, our entire family, to come to the church right away. Surprises or requests like that always trouble Benny. So he asked the messenger many questions, until he felt it was safe. I could hear his mind trying to unravel any dangerous plot.

When we arrived, Pastor Timothy greeted us and invited us into the parlor. He could tell we were confused and a little concerned.

"Just one moment. A little patience," he said. After a while the door leading to the sanctuary opened and in walked probably the second most famous man in the colonies, Dr. Benjamin Franklin.

Benny crossed the room to greet Dr. Franklin and judging by their embrace they had become accustomed to seeing each other, probably at the sessions of Congress that Benny had been attending. Anyway, their resemblance to each other was remarkable and I must once again quote Mother. "Chickens grow chickens."

Benny introduced me, our mother, and sisters. After some very cordial moments the doctor and Benny jumped right into the business of government. They were discussing a proposal that had just passed the Congress that had apparently been written by Benny.

"Sometimes, but not very often, common sense can be found in large groups," said Dr. Franklin.

"But Benny I'm here for another reason ..." he motioned for the rest of us to form a semicircle around Benny. "The Continental Congress is an infant government and yet it has had to make decisions that are usually reserved for wise men. As a legislative body it has made a decision concerning you, Benny. Because of your commitment and bravery and for what you have accomplished for the colonies, the Congress has voted to recognize you. However, given the clandestine nature of the agency you single-handedly established and now direct, and the dangers involved, the recognition was voted to be private. I am the fortunate person who was given the pleasure of presenting you with this, the Gold Medal."

The doctor then handed the medal to Benny. It had no pin on it, for obvious reasons. It's not an award he could wear on his coat but one to be kept in a dresser and looked at on occasion. It would always serve to remind him and those of us who knew about it, that he was appreciated by our fledgling country.

Chapter 25

Handing Down
the Legend

"Mr. Young, Mr. Young are you all right?" I asked.

I was concerned because his bifocals had fallen off his lap and onto the floor, though he didn't seem to react.

As I read the last paragraph of Rachael's book, I couldn't help but get choked up. How could such a great hero of our country go unrecognized? He was reluctant to step forward and take credit for what he did but because of him and others like him, our country had a solid foundation and rose to greatness. Benny was and is a true unsung hero of the American Revolution. So, I could imagine how Mr. Young felt.

"Mr. Young," I said a little louder as I got up to check on him.

"Heard you the first time. Just takes a little time to figure out an answer at my age," he said with a grin.

"Did you know you're the descendant of such an incredible man? And what a fantastic person Rachael was. Had you any idea about them?"

He put his hand into his pants pocket and pulled out a money clip. Handing the clip to me, he responded, "Great grandfather Benny found a way to always carry his medal without displaying it. Been handed down for generations, but now we can hand down

a legend to go with it." Mr. Young paused to look at the medal. Then he handed it to me saying, "No family left for me to pass it on to. Now it's yours. So, now young man, how are you going to tell people about the legend of Benny?"

ABOUT

THE

AUTHOR

Dominick J. Morreale was born in New York City. He attended Adelphi University where he earned his BA and MS degrees. He also earned a doctorate (EdD) at Nova Southeastern University. After a distinguished career in education, Dr. Morreale now devotes much time to literary pursuits. He lives on the North Fork of Long Island, and enjoys its beauty and bounty with his family.

THE LEGEND OF BENNY ...

For more information regarding Dominick J. Morreale and his work, visit his web site: www.DrDominickJMorreale.com.

Additional copies of this book may be purchased online from LegworkTeam.com; Amazon.com; BarnesandNoble.com; Borders.com, or via the author's web site: www.DrDominickJMorreale.com.

You can also obtain a copy of the book by visiting L.I. Books or ordering it from your favorite bookstore.

Breinigsville, PA USA
08 December 2009
228766BV00005B/3/P